THE BOY WITH FIRE

THE BOY
WITH FIRE

APARNA VERMA

NEW DEGREE PRESS

THE BOY WITH FIRE

ISBN   978-1-63676-457-3 *Paperback*
         978-1-63676-359-0   *Kindle Ebook*
         978-1-63676-355-2   *Ebook*

To those who believe that their stories don't matter,
keep a fire burning.

You never know whose beacon you will become.

1
YASSEN

The king said to his people, "We are the chosen."
And the people responded, "Chosen by whom?"

—FROM CHAPTER 37 OF *THE GREAT HISTORY OF SAYON*

To be forgiven, one must be burned. That's what the Ravani said. They were fanatics and fire worshippers, but they were his people. And he was finally returning home.

Yassen held on to the railing of the hoverboat as it skimmed over the waves. He held on with his left arm, his right limp by his side. Around him, the world was dark, but the horizon began to purple with the faint glimmers of dawn. Soon, the sun would rise, and the twin moons of Sayon would lie down to rest. Soon, he would arrive at Rysanti, the Brass City. And soon, he would find his way back to the desert that had forsaken him.

Yassen withdrew a holopod from his jacket and pressed it open with his thumb. A small holo materialized with a message:

Look for the bull.

He closed the holo, the smell of salt and brine filling his lungs.

The bull. It was nothing close to the Phoenix of Ravence, but then again, Samson liked to be subtle. Yassen wondered if he would be at the port to greet him.

A large wave tossed the boat, but Yassen did not lose his balance. Weeks at sea and suns of combat had taught him how to keep his ground. A cool wind licked his sleeve, and Yassen felt a whisper of pain skitter down his right wrist. He grimaced. His skin was already beginning to purple.

The accident had happened on his last job—a simple enough assignment. He had slipped into the large bedroom of the Verani king, pulse gun ready and getaway planned. A small fire crackled as Yassen had crouched beside the fireplace and studied the king's sleeping form. But then something had gone wrong. An alarm had sounded. The king awoke and fired at Yassen, hitting the hearth instead. The sleeping fire had shot up, white and hot, searing right through Yassen's right sleeve and down into his flesh and bones.

By some small miracle, Yassen escaped. His burns had been treated and his arm was saved, but in the eyes of the Arohassin, he was no longer of use.

Yassen pulled down his sleeve. It was no matter. He was used to running.

As the hoverboat neared the harbor, the fog along the coastline began to evaporate. Slowly, Yassen saw the tall spires of the Brass City cut through the grey heavens. Skyscrapers of slate and Sona steel glimmered in the early dawn as hovertrains weaved through the air, carrying the day laborers. Neon lights flickered within the metal jungle, and a silver bridge snaked through the entire city, connecting the outer rings to the wealthy, affluent center. Yassen squinted as the sun crested the horizon. Suddenly, its light hit the harbor, and the Brass City shone with a blinding intensity.

Yassen quickly clipped on his visor, a fiber sheath that covered his entire face. He closed his eyes for a moment, allowing them to readjust before opening them again. The city stared back at him in subdued colors.

The early queen of Jantar had wanted to ward off Enuu, the Evil Eye, so she had fashioned her port city out of unforgiving metal. If Yassen wasn't careful, the brass could blind him.

The other passengers came up to deck, pulling on plastic half-visors that covered their eyes. Yassen tightened his visor and wrapped a scarf around his neck. Most people could not recognize him—none of the passengers even knew of his name—but a police chief might. He could not take any chances. Samson had made it clear that he wanted no one to know of this meeting.

The hoverboat came to rest beside the Receiving platform, and Yassen disembarked with the rest of the passengers. Even in the early hours, the port was busy. Soldiers barked out orders as fresh immigrants stumbled off a colony boat. Judging from the coiled silver bracelets on their wrists, Yassen guessed they were Sesharians. They shuffled forward on the adjoining Collar dock toward the Knuckled buses. Some carried luggage, others came with only the clothes they wore. They all donned half-visors and walked with a resigned grace of a people weary of their fate.

Natives in their lightning suits and golden bracelets kept a healthy distance from the immigrant platform. They kept to the brass Homeland and Receiving docks where merchants stationed their carts. Unlike most of the city, the carts were made of driftwood, but the vendors still wore half-visors and gloves to handle their wares. Yassen could already hear a merchant shouting about his satchels of vermilion tea while another screamed about a new delivery of Cyleon mirrors that had a ninety percent accuracy of predicting one's romantic future. Yassen shook his head. Only in Jantar.

Floating lanterns guided Yassen and the passengers to the glass-encased immigration office. Yassen slid his holopod into the port while a grim-faced attendant on the screen flicked something from his purple nails.

"Name?" he intoned.

"Cassian Newman," Yassen said.

"Country of residence?"

"Nbru."

The attendant waved his hand. "Take off your visor, please."

Yassen unclipped his visor and saw shock register across the attendant's face as he took in his white, colorless eyes.

"Are you Jantari?" the attendant asked, surprised.

"No," Yassen responded gruffly and clipped his visor back on. "My father was."

"Hmph." The attendant looked at his holopod and then back at him. "Purpose of your visit?"

Yassen paused. The attendant peered at him through the pixels of the screen, and for one wild moment, Yassen wondered if he should turn away, jump back on the boat, and go wherever the sea pushed him. But then a coldness slithered down his right elbow, and he gripped his arm. No, he had already come this far.

"To visit some old friends," Yassen said.

The attendant snorted, but when the holopod slid back out, Yassen saw the burning insignia of a mohanti, a winged ox, on its surface.

"Welcome to the Kingdom of Jantar," the attendant said and waved him through.

Yassen stepped through the glass immigration office and into Rysanti. He breathed in the sharp salt air, intermingled with spices both foreign and familiar. A storm had passed through recently, leaving puddles in its wake. A woman ahead of Yassen slipped on a wet plank, her suit flashing red as a merchant reached out to steady her. Yassen pushed past them, keeping his head down. Out of the corner of his eye, he saw the merchant swipe the woman's holopod and hide it in his jacket. Yassen smothered a laugh.

As he wandered toward the Homeland dock, he scanned the faces in the crowd. The time was nearly two past the sun's breath. Samson and his men should have been here by now.

He came to the bridge connecting the Receiving and Homeland docks. At the other end of the bridge, Yassen spotted a tea stall. It was small and held together by rotting wood, but the large holosign grabbed his attention.

Warm your tired bones from your passage at sea! Fresh hot lemon cakes and Ravani tea served daily! it read.

The word Ravani sent a jolt through Yassen. It was home—the one he longed for but knew he was no longer welcome in.

Yassen drew up to the tea stall. Three large hourglasses hissed and steamed as a heavyset Sesharian woman flipped them in timed intervals. On her hand, Yassen spotted a tattoo of a bull, a mark of the Jantari colonies.

The same mark Samson had asked him to look for.

When the woman met Yassen's eyes, she twirled the hourglass once more before drying her hands on the towel around her wide waist.

"Whatcha want?" she asked in a river-hoarse voice.

"One tea and cake, please," Yassen said.

"You're lucky. I just got a fresh batch of leaves from my connect. Straight from the canyons of Ravence."

"Exactly why I want one," he said and placed his holopod on the counter insert. It scanned his pod and automatically transferred the funds. Yassen tapped it twice.

"Keep the change," he said.

She nodded and turned back to the giant hourglasses. Yassen slung his thin backpack onto his other shoulder. The brass beneath his feet grew warmer in the yawning day. Across the docks, more hoverboats pulled in, carrying immigrant laborers and tourists. Yassen adjusted his visor as the woman simultaneously flipped the hourglass and slid off its cap. In one fluid motion, the hot tea arced through the air and fell into the cup in her hand. She slid it across the counter.

"Mind the sleeve, the tea's hot," she said. A compartment at the edge of the counter opened, and a box slid out. "And here's your cake."

Yassen grabbed the box and lifted his cup in thanks. As he moved away from the stall, he scratched the plastic sleeve around the cup.

Slowly, a message burned through:

Look underneath the dock of fortunes.

He almost smiled. So Samson had not forgotten about his love of tea.

Yassen looked within the cake box and found something glinting at the bottom. He reached inside and held it up. Made of silver, the insignia was smaller than his palm and etched in what seemed to be the shape of a teardrop. Yassen held it closer. No, it was more feather than teardrop.

He threw the sleeve and box into a bin and continued down the dock. The commerce section stretched on, a mile of storefronts welcoming him into the great nation of Jantar. Yassen sipped his tea, watching. A few paces down, he spotted a stall marketing tales of ruin and fortune. Like the tea stall, it too was old and decrepit, with a painting of a woman reading tears painted across its front. He was beginning to recognize a pattern, and patterns were dangerous. Samson was getting lazy in his mansion.

Three guards stood along the edge of the platform beside the stall. One was dressed in a captain's royal blue while the other two wore the plain black of officers. All three donned helmet visors, their pulse guns strapped to their sides. They were laughing at some joke when the captain looked up and frowned at Yassen.

"You there!" he shouted.

Yassen lowered his cup. He glanced around him, but there was nowhere to run. The dock was full of carts and merchants. If he bolted now, the guards could catch him.

"Yes, you, with the full face," the captain called out. "Come here!" The other two stopped laughing as Yassen approached them.

"Is there a problem?" he asked.

"No full visors allowed on the dock, except for us," the captain said.

"I didn't know it was a crime to wear a full visor," Yassen said. His voice was cool, perhaps a bit too nonchalant because the captain slapped the cup out of Yassen's hand. The spilled tea hissed against the metal planks.

"New rules on the dock," the captain said. "Only guards can wear full ones. Everybody else has to go half."

His subordinates snickered. "Looks like he's fresh off the boat, Cap. You got to cut it up for him," one said.

Behind his visor, Yassen frowned. He glanced at the merchant behind the fortunes stall, who stood as if the interaction before him were just another part of city life. But then the merchant pointed down, and Yassen saw the sign of the bull on his hand.

Samson's men were watching.

"All right," Yassen said. He would give them a show. Prove to them he wasn't as crippled as the whispers told.

He unclipped his visor as the guards watched. "But you owe me another cup of tea."

And then Yassen flung his arm out and rammed the visor against the captain's face, stunning him as the other two reacted. They leapt forward, but Yassen swung around and gave four quick jabs, two each on the back, and the officers seized and sank to their knees in temporary paralysis.

"Fucking refugee!" the captain cried, reaching for his gun. Yassen jumped behind him, his hands quick and deft as he unclipped the captain's helmet visor.

The captain whipped around, raising his gun, but then sunlight hit the planks before him, and the brass threw off its unforgiving light. Blinded, the captain fired.

The air screeched.

The pulse whizzed past Yassen's right ear, tearing through the upper beams of a storefront. Immediately, merchants took cover. Someone screamed as shoppers and immigrants on both docks began to run. Yassen ran forward and joined the chaotic fray. He let the crowd push him toward the dock's edge, and then he dove into the sea.

The water was cold, colder than he expected, and it took Yassen a moment to gain his bearings before he swam forward. He surfaced underneath the dock, coughing. Footsteps thundered overhead as soldiers and guards barked out orders. Yassen caught glimpses of the captain in the spaces between the planks.

"All hells! Where did he go?" the captain yelled at the merchant manning the stall of wild tales.

The merchant shrugged. "He's long gone."

Yassen sank deeper into the water as the captain walked overhead, his subordinates wobbling behind. Something buzzed beneath him. Yassen tensed, reaching for his backpack, but the dark shape remained stationary. He waited for the guards to pass and then sank beneath the surface.

A sub, the size of one passenger, lay on the rocks as if it had been waiting for him.

Look underneath the dock of fortunes.

Samson, that bastard.

Yassen swam toward the sub. He placed his hand on the imprint panel of the hull, and then the sub buzzed again and rose to the surface. The glass screen pulled back and Yassen climbed in. The cockpit was small with barely enough room for him to stretch his legs, but he sighed and sank back just the same. The glass screen closed and the rudders whined to life. The panel board lit up before him and bathed him in a pale, blue light.

Yassen touched it, and a holo emerged. A note. Handwritten. How rare, and so like Samson.

See you at the palace, it said, and before Yassen could question *which* palace, the sub was off.

2
ELENA

*When the future king arrived at the unforgiving desert, he called
to his followers, "There, we will build our city." He led them under
the cloak of night when the sand had finally cooled. They built
bricks of clay until their hands were coarse and peeling. The twin
moons watched, compelled. They stayed in the sky longer to give the
followers relief from the burning day.*

—FROM CHAPTER 41 OF *THE GREAT HISTORY OF SAYON*

Elena ducked underneath an arch brimming with loyarian sparks.
They rained down on her, coating her hair and singeing her skin. She
didn't mind. When she blinked, the sparks caught on her eyelashes,
and she saw the world through a rim of gold.

As she passed a merchant selling holy offerings of lotus petals
and chipped gold, a large man with iron bands up his arms sneezed
so violently that he threw himself right in front of her path. Elena
sidestepped him just in time, scowling.

"Sorry, miss," the man said as he rubbed snot onto his iron bracelets.
"Looks like I'm coming down with the sands."

Elena gave a tight-lipped smile and motioned with her hand behind
her back, indicating to her guards to leave the man alone.

"Try some soothsayer tea," she said. "Or a mask."

The man's face twisted, and Elena hurried off before he sneezed again.

She brought the collar of her cloak closer, her face hidden behind large sunglasses. Though it was not even midday, she was already beginning to sweat in the desert heat. Her guards pulled up behind her, and out of the corner of her eye, Elena saw Ferma make a sour face.

"I still don't know why you want to come to Radhia's Bazaar, Your Highness," her Spear said. "Especially with all these dirty refugees."

Elena hopped over a stray shobu sprawled out on the sand. On the balcony above, an artisan flapped out a newly dyed scarf, sending droplets of carmine and amber raining down.

Someone shouted, and Elena turned to see two black and blue-haired Sesharian teens whizz by on floating bladers, laughing as a merchant gave chase. On the corner, a group of drunk fans let out groans. The floating bank of holos played back the Cyleon goalie blocking Ravence's shot and winning the Western Windsnatch Title. One fan threw down his drink, spraying the running merchant with beer.

"It's never boring." Elena smiled.

Despite the cloying heat and dust, she enjoyed Rani's winding streets and congested bazaars. The capital city was a jumble of incongruous sounds and architecture, of the stubborn past and marching modernity; tall pillars of blasted sandstone housed storefronts of holo-infused gauntlets, floating bladers, and neoprene gamesuits while merchants wheeled their sand-filled carts, crying out the prices of the day for this sack of purple sage, that exotic pet, or the greatest, biggest map you have ever seen. It was an uproar of hovercars beeping, drivers shouting, and pedestrians calling out as they crossed the road without the faintest fear of traffic; a whirlwind of people rubbing elbows, knees, palms, and dreams; a medley of orphans crying, fathers begging, and businesswomen cursing as they rushed to the hovertrains in their pincer heels. She could feel their collective breath, their sweat, their liveliness that was so unlike the long, cool halls of the Palace.

It grounded her.

Elena flicked a bead of sweat and pushed past a heavy-breasted woman selling sleeping pills. She went down an alley so narrow she had to walk sideways to get through, underneath arches adorned with crimson garian flowers, around a corner and then a side street before she arrived at the dark awning of her favorite spot in the city—Jasmine's Tea Garden.

As she breathed in the sweet, flowery aromas wafting out from the store, Elena heard Ferma grumble out orders to the guards. She smiled.

"Come on, Ferma," she said. "Lighten up. We've done this for many suns."

"Yes, but this time it's different," the Yumi woman said. She pulled her scarf tighter, hiding the trademark hair of her race: thick, long, silky strands that could harden into sharp shards and cut a man's throat.

Like most Yumi women, Ferma had been trained from infancy to be a soldier. There were only a few Yumi left in Sayon after the Burning of the Sixth Prophet, but the ones who had lived served as army captains. Only the very best graced the royal halls. Ferma had been her mother's Spear, as well as Elena's mentor. She was the one who had trained Elena in the art of holding a slingsword between her shoulder blades and how to keep it undetected before brandishing it with a quick flourish of her hips.

When Elena's mother had died, Ferma had presided over Elena's studies of history and politics, tended to her wounds after a long round in the dojo, and broke her fever in the depths of the night. Elena admired the Yumi's elegance. Without a word, Ferma could command a room. Without a sound, she could murder a man.

"I'm not queen yet, Ferma, so you can relax," Elena said.

"No, but every day we get closer to the coronation, we receive more threats," Ferma said. She motioned for the plainclothes guards to take their posts throughout the small square and its adjoining alleys.

"The silver feathers have already swept the area, so let me enjoy this while I can," Elena said and added with a wink, "especially if you're going to hound me until the end of my days."

They ducked inside the old teashop. It was empty with long, cool shadows stretching down the walls. The shopkeeper, Jasmine herself, emerged from the backroom with a platter of tea and cloud cookies—Elena's favorite. She smiled and put them down at their usual table.

"Thank you, Jasmine," Elena said, and the old woman bowed.

"Back for your monthly performance?" she asked.

Elena grinned. She shrugged off her cloak and handed it to Ferma, who in exchange offered her a scarf and a wooden block. Elena twisted her hair up and tightened the scarf around her head, covering her face.

People in the square called her the Masked Dancer. Some had even teased her to lower her scarf and let them catch a glimpse of her smile, but Elena had always refused. It was better if they did not know who she was.

She nodded to Ferma and then stepped back out. In the middle of the square, Elena set the block on the ground. She placed her hand on its surface, and a light scanned her fingerprints and the map of her veins before blossoming like a lotus. Its petals connected and grew, creating a wooden floor.

Passersby, the ones who always came for her show, arrived with eager expressions. Some were Sesharian refugees with faded bull tattoos; others were office workers on their lunch breaks. They dropped coins in the bag Ferma made out of her linen cloak. Elena chucked off her shoes and clapped her hands. Low notes of music floated from the platform speakers. She closed her eyes and began to move, slowly, gracefully, warming up her limbs and stretching out her calves. Her fans rapped the wooden board.

"What is it this time, Madame?" asked a young woman. Freckles splashed across her ears and cheeks, her hair streaked purple in Verani fashion.

"You'll see," Elena said without opening her eyes.

With one more squat and toe raise, Elena came to the center of the board and opened her eyes. A thin ring of people circled her makeshift stage. Others, mothers rushing to grab groceries, urchins dodging under carts and swiping goods, bored teenagers smoking Lynthium grass and prophesying about the clouds, pushed on.

Elena smiled.

Today would be a good challenge.

She stamped her feet and the music stopped. A hush fell over the square. Staring at the crowd with her kohl-rimmed eyes, Elena swirled and brought her hands to the sky. She hit her heels together, and the show began.

Tablas and sitar strings guided Elena as she danced, swerving her hips and shoulders as the crowd began to grow. She could feel their eyes on her, their awe, their captivation. She kept her eyes on them, taunting them to come closer.

They began to clap in rhythm, faster and faster as the music swelled. Elena felt her blood hum with the beat of the tablas. Heat flushed her cheeks as she danced, the ends of her scarf fluttering behind her like wings. Without warning, she leaped, suspended for what felt like an eternity, her legs long and brown in the afternoon sun. And then she came down, soft like the feather of a desert bird.

The crowd broke into applause, tossing coins onto the wooden floor. Elena grinned at the roar. It filled her, completed her, warmed her with an energy she could not feel elsewhere. For only here could she find the adoration she sought—the love of her people.

She was so enamored by their cheers that she did not notice the shadow from above until Ferma suddenly grabbed her wrist and pulled her into the shop, shoving her to the back wall.

"What are—" Elena said, but Ferma stopped her and pointed.

Outside, the shadow grew. The merchants, mothers, orphans and even the teenagers with their pipes all looked up.

Elena opened her mouth to speak again when she heard the telltale drone of the hoverpod. The black oval, smooth as a riverstone, descended from the sky and into the square. It blew sand and rubbish up into the air. Ten feet tall and as wide as three merchant carts, the hoverpod dwarfed her small stage. A shobu leapt up and growled, but it knew not to approach. The crowd shrank back as they saw the sun glint off the pod's onyx finish and the royal insignia of the Phoenix on its door. Without a sound, the door slid up, revealing a black abyss within.

Elena cursed underneath her breath.

"Come on," Ferma said and poked her between her shoulder blades.

Elena sat down heavily. "No," she said. "They know not to come like this."

"The longer it stays out there, the more attention it'll get," Ferma said.

Behind the counter, Jasmine rotated the hourglasses as if nothing had happened. She poured bright red Ravani tea into a twisted vial and set it by the register.

"For the road," she said.

Ferma hauled Elena to her feet. She grabbed the vial and thrust it at her while slipping on her linen cloak, fussing and clucking like a monstrous mother hen.

"I got it. I got it," Elena said. She yanked on the sleeve and stalked out. She could feel the merchants and children staring at her—not with admiration, but with a quieter, colder sense of fear. Elena hid her face and walked into the hoverpod. She heard her guards follow and the door shut.

"So what is it now?" Elena asked as the pod rose.

Ferma drew up beside her and placed her hand on the console. Holos shot up as the lights blinked on.

"It looks like you're being summoned," the Yumi said as she read the holos. She looked more at ease now that she was out of the sun, sighing in relief as she sat down.

"But why?" Elena said. She waved her hand and a black slab emerged from the wall. She sat, watching the city recede beneath her. Sand-scrapers and chhatris gave way to sprawling mounds that melted into the greater landscape of the rolling dunes.

"Wait," Elena said, leaning closer to the bulletproof window. "Are we not going back to the Palace?"

She watched Ferma point into the distance, into the bordering mountains and the impossible swath of forest that ringed the desert.

"No," she said. "Your father wants to see you."

3
YASSEN

When the dragons began to leave, no Sayonai noticed. Not at first.
It wasn't until the droughts came and fires raged throughout the
countrysides that the people raised their eyes to the heavens and
realized—no one was there.

—FROM CHAPTER 17 OF *THE GREAT HISTORY OF SAYON*

Yassen watched the sea glide past him as he sank lower to the murky depths. Torn visors, driftwood, and plastic cups gave way to darker waters. The sub shuddered as it neared the mouth of a cave along the rocky grade. A holo flickered onto the control panel.

"Please place the seal before you," a robotic voice intoned. Yassen set the small feather on the panel. A laser scanned it as the engines whined.

"Entry granted," the voice said. "Please sit back."

The sub suddenly shot into the cave at a breakneck speed, throwing Yassen back into his seat. He realized then that the cave was actually a tunnel, and that it glinted with blue light. Up and up they went until Yassen saw a small opening, a shining patch of water shaped like a silver coin. The vessel bolted out and the sky opened above him with mountains jutting the horizon.

Yassen let out a shaky breath. The sub bobbed gently as the glass covering slid back. He was in the middle of a lake surrounded by the white peaks of the Sona Range. On the shore, a figure stood, waving.

Slowly, Yassen recognized the set of broad shoulders and chest, the wide-legged stance and bowed knees befit a warrior, or a man who rode his horses hard. As the vessel came closer, the man lowered his hand, and Yassen saw something flash on his outer finger.

After all this time, he still wore his family crest.

"Welcome, Cass," the man said. His voice was deeper now, a steady rumble like that of a waterfall. It expanded and lingered in the air long after he had spoken. The voice of a Sesharian who had never forgotten his island past.

The sub docked, and Yassen hopped on shore. "Hey, Sam."

Samson Kytuu was taller, straight-backed like steel with a high forehead and an aquiline nose. But when he smiled at Yassen, he gave that same wide grin that reached the corners of his eyes, the same one he had given when they had crouched along the stone wall of a Ravani bakery many suns ago. The smile had promised a distracted baker's daughter and three loaves of honeyed bread.

Yassen held up the metal feather, and it glinted in the sun.

"Why this?"

"Don't tell me you didn't notice," Samson said, and Yassen brought the insignia closer. In the gleams of the sun, he saw that it was not a feather after all, but a single, flickering flame.

"Of course," he murmured. "Ravence."

He had met Samson in his childhood home of Rani. They had been new orphans, hungry and stranded. While Yassen scoured the desert for castaway trinkets to sell, Samson pickpocketed. They would pool their money to buy food and when they had too little, they stole. Together, they had survived.

Yassen could feel Samson watching him, studying him, possibly experiencing the same shocks that came when meeting a childhood friend after a very long time.

The distance between them wasn't long, but an awkward silence loomed. Yassen hesitated and just then, the sub gave a loud hiss that made them jump and draw their guns. They looked at each other and then the vessel, and a slow laugh started in their bellies before erupting in the air—a laugh that warmed the arid silence and melted guarded fronts, a laugh that they had shared as boys.

Samson holstered his pulse gun with a grin. He kissed his three fingers and pressed them against Yassen's forehead, the customary Sayonai greeting given to friends and family.

"It's been too long, Cass."

They took a stone path that curved along the mountainside. Retherin pines and molorian trees covered the grade. A mountain lark flitted above them, giving its three-note call of peace. The Jantari were known to mine these mountains, yet Yassen did not see the ugly metal hulls of the rigs.

"I've bought the entire land from here to the next summit," Samson said as if to answer his thoughts.

"And they just let you?" Yassen asked.

"Only if my soldiers protect the mines on the northern range," Samson said. "Easy work, though. I even made a small base in the middle—a training grounds of sorts. Perhaps I'll show you sometime."

"There has to be more to it," Yassen said, eyeing him. "I've never heard of the Jantari king being the generous type."

Samson smiled slowly, though he stared straight ahead. "Always the observant one, Cass."

The path grew steeper. Yassen felt his calves begin to burn when they finally crested the hill, and the house suddenly rose above him as if to stun him with all its glory.

It was a behemoth, more palace than a mansion of a successful militant. Melded of black Sesharian marble and Jantari steel, the palace curved around the mountainside like two great wings of some beast.

"You put a *mountain* in the middle of your house?" Yassen asked, turning to Samson.

"Welcome to Casear Lunar, Cass," his friend replied.

Twin towers, modest in height yet ostentatious with their embellished ridges of lapis lazuli flowers, stood on the edges of the sprawling gardens. Soldiers stationed there lowered their pulse guns and saluted as they passed.

Intricate flora—from pale kissed roses to dancing tiger lilies—swayed in the delicate wind, spreading their aroma across the grounds. Yassen spotted gardeners snipping away vines. Though they wore gloves, Yassen could tell by their raven-black hair that they were

Sesharians. They stopped and bowed as Samson approached, but he paid them no mind.

Eventually, they reached the black, yawning entrance of the palace, with its arched marble columns and sculptures of dragons. The guards beside the entrance bowed, and Yassen watched Samson raise his hand, murmuring some command to put them at ease.

"They treat you like a king," Yassen said as they entered the foyer.

To say the outside of the palace was magnificent compared to its interior was an affront. Two spiraling staircases swept up and diverged in opposite directions toward two wings. A gem-encrusted dragon coiled across the marble floor. Above, a million tiny glass tiles reflected the sunrays so it seemed that the very stars were within this room, within his reach. Yassen tried to stop himself from staring, but he couldn't.

"Some say so, but it's more out of respect than divine right," the militant replied.

Yassen tried to compose himself, looking back out the doorway where the gardeners, relieved of their master's presence, resumed their task of snipping away the pernicious mountain vines.

"Do they know who I am?"

"A half-Ravani and half-Jantari mutt," Samson teased, but then he slung his arm around Yassen's neck, his voice lowering. "We're more than orphans now, Cass." He gazed up at the ceiling that captured the heavens. "That's all they need to know."

Yassen gazed around him. How different this was from the derelict ruins they had once slept in. Here, they could host and feed an entire army and still not know the pang of hunger. Perhaps this was what Samson had intended—to create a palace so grand that no one could even mention his wayward upbringing.

Their wayward upbringings.

Yassen felt a numbness in his right arm, and he flexed his fingers with great difficulty. Samson had chosen a different path, and this was what he had to show for it.

"Let's eat, I know you must be starving," Samson said.

As if on cue, a servant with lips stained blue from indigo snuff appeared from the adjoining wing.

"Sires," he said, bowing. Yassen spotted the same bull tattoo on his hand.

"Yassen, this is Maurilis, my most trusted man. Maurilis, this is Yassen, a childhood friend," Samson said. He gripped his shoulder, hands harder, meaner than what Yassen remembered. "A brother, actually."

Yassen warmed at the distinction, but he smiled warily. Though Samson squeezed his shoulder, Yassen suspected his old friend still harbored doubts about his loyalties. He would have to convince Samson that he was done with the Arohassin. Forever. That what he truly desired, above all else, was a quiet morning on this mountainside.

"A pleasure," Maurilis said, his eyes lingering on Yassen's rumpled clothes. "The refreshments are ready for you."

"Splendid," Samson said. He pulled Yassen closer, grinning. "A little bird told me that you still like Ravani tea."

The blue-lipped servant led them down a long hall full of light and crystal. A dragon coiled across the ceiling, its scales fashioned with mirrors that reflected their steps. They came to two great doors at the end of the hall. A river curved along the edges of the gate and swirled inward toward the doorknobs. Samson stepped forward. A pale light scanned his hand and fingerprints. Another thin beam swept across his face, zeroing into his eye. Samson blinked, and then the beam closed, the river hissed, and the door unlocked to reveal the mountain.

A pathway of metal and stone cut its way through a courtyard filled carefully pruned palehearts. Above, a mountain peak glimmered in the glare of the sun, but Yassen did not squint. He could not appear weak before Samson.

The path led to a terrace furnished with ivory chaises. Samson motioned for them to sit as two Sesharian servants placed pots of tea and platters of sandwiches and sweets before them. As they poured tea into their cups, lazy wafts of steam uncurled in the air. Yassen drank in the smell of Vermi leaves and lemongrass. Arranged on a three-tier platter were an assortment of sandwiches filled with apricot jam, gingerberry beads, and smoked meat. Another servant brought out a selection of powdered dew nuts, syrup-coated figs, and cloud cookies that, when bitten, dissolved into honeyed air.

"They still your favorite?" Samson smiled when he caught Yassen staring at the cloud cookies.

Yassen nodded and sank back in his seat. His right arm felt cold and numb, but he ignored it.

A flutter of color made him turn, and Yassen caught the fleeting image of a clawed falcon diving into the canopy for unseen prey. Its descent sent off a flurry of calls. Among them, Yassen recognized the flute-like voice of a mountain lark.

"They can be a nuisance sometimes, but I swear, come dawn, they make the most beautiful chorus you've ever heard," Samson said. He sat back in his seat and bit into a cloud cookie, vapors of red escaping from between his lips.

Along the edge of the courtyard, Yassen saw a gardener rip out a cropping of silver-headed mushrooms that gave off such a strong, sulfurous scent that he could smell it from the terrace.

"Are we having mushrooms for dinner?" he asked and turned to Samson, who was carefully applying a layer of gingerberry beads to a piece of toast.

"They still make your stomach turn?" Samson asked. "Remember the time when you threw up all over Akaros's shoes? Skies above, he was livid. He must have made you scrub those filthy leather loafers a hundred and fifty times before he put them back on."

"I spat in them just in case," Yassen said, and Samson laughed.

"How is that old man? Keeping the boys miserable as always?"

"I thought you had given up on the family name," Yassen said, indicating the signet ring on Samson's pinky. "Or at least that's what the reporters say."

"What do you think?" Samson asked, and Yassen heard the subtle downturn in his voice. Samson was testing him, just like he had suspected.

He hesitated, eyeing his friend. Though he had the same smile, Samson was a stranger in the shell of the eighteen-year-old boy Yassen once knew. The boy who had clutched his arm so hard that Yassen found marks in the morning; the boy who had promised that he was done with his name, done with the Arohassin, and that he was leaving and would one day come back for Yassen.

Yassen felt the ghost of Samson's hand pressing into his flesh.

"I think that—as much as you decry your family name and the horrors it's brought upon you—you still miss your home. Maybe not all the people, but at least the horses." Samson laughed again and Yassen pushed on, picking his words with care, mindful that the person before him was not truly the boy of his childhood. "But what I still don't understand is, after all the wealth and power you've accumulated, why haven't you gone back. Why haven't you punished the people who killed your family?"

"I see you haven't changed a bit," Samson said. He lowered his leg so he sat straighter like a solider. He sipped his tea, but something cold was in his voice. "You're still obsessed with punishment. They drilled that one deep. Didn't they?"

"You were supposed to come back," Yassen said.

"We both know the Arohassin would have cut off our heads if I did," Samson said softly. He brushed crumbs from his sleeve, but Yassen saw the pain in his eyes. Samson had abandoned him to a miserable fate. And now here Yassen was, burnt and thin, a reminder of Samson's shortcomings. Perhaps the militant knew of guilt, too.

"I see you've employed your people though," Yassen said, nodding to the gardeners and the servants. "Are they all Sesharians?"

"Every single one."

"And Farin gave them to you?"

"You don't give men. They're not slaves," Samson said, a hint of reproach in his voice. "I just convinced Farin that not all colonized people make good miners."

"They make better soldiers," Yassen said, looking at Samson.

The militant paused and then gave a slow nod. "Some better than others."

A servant came to refill their cups. When she finally left, Samson cleared his throat.

"The reason I took your call, Cass, was, well, it was the first time you've ever asked for my help," he said. His eyes crinkled with warmth and a lingering darkness. It was the same look Yassen had seen Samson give to their teachers when he had completed his assignment but left a surprise in his wake.

"But when you decided to defect, I had to take safety precautions. You see, Cass," he said and placed his hand in the space between them, the dragon insignia of his ring flashing in the light. "I already have an assignment for you, but I won't force you to take it. It's your choice. Heavens know you deserve rest."

But Yassen knew he really had no choice as Samson tapped the table and holos shot up. News clippings, images, and files opened before Yassen, but he already knew what they contained.

"Ravence," he said before Samson could say anything.

Samson froze but then shook his head. "I knew you'd figure it out. Ravence is about to crown its new queen, and they've asked me to provide security. You know why?" he asked, his eyes boring into Yassen.

Yassen met his gaze without flinching.

"Because the Arohassin plan to attack and assassinate the Ravani family on the coronation day."

"Did they tell you anything else before you ran?"

"Everything I know, I give to you," Yassen said and withdrew a holopod from his pocket. More holos shot up to reveal names, meeting points, and—the mother trove of all—a map of the Arohassin sleeper agents in Ravence. "This is proof that I've truly defected. It's all there, Sam."

"Then you already know what I'm going to ask you," Samson said. He paused, hesitating for a moment, and then pushed on. "Come with me to Ravence. I've already spoken to the king and he's agreed to give you a royal pardon if you help the family take down the Arohassin. Freedom, Yassen. You'll finally have it."

Yassen looked down at his hands. Freedom, what a funny word. Here, he felt so close to it. The mountain air almost made him heady with the notion of quiet mornings and undisturbed peace. Yassen pinched the nerve between his finger and thumb. Ravence was his home. And despite the fragrant mountain breeze, he knew what he really longed for was the desert. The endless, rolling dunes. It was the place he understood and where he would have to return.

He watched Samson sit back and look at him, not with the pretense of childhood familiarity, but with the cold, calculated air of a businessman.

"Pull out that flame I gave you," Samson said.

Yassen pulled out the metal insignia from his pocket and placed it on the holopod. It scanned the flame, and a confidential file opened— his own.

"You see, it has everything I have on you. Names, dates, even the serial number of guns. It could lock you away for life. But I give it to you as a measure of good will," Samson said. "I want no secrets between us, Cass. I said long ago that I would help you get home, and I mean to fulfill that promise. People are going to question my decision, but I know you. You haven't changed."

Yassen studied Samson, searching his face for a trace of hesitancy or dishonesty, but either he was true to his word, or well-trained to hide his thoughts, to give anything other than a look of belief. Actual belief. The same burning belief that opened a floodgate when Samson, gripping Yassen's arm in the middle of the night, had babbled about revenge and defection. The same belief that shone in his eyes when he told Yassen, in a rare instance of drug-induced clarity, that he, Yassen Knight, would survive. Survive out of all of them. Survive to live out old age and perhaps even forgiveness from the gods.

What Samson hadn't known was that Yassen did not find himself to be in the ranks of the forgiven. He was well beyond that point. The burns up his arms told him so. His long flight across the sea told him so. The faces he saw in the night told him so. Guilt, that snake-like poison, wormed its way down his throat as Yassen smiled—a smile he knew would break the cold, calculated air Samson propped as a shield because he too hadn't changed.

Yassen reached for the flame and slipped it back into his pocket. The holograms disappeared in the breeze.

"I'll go to Ravence with you if you get me amnesty," he said. "And then I'll be free."

Samson kissed his three fingers and held them in the air. Yassen did the same, and they touched their fingers together, sealing the promise.

"I was saving this for tonight, but I don't think it can wait," Samson said and withdrew a gold bottle of Cyleoni wine from beneath the table. With a grin, he popped the cork and dumped out their tea, scattering the birds on the terrace. He poured the clear elixir into their cups and raised his in the air.

"To freedom," he said.

"To Haku and Cassian," Yassen said, referencing the code names they had given each other that fateful day in front of the Temple's stone steps.

At this, Samson's smile softened, and he merely dipped his head. They drank in silence. Yassen pretended to take a sip, and then set his glass down, untouched.

He wondered if Samson remembered that he didn't drink.

4
ELENA

The Prophet is justice in the corporeal form. Blessed by the Phoenix, the Prophet never dies but is reincarnated—life to ashes; ashes to life. The last Prophet, the Sixth Prophet, was known to live in this world five hundred suns ago. There are no records of her death, but after her disappearance, Alabore Ravence led his followers into the desert and created what we know now as The Kingdom of Ravence.

—FROM CHAPTER 3 OF *THE GREAT HISTORY OF SAYON*

The hoverpod flew across the sea of dunes toward the mountains along the western border. Despite the arid desert, the Agnee mountains were filled with lush, towering pines. Legends said that when the Sixth Prophet rose, she created the desert to deter armies, but kept the mountain forests to protect the Temple.

If it had been up to her, Elena would have burned it all down. It was easy for enemies to hide in the forest, but the desert left no room for secrets.

Low clouds hung over the Agnee Range and turned the trees into silver spears. The hoverpod rose, climbing through the grey expanse before the mist gave way to the looming Temple.

The Temple of Fire was older than the Kingdom of Ravence, older than the desert itself. It sat on the edge of a steep cliff, overlooking the forests. Shaped in the form of a lotus, the Temple had eight ivory wings, or petals, that represented a tenet of the Phoenix: Truth, Perseverance, Courage, Faith, Discipline, Duty, Honor, and Rebirth. A lantern was fixed at the top of every petal. The priests took rotating shifts to refill the diyas with mustard oil and keep the flames alive. In the heart of the lotus, a pristine white marble dome held court. A thick plume of smoke curled from its center.

The pod docked and Elena walked out, breathing in the smell of ash and pine. Two royal guards, dressed in black uniforms with a red feather above their hearts, stood by the bottom of the steps. They bowed as she and Ferma approached. Elena craned her neck to take in the white granite staircase chiseled into the face of the mountain.

Her heart sank.

Couldn't we have docked behind the Temple?

She knew it was the king's way of condoning her rendezvous within the city. Elena sighed and began the long process of ascending the steps with Ferma close behind. The climb was steep and winding, but Elena was determined not to show discomfort. Her father could sense weakness.

"Give the money we collected to the Orphanage of Sand Children," she mumbled to Ferma when they reached the fountain of the Phoenix. It sat midway up the flight of stairs, gurgling softly. A statue of the Phoenix soared above it, Her red eyes glowing despite the lack of sunlight.

"You give them too much," Ferma responded. She moved easily, her long limbs unfolding and rising like a dancer. Meanwhile, Elena could already feel her cheeks starting to flush.

"If you say another word, I'll throw in your pay too," she said.

Ferma grinned. It took them fifteen minutes to climb the stairs. When they finally reached the landing, two men awaited them. Elena recognized Marcus, her father's Spear. He was a large brute of a man with downy eyes, and he dwarfed the short, white-haired man beside him.

"Alonjo." She smiled.

The Astra, her father's highest-ranking advisor, bowed deeply.

"Your Highness," he said in his soft, whispery voice. "His Majesty is already inside for the Ashanta ceremony."

How many times will he consult the heavens? Elena squeezed Alonjo's arm and then brushed past him.

"Wait out here," she called back to Ferma.

The Temple's entrance was made of firestone and pink marble, laden with jewels burnished from the heat of the desert, but when Elena stepped inside the dark stone hall, shadows awaited her. She could hear the hypnotic drone of the priests coming down the main hall. Carefully, she took off her shoes. The stone was cool underneath her feet but grew warmer as she neared the Seat, the center of the Temple. The chanting of the priests grew louder. She smelled sandalwood-scented incense intermingled with smoke. Shadows danced along the wall, a mirage of the fire that awaited.

When she reached the curve, Elena stopped and closed her eyes. She breathed in and out. Felt the warmth of the stone. Emptied out her mind and then walked forward.

It was if she had stepped into a furnace. The heat slammed against her face, chasing the air from her lips. Despite her resolve, Elena stumbled back. The Eternal Fire roared and shot up toward the domed ceiling and the golden statue of the Phoenix that soared above. A semi-circle of priests stood around the pit of the Fire, chanting.

Within the flames, on the raised dais, Elena saw a man sitting straight and tall. The High Priestess, dressed in a golden shawl, stood before the steps of the dais. She threw lotus petals into the Eternal Fire, and the flames grew larger. The heat intensified. But the figure did not even move or tremble. No wonder people feared her father.

Elena sank to her knees behind the circle of priests. The flames greedily licked the air as her father sat there, head bowed, stoic in the heat.

She felt her chest begin to constrict like the windpipe of a desert bird in the hand of a butcher. Her palms grew sweaty. She rubbed them against her knees and blinked smoke out of her eyes. Elena forced herself to sit still, to stop fidgeting, to look into the Eternal Fire and not be blinded by its light.

The priests gave one last chant, and then the High Priestess poured an urn of mountain water into the pit.

She opened a leather-bound book, a rarity in Sayon, and smoothed the pages.

"Here sits the servant of Alabore Ravence, the one true king. The one chosen to lead his people to their promised land," she sang. "May the Phoenix bless Her followers from the ash of Her Fire. May we take this ash and see the world with eyes unclouded by hatred. May She bless the son who carries Her legacy."

Her father stood up. Ash sprinkled down his shoulders as he stepped off the raised dais and walked down the stairs. The High Priestess pinched vermillion powder between her fingers and drew three diagonal lines across the king's forehead.

"And so we the blessed few," she intoned.

"So we the blessed few," both Elena and her father returned.

Elena rose slowly as her father accepted offerings from the priests. He raised them to his lips, kissing lotus flowers, sweets of diamond rock, and petals of desert rose. The High Priestess saw her and smiled. Elena bowed as she pressed her hand against Elena's forehead.

"When you are queen, you too will sit in the flames," she said, and the wrinkles around her eyes deepened.

"Thank you, Saayna," Elena said, but she could feel her father's eyes on her. He probably sensed the insecurity in her voice. Because try as she might, she could not hold a flame, let alone sit in a fire. She could not withstand the burn.

"Elena," her father said, and she turned to the king.

Her father was a tall man, straight-backed like the tall pines lining the desert, broad shouldered like the mountains, and with the same high forehead as hers. He was nearly sixty suns but gave no signs of his age. Perhaps his rigid constitution and ability to withstand coups, wars, and the Eternal Fire made him so. Perhaps it was the fact he lost his wife to madness while managing a kingdom constantly threatened by religious fanatics and greedy neighbors. Yet when Elena bowed and King Leo placed his heavy hand on her head, she knew the reason her father still stood on the throne was not because of his cunning and tenacity but because his sense of fear had died with his wife.

Her father feared nothing. And that made him a dangerous and capable man.

"I heard you were dancing for the beggars again," her father said as the Eternal Fire hissed. "There are better ways for the people to love your name."

"*Our* name," Elena corrected.

King Leo flicked ash from his hand. The ground rumbled as the stone seal before the entrance slid away, revealing steps. The priests retreated into their underground chambers while the High Priestess remained. She pressed a small, leaf-bound package into Elena's hands.

"The Holy Bird's gifts."

Elena nodded. Saayna always made her feel uneasy. The High Priestess was nearly as old as her father, if not more. Wrinkles crept around her eyes, but her skin was otherwise smooth and unblemished, her brown eyes clear and full of serenity. There was something surreal about her, superficial even. Elena accepted the gift, and the High Priestess bowed and descended into the chamber below.

Once they were alone, King Leo sank down to his knees before the dais steps. Elena followed suit. They sat looking into the Eternal Fire. Though she could not stand its heat, the Fire was mesmerizing in a way. The way the flames danced. The way they soared and licked the feet of the Phoenix like loving, devoted servants. Fire knew how to love and when to destroy.

"There's some news I want to share with you," he said. A fine layer of soot lined his saffron-colored kurta and white shawl. Her mother's necklace, a golden chain with a jade and purple desertstone bird pendant, hung around his neck without a single speck of ash. "The Arohassin attacked a sand port in the Rasbakan."

She breathed in sharply. The Arohassin were an ideological criminal organization bent on destroying kingdoms in the name of a new world order, an order of governments created by the people and not kings. But Elena had seen the work of the Arohassin. They claimed freedom but brought anarchy. They quoted martyrs, yet spawned more in their wake. What good was their liberation if it only led to ash and ruin?

"Do you think that's somehow connected to the skirmishes with the Jantari on our southern border?" she asked.

"Perhaps, but Farin is too proud to hire someone to do his dirty work," Leo mused. "Muftasa tells me that the Arohassin acted on their own."

"Great, now we have storms in our east and south." She shook her head, her voice fierce and low. "But we're losing to the Jantari, Father. Every day, we lose three men compared to one of their own. Ferma told me they found a bomb planted during one of their southern patrols. If only—"

"We can handle the Jantari. It's the Arohassin I worry about. I ought to cut off their heads, but I found something better," he said and paused. The Fire hissed and spat out sparks. "I made a deal with Samson Kytuu. He'll strengthen our forces in the south with his army and use his intelligence to root out the Arohassin."

"And what does the Landless King want in exchange?" she asked. Her father looked at her with his stark, grey eyes, the ones she never inherited. She knew the answer before he even said it, and it was as if the air was sucked out of the room and into the roaring flames.

Her father turned back to the Fire. It threw shadows of light and smoke across his face.

"The marriage would help solidify our position," Leo said. "Despite his past, people love Samson. They adore him—"

"They're stupid."

"—I know," her father continued, "but we can't deny that Samson is a powerful man. Yes, he's one of those snake-oil types, but his track record is flawless. Annoyingly so. We've seen him turn the fate of wars with his Black Scales. He's smart, fast, crude. With a man like him at your side, Ravence will never lose."

Elena said nothing. She stared down at her hands, which suddenly looked so small and far away. In between the crackles and hisses of the flames, she heard the voices of history, those past kings and queens who had suffered and sacrificed for this altar before her, this mounting Fire that ate everything in its path. She felt its heat, its claim on her destiny. The smoke closed around her, narrowing her field of vision until she was only looking at the haunting, dancing flames. How did her father do it?

Without thinking, Elena reached her hand toward the pit. The inferno roared and singed her skin. She yelped and yanked her hand back.

"Don't worry," her father said after a moment, "you'll learn."

Elena fought back a grimace. She curled her hand in her lap to hide the burn.

More ash sprinkled down Leo's arm as he leaned forward and scooped up a single flame. It almost leaped into his hand, ready to claim new flesh.

"I would burn them all, just like your great grandmother did in the Red Rebellion," he said. Elena felt her skin prickle as he brought the flame closer and held it up between them. "But there are more ways than burning and fighting to change the course of this land. Sometimes, all you need is to present the threat and then watch them cower like shobus with their tails between their legs."

Gently, her father returned the flame back to its awaiting hearth. He laid out his unscathed palm.

"Yassen Knight is coming back to Ravence with Samson. He'll join your Spear and be a part of your guard until the coronation."

"Yassen Knight?" she said. She was sure she had heard incorrectly.

"Don't sit there with your mouth hanging open," her father said, not unkindly. "He defected from the Arohassin, and Samson picked him up. Apparently, they're childhood friends."

She scoffed. "Isn't he crippled? The Arohassin burned his name in the sand."

To burn one's name in the sand was to call for their death. She had seen the Arohassin do it before to defectors. They never lived for long.

"Having Yassen Knight in Ravence will only attract their attention," she said.

"Yassen and Samson both know more about the Arohassin than we do," Leo replied.

"But father, it's *him*. The same man who assassinated the Cyleon ambassador and General Mandar. We almost started a war because of that murder."

"I know," her father said.

Ash skittered as the king stood and bowed to the Eternal Fire. In the wavering shadows, he looked more than a man, close to a god.

"That's why I've chosen him."

5
LEO

*The Prophet raised her eyes to the heavens and said today justice
would burn the land and cleanse it of its sins. But she does not know
what it means to burn.
The pain of it. The sorrow of it.*

—FROM THE DIARIES OF PRIESTESS NOMU OF THE FIRE ORDER

Leo watched the Eternal Fire roll back into itself, satiated. The Ashanta
ceremony had calmed it for now.

Elena had left in a huff, leaving him alone in the Seat. He knew she
wouldn't like Yassen Knight being a part of her guard, but Leo wanted
that bastard close. The assassin wouldn't dare make a false move with
so many eyes on him. And, with Yassen so close, Leo would enjoy
watching him sweat.

The Eternal Fire grew taller and licked the Phoenix's feet. Leo
looked up at the great bird. The first followers of the Fire Order had
carved the ancient language of Herra into the Temple wall. Though
Leo could not read the writing, he knew it told the story about a
vengeful god and an all-powerful Prophet who could make the world
bend. A man who could raise fire from nothing.

Leo had once believed he would be the Prophet. Any young Ravani
brought up on tales of the beast of fire thought he was the one to ride
it. But then he had learned how to sit in the flames. Learned how to

respect fire and withstand its heat long enough to give the country a show. He had come to know the truth. There was nothing special about fire. It burned and raged. Demanded sacrifice, worship. It had no need for a Prophet.

His dream had crumbled to ash, hardening to a cold, steady demeanor of a king who knew how to inspire both fear and respect. Fire had taught him one thing—the power of myth. Give the people something to believe in. Make it strong enough, fearsome enough, and they would all bow.

The king turned at the sound of stone scraping. The High Priestess emerged from the chamber below. She had taken off her golden ceremonial garb and was dressed in a plain red robe with an orange shawl to cover her hair.

"Your Majesty."

"Saayna," he said and then, seeing the drawn look on her face, "What is it?"

"There is something you need to see."

They descended into the chamber, the heat of the inferno gradually seeping away as the cool damp of the mountain wrapped around them. A vast network of tunnels spidered beneath the Temple. Here, the priests slept and worked, emerging only to tend to the Eternal Fire and the diyas. The irony of the priests of the Fire Order living in constant shadow had always amused Leo. He regarded them all with the healthy skepticism of a ruler. The Fire Order was necessary to his reign. A Ravani king and queen could only rule after receiving blessings from the High Priestess and the Eternal Fire. Throughout the suns, he had increased the budget meant for the upkeep of the Temple and encouraged citizens to give hearty contributions. Leo gave the Order their worshippers, and they in turn gave him access to the heavens.

Small floating orbs lit the underground chamber. Leo and Saayna followed it to the end, took a turn, and then emerged into a larger room. The roof was not made of stone like the rest of the tunnels; instead, banyan roots and moss intertwined to create a living ceiling that let pale sunlight filter in. Herbs hung around the wall, filling the room with the smell of turmeric and dry pine. A young priest lay in a cot on his stomach, covered by a thin blanket. A small priestess sat beside him, but stood immediately as they entered.

"Your Majesty," she muttered. A star-shaped birthmark on her cheek collapsed and expanded with the movement of her lips.

"Leave us," Saayna commanded.

The small priestess dipped her head and scurried away. Leo approached the young man spread out before him.

"What's wrong with the boy?" he asked. The young man's face was grey and slack. A slick sheen of sweat covered his body.

"Yesterday, the Eternal Fire burned him across the back. It will take him weeks to recover," the High Priestess said from behind.

The Eternal Fire often lashed out. During his crowning, it had leapt from the pit, burning his foot. He still had a scar that roped around his heel like a serpent. Yet, over the suns, Leo had learned how to control the flames. The Phoenix and Her Fire commanded respect, like any god. Give that, and it would stay at bay.

"He should have been more careful."

"But, sire," Saayna said. "It burned a message."

Leo froze. "A message?"

The High Priestess removed the blanket covering the young priest. A burn spread across his back. It was as if a hand had taken a dagger and carved into his flesh. The priest's scalded skin shaped into two runes. Leo peered closer. The only symbol he recognized was the feather of the Phoenix.

"Do you know what this says?"

"Daughter of Fire," the High Priestess answered, her voice soft. Reverent.

Leo glanced up at her and saw the fervent look in her eyes.

"*Daughter* of Fire?" he repeated. The meaning slowly dawned on him. He looked at Saayna and then the poor boy. The runes smoldered in the low light.

"The Prophet comes," the High Priestess whispered.

Leo felt something unspool within him. Disbelief perhaps, denial even, but deeper within, disappointment. *Daughter of Fire*. The next Prophet would be a woman. It would never be him.

After learning the nature of the flames, he had believed in the Phoenix and Her Prophecy with a grain of sand. He went through the rituals and ceremonies because that was what he needed to do as king. Put on a show. A feigned devotion. Ravence was built on the back of an old religion. He had to cater to it. But this, this was something his predecessors had never prepared him for.

Leo looked to the High Priestess.

"When?" he asked.

"I know not, only that the time draws near," she said. "She will come for Ravence."

His father had told him this as he slipped into old age and madness—a prophecy that warned of the Phoenix rising again.

"She will call forth a Prophet who will turn all of Sayon into a dry, brutal desert," the old king had gasped, his eyes red and swollen. "She will burn everything in her path, including this kingdom. All gone in a single swipe of a vengeful god."

"We struck a deal," Leo said to the High Priestess. "Alabore Ravence struck a deal with the Phoenix, and he was blessed with Ravence. Why would the Prophet take the blessing back?"

"The Phoenix is mysterious in Her ways."

"Heavens be damned, Saayna!" He gripped her shoulders. She flinched, but her gaze was steady. "I've made my mistakes, but don't let Elena suffer for them. Tell me, do you know what the Prophet intends? Where is she now? Has she already been marked?"

Saayna's lips hardened, and she removed his hands with soft fingers. Slowly, she covered the young priest, moved to the wall and, with a wave of her hand, summoned a holo. A map of Ravence floated before them, along with pictures of the two runes. She plotted the symbols over Ravence, and Leo watched as the black lines cut through the desert, leading to Rani.

A map within a map.

"The girl has been marked," the High Priestess said. "She is here, in the capital, but she has not come into her full powers yet. That day will come. I can feel it. The Eternal Fire grows hungrier. Soon, we all have to answer for our sins."

She turned to him, her eyes dark and deep. "Especially you, Your Majesty."

Leo disliked the undercurrent in her voice, but he forced himself to stay calm. He knew he could not trust Saayna. He sensed a lie dripping from her lips like rattlesnake venom. She would defend the Prophet. It was her duty; but it was also his duty to protect his kingdom.

For a split second, he wondered if Elena was the Prophet, but no. She could not hold flames. She could not withstand their heat like he could. Rage welled inside of him.

Damn this Prophet! Damn the skies above!

He needed to hunt down the lunatic. Fire brought only destruction, while he and his ancestors had brought peace to this wild desert. He would not let it burn.

"Saayna," he said, his voice measured, calm. "I'm placing you under arrest for treason. The guards will escort you out of this Temple, and you will only return on coronation day. Until then, you will help me find this Prophet. You *will* defend Ravence." He looked at her and then the young priest. "Or else I will make sure he is the first to burn."

Saayna nodded, her face composed and shoulders straight. She seemed to accept her fate willingly. These religious fanatics were always like that. They gave in to the gods without so much a squeak of protest.

"As you wish, Your Majesty," she said. The edge in her voice made him clench his jaw.

Saayna moved toward the young priest, but Leo stopped her.

"We are leaving. Now."

She threw a look at the boy but walked to the door. Leo followed her up and out of the chamber. The stone slab slid back and they re-emerged into the Seat. The Eternal Fire hissed. It elongated, the flames curling and dancing as if they could sense Leo's distress. As if they were laughing at his fate to come.

When they walked out of the Temple, the mist had evaporated. Golden light dusted the great pines, and beyond the dunes spilled out, still and majestic. The desert knew of fire. It could withstand its heat, just like him.

Leo motioned to Marcus who stood waiting by the Temple's entrance.

"Arrest the High Priestess," he said. "Take her to Desert Spider, and do not let her get close to fire."

Leo watched his Spear lead the High Priestess away, her hair shining like spun bronze. She was a proud one. He would give her that. But he would make her bend like everyone else.

6
YASSEN

The Sky People were said to build their kingdoms in the clouds. They flew on ancient lily pads guided by a Sky Scout to the upper mountains of Seshar. We have discovered some vestiges of their civilization, but most were destroyed during the Jantari invasion.

—FROM CHAPTER 13 OF *THE GREAT HISTORY OF SAYON*

Yassen undressed and examined the marks on his arm. He had woken up from a strange dream filled with long shadows and smoke. A dull sense of pain spiraled up his arm to his shoulder, and when he tried to move his fingers, they were unresponsive.

It was a moonless night. Tiny stars pinpricked the dark, heavy fabric of the sky. This was the time he had often slipped out to do his work. He would move like a shadow—smooth and supple. By the time he had found his target, Yassen felt as if he was a part of the night. And then it had been so easy. He would raise his pulse gun and lock in the sensor, as if he was a conductor raising a baton. Then, it was just a simple, little pull.

He almost missed it.

But everything had changed that fateful night in the Verani kingdom. Now the night felt long, barren. It did not call to him like it used to.

Yassen began the slow work of awakening whatever life was left in his arm. He massaged his numb hand, pinching the nerve between his thumb and forefinger, counting until ten, then fifteen, then twenty, until he felt some semblance of sensation.

When they found him after his injury, the Arohassin had sent a doctor—a small, steel-glasses type of man with long, dainty fingernails—who told him to try electrical pads, or submerge his arm in ice water, and then boiling. If that didn't work, they would have to cut off his arm. Yassen had tried, and, for days, he felt nothing in his arm. He did, however, feel the weight of their gaze. Akaros, Taran and the rest. He could feel them debating the risk versus the reward, whether he was still an asset and, if not, how exactly to execute him.

Every time his arm became numb like this, Yassen felt a cold, slow panic. He was still useful. He knew that, but his injury told otherwise. It spoke of his mistake, his replaceability.

Yassen pinched the soft pad of skin between his thumb and forefinger harder. His fingers twitched, and he sighed in relief.

He was already dressed when Maurilis knocked on his door. Dawn had yet to color the sky as the Sesharian guided Yassen to the main foyer. Despite the moonless night, the mirrored ceiling sparkled with stars, as if the heavens were already awake and within his reach.

A hoverpod was docked outside the entrance. Samson stood on its ramp, wrapped in a milky fur coat that looked as if it had recently been skinned off a fyrra.

A servant took Yassen's bag while several others rolled Samson's suitcases up the ramp. Yassen watched them go like ants marching up a hill.

"Mother's Gold, how much are you bringing?" he asked.

"You need help with your wardrobe," Samson said as he looked him up and down. "We can't go to the holy kingdom looking like soldiers."

"I dress just fine."

Samson surveyed Yassen's asymmetric white shirt and slacks. He stopped a servant guiding a floating rack up the ramp and grabbed a coat.

"Here," he said and threw it at Yassen.

Yassen caught it. The coat was soft, with a powder blue finish and onyx buttons fashioned into lotuses. Yassen flipped the lapel and saw his initials woven beneath.

"I had it made and delivered late last night along with a few other things," Samson said. "We don't want you to look like you just came off the sea."

Yassen scowled. "They know who I am."

"Still, deception," Samson began.

"Is not a felony," Yassen finished. The words came on reflex. It was a saying the Arohassin had beaten into them. That and: *Murder is not a sin, but an awakening of one's own mortality.*

It felt odd to hear Samson say it, for him to remember. He had sworn off the Arohassin, calling their tactics egregious, animal-like, but here he stood reciting their mantras.

Yassen followed Samson into the hoverpod as Maurilis barked out final orders to the servants. The two friends sat across from each other in plush leather seats. A bottle of Marin Light champagne chilled in a pitcher while an assortment of fruits and a pot of steaming tea sat on the table.

As Samson poured their tea, Maurilis stumbled and dropped a package. It rolled and hit Yassen's foot. Before the Sesharian could grab it, Yassen picked it up, the suede cover falling back to reveal a corner of a map.

"Paper?" It was rarity in Sayon. Only scholars of ancient texts had access to such fragile material.

"It was a gift from Farin," Samson said, watching him.

Yassen slid back the cover and unrolled the map, smoothing out the corners carefully. He wished he hadn't.

In faded ink, the map showed a network of tunnels beneath the Sona Mountains. The tunnels spanned underneath the entire mountain range, running north to south. Only a jumble of lines crisscrossed at the center and southern point of the range, notating the chambers that ran east to west.

Yassen glanced at Samson, his heart hammering. Did he know about the cabin?

"It's just an old souvenir. Half of those tunnels are defunct anyway," Samson said. "Still, best not let it get too much air." He took the paper from Yassen, gently returned the map to its cover, and handed it back to Maurilis with a look.

Yassen stared at him, his mouth suddenly dry. He wanted to believe Samson. He wanted to believe that the map was just a faded memory, the tunnels nonexistent, but he knew they weren't.

After all, his Jantari father had died after discovering them.

A holo popped up from the console on their table, and the pilot announced they were ready for takeoff. Maurilis returned, empty-handed.

"Everything is ready, sire," he said. "The troops will be arriving after sundown."

"Thank you, Maurilis," Samson said, and the Sesharian took his leave.

Yassen sank back into his seat as the hoverpod rose and the sun began to peek over the horizon. The sky slowly blossomed, shaking off its dark slumber. Blue leached to purple to pink. The sun warmed the underbellies of the clouds, and Yassen watched Casear Lunar grow smaller and smaller until it disappeared. He tried to sit back and relax, but he couldn't. Samson, on the other hand, curled into his coat, fast asleep, his tea untouched.

Behind them, the famous Sona Range unfolded, a series of lush mountains peppered by silver mines. Here, the Jantari drilled for their infamous metal. They sent the conquered island folk deep within Sayon until Sesharians could no longer see their hands before their eyes. Though Yassen was accustomed to the dark, he had always hated the pitch black of the underground. He did not know how his father had done it: mined in the darkness; rubbed his hands raw so that the cracks of his skin were filled with dirt.

As the hours passed, Yassen felt the knot in his stomach grow tighter. Soon, he would return to the country that disowned him. There he would be judged, spat out, shunned. He knew the Ravani held no warmth toward him, and he couldn't blame them. He looked more Jantari than Ravani with his pale eyes, yet he spoke with the same rolling accent of the desert. They would not know what to make of him. Sometimes, he did not know what to make of himself.

After his mother died, Yassen had only returned to Ravence twice. Once, to take out a target, a fat, rich general with jade piercings down his neck; the other, to escort Taran to safety after the Kingdom of Pagua had gotten wind of their whereabouts. Yassen had smuggled the leader of the Arohassin into Ravence. It was the last place the Pagui would go. At the time, they still feared King Leo.

"Yassen."

He whipped around to see that Samson was awake, staring at him.

"There's something I need to know," he said. He shrugged off the coat and leaned forward, clear-eyed and alert. Yassen wondered if he had even fallen asleep at all.

"Your arm..."

Yassen froze. "What about it?"

Samson narrowed his eyes. "Word is that you burnt it. That you can't use it anymore. Is that true?"

"It still works, and I shoot with my left," Yassen said, flexing his right arm.

But the intensity in Samson's eyes did not change. "People know about the accident. The Ravani Intelligence, the king, hells—even the High Priestess. The Arohassin burned your name in the sand, Cass. They're looking for you," he said and leaned closer. "I need to know, are you taloned?"

"Your men must have told you about the guards in the port," Yassen said, squaring his shoulders. "Did that look like a man who can't fight?"

At this, Samson drew back. He regarded Yassen for a long moment and then turned to the window.

"There it is."

Yassen looked out and saw, unfurling beneath the clouds, the dunes of his childhood. The Ravani Desert spread out before him, sloping in easy, natural curves. To the west, far off in the distance, the mountaintops of the Agnee Range kissed the blooming sky. Somewhere within those mountains was the Eternal Fire, the incestuous power that had beguiled men for centuries. Sons had slain fathers and mothers had killed daughters in hopes of one day controlling the flames. For to conquer the Eternal Fire was to conquer the gods.

Waves of heat danced upon the horizon. Toward the southwest, Yassen glimpsed the red, dusty canyons that connected the southern cities of Magar and Teranghar. The hoverpod flew forward, its shadow flitting over thorny brush and narrow valleys. The dunes unfolded and then Yassen saw his home; the capital of Ravence—Rani.

Sandscrapers rose as if to defy the heavens themselves. Hovertrains zoomed from the city center to the outskirts, carrying tired laborers and overworked refugees. Crammed between the pristine buildings and extravagant chhatris were booming bazaars and poorly plotted side streets. Yassen had often snuck away to the city from his home in the outskirts. After docking at the hovertrain platform, he'd pick a random alleyway and follow its twisting path. At every turn, he found himself in a different village—no, a different country—with various languages and sounds, from the rolling, heavy vowels of the northern Ravani to the rumbling growl of the Karvenese. There was always something new to see, a new street food to try.

When he didn't have the money, which was quite often, Yassen had watched the street urchins and learned their ways. He learned how to pickpocket soft-hearted Nbruian tourists while he handed them satchels of spiced lotus puffs; how to evade the silver feathers during their routine rounds; how to use the alleys to his advantage when an officer gave chase.

As they approached the city, Yassen craned his neck to see flashes of familiar buildings and new, developed squares. He could feel the desert heat pressing against the hoverpod's glass. Yassen rested his head against it. He could almost hear the cacophony of the city: the blare of hovertrains and ring of sky bells interspersed with bellows of merchants and curses of drivers; a city breathing the lives and dreams of three million people, twelve nations, seven districts, and one, wayward boy.

And there, rising among all the chaos, was the amalgamation itself—the Fire Palace.

Sitting high up on a hill, the Palace overlooked the city. Its ivory chhatris and sandblasted towers glowed in the morning sun. Marble lattice work and fiery red gems adorned its windows. Three twisting spires—one each to look south, east and west (but never the sacred north)—stood like stoic guardians. There were no walls around the Palace; the hill and the towers were enough.

"She's a beauty, no?" Samson said.

The hoverpod rose up the Hill. Yassen caught glimpses of luscious courtyards and fountains before the hoverpod lowered onto a platform behind the Palace.

Samson stood, his fur coat spilling down his shoulders.

"Do you remember the Desert Oath?"

"I could never forget it," Yassen said.

"Good, make sure you put some heart into it." Samson grinned. "Ready?"

Yassen stared out the window, rubbing his arm before he stood.

"Yes," he lied.

7

ELENA

When Ravence was still a young kingdom, sandstorms raged along the borders. Queen Aesheya had claimed that her god brought the storms to ward off invaders. This is a lie. When examining the weather patterns of that era, one must note the freak occurrence called Barru. A passing of a comet amplified the northern winds and thus, the storms. This all goes to show that the Phoenix is a myth and the kingdom a sham.

—EXCERPT FROM AN OPINION PIECE IN *THE JANTARI TIMES*

Elena sat beside her father in the large, golden throne room. Over twenty thousand intricate mirrors shimmered within the walls, reflecting the golden light of the sun. She watched marigold flowers on the ceiling blossom as the sunlight touched them. They emitted a sweet, hazy smell, a tactic Leo used to lull heads of states into a false sense of security. Elena found the smell sickening. She had already decided that once she sat on the throne, she would rip out the flowers. Grind them with her palm and throw them into the Eternal Fire.

How was that for an offering?

Alonjo kneeled on a modest cushion beside the throne, on her father's right. He checked the holo floating before him.

"They have just docked, Your Majesty," the Astra reported.

"They're late," the king said.

Her father was dressed in a white silk kurta with an embellished, golden scarf draped elegantly down his shoulder. Kohl rimmed his eyes and a singular jade earring glittered in his right ear. Thick ropes of fire chain and a brooch of the Phoenix hung across his chest. Though Elena did not see it, she knew that beneath it all, Leo wore her mother's necklace.

The king sat upright on the throne with the crown of Ravence resting on his temples. The circlet was neither large nor glamorous. Alabore Ravence had had the foresight to create a humble token—a symbol worthy of the Phoenix.

And so, the crown that many nations had slain for, warred for, was merely a band of gold cut into the shape of dunes. In its center, Alabore Ravence had fitted the Featherstone, a jewel that contained the only feather the Phoenix had granted men. It glinted softly as her father and his thousand reflections turned to her.

"Did you bring the white sands?"

Elena unwrapped the bundle her guards had brought in, revealing a gold basin filled with ignitable white sand.

"Do you think they know the Desert Oath?"

Leo settled back into the throne, his eyes watching the great, bronze doors. "If they're not stupid, they should have already practiced it."

Elena nodded. She had taken the oath the same day she had, for the one and only time, worn the crown. It had been on the eve of her seventeenth sun, the day she had returned from her Registaan. It was a right of passage for every Ravani heir. Half a sun spent in the grueling depths of the desert, alone. She had been sent with no guards, no food, no water. She had only her wits, her training, and her Ravani blood.

Elena had learned how the desert moved and slept. She had learned how to coax water out of hardy plants, how to find the shady groves of a sandtrapper, how to, when the heat became too unbearable and the nights too cold, sit still and mediate: to slow down the life in her body so that every second became a day, a day a week, a week a month. So slow was her heartbeat that rattlesnakes mistook her as a stone and slithered past her. When she finally opened her eyes, Elena had felt balanced and light, as if she could dance out the rest of her days.

And she had. She'd danced to the songs of the desert as sand skittered in the wind. She'd danced to the ancient forms of Kymathra and

Unsung, steeled herself into the warrior poses of the famed Desert Spiders, the lithe female soldiers who had once guarded Ravence.

When she finally returned to the Palace, her skin had warmed from olive to burnished gold. Even her father had barely recognized her. Maybe that was why, when she was alone with him for the first time since her return, he had taken off his crown and rested it on her head.

"Only a desert wind can withstand the desert heat," he had said.

Elena had nodded, pretending to understand. Despite its delicate form, the crown felt heavy and small. It pinched her temples.

Gently, she had removed the crown and placed it back in her father's hands.

"Until then, it's yours," she had said.

The doors of the throne room swung open, and two men entered. Alonjo stood while Elena and Leo remained seated.

"Samson Kytuu and his party, Your Majesty," the Astra announced.

The two men bowed. Elena instantly recognized the famed Sesharian militant. He was handsome, strikingly so, with a gait that reminded her of a lion in the desert, slowly circling his prey. But then her eyes rested on the tall, pale man beside him. He was shorter than Samson and less beautiful, with golden hair and a long, pointed face. Yet he walked with the ease and grace of Ferma, like water gliding across a surface.

Jealousy gripped Elena. Only a skilled fighter could move like that. The sun dusted the man's head, but he seemed to shrink back from it. And then Elena realized who he was.

Yassen Knight. Assassin. Terrorist. And, Mother's Gold, a Ravani.

"Your Majesty, and Your Highness," Samson said as they knelt. "It is our honor to be graced by your company."

"You honor us by being late." The king gave a cold, hard smile. "Now stop kneeling."

They stood. Samson stepped forward while Yassen Knight kept his eyes on the red marble floor.

Coward.

"Your Majesty, my apologies," Samson said. If the king's rebuke threw him off guard, he gave no signs of it. His smile was easy, sloping, and it warmed the corners of his eyes. "We were finalizing placement of my troops. A selected few will remain in the capital, as we discussed, while the others will be sent to the southern border. I will even send some of my men to guard the Temple—"

"The Temple will only be guarded by Ravani forces," Leo said. "It is our sacred duty as wardens of the holy land."

"Of course." Samson motioned at the servants who had followed him in. "We come bearing gifts for you and Her Highness."

The servants laid down the packages and pulled back the cloths, revealing a wide array of gifts: Sesharian swords with silver hilts, jade elephants with diamond trunks, dresses of gemini crystals, silk scarves of every color imaginable, and pile upon pile of glittering necklaces, bracelets, and gauntlets.

Elena sighed. She glanced at her father, whose face remained smooth and plain like summer marble. He hated when guests brought him such trivial gifts. It was an act of complacency, he had told her, a way visitors tried to swoon them like the marigold flowers showering their scent from the ceiling.

Leo waved his hand and the servants wrapped up the gifts and took them away. After their reflections receded, Leo stood. Elena shot up to her feet. Even the pale assassin looked up.

"You come with a proposition," Leo said. "State it."

Again, if her father's candor derailed him, Samson made no sign. He turned to her, his eyes bright and clear, his voice steady.

"Your Highness, I come with a humble offer. Ravence has many enemies along her borders, yet she has opened her doors for Jantar's island refugees. As a Sesharian, I am thankful for your service to my people. I am willing to give you my strength, my armies, if—"

"If I take you as my king," Elena interjected. She looked long and hard at Samson, long enough to make him sweat, before continuing. "I've gotten many proposals. What makes yours different?"

Samson glanced at Yassen and then to her father.

"Do you have the list?" Leo asked.

Samson withdrew a holopod from his pocket and called up the holos.

Names, codes, and maps spilled out. Elena recognized the city grid of Rani, but there were plotted points that she did not recognize.

"These are the active Arohassin agents in Rani right now," Samson said. "Their entire Ravani operating network is also in here. We have names, locations, holo references—everything. I've had my men cross-check the names and they all hold."

"But have you tracked any of them down?" Alonjo asked.

"With the king's permission, we will." Samson placed the holo-pod in Alonjo's outstretched hand and took a step back. "This is my offering—redemption. A final blow on the locusts that have plagued Ravence. And it will all be under your name, Queen Elena."

Elena regarded him. It was wrong to call an heir queen before she took the throne, but he had done so to please her. To stroke her ego. Elena cautioned herself from gloating. Samson was a crafty one. He, like all the common born, thirsted for power.

But Ravence needed his men. The Black Scales were infamous for their efficiency, their cold-hearted accuracy. No kingdom that had employed Samson's forces had ever lost. Her father had failed to rid the country of the Arohassin, failed to capture the love of the people. She could finally be the one to free Ravence from its dissenters.

Elena squared her shoulders and squelched the numbness in her stomach. The people loved a war hero; that was what she would give to them.

"I accept," she said. "Let us come together in union to rid Ravence of her troubles." Her eyes rested on Yassen. "All of them."

Yassen Knight did not flinch from her gaze. She had heard of his accident; they all had. She had imagined a limp, a weakness, but Yassen Knight stood as still and impassive as the dunes on a winter night. It made her uneasy. There was something familiar about him, yet also something alarming.

"It's decided then," Leo said.

Elena lifted the golden basin and set it between her father and their guests. She then produced two long matches from her lehenga and handed them to the king.

"Now, let us seal it with the Desert Oath."

The two men knelt, their reflections following. Elena watched as Leo struck the matches and threw them into the basin. A fire roared to life.

Together, Samson and Yassen held their hands over the flames, their voices unwavering.

"The king is the protector of the flame, and I its servant. Together, we shall give our blood to this land. I swear it, or burn my name in the sand."

Together, they brought their hands down into the basin. Pressing their palms into the flames, they left the imprint of their fingers, and their oath, in the ivory sand.

"So it is thus sealed," Leo said, and with a clap of his hands, the flames died with a whisper.

Alonjo brought forward a silver bowl of water. Samson and Yassen dipped in their hands to cool their burns. Neither flinched as Alonjo wrapped cool, jasmine-scented cloths around their palms. Elena caught Yassen's eyes, and she breathed in sharply. In the light of the room, they looked white as the tips of the summer dunes. As white as the blinding glare of the sun. Unholy and unnatural.

He truly is one of the unforgiven.

"You have come a long way," Leo said. "Retire to your rooms and get some rest. We will reconvene with my generals, and I expect your troops to be in position by then."

"You have my word," Samson promised.

Leo turned to Yassen and gave him a hard look that even Elena could not withstand. The king leaned forward and whispered something in his ear that she could not hear. The traitor bowed deeper in response.

"The guards will escort you to your chambers," Alonjo announced.

The three men dipped their heads as Elena and Leo exited through the door behind the throne. They entered the adjoining office, where Ferma stood waiting.

"Well, did he propose?" Ferma asked.

"I accepted," Elena said sourly.

"Then a celebration must be in order." Her Spear grinned. "What say you, Alonjo?"

"Yes, we must announce the union soon," he said, closing the door behind them. "A ball perhaps. Or an appearance from the landing."

Elena turned to the king, who took off his crown and set it on a cushion. He had been silent through all this.

"What do you think, Father?" she said.

"Whatever you wish," he said as he sank into the chair behind his red marble desk. Elena waited, but he said nothing more. Not even an utterance of congratulations.

"What about Yassen Knight?" she said finally. "What are we going to do with him?"

"He'll be a part of your guard, like we discussed," Leo said.

"But he's half Jantari. What if he has something else planned? What if he smuggles in guerrilla fighters or plants a bomb?"

"You can keep eyes on him," Leo said.

"But—"

"Enough!" he said, and she fell silent. She felt Ferma stiffen beside her. Even Alonjo shrank back. "I know how to keep this kingdom safe, at least until you are crowned its queen."

Elena bit her lip. She wanted to tell him that she could keep Ravence safe too—that she would hunt down bastards like Yassen Knight who threatened their kingdom, not welcome them in with open arms—but she held her tongue. The desert picked its battles.

Without another word, Elena turned, her lehenga swishing behind her. She returned to her room where Diya, her handmaid, had opened the windows. The sheer curtains danced in the late summer breeze as Elena sank onto a bench before the large window. Below was her private garden filled with lotus flowers and the sweet jasmine her mother loved, or at least that's what Diya told her. A sand-colored yuani bird washed itself in the golden fountain. Elena watched it as Ferma sat down beside her.

"Don't get upset over this," the Yumi said. "Your father is right. We can watch Yassen Knight closely."

"I don't believe him," Elena said. She recalled the distracted look in the king's eyes. "Yassen Knight is too crafty. He'll escape when he gets the chance."

"Elena, there's no place to escape to in the desert," Ferma said gently.

"You don't know that," she said, more as a whisper to herself. The desert was full of hidden places. She had seen them, curled up in them. The desert opened itself up for those who knew how to use it, and something told her Yassen Knight was smart enough to realize that.

"In any case, I need to prep your new guard," Ferma said, beginning to rise.

"Aren't you bothered?" she asked as she looked at the bird. "Yassen Knight will be a part of my guard. If my father really believed in you, he wouldn't have added a newcomer."

Elena did not need to turn to know that she had hit her mark. Of course she believed in her Spear. But the Yumi was growing close to her retirement at fifty suns. Perhaps her father had sensed her declining utility.

"He made Yassen Knight your guard to keep him close," Ferma said. There was an edge in her voice, a sharpness that made Elena flinch. "If he is planning anything with the Arohassin, or the Jantari, we will know. This is to keep you safe."

"But you and I can keep me safe," she insisted. She turned and squeezed the Yumi's hand. "We're more capable than a crippled castaway."

Ferma said nothing, only patted her hand and broke away. "You have training in a few hours. Don't be late."

Elena waved her off. She heard the door open and then a man's voice. Yassen Knight stood in her doorway. He had changed into the black and red of a royal guard, but the suit was too small, and she caught a glimpse of a dark band on his wrist before he pulled down his sleeve.

Ferma stepped in front of him. "You can't be here."

"The king instructed me to come," Yassen said.

"Not before your orientation."

"The king sent me here," he said simply.

"It's alright," Elena said. She walked over and crossed her arms. Closer up, his eyes looked less frightening, though still unusually pale.

"What kind of training do you have?" she asked.

"All kinds," he responded.

The Yumi bristled at the arrogance in his voice, but Elena touched her arm. "My father may have picked you, but I decide whether you stay." She nodded at Ferma. "Training is after the war meeting. You'll go against Ferma."

He glanced up at her guard. "Against a Yumi?"

"If you have 'all kinds of training,' you should know how to fight a Yumi." Elena grinned.

"As you wish." He stepped back, and the light from the hall's window slanted down his face. His eyes turned translucent. For a moment, Yassen hesitated, but then bowed his head. "You have a wonderful garden."

"See you in a few hours," Ferma said and slammed the doors shut.

The Yumi whipped around, glaring, but Elena only shrugged and made her way back to the window. The bird was gone, the fountain still. She leaned forward, her elbows brushing the warm, pink stone. An orange haze hung around the hill and the city below. Waves of heat shimmered above the distant dunes. Elena could feel the desert call to her, beckoning her to lose herself in its canyons and craters.

"Inform the gamemaster," she said to Ferma. "I want to see him crumble."

8
LEO

During the Golden Reign of the Third Prophet, storms washed the world until it was bright and new. Crops burst into valleys and along mountainsides. Children knew not of hunger. The world knew not of war. Will a time like this ever return?

—FROM THE DIARIES OF PRIESTESS NOMU OF THE FIRE ORDER

Leo sat at the head of the War Room table as his generals bickered about Yassen Knight. He had told them as soon as he entered that the assassin was in the Palace, and the room had broken into an uproar. They debated and haggled, but when he only sat there in silence, they turned among themselves to discuss what to do with the traitor.

"As soon as his list checks out, I say we hang the Jantari half-breed," General Rohtak snarled. He was a big army man with a hatchet nose and eyes of weathered steel. "Or better yet, flay him on the noose."

"It could be a display of strength and unity," Mahira, his Sand Raider general, replied. She was long-boned like a Yumi with half the grace. "There's nothing better to bring the people together than a scapegoat."

"No, it would only cause further insurrection. The Arohassin have burned his name in the sand. If we take his life, we cheat them out of it," said a thin voice. Leo turned to Muftasa, the head of Ravani Intelligence. She was a small bird of a woman, dressed in all black, with a peckish nose and mouth that puckered as if she were perpetually dehydrated or scrutinizing those around her. After thirty-five suns, Leo knew it was both.

"He can be of use to us, all of us," she said and looked pointedly at Samson.

Samson sat beside Leo, his leg propped up on his knee. He had been silent through the whole exchange, watching the generals with an amused expression. Leo had to give it to the young militant. He knew when to wait and when to strike. But heavens, the boy had to rein in his pride.

"Yassen can be trusted," Samson said. He leaned forward, looking between the generals and Leo. "You forget that he was born here. Sand runs through his veins. He's already given us a complete list of Arohassin agents, from their gathering points to their connects. If we act now—quietly, of course—we can take them down without their leaders getting wind."

Behind Samson on the northern wall, a holo of Yassen Knight floated beneath backlit slabs of nero-granite resembling the Phoenix. Their red light spilled onto Yassen's face and the black glass table.

Leo was no fool; he knew Yassen Knight could not be trusted. He could feel it deep in his bones, an intuition that had guided him through many rebellions, wars, and assassination attempts—an intuition that had never failed him. After all, here he was, alive and whole.

Yassen Knight was a man tired of running, and that made him weak. Like Samson and his generals and those groveling heads of state, Yassen worked to please him. He would do anything for his freedom, and that's where Leo's advantage lay.

The king had seen the look in those colorless eyes. It was a look of desperation, perhaps even exhaustion. Either way, Leo would work him. Rip out every secret until nothing was left to give. If Yassen had not truly defected, he would find out. Desperate men always made mistakes.

"My men are already taking their stations in the capital and the desert outposts as we speak," Samson continued. "We've got holotracking sensors, desert suits, missiles, pulse guns, and slab grenades." He smiled as Mahira let out a low whistle.

"Sounds like you're building up your own army," she quipped.

"I already have one," he replied. His gaze never wavered, and eventually Mahira leaned back in her seat. "Every man of mine is ready to defend Ravence. To scare off her enemies."

"Show me," Leo said suddenly. His eyes met Samson's. "Let's have a military exhibition on our southern border. Your Black Scales marching under the Ravani flag."

"But Your Majesty—" Mahira began.

Leo held up his hand. "Farin's too smart to strike first, but he's growing impatient. I can sense it. If we don't act now, we'll have a war on our hands."

Jantar's army lay to the south where Jantar and Ravence touched borders. Every day, Ravani soldiers tensed as Jantari soldiers marched along the border, carrying their crude zeemirs and massive pulse guns. Sometimes, a soldier overstepped. There would be pulse fire, grenades, but never an outright war. Farin was biding his time, and Leo could feel the steady beat of his army bearing down on his kingdom. The slow suffocation. He had lost more men on the border than Farin. Draped countless Ravani flags over their bodies before burning them to the heavens.

If the metal king saw Samson's Black Scales with the Ravani army, saw the brute force of their numbers, perhaps he would falter. Perhaps that could buy Ravence more time.

"But Your Majesty, should we not pursue peace talks as our first course of action?" Samson asked.

"And how did that turn out for Seshar?" Leo asked.

Samson fell silent, his eyes growing dark. Even the generals shifted in their seats. General Mahira threw a look at Samson and then patted his hand.

"It's alright, boy," she said quietly. "We all know the work of the Jantari."

"Then let's arrange for it and give it a name," Leo said. "We will have the demonstration at the end of the week."

"A name?" mused Saku, the Minister of Defense. His mouth screwed up in thought, and then his thin eyebrows creased. "What about Black Sands Day?"

Black sands. It was an omen in the desert, a sign for storm winds and catastrophe. Leo himself had never seen black sands, but his father had told him stories of the phenomena appearing before invasions.

"A tad dramatic, but it will do," he said.

Samson clapped his hands, an easy grin curving across his face. Whatever hesitation he had felt, whatever demons the mention of Seshar had rucked up, were gone. "I'm sure Farin would love it."

There was a chuckle around the table, one that Leo did not share. Samson turned and pointed to a holo on his right. It displayed a map of Ravence with several points scattered throughout. He zoomed into Rani as a carousel of faces floated along the wall. He stopped on a woman with red hair and an upturned nose.

"There are more instigators than Farin to consider, however," he said. His tone grew deeper, more serious. "The Arohassin have operated within Rani for decades, always evading your grasp. But I, gentleman, and ladies," he said, dipping his head toward Muftasa and Mahira, "bring you the trap that will ensnare them all." Leo watched his generals take it in, their faces carefully composed and their eyes alert. Like him, they were judging this young cub who had strutted into the lion's den with a fresh kill. "Yassen Knight provided us with a thorough list. Let's not waste time. This agent operates right in the heart of old Rani, by Radhia's Bazaar," he said. "My men are ready to bring her in. I just need your word, Your Majesty."

Leo had studied the list in his office and had been surprised by it. Of course he knew that the Arohassin operated in many nations, but to see that so many had wormed their way into his kingdom...

He had tried to diminish them, stake them out until they withered and died, but when one head was cut off, another grew in its place. In his long reign, the Arohassin were a constant reminder of his failure. They were the only flaw in his legacy.

Yet here was his chance to finally crush them. Leo brought the holo closer, scrutinizing the names. He could bring them in, but the situation was delicate. One wrong move would alert the Arohassin network. One wrong move could endanger Elena and his kingdom.

"Locate three agents," he said finally. "They should be important, but not enough that their absence will tip off their leaders. If any of these agents recognize Yassen Knight as a defector, we will not burn him. At least not yet." He looked at his generals and Samson. "Understood?"

"But we will burn him. Won't we?" General Rohtak asked.

"Yes," Leo said, his eyes on Samson. "That was our deal."

Samson merely dipped his head in acquiescence.

"Then let us turn to the matters of the coronation," Saku said.

Leo nodded, but he barely listened as the generals drew maps of the coronation parade route and discussed the blessing ceremony at the Temple. He kept his gaze on Samson, who sank into his seat with a pinched look on his face.

Eventually, Alonjo tapped his shoulder, and Leo turned to see Muftasa looking at him expectantly.

"Yes?" he asked.

"Your Majesty, we were just discussing the blessing ceremony in the capital after the coronation. Will the High Priestess come by hoverpod or desert carriage?" she asked, and Leo thought of Saayna locked within Desert Spider. His thoughts drifted to the runes, and his stomach twisted.

"Desert carriage," he answered, trying to keep his voice as level as possible.

Muftasa blinked. After suns of service, she likely detected his unease, but, to her credit, she merely turned back to the generals and laid out the security plan for the High Priestess of Ravence.

Afterward, the meeting broke. The generals rose and bowed. One by one, they filed out, casting a look at Samson, Alonjo, and Muftasa, who continued to remain seated.

"Alright," Muftasa said once they were gone. "What is it? Tell me."

Leo smiled. Only Muftasa could speak to him with such candor.

He motioned to Alonjo, who drew up the holos of the burnt priest and the runes on his skin.

Samson inhaled sharply. "Skies above," he whispered.

"Well, I suppose you could say the heavens have spoken to us," Leo said. "The Prophet will come."

Silence filled the room, sudden and heavy. It dragged down their shoulders to their chests. Even Leo could not shake it off. He watched their faces. They all wore matching looks of shock and disbelief.

"It will be a woman," he said finally. "A young girl who has already been marked. If what Saayna says is true, if the Prophet is to come, then we are dead men walking."

He rose and motioned for them to stay seated. He walked to the northern wall before the rendition of the Phoenix. With a wave of his hand, he dismissed the holo of Yassen Knight and pulled up a map of Ravence.

"According to Saayna, the girl is in Rani. Samson, Muftasa, arrange a covert operation to find girls who fit the description. They will be marked. Maybe with a rune or a flame... I'm not sure. But I know they will not burn. You will find them, and you will bring them to me." He turned, the red light of the Phoenix spilling down his shoulders. "We will not allow a religious heretic to dismantle our kingdom."

"But if the legends are true, we won't stand a chance before the Prophet," Muftasa said.

"Not if we execute her before the Phoenix rises," Leo said, and the silence that came after was even more damning. He could feel the weight of the heavens and seven hells bearing down on him, judging him.

"Find her," Leo said and looked pointedly at Samson. "If you want Ravence, you will bring me the Prophet."

Muftasa coughed. "It's funny you say this," she said slowly.

Leo turned to face her as she summoned a holo. It showed the face of a young girl with hair the color of starlight.

"We've kept tabs on arsonists in Rani," she began. "Most tend to be gold caps or the religious type. Often harmless. They usually crop up around the Fire Festival. Anyway, an agent of mine brought this case to my attention. It was unusual because the girl was so young."

She gestured at the holo. "She's twelve suns but has already accrued a record of setting buildings and animals on fire, particularly in the last two months. Her neighbors have complained of her trying to burn their houses down, but..." Muftasa hesitated.

"Out with it," Leo commanded.

Muftasa looked between him and the holo. She sighed. "Recently, a silver feather had to bring her in after she set a squad car on fire. It was his hovercar," she said, and Samson laughed. She shot him a look. "When he brought her in, he said he found burn marks on her. Recent ones."

"Burn marks?" Samson asked. "I thought the Prophet didn't burn."

"The Prophet does burn, but only once," Leo said. "The Phoenix burns the Prophet to mark her. After that, she doesn't burn anymore."

As he said this, Leo felt a cold fist clamp around his stomach. This girl perfectly fit the description. He should feel relieved, calm even, but he could only feel an impending sense of dread. If this girl was the Prophet, he would have to commit the highest sin in all the heavens. He would be hated, cursed. No amount of Ashanta ceremonies would save him. But if the Prophet came into her power, his sins would pale in comparison.

Leo held no delusions about the Prophet's intentions; she would kill him, burn him for all of Sayon to see. And then she would turn the rest of Sayon into one long, arid landscape. Ravence would crumble. This dream of peace, however bloody it became, would vanish in the desert winds.

"Where is she?" he asked.

"In the western slums of Rani," Muftasa said. "Her name—"

"Don't tell me," Leo cut her off. The fist in his stomach tightened and turned. "I don't need to know."

It was better that the girl remained unknown to him. Names held power. They could corrupt, sway a man. Knowing her name would only make the job more difficult. Seeing her face made it hard enough.

"Shall we bring her in?" Muftasa asked.

Leo hesitated. He looked at the young girl with hair of spun starlight. She had unusually clear eyes that bore into him. He felt a pang in his chest—guilt perhaps, remorse even—but he pushed it down.

If he was to be burned, so be it.

"Round her up," he said, "and begin a search in the capital. Look for other women with recent burns and bring them to me."

And then, to himself, *before she kills us all.*

9
YASSEN

*The Yumi are proud, powerful warriors. The women are gifted with
weapon-like hair while the men serve as healers. For centuries,
they led the most fearsome armies, some even going on to lead
as queens. However, the Sixth Prophet killed many of the Yumi.
Only a few hundred remain, mostly serving as mercenaries in armies
around Sayon.*

—FROM CHAPTER 30 OF *THE GREAT HISTORY OF SAYON*

The gamemaster rapped on the changing room door.

"You ready?" she asked.

Yassen bit his lip as he slowly pulled the bulky gamesuit over his
right shoulder. His arm had grown stiff since the morning flight. He
had tried to slip it in the sleeve and had failed thrice already. He felt old,
clumsy. How could he expect to fight? When he had told Samson about
the princess's challenge, the militant had begun to pace the room.

"It's a test," Samson had said finally. "You can't win."

"But if I lose, I won't be a part of her guard," Yassen had responded.
It wasn't a test. It was a balancing act. If he lost, Elena would cast him
out. If he won, he would dishonor her Spear *and* the princess herself.

And nothing was worse than an heir with wounded pride.

Sucking air through his teeth, Yassen managed to zip up the suit
and walk out. The gamemaster tapped his chest twice. The suit sucked

in, morphing to fit the grooves and ridges of his body. Yassen flexed his hands, and the suit rippled in response, smooth like silk.

The gamemaster eyed the cut of his muscles and sniffed. "Not bad."

Yassen allowed himself a small smile. He hadn't been in a gamesuit since his training days. Back then, the Arohassin fitted each recruit with a specialized suit.

Kavach, they called it. Armor.

It was a type of gamesuit specifically manufactured by the Arohassin. It tracked every vital of the body—from heart rate to temperature fluctuation and reaction timing. The operators used the data to create personalized weapons for each recruit, given upon graduation. Yassen had been the first in his class to receive his pulse gun. He was better than most, which he had learned early on. When the other recruits balked, he had stood calm and steady. Firm, like the roots of a banyan. Even Sam, with all his wit and charm, could not hit a target as well as he could.

Yassen followed the gamemaster into the console room. It was a glass-encased chamber that overlooked a training floor covered with black sand. Lotuses carved from onyx granite lit up the ceiling, casting the field in a pale, blue light. On the far wall of the dojo, the insignia of the Phoenix smoldered.

The gamemaster walked to the command console covered with various holos and dials with which she could control the sand. When she activated the field, the sand would rise and twist, adding a further challenge to the fighters.

Samson sat before the console but straightened as Yassen entered.

"I thought you went to see the king," Yassen said.

Samson pulled him close.

"Be smart," the militant whispered into his ear. "One false move, and we're both done for."

A hiss of gas made them turn as Ferma walked out of the suit chamber, a shimmer of steam clinging to her gamesuit.

"Your turn," she said.

The gamemaster closed the door of the chamber behind Yassen. Sensors locked into their dockets on his suit, and he felt a familiar twinge of electricity zip through his veins.

"Configuring," the gamemaster said, and the chamber activated. A laser scanned Yassen's body as the suit cooled and expanded, testing his pressure points and reading back his vital signs to the screen in front of the gamemaster. There was a soft beep as the suit squeezed his right arm. The gamemaster narrowed her eyes. She cast a glance at Yassen but said nothing. She tapped something into the screen, and the suit tightened around his right arm, adding more armor. Within a minute, it was done. Yassen walked out and looked down. The suit felt even sleeker now, akin to his own skin, except it was unblemished. Whole, not broken.

"You look like you've seen a ghost," said a voice.

Yassen looked up to see Elena standing beside Ferma. Her eyes traveled over him, sizing him up.

"I haven't been in a gamesuit in a while," he responded.

"Why is that?"

"Too many memories." He remembered how light the pulse gun had felt when his master, Akaros, had presented it to him upon his graduation. How natural it felt to load the chamber. How cruel it all seemed now.

"Alright, fighters, get down into the field," the gamemaster called out. Two opposite doors at the end of the room opened. Yassen gripped Samson's elbow and squeezed.

"I think if I make one false move, *I'm* done for," he whispered and descended into the training field.

The blue lights flashed. The lotuses on the ceiling began to spin as the magnetic field thrummed to life. Yassen spotted Ferma on the other end. The suit revealed her lithe body and coiled muscles, the result of a lifetime of training, fighting, protecting. He wondered what scars the suit hid for her.

She untied her hair, and it fell around her shoulders in long, silky strands.

For now, Yassen thought. He knew of the power of the Yumi. Their hair was their shield, their strength. It could harden into a million sharp shards that could cut through a man. He had seen it once when pickpocketing in Rani's financial district. An off-duty Yumi solider had caught a man trying to force himself onto a young girl. She had pierced his hands with her hair and then dragged him into Coin Square for all to see. Only then did she take him to the hospital, handcuffed.

"Fighters, ready," the gamemaster's voice rang out.

Ferma kneeled, and Yassen did the same. The sand felt warm underneath his fingertips. He glanced up and saw Elena watching. An unspoken challenge shone in her eyes but also a curiosity. He let his gaze linger, and then the bell rang and Ferma shot forward.

She was fast—surprisingly so. Yassen barely had enough time to move away as she whipped her hair. The shards scraped across the floor but Yassen twisted and spun, kicking her shin. Her hair swung around, and he fought back a yelp as it pierced his foot.

He hopped back as his suit recalibrated, soothing the bruised skin and reconstructing his torn muscle. Ferma turned slowly, her hair coiling. Her tawny eyes were bright and yellow like a cat. Yassen sucked in a deep breath as she stalked forward, wishing he had a weapon as lethal as Ferma's locks.

But then the sand hummed and shifted below his feet. Yassen lunged backward as the ground caved in, forming a pit. Ferma tried to scramble back, but her foot slipped; the sand began to swallow her. She growled and twisted, her hair finding purchase over the lip of the pit. She began to climb, and Yassen found his opening.

When she crawled from the pit and leapt to her feet, he landed his first blow, square on her torso. She stumbled back but did not lose her balance. Her hair lanced up, black and sharp. One shard sliced Yassen on his cheek, and he felt warm blood spray out.

Clever. The gamesuit protected the body but not the face.

Yassen wheeled around, sweeping his leg out, but Ferma was quicker. She jumped lightly out of his reach and then rushed him. Yassen weaved in and out of her blows as sand sprayed against his face. He felt the rhythm of her moves, the pattern of her advances.

And so began their dance. Every time she advanced, he retreated. Every time she twisted, he shot forward. Above, Elena, the gamemaster, and Samson watched. On the screens, they could see Yassen and Ferma's escalating heartbeats, the tear and energy in their muscles.

Sweat beaded on his brow but, despite himself, Yassen enjoyed this. This waltz. It all came back to him now. The flush of battle. The exhilaration of landing a blow. The adrenaline pumping through his veins.

Yes, he might regret the things he'd done for the Arohassin. *But nothing,* he thought as Ferma spun low, *nothing can beat the rush of a game.*

The sand hummed again, forming columns. Ferma disappeared behind one, her hair hissing. Yassen crept forward, glancing around the column when Ferma pounced from behind. Her hair jabbed his right shoulder, quick and savage.

Pain burst down his burned arm. Yassen bit back a shout as he slipped behind the sand column to escape her following blow. Ferma turned, and he noted the subtle catch of her breath, the slight slowness of her movements.

Yassen waited until she was close and then, at the last second, grabbed her arm, ducking underneath her writhing hair as he launched forward, delivering an uppercut with such force that it hit her squarely on the jaw, sending her sprawling. Ferma hit the floor, and the bell rang out.

"End of round," the gamemaster announced.

Yassen panted as the Yumi sat up. She looked stunned, angry even, as she collected herself and rose to her feet.

"We're the same, you and I," Yassen said quietly so that only she could hear.

"We're nothing alike," she spat.

"We're both warriors," he said. "And we both want the same thing— the best for Ravence."

"You only want what's best for you," Ferma said, taming her hair.

The door behind her opened, and Elena stepped out.

"That'll be all, Ferma," Elena said. She was dressed in a gamesuit that revealed her supple curves and carved muscles. "I'll have to test him myself."

Ferma glared at him, and he saw the unspoken threat. He would not dare hurt Elena; he would be a fool to even land a scratch on her. And Elena knew this. He saw the wild hunger in her dark eyes as she watched him. She meant to hurt him, and he could do nothing but accept the blows.

The Yumi slowly slunk out of the training field. The door closed behind her, and then he was alone with the heir of Ravence.

Yassen bowed as the bell rang out again. Though she wore a game-suit, he was hesitant to strike Elena. She moved quickly, not with the grace and agility of Ferma but with a sureness that made every movement purposeful.

Yassen shook out his hands as they circled each other. His injured arm still rang, and a numbness began to creep up his elbow. He knew she was waiting for an opening, just like he had with Ferma. The columns hummed and bent. He faked left, a move so obvious that when she came up on his right, he tensed for the blow.

She hit him in the chest, a deep jab that made his breath catch as he stumbled back. The sand hissed and crashed down. He dived out of the way as Elena advanced. She was light on her feet, determined. She didn't let a missed blow get to her as she swung again. Yassen rushed her, grabbing her arm, but she recognized the move and brought her knee up to block his punch.

Yassen spun out of her reach, breathing hard. She smiled. This time, when she shot forward, he stepped forward and let her foot hit him in the stomach. Pain whiplashed through his body, and Yassen gasped. She made quick work thereafter. Blow after blow rained down on him.

He could feel the sheer loathing and calculated precision in every strike. He raised his hands up to protect his cheek when she whirled, delivering a kick square into his chest. He smacked into the sand.

"Enough," Samson's voice rang out.

Through bleary eyes, Yassen looked up to see Samson at the glass box above. His face was pinched, his mouth a hard line.

"I think you've proven your point, Your Highness," he said through the intercom.

Elena sniffed, shaking out her arms. She looked down at Yassen sprawled out on the black sand.

"Clean him up. I don't want a bloodied guard following me around," she said and walked out.

In the glass box, Yassen saw her say something to Samson, and then Ferma followed her out. Slowly, Yassen got to his feet. He sucked in air through his teeth as pain lanced through his ribs. He hadn't taken a beating like that in a long time, and the man who had done it to him was dead.

Samson waited while he disrobed and donned fresh clothes. The gamemaster took his suit, and handed him a block of ice with a sympathetic smile. Yassen pressed it to his cheek.

"Your arm," she said in a low voice. "You need to see a doctor."

"I will, thank you," he said.

She drew back, her mouth screwed up in distaste. "That's what they all say."

She left without another word, leaving them alone in the room with its glass panels and pale blue light.

"I'm sorry," Samson said finally.

"It's alright, Sam."

"No, Cass, it's not." The militant shook his head. His eyes held the same brazen look as on the night he had promised Yassen of escape. "I gave you my word that I would help you, but these people... They'll learn."

"I'm taloned, Sam. Quit pitying me," Yassen said. He dropped the ice in a waste bin and gripped his friend's shoulder. "If we stick through this, you'll be king, and I'll be absolved of all my crimes."

Samson looked as if he was going to retort, but then he sighed.

"You're right," he said. "Go, you deserve some rest. I'll call for you later."

Yassen clapped him on his back and left Samson standing alone in the blue lights.

He hurried toward his room, avoiding the stares of servants as they glanced at his bloodied face. His sleeve began to edge up. Yassen went to pull it down when he saw that the marks had changed; they were beginning to warm, to grow red. He could feel the creeping heat, the tinge in his nerves.

Yassen walked quickly as hot, blistering pain cracked up his arm and drilled into his shoulder. Spots swam in front of his eyes. He turned into the hallway to his room when the world began to tilt. He stumbled, his knees going weak. A salty, iron taste filled his mouth.

He grabbed the wall with his good arm and slunk forward. Darkness ringed his vision. His fingers brushed something cold, sleek. *The panel.* He pressed his hand into the scanner as a laser shot out to confirm his identity. The door swung open, and Yassen stumbled in, falling to his knees.

A desert breeze licked his face. Warm and delicate. He was faintly aware that the window was open. Strange, he had not left it like that. Yassen tried to crawl forward, but his right arm stuck to the ground like molten lead. The breeze whispered, and he smelled the sweetness of a summer storm mixed with the promise of wet sand as he slowly lost consciousness.

10
LEO

*There are three types of fire. There is that of the Phoenix—a wild,
vengeful power. There is that of the dragon—a cold, haughty power.
And then there is the third—a fire that provides, nourishes, and heals.
I have only read of such fire in the scrolls. I have yet to find it.*

—FROM THE DIARIES OF PRIESTESS NOMU OF THE FIRE ORDER

Leo and Alonjo came to his private office—the real one fitted beside
his chamber, not the façade behind his throne room. As he entered,
Leo breathed in the smell of wet sand. There would be a storm soon.
Good. The city needed a little rain.

The study was a large circular room, full of lavish red curtains and
an intricate rug his grandfather had loved. A black granite table with
golden veins sat before the large bay window. Overhead, a glass dome
allowed ample light onto a seating area with floating orbs, sandalwood
chairs, and a chaise large enough to fit three men. Yet what Leo loved
the most about his study was the fire.

A ring of flames writhed around the room, their hiss a comfort to
Leo. In the beginning, he disliked their heat, their unpredictability,
the way a single flame blinded his eyes and made him see shadows
afterward. But he had grown to appreciate the power of a fire. Its
chaotic beauty. His forefather had founded Ravence with a respect
for fire, and it was a discipline Leo's father had instilled within him.

Leo went to his desk and projected an encrypted hologram. He placed his hand down on the panel. The system read his fingerprints and the map of his veins while a beam scanned his face and retinas.

Please verify, the holo read.

Leo glanced at Alonjo and then tapped in the password he had set his first day as king. The floor rumbled, and the emblem of the Phoenix separated to reveal stone steps that disappeared into darkness. Alonjo took a floating orb beside the chaise and sent it down the stairs to light their way.

"Wait," Leo said. He tapped the holo again and the flames surrounding the room shot to the ceiling. They crackled and spit out sparks—a barrier should anyone enter his study unannounced.

He followed Alonjo down the stairs and into the Palace's underground tunnels. King Fai had built them as an escape route. He had ordered his men to create tunnels for the Palace and the city's people as Jantar's army had trekked its way through the dunes to lay siege on the capital. But he never had to use them. Fai had been preparing for the wrath of men—not the wrath of the gods.

The desert storm had come at night. It started as a whisper, a slight touch against the skin, but in a matter of minutes, it snarled and wreaked havoc on Jantar's army, making them easy pickings for Fai's skilled desert raiders. When morning came, Jantar's army lay scattered and dead.

Fai's successor, Queen Jumi, had taken a curiosity to the tunnels and ordered for their expansion. Soon, a vast network of tunnels and chambers snaked underneath Palace Hill, slithering into the desert and the city. Here she built the Royal Library, a tall chamber that housed ancient scrolls and physical books.

Leo breathed in the musky scent of time-worn paper as they stood in the middle of the library, a round room like his office. When Leo looked up, a mass of darkness awaited.

With a push, Alonjo sent the orb up to reveal bookcases that rose further than Leo could see. Scrolls upon scrolls, spines amongst spines, packed into the dusty shelves. As the orb rose higher, more orbs floating quietly along the wall awakened until the library basked in a warm, gentle light.

As Leo scanned the multiple shelves, a slow dread rose up his throat. How in heavens could he decipher the runes when he did not even know where to start? He summoned a holo of the burnt priest. It floated beside him as he approached a shelf and studied the faded parchments.

He visited the library rarely and never for very long. The first time, he had come with his father, King Ramandra. The second, Leo brought his new bride to show her the wealth of information she had just inherited. And the last was when, a few months after his queen's death, Leo had returned to the place that had brought her so much joy. Aahnah had studied and read the scrolls. She knew how to navigate its shelves. She had learned the truth about Ravence and had taken its secret to the grave.

Leo wished he had asked her how she created order among the scrolls, but he had been distracted by the demands of the throne. Absentmindedly, he traced the lip of a shelf. Dust and grime filled his nails.

"I suggest we begin by searching the Immortal section," Alonjo said.

Leo nodded. The Phoenix was an Immortal, and Her feather had been burned into the priest. He followed the curve of the shelves until he found the westernmost point. Golden script inscribed into the wood told him that shelves 1 to 322 housed texts and histories of the Immortals. He pulled down a scroll and opened it, coughing away dust. He searched for the Phoenix's feather but there was no such symbol.

He returned the scroll and opened another as Alonjo joined him. It was slow work. The floating orbs bobbed overhead as the hours passed. When he could no longer reach the higher scrolls, Leo stepped onto a stone circle before the shelf. He hit his heel against it twice, and the stone lifted, carrying him up in the air. Alonjo did the same.

"Any luck?" he called out after some time.

The Astra sighed and replaced a scroll. "None, Your Majesty." He checked the time on his holopod and started. "Mother's Gold, look at the time. You're supposed to have lunch with Her Highness now."

Leo tapped his foot twice. The stone platform began to descend when Leo noticed it. Shelf 52. He stopped the stone circle. There, right beneath the golden number, were his wife's initials. A.M. Aahnah Madhani. Her maiden name.

She had once told him that she marked the shelves that held something of interest to her or contained a text he would find amusing. Leo floated before Shelf 52 and scanned the scrolls. He pulled one out and then another. He did not know what he was looking for, only that he would recognize it when he saw it.

He pulled out a parchment with a metal band. Stamped onto the metal was the feather of the Phoenix; it glinted red in the light.

Leo opened the scroll gingerly. The paper was delicate, as if it would dissolve in the slightest breeze. But there, in the lines of text, he saw the feather and the rune that matched the ones burned onto the priest. He rolled the scroll closed and put it into his coat. Two more scrolls had metal bands; he took them as well.

The stone circle descended and Leo returned to the ground. Slowly, the light diminished until only one orb was aglow. They followed it up the stairs and into his study where the crackling flames rose to welcome them.

"Reschedule my lunch with Elena," Leo said as he set the parchments on his desk. "I don't want to be bothered for the next two hours."

With a wave of his hand, Leo calmed the fire. The flames shrank back to their embers, purring.

"Your Majesty," Alonjo said, but he did not turn to leave.

"Is there anything else?"

"The engagement of your daughter, I believe we should announce it. Tomorrow even. Having Samson appear next to Her Highness on Palace Hill will send a message to the Arohassin."

Leo looked down at the scrolls and at the holo of the priest. The marks stared back at him, dark and raw.

"Arrange for it," he said and sat down.

Alonjo bowed again. The chamber opened and shut softly behind him. Leo unrolled the first scroll, the one he had already read. It looked even more fragile above ground.

Gently, he flattened the parchment and studied the rolling script. It was written in Herra, the ancient language spoken in the early days of Ravence before King Mahabir mandated that everyone to speak Vesseri.

Leo was careful not to smudge the handwritten ink as he tried to make sense of the ancient symbols. He recognized the feather and the rune shaped like the eye of a hurricane, an inward storm. He searched for some clue that would unlock their meaning, but the scroll held no such key. Perhaps by association, by comparing the scrolls together, he could find something.

The second scroll was longer, and Leo spotted the feather and the rune several times throughout. He placed the texts beside each other. Both had the feather in the upper right-hand corner, followed by a rune. On the priest's back, the feather was the first symbol while the inward storm was the second.

Leo looked to the flames as they wavered and hissed. The feather represented the Phoenix, he knew that, and the second rune always appeared beside it in the scrolls. Was it an adjective? A description of the Phoenix's power? The High Priestess had said that the runes meant Daughter of Fire, so did the second rune prescribe gender? Or was Saayna leading him through a wild shobu chase? Leo racked his brain. He felt as if he had seen this rune before, but he couldn't pinpoint where.

He unrolled the last scroll and set the metal band to the side. This one was shorter than the rest with no symbol other than the feather. Leo peered closer. There, at the bottom of the page, written in tiny scrawl, was a familiar phrase.

Nebrium fe ruin.

So we the blessed few.

It was the phrase he always recited at the end of Ashanta ceremonies, the same one he whispered to himself before war meetings with ministers and generals. Yet, the one written before him stood out. At the end of the phrase, looping out of the last letter, was the second rune. It looked almost as if it was written by mistake—a stray dash of a quill. Leo peered closer, but then there came a rumble as the hall to his study opened. He slipped the scrolls into his desk drawer as Elena entered.

"I thought I told Alonjo not to let anyone in," he said.

"Not even me, Father?"

"Don't be coy," he said. The chamber remained open, but no one else came through. "Where are your guards? Where's Yassen?"

"He went to dress his wounds." She sat down and reached forward, picking up the metal band he had tossed aside.

Leo cursed inwardly as she held it up to the light.

"Reading something?"

He pressed his hand against the desk drawer to ensure it was fully closed before grabbing the band. "Old texts that don't concern you," he said and deposited the band in the drawer.

She eyed him. Of course she must know that it came from the Royal Library, but Leo did not wish to tell her why.

"Alonjo is organizing a public viewing on Palace Hill to announce the engagement. You should prepare a statement with Samson," he said, but she waved him off.

There was an intensity in her dark eyes, her mother's eyes, as she leaned forward, her voice earnest. "I need you to teach me about the fire," she said. "Teach me how to hold the flame."

The surrounding fire crackled as if responding to her request. She wasn't ready. The last time she had tried to hold a flame, she had burned herself and filled her room with so much smoke that it could be seen all the way from the capital. Newscasts speculated as to the cause before Leo sent out a statement to claim there had been no blaze; that the High Priestess had come to cleanse the Palace with incense-sweetened smoke.

No one could know that the heir of Ravence was not capable of withstanding fire.

Elena drummed her fingers against the desk to call back his attention.

"You're not ready yet," he said.

"You keep saying that, but how will I ever be ready if you don't teach me?" she said. "How can I be queen if I can't even get through the Ashanta ceremony?"

He could not tell her the truth, not now.

Fire brought pain. Sacrifice. A sacrifice she was not yet ready to give.

"The viewing will be tomorrow morning," he said.

Elena sat back, her mouth a hard line and her eyes, Aahnah's eyes, judging him.

"You're making a mistake," she said finally.

But he summoned holos of his upcoming meetings to divide the space between them.

Elena gripped the edge of his desk, a muscle working in her jaw. But he said nothing more, and after a few wordless minutes, his daughter swept out of the room.

The flames hissed. Leo sat back in his seat and pulled out Aahnah's necklace from underneath his kurta. No one had told him he would have to sacrifice the one he loved when he came before the Eternal

Fire for his crowning. His father had hidden the truth, and at first, Leo had been angry. He had refused to sacrifice Aahnah. The flames had ripped him apart in response.

Miraculously, he had survived. But he had lived under the delusion that the test was over, that the Eternal Fire was satisfied. Aahnah was the one to discover it was not.

She had found the truth in the scrolls. Elena was but seven suns when they went to Temple for an Ashanta ceremony. The Eternal Fire had been hot, angry. It had snapped at him, and Leo had stumbled down the steps of the dais when Aahnah, face resolute, jumped into the pit. Within seconds, the Eternal Fire devoured her. Completely. It left no traces, not even ash.

In one moment, she had been there, holding Elena and then, she was gone, leaving Elena alone by the dais.

After her sacrifice, the Fire had fallen back, quiet, satiated.

Only then did Leo realize why his father had hidden the truth. He wanted to protect him as Leo wished to protect Elena now.

The scrolls rustled as Leo opened them. Elena could not hold the flames because he had refused to give penance when it was due. She bore the crux of his sin.

Leo studied the rune shaped like an inward storm; he understood it now. The Eternal Fire had given him a warning—a reminder of his transgression.

But he would protect Ravence until his dying breath. Without him, the nation would fall into chaos. Elena would be alone to fend off the hyenas who stalked Ravence.

No, he would find a way. He had to. The runes smoldered before him as Leo put in the call to Muftasa.

"The girl," he said. "The one with the hair of starlight. Bring her to me. Let's see if she burns."

THE LAST PROPHET

When the Phoenix rose from the Temple, She spoke to the priests in a voice made of ash.

"Why are they fighting for this land?"

As She spoke, armies waged war at the foot of the mountains. If one walked to the front steps of the Temple, one could hear the faint sorrows of battle: the clash of metal and the short-lived screams of obsessive men. The Phoenix looked from priest to priest, but none could meet Her eyes—not only because of their shame, but also because they could not see past the clarity of Her flames.

All except one.

A priestess met the golden eyes of the Phoenix and spoke in a small yet steady voice.

"It is because they do not realize their mortality," she said.

The Phoenix stared down at the priestess, but she did not waver. She did not break her gaze.

"Then it is you," the Phoenix said, and so it was done. Her Fire rose in answer to its new master and wrapped around the arms and limbs of the priestess. It enveloped her, covered her, welcomed her. The Phoenix raised Her wings and a beam of light erupted from the heart of the Fire to the sky above. The armies below saw it. The whole world saw it.

The Prophet was chosen.

With a wave of her hand, the Prophet unleashed the rage of the Phoenix. A fierce inferno tore down the mountainside. Those who resisted perished. Those who begged for mercy perished. Those who simply sank to their knees in defeat perished.

There is no forgiveness in the eyes of the Phoenix.

When the last king had burned to ash, the Prophet turned to the priests.

"There will be no more wars for this land," the Prophet declared. "Though we cannot stop their ambitious nature, we can prevent the Sayonai from reaching this Temple."

And so it was done. The flames pushed past the mountain to the land beyond, burning rivers, streams, trees, birds and men alike. The priests watched as the land transformed from a fertile, green forest into an arid desert that shielded none from the unforgiving gaze of the sun. Only the forest that grew along the mountains continued to exist.

The Phoenix saw this and more.

She spread Her marvelous wings, and in each glistening feather, the Prophet recognized the colors of the world—from the dark depths of the sea to the warm shades of a sunrise. And as she saw these colors, the Prophet felt her body morph. Her limbs grew and her eyes changed.

The priests say her eyes melted into the same eternal gold of the Phoenix; her veins pulsed with the heat of a fire; her hair unfurled into curls of smoke; and her lips, which once sang hymns, became small and hard.

When she spoke, she spoke with the multitude of her former reincarnations.

"This Fire will protect the land. Do not let it die."

And so the Eternal Fire came to live in the heart of the Temple. The priests watched as the Prophet and the Phoenix rose as one, growing brighter and brighter until the priests were forced to look away. When they finally reopened their eyes, the Prophet and the Phoenix were gone.

Only the sun, bright and unmerciful, remained to see all that would come.

11
YASSEN

Jantar's shining city of brass, Rysanti, was created five hundred suns ago by Rydia the Tyrant. When workers complained about the bright reflection of the sun on the brass fixtures, she ordered them to wear visors. Hence, the Jantari began to lose the color of their eyes.

—FROM CHAPTER 33 OF *THE GREAT HISTORY OF SAYON*

Yassen awoke to someone banging on his door. Still groggy from sleep, he slowly crawled onto his knees. There was a dry, ashen taste in his mouth. Yassen licked his lips as he pinched the skin between his thumb and forefinger. Needles of pain pricked his arm. He winced, trying to move toward the door when it burst open, and Samson tumbled in.

"Dragon's tit! What are you doing on the floor?" he demanded.

Yassen leaned his head against the wall. "It's comfy."

Samson took in his unkempt clothes and tousled hair. He squatted down and gripped his chin.

"Did you pass out?" he asked, a genuine hint of worry in his voice.

"She kicked my ass," Yassen replied.

Samson turned his face side to side, squinting. "Actually, I think she improved your looks."

Yassen snorted and turned away. Samson straightened, wiping his hand on his pants. He surveyed the room, taking note of the untouched clothes laid out on the bed.

"Is it your arm?"

Yassen rose to his feet. The sky was already growing dim, the twin moons beginning their nightly watch. He vaguely remembered a storm, but only a few dark clouds loomed on the horizon.

Samson walked to the open window and looked out at the fading sunset, its violet glow touching the tips of his ears. "The gamemaster told me. She saw it in the scan. I told her I would tell Elena myself."

Yassen recalled how Elena had watched him, like a desert hawk tracking its prey before smashing it against the rocks. She must have sensed his weakness. Perhaps that was why she wanted to fight him in the first place.

Yassen sat down on the edge of the bed. Silk shirts from Nbru, linen jackets from Monte Gumi, and cotton pants spun on the quaint foothills of Beuron lay out across the soft sheets, untouched.

"Try one on. See if it fits," Samson said. He pressed a button on the windowsill, and the glass panels closed.

Yassen hesitated. He looked down at the clothes and gingerly picked up a blue linen shirt with golden buttons. "Give me a minute," he said and began to move toward the washroom when Samson stopped him short.

"Try it on here," he said.

They stared at each other for a long moment. Finally, Yassen sighed and sat back.

"I knew it," Samson said. "Is it really that bad?"

Yassen slowly peeled off his sweaty shirt to reveal his right arm. Deep, dark welts sliced across his shoulder and bicep, his skin brown and wrinkled like a date left out in the sun. Touching his elbow, Yassen felt a familiar ache echo through his bones.

"What did the Arohassin do to you?" Samson whispered.

"They did nothing. I made a mistake," he said and stopped. The memory and the pain it brought was still too raw. He remembered how the fire had grabbed his arm. The smell of seared flesh. The deep, blistering heat. "They were barely able to save it."

Samson slowly sank into a floating ottoman and folded his hands beneath his chin. It was an old mannerism. He had done the same when they had received their first assignment to kill. Akaros had told them the job, and, afterward, Samson had grown silent. Withdrawn. As if he already regretted the actions he had not yet committed.

They had been sent in the night, except this time, it wasn't for training purposes. Their targets were fleeing prisoners. The Arohassin called it the Hunt. They took in prisoners of wars, flayed them, drowned them, hung them, and, if they had survived, let them serve as target practice for their newest recruits.

In all the time it took to gather their weapons and head over from the barracks, Samson had said nothing. The twin moons had hidden behind the clouds that night. It was hard to see from their perch on the hill, but the escape door of the underground prison stood directly across from them. Five were in their party: Samson, him, two other recruits that had survived camp, and Akaros, who lay beneath a camouflage of thick vines.

"Alright, boys," he had said, "they're coming out."

The first prisoner had peeked out from the gate and scanned his surroundings. He looked hesitant, his lips pale and eyes haggard as Yassen watched him through his scope. Three more peered out behind him. They talked among themselves, debating. Yassen tried to read their lips when the first prisoner took off running. One of the boys fired. The pulse echoed through the valley. The man stumbled and fell.

"Quick now," Akaros had drawled.

Another prisoner screamed and dashed to the right. Yassen followed him. He could see his head perfectly centered in his viewfinder. This man was somebody's son, likely a brother and father. He could have been a decent man. But Yassen had pushed away these thoughts as he felt Akaros watching him, testing him, waiting to see if he would crumble.

His shot had been clean; it hit the man right in the head. His body had crumpled, his legs folding beneath him as if he were made of string, not bone. When Yassen exhaled, his heartbeat thundered in his ears. His whole body trembled. For he understood in that moment, in the split second when the pulse ripped the man's consciousness out of his body, that it also tore a part of him—a part he could never, ever mend.

The other recruits found their targets. Only one prisoner remained, and she ran for the hills. Yassen had glanced at Samson, who lay frozen. Even his grip was slack.

"Come on," Yassen had whispered, but Samson did not move.

The prisoner was eventually caught and executed. Samson was whipped a hundred and fifty times; all the recruits had to watch.

Yassen did not remember if Samson had cried. He only remembered how, when they had returned to the barracks, Samson, addled by drugs, had whispered something in the dark.

"She reminded me of my sister."

In all the time he had known him, Yassen had never guessed that Samson had siblings.

Raindrops hit the windowpane, and Yassen jumped. Samson went to the window and opened it again. A gust of fresh air—that raw, grainy scent of wet land—filled the room. Yassen felt the cold touch of raindrops on his burnt skin. He curled his hand into a tight fist until thin, crescent moons appeared on his palm.

"There isn't anything like a desert storm," Samson said.

Yassen flexed his fingers, waiting for the needles to return.

"I can still fight," he said.

"I know you can," Samson said, his back turned to him. "But I wonder if this kind of fighting will kill you."

"I've been through worse," Yassen replied. He tried to sound nonchalant, but his hand trembled, and he curled it back into a fist to stop the shaking.

"There's an Arohassin agent on your list that we want to bring in," Samson said. "She operates in Rani, out in the southern district. We need to make sure she check—"

"I'll do it," Yassen said, standing. "I can bring her in."

In the fading light of the sunset, Yassen saw Samson's shoulders slump. His head bowed. After a moment, Samson turned and met his gaze.

"If she doesn't check out, they'll kill you on the spot."

Yassen nodded, but he knew Samson had more to say. He could see the words in his eyes, could read them in the way he clutched the windowsill. "Is there anything else?"

Samson glanced at Yassen's arm, his mouth twisting.

"You always were the one who could make the kill," he said, eyes flashing with pity and disgust.

Yassen detested that look. His neighbors had stared at him the same way when he had lost his parents, as if he were a wounded shobu. Filthy and unwanted. They had whispered about him, the poor boy with the Jantari eyes. *No one will adopt an orphan like him.* He had wanted to pluck the pity from their eyes and bury it deep in the desert.

Samson bent toward the bed and chucked a white shirt at Yassen. Gone was the look, replaced by an easy, if not cautious, smile.

"This would look better on you," he said. His eyes lingered on his burnt flesh. "Does it hurt?"

"Sometimes, like a ghost is traveling through my body," Yassen said. He straightened and grabbed a pair of cotton trousers. "Now, if you could leave."

Samson paused before the door. The rain fell harder, thick wet drops that sounded as if a million tiny soldiers waged battle on the roof.

"We leave right after dawn," he said. The door closed softly behind him.

Yassen dropped the shirt to the floor. He crossed the room and leaned out the window. The rain splashed his face, soaked his hair, trailed down his naked torso. He wanted to feel its chill in his bones. To feel anything in the cold dampness that bogged down his chest.

Through the mist, Yassen could make out the silhouettes of the sandscrapers and chhatris. Beyond them lay the desert suburbs and, somewhere in the outskirts, his home.

Home. What a strange word. It was meant to be a haven, a place where he could finally die in peace, but it felt more like a curse. A dream that perhaps he would never achieve.

He had never fit in with his cursed, colorless eyes in Ravence. The Jantari spurned him as soon as they heard the desert on his tongue. He had always been an orphan, even before he became one. His parents had tried to shield him, but they too bore the same ostracization. *Traitors,* they had called his parents. *Abomination,* they had called him.

Yet here he was on Palace Hill, in the Palace, looking down upon the city that had spawned him. He, who had never even dreamed of setting foot within the royal courtyards, slept in its chambers. Yassen turned his face up to the lumbering clouds. He knew these people would never accept him. They would doubt him even if he killed the leader of the Arohassin and served him on a platter to the king. The Ravani wished for his death, no matter if he crawled in the desert, repenting.

Yassen closed his eyes and tasted the salty rain.

But he, the orphan from the desert outskirts, would show them. He had to.

12
ELENA

There is a rage that comes with fire. An all-consuming fury that boils away any sliver of fear. This is why the Prophet is so powerful. She serves the heavy hand of justice without the fear of death. Her lifetime contains a multitude of generations, and our life is only a blink in hers.

—FROM THE DIARIES OF PRIESTESS NOMU OF THE FIRE ORDER

The library still smelled like old stone and stale sand. The orbs lit up one by one, and Elena looked up to see the tower of books and scrolls spiraling above her.

She had recognized the metal band on her father's desk. Her father rarely ventured down into the Royal Library; she knew it reminded him too much of her mother. But if he had pushed away his hesitance to consult the scrolls, it meant something larger was at play.

Elena turned to the sound of footsteps. Ferma descended into the chamber, brushing dust from her long, silky hair.

"I've moved the guards outside your door to the end of the corridor. They didn't hear the passage opening."

Elena nodded. Every member of the royal family had a private entrance to the library. It was something Queen Jumi had insisted upon when she had enlarged the library. Though Elena trusted her guards, she did not want her father to know she had come here. He obviously was hiding something, so she would do the same.

She approached a bookshelf along the eastern wall, running her hand along the stone and unsettling centuries of dust. She visited the library more often than her father although not to read. That had been her mother's calling. She came to escape nagging tutors and Ferma's constant drills. Something about the cold stone and the musty scent of timeworn pages calmed Elena. Here, she could clear her thoughts. Here, no one could call out her shortcomings.

She followed the curve of the shelf as Ferma ascended on a stone platform.

"His Majesty has definitely been here," the Yumi called out. Her voice rang through the tall chamber.

Elena stepped onto a stone circle and joined the Spear before the western shelves.

Ferma pointed at a section. "The dust is unsettled there."

"Why would my father study the Immortal scrolls?" Elena muttered.

She knew these ledges like the back of her hand. Her mother had taught her how to navigate the library; Aahnah had been its keeper, dusting the shelves and organizing the scrolls into a secret order that she had taught her daughter. Often, Elena would find her here, buried in scrolls, reading runes and ancient prophecies about the world that came before. The former queen had lived in her own realm, with her own rules and characters. Elena and her father were but minor reminders from the realer, plainer world. As she grew sicker, Aahnah had spent more time in her books and less time worrying about Elena's growing pains. She had cared more for these scrolls than her own child.

Elena swallowed a wave of childhood bitterness. Aahnah was dead now. There was no point in distressing over the past.

She turned her attention back to the shelves, searching for disturbed dust. Her fingers brushed against the ends of the scrolls. One jutted out, and Elena made to push it back when she spotted her mother's initials scratched into the shelf's edge.

Aahnah liked to leave behind signs of herself. She used to scribble her name everywhere, from the inside lapels of her coat to the margins of historic texts. When Elena had asked her why, her mother had become quiet. She had a distant look in her eye, as if to tether herself to some far-off point.

"Your name is important, Elena. It tells you who you are. It tells the world who you are," she had finally said.

It had taken her mother's death for Elena to understand why she had marked everything. It was not so much a claim of ownership but rather a quiet, desperate act to be remembered. To keep herself from disappearing by scattering parts of herself for others to find.

Elena rubbed her mother's initials, wondering if Aahnah were here now, what she would say about the daughter who could not hold fire.

"What exactly are we looking for anyway?" Ferma asked. "Was His Majesty searching for something?"

"I think the king might actually be out of his element." Elena stared at her mother's initials and then at the dark hole where a scroll had been. She thought back to the metal ring on her father's desk; the look on his face when he refused to teach her about the Eternal Fire, about her own kingdom. "He's searching for answers, which means he has even less time for me."

The coronation was a little over a month away. If she couldn't get the answers from him, she would take her chances with the dead.

Elena pulled out a scroll and unrolled it carefully. The paper crinkled at her touch. She recognized neither the language nor the symbols scrawled along the edges. Carefully, Elena set it back and grabbed another.

Ferma joined her. They floated before the shelves, going from section to section, but after hours of searching, they found nothing sensical.

"This all looks like gibberish," Ferma groaned.

"No shit," Elena said. She jammed a scroll back into the shelf.

She was running out of time. Samson would arrive soon to discuss their announcement, and she suspected her father would return to the library tonight and post sentries at all of its entry points. She had no chance of coming back if that happened.

Elena swatted away dust as she unrolled another scroll. Her eyes glazed over the sloping runes. She was just about to close it when she stopped.

There, in the margins of her paper, were her mother's initials. She had held this same scroll, pored over these same runes. Though the queen had not been a great mother, she had been an astute scholar, and Elena trusted her judgment.

Elena motioned for an orb and it floated downward. She watched, fascinated, as the runes unlocked in the light, unspooling and lengthening, forming new figures and characters until she realized they weren't words but drawings of women surrounding a single flame.

She studied the scroll further.

No, it was the same woman.

And she was dancing around the fire.

"What is that?" Ferma asked.

Elena stared at the scroll, her mind racing. It showed seven different stances. Elena recognized none from her training in the Unsung and Kymathra, but she recognized one thing, felt it deep in her bones. A deep, instinctual knowing. Here lay a path to power.

"This is the way to hold fire," she whispered.

There were translations beneath the runes, and Elena recognized her mother's handwriting. The seventh form was faded however, the text and woman scratched out. Elena smoothed the lower corner of the scroll. Someone had drawn a small flower. A jasmine. Below it was her mother's signature, like the mark of an artist: A.M.

Elena descended, the orb and Ferma following. She rolled the scroll and slipped it into her blouse, already making for the exit as the orbs began to dim.

"Elena, wait," Ferma called, and she stopped and turned to the Yumi. "Maybe we should inform your father about this."

"Your gracious king doesn't even want to teach me about fire," she said. "This will be our secret."

"Did you ever consider *why* he's hesitating?" Ferma asked. Her tawny eyes seemed to glow in the darkness of the library. "Do you even remember that day?"

No.

"Yes," Elena said, her throat tight. In truth, she only remembered moments: her mother's reverent eyes, her father's horrid scream. It was the only time in her life that she had seen him fall to his knees.

"He doesn't want you to have the same fate as your mother," Ferma said.

"She was a fool," Elena spat.

The scrolls had filled her mother with madness. Leo thought it was her illness, but Elena could not forget the look in her mother's eyes before she leapt into the flames. The fervor in them. Like all the fire lunatics, Aahnah had come to believe redemption could only be achieved through burning. She had leapt into the pit of the Eternal Fire, leaving Elena not even her ashes to scatter in the wind.

"Maybe if she had known how to hold fire, she wouldn't have burned," Elena said.

"Fire is dangerous. It's pure chaos," Ferma insisted, gripping her arm. "You can't learn to wield it with only a scroll. You almost burned down the Palace the last time you—"

"You think I can't do it." Her eyes bore into Ferma. "You sound just like your king."

"I just don't want to lose two queens," Ferma replied.

At this, Elena felt her anger dissipate. She turned away so the Yumi could not see her face flush with guilt.

"Leave me," she whispered, but her voice echoed through the tall chamber.

Ferma hesitated, but then she bowed deeply.

"Your Highness," she mumbled.

Back in her room, Elena unrolled the scroll as it began to rain. In the third form, it looked as if the woman cupped a flame to her chest, almost like a babe. Elena could not imagine her father mimicking these moves and holding fire so tenderly. How had he learned to overcome its hungry heat, its unforgiving desire? How had he learned to be so ruthless?

A holo popped up above her desk, and Elena opened it to see a message from Samson.

Congratulations on our engagement. Attached was a statement he had already drafted. As she read it, Elena felt a cold numbness slither in the pit of her stomach. Marriage was an inevitable fact of life; she had to marry and bear an heir for the next Ravani generation. That was her duty. But Elena had always believed she could rule without a partner, just like her father had without his. It would be harder, yes, but at least she could focus on protecting her kingdom rather than appeasing the desires of a man.

There came a knock on the door. Elena quickly stowed the scroll in her desk drawer as her guards announced that her fiancé had arrived. She ordered them to let him in.

"Your Highness," Samson said and bowed deeply.

"Skip the formalities." She beckoned toward the covered terrace. "Let's discuss out there."

"Have you had time to read over what I sent?" he asked as her handmaid brought out tea and a platter of cloud cookies. The rain drummed against the balustrades and down in her garden as the banyan trees rustled in the wind.

"It's a bit rough around the edges, but I can fix it." Elena poured their drinks, examining Samson. She had heard stories of his military feats and, in person, he looked like a warrior with his broad shoulders and warm, bronze skin. But she also saw the makings of a royal within him: the confidence and arrogance in his posture, the sureness in his gaze. He would make a pretty king.

"Let's be frank," she said as he reached for his cup. He hesitated and sat back without it. "Is Ravence your only play for a throne?"

If the question surprised him, Samson made no sign of it. He merely regarded her with dark blue eyes. *Too much water*, she thought and stopped herself from rubbing the back of her neck. Such eyes were considered bad luck in Ravence. They held an abundance of water, and out here in the desert, it drove men mad with greed.

"No," Samson finally said.

She ventured a smile. At least he knew when to be honest.

"What other young queens have considered your hand?" She took a sip from her tea, never averting her gaze.

He held it. "Two, actually—from Cyleon and Mandur. Both are strategically sound, but Cyleon is only suns away from a civil war, and Mandur can't get over its grievances with Pagua."

"Sounds like Ravence and Jantar," she mused. And then the realization dawned on her. How had she not seen it before? Samson was Jantar's rising star—the islander turned star general. If there was one throne he sought above all else, it would be Ravence.

"They say the Jantari love you more than their own king." Her eyes dragged over him like a whip. "Is that true?"

"Who am I to uproot a king?" he responded. A wisp of a smile played across his lips. "Besides, queens hold more favor in court."

"Is that so?"

He leaned forward, so close that she could see the vivid sea trapped within his eyes. His fingers brushed the back of her hand.

"'A steady hand and a quick sword,' isn't that what your scriptures say?" He slid his hand down, touching the soft skin of her wrist. "You're the hand, I'm the sword. You command, and I'll burn their names in the sand. Imagine the Arohassin gone and peace with the Jantari. Your reign—our reign—will bring back the Golden Suns. An age of splendor."

Elena pulled her hand away.

"What do you think of fire?" she asked. "What does it do?"

It was an odd question, but she needed to know if the same obsession ran through Samson as it had with Aahnah. If she would have to lose his ashes in the Eternal Fire.

"Fire brings life. Domination. Reverence," Samson answered, each word soft and slow. "But it's an insidious power. It can burn one from within if you're not careful." And he looked at her with such intensity that for a moment, Elena wondered if he knew about the scroll.

"I've seen how fire can tear apart its followers," he continued. "It leaves marks that can never be erased. The Ravani know all this yet continue to worship the Phoenix. Others call it madness, but I think your people have tapped into an ancient force that no other nation understands." He paused, and they turned to look at the desert that lay beyond Palace Hill. The rain shimmered over the dunes like silver dancers. "Ravence has survived because it knows what it means to burn. It knows loss, yet its people continue to believe."

"'Faith is stronger than any king,'" she whispered, quoting the scriptures.

Samson nodded. "And your father knows this. He entertains the Fire Order because he needs the image of myth and divinity to ensure his power. He sits in the flames to keep your people in line."

Elena let out a low breath. "I can't hold fire," she said. The words came before she could stop them, a tumbling rush. She had never admitted this to anyone; only Ferma and the king knew. Shame and relief colored her cheeks, and Elena bit her tongue. To his credit, Samson only shrugged.

"Does it matter?" he asked. "It's all a show. You just make the people believe you can hold fire, and they'll worship at your feet."

"Perhaps," she said. Appearances and deception were the first rules of any statecraft. Truth, when applied strategically, was a finely edged knife. "But if the Prophet were to hear you, you'd be the first to burn."

At this, Samson laughed—a deep, booming sound that resounded off the walls and leapt to meet the rain. It was a type of laugh that did not often frequent the Palace halls. Elena felt herself warming to it.

"I'm sorry about your friend," she said. "I may have been a bit cruel."

"He can handle it," Samson said. His laughter subsided, and he looked at her with a faint smile. "Give him a chance. Will you?"

Elena looked out at her garden, at the darkening sky. A soft breeze whispered through the trees, bringing the scent of wet sands. Beneath the hill and beyond, the dunes sprawled out into the deep desert.

Her desert.

Elena rose, and Samson rose with her. She led him to the door, and when she offered her hand, he kissed it, his lips lingering against her skin.

"Think about it," he said and bade her goodnight.

Long after he had gone, she touched the back of her hand. It wasn't the kiss that had shocked her, but the heat of his lips. They burned her skin.

The next morning, Elena joined her fiancé and father on the terrace looking down on the capital. Ferma and the royal guards stood behind them while Yassen waited in the wings. When she saw her guard in the morning, Elena had ignored him. There was a mark beneath his brow where she had hit him, but otherwise, he looked composed. Oddly, she had felt relief, but Elena quickly pushed it away. He did not deserve her pity.

A wide sea of reporters and civilians jostled at the base of Palace Hill. Some projected holosigns displaying the royal family. Others waved tiny flags. Most regarded her and her father silently. She could feel the weight of their gaze, the guarded look in their eyes. Elena had not forgotten the way the pedestrians had watched her in front of the tea shop when the hoverpod descended. They had repelled from her as if she had been a rattlesnake, ready to strike.

Slowly, a chant began through the crowd. Elena leaned forward to listen.

"Son of Fire, Son of Fire!"

She spotted the telltale gold caps. At once, she knew they had started the chant.

The gold caps pushed their way to the front of the crowd like a wave, their chant growing louder and louder. They were a boisterous lot prone to epic tantrums of nationalism. Though most of Ravence believed in the Phoenix, the gold caps believed in the Holy Bird with such ferocity that they would burn themselves to show their piety. They shamed the nonbelievers, ridiculed the royal family's skeptics, and threatened the ones who dared to speak of revolution.

Leo raised his hands, and the gold caps let out a loud roar. Elena saw him smile. They were her father's most ardent supporters, the ones who would not bat an eyelash if he were to kill a man with his bare hands. Their support had spurred Leo's reign for decades.

Elena despised them.

When the king lowered his hands, the crowd fell quiet. Leo was dressed in golden robes that shone despite the dark morning. He wore the crown, the Featherstone pulsing as if alive. Elena stood to his right, Samson to his left. She glanced at her fiancé and found him looking straight at her.

Samson winked.

"May the sun dawn upon our lands," Leo said.

"And the fire burn within our hearts," the crowd intoned.

Their collective voices lifted up from the bottom of the hill, a warm, cohesive drone that seemed to dispel the dark clouds lumbering above. Elena mumbled the words to herself, shivering in the early desert morning.

"The time has come for a new queen to rise," Leo said, and at this, the crowd gave another wild roar. A hovercam floating before the terrace zoomed in on Elena's face. She tried not to grimace.

"It is tradition that when the heir turns twenty-five, the old sun must set. He must dim his light for the new dawn," Leo said, his voice amplified by the mics surrounding them. "As a king, I cannot be more delighted. This heir is more radiant than our past monarchs."

He turned to Elena, and she bowed her head. "But as a father, I must tell you that there is something that the heir needs."

A murmur went through the crowd. The hovercams moved closer.

"The sun governs above all. But the flaming sword will make us bow." Leo raised both hands, beckoning for Elena and Samson to step forward. They did so at once. She could hear the crowd inhale sharply, feel their eyes narrow as they began to realize the meaning behind their king's words.

"It is with great pleasure that I announce the engagement of our heir. Ravence, after so long, will once again know the power of both king and queen."

The crowd erupted. The gold caps, as always, were the loudest. Samson held out his arm, and after a moment's pause, Elena took it. He raised their clasped hands, and the crowd cheered.

When the people finally came back to their senses, it was her turn to speak. Her stomach suddenly a pit of stinging ants, Elena squeezed Samson's hand. He squeezed in return.

Gulping down her nerves, Elena stepped forward.

"My fellow countrymen," she began, and she heard Leo start behind her. Royals often began their speech by calling upon the heavens, not the common born before them. She heard the crowd whisper nervously, confused by her greeting, but she forced herself to smile.

"Yes, countrymen," she said. She gripped the podium, willing her voice to lose its warble and become steady. She could feel her father and Samson, her past and her future, watching her. "The people of Ravence create the beating heart of this kingdom. Your blood courses through its veins. I may be blessed with the Fire of the Phoenix, but your passion stirs the winds of the desert."

She stood taller, her chest warming, her voice slowly losing its nervous tremble.

"They say that it is the sovereign that leads a nation to enlightenment. This is true. As queen, I intend to lead us to great prosperity. But the people, the people of salt and sand, the ones who built Rani alongside Alabore Ravence, bring enlightenment to life. Without her people, Ravence is nothing. Without your faith, she is merely a dream in the desert.

"Every day, we are threatened by those who dare to destroy this dream. Those who speak of revolution and a path without Agnee," she said, and somewhere within the crowd, a person booed. A gold cap yelled something, and others shuffled their feet in discontent.

Elena was no fool. She knew some in the crowd despised her family, despised everything she stood for. But they were still her people. Born of salt and sand, just like her.

Her eyes swept the crowd. One by one, the crowd quieted under the weight of her gaze. It was a trick she had learned from her father—to stretch out silence and use it to her advantage. When the murmur finally died, replaced now by a tight awkwardness, Elena raised her chin.

"I know there are those of you who disagree with the throne. Those who believe this government has failed you, silenced you. But hear this—I welcome you.

"This kingdom, this dream of peace, will always serve its people first. As queen, I will protect you. As sovereign, I will lead you. But as a Ravani, as a daughter born of salt and sand, I will work beside you.

"My countrymen, we are the guardians of this kingdom. We are the defenders against the violent barbarians who seek the Fire. Will we let them so easily dash our dream?"

"No!"

"Never!"

"Burn them all!"

Elena raised her hand to quiet them. "Then defend this dream. Jantar, the Arohassin, they know little about the power of Ravence or her kindness. Where were the other kingdoms when the islander refugees came to their doors? Who let them in? Who clothed them, gave them purpose? You, my countrymen. You opened your arms to strangers, and this is a feat no other nation can claim."

She turned to Samson and let her eyes soften as the cameras zoomed in. "A new era dawns upon Ravence. One in which we are not just defending our borders but strengthening them. With the help of my beloved, our future king, we will protect the dream of our forefathers."

She turned back to the crowd, her voice rising. "So lend me your hearts, my countrymen. Let us work together to show the world what Ravence can really do. So we the blessed few."

"So we the blessed few," the crowd cheered. Their voices rumbled up the hill and rolled through Elena with such force that she took a step back. Her bones buzzed with the energy of their chorus. Even the hesitant onlookers raised their voices in triumph. She laughed, stunned. She had always been wary of a mob's power. Of their mindless devotion. But if she knew one thing, it was that reverence was in their blood. The Ravani bowed to her because that was all they had ever known.

Samson helped her down from the podium. In the doorway, they turned and waved—the perfect picture of Ravence's royal couple.

"I thought you said you were going to sand down the rough edges," Samson said once they were inside.

"I just made them sharper." She smiled.

"Was 'the countrymen' your idea?" Leo asked, looking at Samson.

He shrugged. "It was merely a suggestion, but everything else was all Her Highness."

Her father turned to her, and Elena bristled, prepared for his usual retort of disapproval. But instead, he placed his hand on her head.

"Preaching unity was a smart move. You will make a mighty queen," he said.

Elena blinked. His hand was heavy, but she felt pride flutter in her stomach, making her feel light. Buoyant even. When her father left, she grinned from ear to ear. Not even the sight of Yassen Knight could dampen her joy.

"We must take our leave." Samson looked at Yassen. "We've got some hunting to do."

"Good hunting." She squeezed his arm. "And thank you."

Samson bowed, Yassen following suit. He had still not said a word to her, but she did not care. Days from now, she knew the whole nation would be abuzz from her speech. They would revere her, love her, swear their lives to her. Never mind the fact that she still could not hold fire. The people believed in her, and that was all that mattered.

13
YASSEN

Belief is stronger than a god, more fragile than a feather.
—FROM THE DIARIES OF PRIESTESS NOMU OF THE FIRE ORDER

Yassen stood at the corner of the meat bazaar as Samson's men got into their positions. They were in old Rani, near Radhia's Bazaar, a portion of the capital he had frequented when he was younger. His mother had grown up here. They had only moved to the desert outskirts after his father had insisted they stay closer to the wide expanse of the desert.

Yassen could not blame him. His father was as skittish as a hare, constantly searching for exits should the need arise. In old Rani, the buildings crowded each other; neighbors could hear conversations through the walls. Here, there was no escape.

Yassen stood at the end of the butcher's market. Holosigns in front of store windows advertised today's pickings—from hearty lamb to delicate hiran. Shoppers milled about, trying samples and lugging freshly cut venison. The smell of meat hung heavily in the desert heat. It made Yassen feel sick, but his stomach rumbled. He hadn't eaten dinner yesterday.

He pulled his scarf tighter around his lower jaw as a man wearing a gold cap walked past. He did not even give Yassen a second glance. Yassen shivered to think what would happen if the man had recognized him. The Ravani may have mixed feelings toward the royal family, but they all detested the Arohassin. One look, one word, and a mob would be on him.

Elena's speech still rang in Yassen's mind. He had never been the religious type. He hated fire, and he always thought the Phoenix was a cruel, vengeful god who had no time for orphans like him. But he could not deny the power of her words, for there was truth in them.

Ravence was a land of devotion. They worshipped the Phoenix even though it had been a long five hundred suns since they last saw the Prophet. The Arohassin had warned him about the power of faith. But it wasn't until now that Yassen had seen it and felt terrified by it.

His ear crackled.

"Scarlet sighted by Eagle One," a voice said.

Yassen pretended to be preoccupied by the pig's feet hanging within a storefront window. He glanced up at the building to his right. Behind a dark window on the top floor, Samson sat before a panel of holos, tracking all of their movements. *His* movements. This was the test to see if Yassen Knight had truly defected.

Once they smoked out Giorna, the Arohassin agent, he would cut off her escape. Samson's men would then swoop in, and he could finally, hopefully, earn some trust in this forsaken place.

Yassen licked the sweat from his lips. Though the summer was edging away, the heat had not let up. He pulled at his collar, blowing air through his cheeks.

This is just another sting operation. Just follow protocol.

His ear crackled again. "Scarlet heading south down butcher's alley. Eagle One and Two are in positions."

"Hawk in position," Yassen muttered.

"Scarlet in the alley. Do you have eyes?" Samson asked.

Yassen looked up the alley. He saw red everywhere. The canopies covering the stalls, the castaway feathers of a skinned yuani, the blood dripping down the hanging sacks of meat and pooling in the sand below. Then he spotted her.

The rust-colored hair. Giorna.

She was a small woman with thin eyebrows and closely set eyes that gave her an eternal look of disdain. Yet she moved with the fluidity and grace of any Arohassin agent. Yassen could recognize that walk anywhere. It belied suns of gruesome training and long nights of hunger, an obsession for pain and the sharpening of it to create a master weapon who could cut through a man or king without a sound.

"I have eyes," he whispered.

Giorna walked closer to him. She seemed unbothered by the heat and the bloodied pounds of meat. Yassen angled his body so she could not see his face as she drew near. Out of the corner of his eye, he saw her glance at the window beside him.

Quickly, he made to go inside, calling for the butcher's attention. The merchant turned and yelled at him to wait. Yassen spat back, rolling his r's to imitate the rounded southern Rani accent as Giorna passed him.

Her arm brushed against his shoulder.

But it was close enough.

Yassen felt the knife point graze across his spine. He whipped around just as she began to push it into his lower back. He rammed his hand down. The knife clattered to the ground, but she was already gone.

"Scarlet's on the run! I repeat, she's on the move!"

Yassen chased after her. She knocked over a bin of dried hawk bones to block his path, but he vaulted over it. She veered to the right, pushing past shouting merchants. They crowded in, jostling Yassen, but he shoved past them. One vendor pushed a cart piled high with sweet, summer apples imported from Cyleon; Yassen crashed right through it, sending the fruit flying.

"Mother's Gold!" The merchant cried as Yassen hopped over the spilled goods. "My apples!"

Yassen shouted apologies but did not slow. Giorna dashed to the left, and Yassen headed down an adjoining alley to intercept her. His feet pounded against the pavement. He knew this city like the back of his hand. She was heading to the main bazaar. A small woman like her could easily hide in a big crowd. If she did, he would have failed. Leo would have his head.

Yassen ran faster.

He spotted a fire escape on the side of a pub. He swung himself up, wincing as a jolt of pain stabbed up his right arm. The bouncer shouted after him as Yassen quickly hopped up the steps. He scrambled onto the roof and whirled around. For a moment, he thought he had lost

Giorna, and his throat closed in panic, but then she reappeared from underneath a red store covering.

"Hawk? Hawk, where is she?" his ear crackled.

But Yassen ignored Samson's questions. He leapt onto the roof of the next building as Giorna sprinted down the street. He ran alongside her, his shadow flitting over the red awnings of storefronts. Up ahead, Yassen spotted the colorful orange flags of the main bazaar.

It drew closer. Fifty paces, then forty, then thirty.

And then Yassen jumped.

For a moment he was suspended in the air, weightless, free.

But then gravity took over, and he was falling. He landed right on top of Giorna. She screamed and they hit the ground, the impact stunning Yassen. He blinked away spots. Giorna twisted, and her elbow dug into his stomach. Yassen gasped. He reached for her arm, rolling and using his weight to pull her under him and then to pin her down. She shouted, but he grabbed her other arm and twisted it above her head. She spat in his face.

"You fucking traitor," she seethed, her eyes wild. Sand clung to her auburn hair. "Fuck you."

"Quit. Squirming," he gasped. Shouts echoed up the street, and Yassen looked up to see Samson's men in their black and blue uniforms.

"They'll have your head for this," she gasped as he pushed her further into the dirt. "Taran will skin you alive."

"So will they," Yassen said as he looked at the Black Scales. They pointed their pulse guns at the two of them. Cautiously, one approached. He handed Yassen a pair of handcuffs, and Yassen clipped them on Giorna's thin wrists. He tightened them for extra measure.

They hauled her up. Giorna kicked and twisted, landing a blow on one soldier's face before two others grabbed and tied her legs. A crowd had begun to surround them. Yassen drew his scarf closer. Among the onlookers, he saw the sheen of gold caps.

"Go on, nothing to see here," a Black Scale ordered. "Go on! Back to your jobs!"

A hovercar with the silver feather of the capital police parted the sea of people. The guards pushed Giorna in, but not before she shot Yassen another burning look.

"You've got more balls than the king," Samson said in his ear. He gave a soft chuckle. "Squad Dragon and Bear found the two other Arohassin agents. You're cleared, Cass."

Yassen could only nod as he watched the hovercar drive away. With the star of the show gone, the crowd began to disperse. A couple of the gold caps stayed, eyeing Yassen, but they kept their distance. Yassen regarded them warily. They noticed his strange, pale eyes, the eyes of a Jantari, and kept throwing dirty glances his way. If only they knew he had his Ravani mother's smile.

A dull ring of pain spiraled up Yassen's right arm. He was still sore from his spar with the Yumi and the princess, and the fall had rattled his bones. He grimaced, wiping sweat from his forehead with the edge of his scarf before joining the waiting Black Scales.

"Good hunting, Hawk," one of the soldiers remarked. "I bet the old king will rest more easily tonight."

"Sure," Yassen replied dryly. "Now let's get out of here."

The gold caps began to leave, muttering amongst themselves. One spat in Yassen's direction. As he watched them go, he felt something drain away within him.

No matter how hard he tried, no matter how many Arohassin agents he delivered, Yassen knew he would never be accepted. His was the life between edges. Between Ravence and Jantar, right and wrong, holy and damned.

Yassen winced as he touched the knife wound on his back. It was merely a scratch, but it burned.

He only had to survive for one more month. One more month and all of this would be over. Elena would be crowned queen, and his job would be done. He would be free.

Doubt slithered through his chest, but Yassen pushed it away.

He had to believe it.

14
LEO

In the end, we must all burn.

—FROM THE DIARIES OF PRIESTESS NOMU OF THE FIRE ORDER

Leo sighed and pinched the bridge of his nose. The scrolls lay out in front of him, stoic and indecipherable. He had returned to the library in the night and pulled out more scrolls. He had run his eyes over these runes so many times that they burned in his dreams, in his moments of peace, in the empty shadows of his office. It was almost as if they were watching him and laughing at his attempts to understand them. Leo licked his lips. He had to find the Prophet before the Eternal Fire did.

The door to his chambers rumbled open, and Samson entered. He wore a light blue kurta with the top two buttons undone, revealing his smooth, muscled chest—a strong young man.

Like I used to be, Leo thought. His sudden bitterness shocked him, and he pushed it away. He usually wasn't one for such thoughts. *I'm just tired*, he reasoned.

Leo rolled up the scrolls as Samson bowed.

"I have some good news," the militant said, and a triumphant smile spread across his face, "We've apprehended three Arohassin agents on Yassen's list. They all check out. *Yassen* checks out. We can trust him."

"No one can be trusted," Leo said. He met Samson's eyes. "Surely you know that."

A muscle worked in Samson's jaw, but he held his tongue. *Smart boy.*

"Where are the agents now?" Leo asked.

"Held at a black site in the desert."

"Interrogate them," he said. "See if they know anything about the Arohassin's sabotage plans for the coronation."

He suspected it would of little use to torture the Arohassin agents. They wouldn't talk—even Muftasa's men could barely crack them. But he felt it was necessary to send Samson on a fool's errand. Perhaps it would humble the boy.

Samson bowed and turned to go.

"Wait," Leo called out, and Samson froze. Slowly, he faced the king again and met his eyes.

Too much water.

Leo stood and walked around the desk. He slid off the ring on his finger, a fine green amulet with flecks of gold, and handed it to Samson. It was shagun, a present the bride's father gave to the groom as per tradition. Samson slid the ring on his right hand, the signet flashing on his left. It fit perfectly.

"I've never properly welcomed you into the family," Leo said.

Samson rubbed the gem for good luck. "Thank you... Father."

"You'll need to change your name when Elena makes you her king."

"What's wrong with Samson?"

"It's not Ravani." Leo looked at his hand, at the signet ring that showed his family's crest. "The people will never accept a Sesharian as their ruler, no matter how many refugees we accept. But if you take a Ravani name, they'll shower you with blessings."

"It's better to be hated for what you are, than to be loved for what you're not," Samson said. He gave a grim smile and bowed his head. "Your Majesty."

He strode out of the room, the flames hissing behind him. Leo scoffed and shook his head, but an uneasy sensation slithered in his stomach. He made a note to send the next batch of detained agents to Samson as well. He would work the pride out of the boy.

His holopod beeped, and Leo enlarged the holo. Muftasa appeared before him.

"Starlight is in," she said. Her face betrayed no emotion. "We have her down in the tunnels. She has strange markings, but we haven't tried to burn her yet. Should I go and—"

"No," Leo said. His voice thundered in his ears. "I will. If she is the Prophet, I want to be there."

If she was the Prophet, Leo doubted that his men would have the courage to kill her. Their belief would hold them back. He, on the other hand, would not balk.

Leo gulped, his throat suddenly tight.

Something flickered in Muftasa's eyes, but she nodded. "We'll be waiting."

Leo closed the holo. Through the glass ceiling, he could see dark clouds lumbering across the heavens. The muted light painted the room with grey shadows, but it also brought a stillness. The charged quiet before a storm. He closed his eyes to relish it. To drink in the calm and bottle it up—for he knew that after today, there would be no peace for him.

Alonjo and the guards led Leo through the tunnels beneath Palace Hill. Floating orbs lit the bare walls. Dampness clung in the air, and Leo shivered.

They arrived before a metal door that Marcus rapped on twice. It slid open, revealing Muftasa, who looked even smaller in the cramped darkness.

"She's here," she said.

"Take me to her," Leo replied.

They walked down another hallway and came to a door guarded by two RI agents. They nodded at Muftasa. One pressed his hand on a screen, and the door slid open. They entered a small, concrete room. A panel of dials sat underneath a long screen that stretched across the far wall. A door stood in the corner, leading to a smaller room where a little girl sat on a bench.

The fluorescent lights made her hair shine, as if it captured the stars themselves. She must have heard the door, for she spun around and looked through the glass. It was a one-way mirror, but her eyes bore through Leo all the same.

Holy Bird Above, this will be difficult.

Leo stood in front of the panels as Marcus stationed guards along the tunnel and closed the door. Now, it was only the four of them: him, Alonjo, Muftasa, and the girl.

The girl drew her knees in and rested her chin between them. Her eyes held a strange awareness—a clarity Leo had never seen before. She did not seem to be perturbed in any way; she merely watched as they studied her.

Finally, Leo spoke.

"Let me in," he said in a voice too thin. His throat felt dry. "Let me talk to her."

Without a word, Muftasa turned a dial on the panel, and the door separating the two rooms slid open. Alonjo gave him a single match.

"So we the blessed few," he whispered.

Leo grasped the splinter, but he could not muster himself to repeat the phrase. He walked into the other room before he could change his mind. As if sensing his fear, Muftasa shut the door behind him.

The cell felt even smaller now that he was standing in it. On the right wall, a large black hole covered with metal grating stared at him. Leo tried not to think of what lay behind it.

The girl looked up. She was frail with a head too big for her shoulders. She had marks on her hands, light red burn marks that spiraled up her arm like braided rope.

Carefully, Leo dusted the bench and sat on the other end.

"Hello," he said.

The girl blinked.

"My name is Leo," he said and then hesitated. "I'm the king."

The girl said nothing.

Leo felt sweat pool underneath his armpits. On the other side of the screen, Alonjo and Muftasa watched him, and though he could not see their faces, Leo could feel the weight of their judgment. It wrapped around his shoulders like a slow, coiling snake. But they were not the ones who held the match. He had to do it. He must. If the girl before him was the Prophet, it was his duty as king to face her.

"I have something for you," he said and revealed the match.

The girl's eyes grew wider, as if he held a prized jewel between his fingers. He saw the curiosity in her gaze, and a deep, creeping madness.

He held the match between them. "Do you know what this can create?"

"Fire," she said, her eyes shining. "Life."

Life. What an odd choice. For Leo, fire only meant destruction. Chaos.

"And what do you do with fire?" he asked.

The girl blinked. Her eyebrows crossed, and she looked at him as if he were wrong in the head.

"It protects me," she said. Her voice was high and sharp, beautiful even. She reached for the match, but Leo pulled back.

"Can you control the flames?" he asked, but the girl shook her head. She reached for him again, but Leo gently pushed her hand away. "Do the flames hurt you?"

The girl sat back. She looked down at her arms, at the marks that lightened her brown skin. "You're the king," she said. "You should know."

Leo got up. The girl followed him with her eyes. At the door, Leo paused. He looked back at her.

Twelve suns. She had a lifetime before her, a lifetime to grow, travel, fall in love. But if she was the Prophet, it would only be a lifetime of ash. And if she wasn't, well, then whoever the Prophet was, she would burn them all.

Leo knocked on the door, and it slid open. At the last second, he threw in the match.

The door closed with a whisper. Through the screen, he watched the girl scramble for the match. Muftasa wore a pinched expression while Alonjo stood frozen in his spot. Leo glanced at the metal grate and then the girl. With a wave of her arm, she struck the match against the stone bench. It flared to life.

"Do it," he said.

With a heavy hand, Muftasa pressed the panel.

The metal grate hummed.

The girl turned just as the hum morphed to a screech and a torch of fire flared out. It instantly leapt on her body, ate up the shadows, sucked in the air.

The girl screamed.

Beside him, he heard Alonjo gasp and Muftasa exhale a prayer. They moved back.

But Leo did not turn away. He let the sight before him sear into his mind: the girl's flailing limbs, the darkness of her body against the bright, hungry flames.

This was his price to pay. This was his sin to bear.

After the girl was nothing but a blackened heap of bones and flesh, Leo turned to Muftasa.

"Continue the search in the capital," he said, his voice flat and toneless. "We still have yet to find our Prophet."

15
ELENA

At 0600 hours, the Hawk Patrol encountered a landmine hidden along the southwestern region of the wall. All eight members were killed. This has put the total monthly death toll at eighty-five Ravani soldiers. We lose three men for every Jantari soldier. Even our Sesharian recruits are beginning to balk.
Ravence must make a move, and soon.

—A REPORT FROM COLONEL AKBAR, STATIONED AT YODDHA BASE

Elena fanned herself with the edge of her dupatta, which already was beginning to wilt in the unforgiving desert heat. They stood on an embankment overlooking a shallow valley along the southern border. At its edge, Samson's army prepared for the demonstration, their pulse guns glinting in the harsh sun.

Samson stood beside her, dressed in the military navy of a general of his Black Scale fighters. He had lined his eyes with kohl, a custom among the Ravani, and one that brought out the strange blue of his eyes. He saw her staring and tugged at his collar.

"Trust me, I'm sweating beneath this," he said.

"Then imagine the state of your poor men," she said.

"They've handled worse."

"Worse than the Ravani desert?"

Samson smiled slyly, his voice a whisper. "The desert can undo any man."

Elena turned away, hating the sudden flush that rose on her cheeks.

Across the dunes, a wall of red sandstone jutted against the sky, separating the Kingdoms of Ravence and Jantar. Ravani soldiers patrolled the border. On the other side, the Jantari watched, waiting. Elena wondered if Farin was among them. Was he sitting in his metal castle, watching the livestream of the hovercams and journalists below, or was he there among his soldiers, stewing with rage? Both images pleased her. The half-metal king would not underestimate Ravence now. Not after this.

The canopy fluttered above them. Ferma brought up a pitcher of chilled water, Yassen a platter of dates. Elena smiled to see him reduced to a servant.

"Any word from Marcus or Alonjo?" she asked.

"The king should be wrapping his meeting soon," the Yumi answered.

Elena glanced behind her at the Yoddha Base. It was a large, military compound with gated checkpoints and holosensors. Heavy guns sat on top of towers, while Ravani soldiers worked tirelessly under the desert sun. Her father was in there, wrapping up some meeting about heavens knew what. It annoyed Elena that he still held meetings without her. She was only a month away from taking the throne. Surely the old king should include her in all pressing matters.

Suddenly, the sound of a horn ripped through the air. Elena straightened as flag bearers exited the military compound and announced the arrival of the king. Leo strode out, the edge of his red sherwani flapping in the breeze. A golden silk scarf draped across his right shoulder. He had chosen not to wear his military uniform. It was a slight, but one Elena understood. The king, though the protector of the land, was above all else. He did not need to don his brass and medals to show the world of his mettle.

Elena, Samson, and their guards bowed as the king strode up.

"Shall we begin?" he said.

The soldiers in the valley below came to a standstill. They must have seen the flagbearers, and now they stood erect, waiting for a signal.

Samson withdrew the slingsword strapped around his waist. The blue and silver blade flashed as he raised it to the air.

"The king is the protector of the flame, and I its servant," he intoned. "Together, we shall give our blood to this land. I swear it, or burn my name in the sand."

He brought his sword down, and the first Black Sands Day began.

First came the infantry. Rows and rows of Black Scale soldiers in their black uniforms marched through the valley, accompanied by the blare of horns. They moved in unison, their legs and arms weaving in and out like a well-oiled machine. The soldiers held their pulse guns to their chest, their slingswords buckled around their waists. Behind them came the tanks that left no tracks in the sand. Fighter jets shaped like the heads of tridents zipped through the air. They flew low, and as they neared the valley, they rolled off, spreading across the sky like the wings of a bird.

As the infantry neared the embankment where the royals stood, the soldiers swiveled their heads together. Commanding officers barked out orders, and five thousand men turned and snapped their heels to attention. They raised their hands in salute.

"All hail King Leo!"

"All hail the heir!"

"All hail her betrothed!"

Elena returned the gesture. Her eyes swept their faces, each as resolute as the last. These were true fighters, men and women of unbendable steel and remarkable courage. She saw it in the jut of their chins, in the furrow of their brows. As they opened their mouths for the last hail, Elena heard in their voices—a roar of an unwavering people.

"All hail the Kingdom of Ravence!"

The tanks swiveled and fired in the direction of the wall, one by one. The shots rang through the valley. And the holocams flashed, capturing it all. Elena smiled. *Let Farin see that.*

The soldiers turned and snapped their heels. The commanding officers gave the order, and five thousand of Samson's soldiers—her soldiers—resumed their march. The valley shook underneath their feet.

Afterward, when the procession had passed and the fighter jets roared off to dock at the southern bases, Samson touched her elbow.

"Come, let's meet the men," he said.

She turned to her father, who shook his head.

"I have matters to attend to. You two go," the king said. He stood with his back to the sun, his jade earring glittering. There was a strange, dark look in his eyes. Before she could retort, he turned on his heel and swept back into the base.

Elena fought back a curse. Slowly, she unclenched her fists, smoothed the long skirts of her lehenga, and turned back to Samson.

"Lead the way," she said.

She followed her fiancé down the embankment, Ferma and Yassen trailing behind. They reached a tent of the commanding officers. When they saw them approach, the Black Scales snapped to attention, their hands crossing their chests in salute.

"Hail the sun and her flaming sword!" they cried.

"At ease," Samson said, and they immediately relaxed.

As he introduced each officer to her, Elena could not help but notice how the soldiers leaned toward Samson. How they hung on every word he spoke. His very presence engulfed them. She saw their undying devotion, the forged steel of brotherhood, and she understood a very plain truth. While King Leo had built his reign on fear, Samson had built his power through hard-won victories and shared suffering. He knew his men, and they in turn, loved him for it.

She smiled at the last officer and then turned to Samson.

"Excuse me, I just need a moment," she said.

Concern knitted his brows, but Elena squeezed his elbow and offered another smile. She ducked out of the tent where Ferma and Yassen stood waiting. The day had grown hotter, and the sand baked beneath her feet.

"Are you alright?" Ferma asked.

"Could you fetch me some water?" She fanned her face with her hand. "It's too hot."

The Yumi nodded and strode in the direction of the refreshments tent, leaving her alone with Yassen. A sudden, awkward silence loomed between them.

Elena cleared her throat. "Listen, about the game—"

"It's alright. I suppose I deserved it," he said.

She glanced back inside the tent and hesitated. "Samson," she began. "How well do you know him?"

He looked at her. "Why? Are you getting cold feet?"

She scowled. "I don't—"

"You don't often find men like him," he said and gave a mirthless grin.

She clenched her jaw. *How dare he interrupt me twice?*

Yassen looked past her and into the tent. "You've had other suitors, but you chose him. Why?"

"The others were never good enough," she responded flatly.

And it was true. She thought of the allergy-afflicted prince from Cyleon and the overbearing bachelor king of Mandur. They and others had come calling for her hand. She had seen the privilege within them, the diffident nonchalance of men who believed everything and everyone served him. They had all demanded that she would become queen of their kingdom, Ravence a tributary territory. They had all left with bruised egos.

She was Elena Aadya Ravence above all else. No man, she thought as she looked at Samson surrounded by his officers, could ever take her birthright away from her.

Elena groaned as she sat on the bench before her great windows. After the Black Sands demonstration, she had gone from meeting to meeting, discussing preparations for the coronation, the ball, and the upcoming Fire Festival. Somehow, Ferma had managed to slip in an evening training session. The Spear refused to let her use a slingsword, blindfolding her. Elena had to use her senses to predict the movement of the sand and her opponent. She had only lasted three minutes.

Sighing, Elena shook sand from her hair. Night was falling, and the red sky slowly bled into deeper purple hues. It reminded her of plums, her mother's favorite, the sweet, rare fruit harvested only during the summer. Elena glanced at the bowl of fruits in her foyer, but it held only mangos and unshaved lychee. A pang of nostalgia went through her.

She went to her closet, past the racks of silk saris and chiffon lehengas, heading to the dark back corner. Bending, Elena withdrew a brown cloak from the lower shelf. Dust took to the air, and she coughed. The cloak was rough to the touch and held no embellishments, no regal bearings. It would do.

Elena donned the cloak. She grabbed a scarf as well and wrapped it around her neck. Back in her bedroom, she squatted beside the fireplace. A few flames flickered, as if dreaming. She took a glass orb and scooped out a singular flame. It hissed, reeling. Elena almost dropped the orb, but the flame curled back into itself and held. She let out a low breath.

The sky was now pitch black as she descended into her garden. The fountain gurgled softly. Elena turned the stone bird perched on its lip, and then the base of the fountain shifted back, revealing marble steps. Floating orbs lit up as she ventured into the tunnels. Instead of veering off to the right for the library, Elena turned left toward the city. A chill crept beneath the desert, and she pulled her cloak tighter. The scroll rustled within her sleeve.

As she neared the city, the tunnel sloped upward. A metal grate, as tall as a man, covered the exit. Elena peeked out. The alley was dark, empty. Drawing a deep breath, she stepped back and whispered, the sensors along the grate detecting her voice.

"As above, so below."

The metal grate rumbled and then parted a mere two feet. Elena scooted through, and then it rolled back into place. She walked quickly, careful not to draw attention to herself nor the metal grate from which she emerged. The flame warmed her abdomen. She entered the Thar district, a large, winding network of alleys, bars, and small firestone squares. Floating orbs and neon signs lit the wide street as drunken couples stumbled out of pubs. On the corner, she spotted a beggar sitting beneath a gulmohar tree. Even in the night, its scarlet flowers burned against the dark sky, like little tendrils of flame.

Elena slowed as she approached the beggar. A thin wisp of smoke curled from his blue lips. He looked up at her with dazed, drugged eyes.

"You," he said, and then his lips curled back into a snarl. "What are you doing here?"

Elena stopped. Across the street, city dwellers mingled in and out of a pub, oblivious to the commotion.

"What are you talking about?"

"You don't belong here, Sesharian," the beggar cried. He raised a shaky finger. "You and your filthy kind should rot on your island."

She wanted to retort that she wasn't a Sesharian, that she was Ravani, just like him, but something made her hold her tongue. She thought of Samson. How his men had crowded around him. The devotion in their eyes. Though wary of his motives, Elena recognized Samson's power and his ability to unite. Sesharian, Jantari, Cyleoni—no matter where they came from, the soldiers respected him. They swore their lives to him, burned their names in the sand for his cause.

She looked at the man. "Careful," she said, "I heard there's no place for intolerance in the new regime."

The beggar laughed. "The heir is a whore for that vile Sesharian. I heard his men take turns with her."

Her face colored. Underneath her cloak, the fire hissed. Elena took a step back. *He's drugged. He has no senses.*

Yet a part of her wanted to punch the man, to drag him through the sands. Elena glanced around and saw that onlookers from the pub had gathered. There was a heated look in their eyes, and she heard the familiar whisper of danger even before they began to approach.

Elena pushed past the beggar, fists clenched.

"That's right! You go run!" he called after her.

She began to pick up her pace as she felt the onlookers' eyes on her back. She turned the corner but did not slow until she reached the quiet suburbs of Rani. Here, laborers and immigrants bundled into their homes. Only a few windows were lit, and Elena saw the shadows of tired men and women. She walked on, heading for the desert. There was no hard line from the suburbs to the rolling dunes beyond. It was a subtle difference, a slight shift of sand along the western edge.

Eventually, the dunes curved up before her. The twin moons sloped into perfect, mirrored crescents. Nothing stirred nor rustled in the night. The stillness felt like a blanket, its silence a cool relief. Elena breathed in the sharp, cold air, her stomach slowly unknotting. To the unexperienced eye, the desert looked endless. Overwhelming. But Elena knew that the curve of this dune differed from the one before it. She understood how the desert moved in the wind, how it shifted to form new masses. This was her home. And she knew its secrets.

Elena hopped down a rocky face into the bowl of a dune. She came before a stone overhanging. Three lines were chiseled into the rock. She had marked this place long ago when she had trained with Mahira's sand raiders. The cave was small but deep. Perfect to stash a cruiser.

Elena ducked inside as she withdrew the flame. Its light beat back the shadows to reveal a form covered by a black tarp. Elena threw it back to reveal a smooth, silver cruiser. She rested her hand on its glass control panel, and it flickered to life.

She placed the orb inside the back compartment and got on. It had been a while since she had been on a cruiser, but as Elena gripped the worn, leather handles, it all came back to her. Months in the desert flying over dunes, zipping through valleys, barreling through sand hovels. The wild, precarious nature of it. The thrill of it. The freedom.

Elena pressed the pedal, and the cruiser jolted forward. She shot up the lip of the dune, and then she was off.

Wind whipped back her scarf and hood as she zoomed through the desert. Sand peppered her face. The dunes rose and melted past her as she followed their curves and valleys. The sky opened up for her. The stars spilled out, and Elena felt a contagious sense of euphoria bubble up in her throat.

Here, there were no guards, no generals, no king who could hold her back. Here, it was only her. Her and the wide, unspooling desert.

After some time, when she was sure she had not been followed, Elena slipped into a valley and killed the engine. She estimated she had ventured several miles into the desert. The dunes towered above her, blocking out the twin moons, but not the stars. They scattered above her and shone with such brilliance that she almost forgot about fire. Its orange, shifting light paled in comparison to the radiance of the heavens.

Perhaps this was what Alabore Ravence had felt when he first came to the desert, when he saw the stars over the dunes. He must have realized that the night held the same power as the day. And so he had sought the help of the twin moons to build his kingdom—his dream of peace.

Elena opened the back compartment and looked down at the orb, at its single, flickering flame. In the end, she supposed, Alabore had realized what all men came to know.

The stars would come and go.

Fire was eternal.

Elena grabbed the orb as well as the pulse gun stashed beneath. She stepped lightly and quickly so that her feet only left shallow depressions in the sand. The scroll bounced within her cloak, brushing against her arm.

As she neared the top of the dune, Elena froze. There, silhouetted in the pale moonlight, was a man. She could make out the light hair, the pale skin of a familiar ghost-like figure. Yassen sat on the crest with his back to her. He looked perfectly relaxed, as if he had been lounging in the dunes, in this desert, for countless suns.

"What are you doing here?" she called out. Her heart thundered in her ears as she felt for the pulse gun beneath her cloak. They were alone in the deep desert. She had no guards, no Spear. Here, Yassen could kill her. The Palace would not be able to find her body for days.

"Enjoying the quiet night," he said without turning. He ran his fingers through the sand. There was something eerie about him, and a voice in her head whispered to get out, to turn back, but Elena stood her ground.

"I mean, how did you find this place?"

"I didn't," he said.

"No one knows about this spot."

Yassen turned. His eyes almost looked white, translucent. The voice rose again, but she fought back the urge to flee. This was her desert. She would not abandon it.

"I know many things about this place," he said. He stood and wiped sand off his pants. The metal bird on his uniform glinted in the moonlight. A breeze sighed over the dunes, and the desert rustled. Sand brushed against her exposed face.

She gripped the handle of her pulse gun as Yassen approached her. He stopped just a few feet shy. The twin moons peeked over the top of his head like whispering spirits. In their light, he looked younger—his face unlined and his mouth soft. It was as if the desert wind had lifted the weight that bowed his shoulders.

"People only roam the desert when they're running or searching for something," he said and looked at the orb. "What's all this?"

She held it away from him. For some reason, she felt that he would try to extinguish the flame.

"I can handle myself out in the desert," she said.

"But why bring a flame?"

"None of your business," she spat.

Yassen walked closer, and she took a step back. She began to pull out the gun but stopped when he held out his hands in front of her, his fingers splayed out, empty.

"I didn't come to hurt you," he said. "To be honest, I snuck out of the Palace myself. It was too... suffocating. So I came out here. And then I heard your cruiser and saw you in the valley."

"How did you get all the way out here?" she asked, eyeing him. She spotted no pulse gun, not even a slingsword on him.

"I nicked a floating blader from a kid, but it died a few miles in. So I walked."

"Walked?" She stared at him. "That must have taken you hours."

Yassen shrugged. "I needed to clear my mind."

The pulse gun felt smooth beneath her fingertips. She could blow his head off right now. She could finally enact the vengeance her father kept delaying. Yassen still had his hands out before him. If he countered, she could react.

But Elena paused. She couldn't kill him—not like this. If Yassen Knight died, she wanted him to burn, for all to see.

"Looks like you needed some space, too," he said. He lowered his hands and gestured out toward the desert. "All the space you need to practice, with no one to judge your shortcomings. The only audience, the stars. A man could disappear out here, and no one would know it." His voice sounded wistful.

Elena regarded him suspiciously. "Don't get any ideas of running away. Mahira's raiders will track you down. *I'll* track you down."

"I know. That pulse gun you're holding could blast a nasty hole." A corner of his lip curled up. "But what's the point of killing a man like me without an audience?"

He had sensed her hesitation. Elena cursed inwardly and withdrew her firearm. It hummed to life, the chamber glowing an eerie blue as she cocked it in his direction.

"A walk in the desert doesn't absolve you of your sins," she said. "Nothing can erase what you've done."

"Nothing but fire," he said and fixed her with his pale eyes. "But that's what you came out here for, right? You want to learn Agneepath."

She inhaled sharply. Agneepath was an ancient word, reserved for chants and prayers. It meant the path of fire; it was the word the High Priestess uttered before her father sat on the dais. It was the word *she* would utter when she became queen—for the path of Ravence was welded by fire. The monarch must learn to walk amongst the flames, to carry out the destiny Alabore Ravence had spun for them. But if Yassen knew she had come here to practice, he must know she couldn't control fire.

"Who told you?" she asked, aiming her weapon at his chest.

"The servants whisper," he said, "and I listen. I heard you almost burned the Palace down the last time you tried. That's why you've come all the way out here."

Elena bit her lip. Did the whole Palace know of her shortcomings?

He reached out and touched the barrel of her pulse gun, his eyes never leaving her. "You want me to burn. So be it. But I have a right to Ravence as you do. This isn't just your home. It's mine too."

"You lying bastard," she spat. She shoved his hand away and raised the gun. Yassen stepped back. "You've helped the very people trying to destroy this kingdom. You *betrayed* us."

"No," Yassen said, and his voice was thin, frail, holding none of his usual measured calmness. It made her hesitate. "That wasn't me. That was *them*," he said, and the weakness in his voice was replaced with disgust. "The Arohassin tricked us, brainwashed us. We were only kids. I didn't know any better. And now here I am, working with you—working *for* you—to amend what I have broken."

He spoke with a zeal that surprised Elena. She had never seen him so animated, so honest. She blinked, as if to make sure it was truly Yassen Knight standing before her.

He had brought her father the list of Arohassin agents. He served them up like pigs for slaughter. And he had not balked when the red-head woman had called him a traitor. Samson had told her so.

A breeze swept up the sand as Yassen watched her. Despite the gun, he showed no fear. And a fearless man was a dangerous man. Her father had taught her that. Elena steeled herself. Try as she might, she could not bring herself to trust Yassen. Not yet.

The sand drifted lazily across their feet, and Yassen cocked his head, as if listening to it.

"There's going to be a storm," he said.

She could sense the dunes shifting beneath her feet as the desert began to moan. It started as a murmur, an elusive sound, but as the wind picked up, it grew louder. The flame danced in its glass enclosure. Elena cursed and lowered her gun as she hugged the orb to her chest to shield it.

"We'd better find cover," she said.

The dunes shuddered as they made their way down. She knew how to move without sinking, how to read the lines of the dunes and the stars to guide her back to the sparkling city. To her surprise, Yassen remained only a few steps behind. He too moved lightly across the sand, though he only had half of the grace. She could tell he had been raised in the desert, yet had forgotten some of its ways.

They reached the cruiser as the sky clouded over and the heavens disappeared. Elena shoved the orb into the back compartment.

"Get on!" she shouted. She hopped onto the cruiser, and Yassen followed suit.

She slammed on the pedal, and they shot forward. Sand slashed their faces and clothes. The wind roared. A large, dark mass surrounded them as Elena revved the engine. She knew they couldn't outrun the storm. The city was too far.

She swerved, and they launched up a dune. The cruiser jumped the lip, skidding before Elena corrected it and they hurtled past rocks shaped like kneeling men. Elena squinted, spitting out sand. She couldn't see any valleys or land markings, but she had grown up in this desert. It claimed her as much as she claimed it.

"Do you know where you're going?" Yassen shouted into the wind.

She didn't respond. She trusted the sensation in her gut, the well of trust she gave to the desert. Because belief had power. And like a beacon calling a faraway traveler home, the desert called to her, offering her its safety.

The overhang came out suddenly on their left. She nearly passed it but then yanked the controls, cutting across the rocks and launching into the cave. A thick layer of sand shifted around the floor, but otherwise, the hovel was still. Elena gulped in air. The engine's hum filled the space; Yassen reached around and turned it off so that the only sound came from the sandstorm outside.

She dug out a canteen of water stowed in the cruiser's back compartment. Yassen turned, studying the cave as she splashed her face. In its glass enclosure, the flame still lived, though it was smaller now.

"What is this place?"

Elena sighed as she sank to the floor. She cradled the orb, letting the warmth of the small fire seep into her chest. A drop of water curved down her chin, hissing as it fell into the flame.

"I stayed here during my Registaan," she said. After two months into her initiation, she had discovered this spot after chasing a desert hare. The small animal had hidden here, but when she cornered it into the back of the cave, it jumped out, rushing past her. She had been too tired to pursue it. As Elena stared around their small shelter, she knew instinct and memory had pulled her here. Silently, she whispered a thanks to the desert.

Yassen sank down across from her. His long legs splayed awkwardly in the small space.

"You knew the way despite the storm," he said, his voice tinged with awe as he gazed around the cave.

"Your desert walk," she said, "it's proficient but sloppy. You've been gone from Ravence for too long."

Yassen looked down at his hands. His voice was quiet. "I'm here now. Aren't I?"

And he hadn't killed her. Perhaps he truly had defected, but Elena couldn't let go of her suspicion.

"These storms don't last long," she said.

"Ferma will be outraged."

She shot him a look. "We'll be back before morning."

Sand fell as Yassen ran his hand through his hair. He leaned back and closed his eyes. Elena placed her chin on her knees and listened to the storm outside. After a while, she heard him snoring softly.

She studied him. It was hard to imagine he was capable of assassinating kings and queens. Before her, she saw only a man too tired to be afraid of her.

As Yassen slept, Elena withdrew the scroll, unraveling it carefully. The fire flickered beside her. She used its light to trace the movements of the dance.

The forms of the woman looked even starker, her expressions fiercer. The text was written in Herra, the same ancient language the priests spoke in, but underneath each phrase, her mother had translated it into Vesseri.

Elena whispered the words underneath her breath. "Agneepath netrun. Fijjin a noor."

The path of fire is dangerous. Tread it with care.

Care. Did it mean *caution* or *love*—like how Aahnah had taught her how to navigate the library and keep it a secret between them?

Elena thumbed the corner where her mother had drawn the jasmine. It was her mother's favorite flower, and she had grown large bushes of it in her garden. She remembered watching Aahnah prune the delicate stems, her fingers lifting the leaves, her voice soft and secretive as she spoke to the flowers as if they were listening.

Elena pressed her hand against the warm glass. She needed to hold the flame with care, tenderness—that she knew, but how?

Slowly, she rose, shaking off sand. Yassen lay as still as before. Elena set the orb before her and began to imitate the dancer.

It felt like her excursions into the city, except this time, there was no platform, no crowd, no hot tea to follow her performance. Elena folded her hands behind her, as drawn in the second form. The flame flickered. She tried to balance on her right foot, but she teetered. She flung out her arms to steady herself, and her left foot hit the cruiser. She nearly yelped.

Elena hopped on one leg and threw a sour glance at Yassen. His chest rose and fell in a steady wave. She let out a breath and resumed the first position.

It resembled the Warrior pose of the sun meditations—one that Ferma had drilled into her. This was a dance that required poise, rigidity, yet also softness. Dance, like many things, was an act of balance. It required her to regulate her breathing, to give and take from the air around her. To empty her mind and heart and fill it with the brilliance of song. Except there were no drums to accompany her—there was only the singing wind.

Elena rose from the Warrior and tried to balance on her right foot again. This time, she held steady as she folded her hands behind her back like the wings of a bird. She tried to intensify the strength of her pose, the fluidity of her movements. Sweat beaded down her brow, mixing with sand and dirt.

As she unfolded her arms and dipped her head, the fire bowed. Elena gasped. The flame rose and licked the side of the glass bowl. She watched, transfixed, as it grew taller.

"You keep that up, and you'll set this place on fire."

Elena spun around, and the flame sputtered and died in a pile of ash.

Yassen lay as before, but his eyes were open. He held Elena in his gaze. For a moment, she felt like she couldn't move, that ice had lodged into the space between her bones as she stared into his strange, pale eyes.

But then sand brushed her foot, and she hopped back.

"So that's how the Ravani control fire," he said.

Elena did not reply as she rolled up the scroll and slid it back in her cloak. Yassen overturned the orb, ash spilling onto the cave floor.

"I've never heard of dancing to control flames, though," he continued.

"Only those with divine rule can do it," she retorted hastily.

"So only your family and not us lowly commoners?" He looked up at her with his colorless eyes. "Don't you think that's a bit unfair?"

"It's the way the world works." She grabbed the orb and stowed it within the cruiser's compartment. Outside, the storm still hid the twin moons and the star-filled sky.

"But the Prophet can be anyone," he said. "He or she could be a commoner and learn to wield fire."

She scoffed. "As if you believe in the Prophet."

Yassen smiled faintly and looked down at his hands. Elena saw the mark on his wrist. The blackened skin.

"Have you been burned?" she whispered. When he didn't respond, Elena crouched before him and lightly tapped his arm. "I saw the mark."

"It's nothing," he said.

"Sounds like you're lying," she said and grabbed his wrist. He resisted, but when she shot him a look, he allowed her to roll up his sleeve. She gave a tiny gasp.

His arm was covered with burn marks—deep red welts ready to burst. In the spaces between the marks, his skin was shriveled and brown.

"What happened?"

He met her eyes with a cold, hard look. "The Arohassin."

She dropped his arm, empty of words. She had heard of the Arohassin's cruelty. They recruited young orphans and drilled them with such intensity it made the Yumi's training pale. But she had not expected this.

Yassen rolled his sleeve back down, not meeting her gaze. It occurred to her then how little she knew about him. She had been so blinded by hate that she had failed to consider what the Arohassin meant to him. Yassen Knight was too smart to be a blind follower. Their ruthlessness may have hardened him, but it could have also nurtured a deep resentment—a resentment he now turned against them.

"No wonder you don't like fire," she said softly. Though the wind still roared, she sensed it beginning to tire. The storm would end soon.

"I don't know why I'm telling you this," she began. "But I hate fire too. I hate the burn. It feels so... wrong. I don't understand how my father does it. Only that I need to learn his secret before my coronation."

Yassen said nothing for a long moment. He merely looked down at his hands, at the mark on his wrist.

"The path of fire burns everyone in the end," he said finally.

Elena gave a pained smile because she knew it was true.

They passed the time in wordless silence until the wind fell and the sky cleared. Through the mouth of the cave, they saw the faint colors of dawn splinter along the horizon. Elena started up the cruiser as Yassen dusted sand from his pants.

"We will not speak of this," she said. "Any of it."

He nodded and got on behind her. They zipped through the desert that lay open for them with new, unbaptized curves. It was so peaceful, so still, as if there had never been a storm.

Elena breathed in the early morning air and felt Yassen inhale with her. When they reached the city outskirts, Elena stashed the cruiser in a rundown hut that had long been abandoned by its owners. She had no fear of anyone stealing it; any thief would need her fingerprints to start the vehicle.

The sun peeked over the dunes and slowly chased away the night's long shadows. She saw Yassen stretch like a cat in the sun, the light picking out the gold in his hair. When he noticed her looking, he stopped. Something strange shone in his eyes, but she couldn't tell what from this distance.

"I'll go on alone from here," she said.

"You should be careful with fire," he said. "It hurts more than just you."

"Trust me, I know."

She left him standing there as sunlight spilled into the narrow alleyway and the city began to wake. She could hear the shouts of mothers, the creaky wheels of merchant carts, and the thrum of the hovertrain as it carried day laborers from the outskirts to the city center.

It was true. He didn't need to tell her the consequences of Agneepath.

She rubbed the sore skin of her fingers. Her entire family was plagued by the honor of carrying fire.

16
LEO

Beware of the Desert Spider.
For she is fearless, and therefore, powerful.

—A RAVANI PROVERB

Leo rubbed his temples. He could feel the beginning of a migraine crawl up his neck and the back of his head. A cup of soothsayer tea would help, but he had no time. He had yet another war meeting with his generals, and the plans for the ball still needed to be addressed, on top of overseeing the ongoing operations to bring in the other Arohassin—

"Your Majesty," Samson said, interrupting Leo from his thoughts.

Leo closed his eyes for a moment longer. He took a deep breath and then regarded his future son-in-law with hooded eyes.

"Regarding the ball invitations—I think it might help if we invite King Farin," Samson said.

Leo tried his best to keep the venom out of his voice. "The King of Jantar? Really?"

They were seated in a hoverpod heading north for Desert Spider, a black site that lay deep within the dunes. It was an unmarked location, invisible on all military maps. It was where they sent high-level prisoners or any enemies of state. Ravani Intelligence oversaw its daily operations. Muftasa reported occasionally about the site's inner workings, but Leo was careful not to ask too many questions. As far as he was concerned, the base did not exist. Except for today.

Saayna was imprisoned at Desert Spider, but he knew he could not keep the High Priestess there for long. Elena was due for an Ashanta ceremony in a matter of weeks, and the coronation would follow. They would need Saayna for both. But until then, Leo intended to make the High Priestess sweat. She had sworn herself to Ravence, yet her loyalty lay with the Fire Order. She would protect the Prophet, at any cost. Leo would rather try breaking her than rummaging through scrolls for his answers.

The girl with hair of starlight had not been the Prophet. Neither were the other girls they had rounded up in the capital. Leo had taken the child's ashes and thrown them off Palace Hill, watching the grey flakes scatter in the wind. How many more women would he have to burn before he found the one who would turn the flames on him?

"I know, but hear me out," Samson said, splaying out his hands. "The Jantari regard me as their hero. Their king practically regards me as a son. If we ever want peace for Ravence, we need to make amends with Jantar."

"King Farin and I cannot sit in one room for long," Leo said. He did not mention how much he hated that vile man's metal guts. "Besides, he's a horrible dancer."

Samson grinned. "Jantari metalmen usually are. You just have to grease their joints a bit. It's nothing Elena and I can't handle."

Leo pursed his lips. He wondered how well his daughter and Samson were getting along. Alonjo had informed him they often went for long walks in the courtyard. Elena could charm anyone. That was her gift. But did she know of the gravity of marriage? His had not been long, but still, a healthy royal couple meant a strong kingdom, a continued royal line—heavens, he was starting to sound like his own father.

"Fine. Send an invitation," Leo said finally. "Though I hardly believe Farin will come."

"Oh, he will," Samson said. "Especially if Elena and I send our personal greetings."

As if that would make any difference to Farin. But Leo kept that thought to himself.

Alonjo joined them at the upper level of the hoverpod, bearing a cup of soothsayer tea.

"For your headache, sir," he said, and Leo smiled.

"Heavens bless you, Alonjo."

After forty suns, Alonjo had learned to read all his mannerisms. The Astra also proved to be the most insightful person in his court; he had an uncanny way of recognizing and predicting the future. He was the first to tell Leo about Yassen Knight's defection, and when Leo had pushed further, Alonjo had simply answered that he had heard so from a nomad in the market. Leo had no need to doubt him. Alonjo had strange ways of procuring information, but his information had always proven correct. And he made great tea.

Leo took a sip. The drink was delightfully warm and, like its namesake, soothing.

He looked out the window as they flew further north. Thick clouds layered the horizon, the air pregnant with a storm not yet ready to break. As Alonjo informed him about the guest list for the ball, Leo studied the dunes. Without the sun, the desert looked harder, full of sharp edges rather than the delicate curves he knew. And there were shadows. Long, black specters that cut across the sand to claw their way toward him.

And then a creeping sensation chilled the blood in his veins. Leo suddenly felt as if his body was not his own, that he was floating. He looked down and saw himself sitting by the hoverpod window, Alonjo and Samson sitting before him. He could see Alonjo's lips move, but there was no sound. He tried to cry out. He tapped the window, but neither Alonjo nor Samson turned.

The world turned and shifted into watercolors of grey. The hoverpod dissolved. He was floating over the desert, the dunes stretching on for miles in every direction. The sky began to melt in thick, heavy drops. When it hit the ground, the sand hissed. It blurred beneath him, stretching and mutating until he was floating over a valley.

Leo gasped.

There, burned in the valley, freshly smoking, were two shapes.

Two runes.

One was a leafless tree. The other was a simple circle with a singular dot in its center. Leo reached for them.

The desert screeched. Shards of sand cut through his body. He screamed, falling.

"Stop," he cried. "Stop!"

"Your Majesty?"

Leo opened his eyes to see Alonjo and Samson staring at him.

"Stop what?" the Astra asked. "We're nearly at the outpost."

Leo stood, his heart hammering. He was back in the hoverpod, the dunes rolling beneath him without pause. Gone were the harsh shadows. Had he imagined them?

Leo swiped sweat from his brow. His vision swam, and he stumbled. Alonjo flung out an arm to steady him.

"I, I—," he stuttered.

Alonjo gently lowered him back into his seat. His head felt as if someone were pushing several needles into his brain. Leo looked down at his hands. They were shaking.

"I saw something in the desert," he said. His voice was thin, raspy. "Runes. There are two more."

"But Your Majesty, you were here. I'm afraid I may have bored you to sleep—"

Leo straightened. *Had it been a dream?*

Samson offered him water, and Leo drank greedily. When he set the glass down, the hoverpod began to descend.

At first, Leo did not see Desert Spider, but as they flew closer, he noticed the subtle difference in the curves of the dunes.

The outpost was a series of sand-colored buildings that blended into the landscape. A man could walk past this place and not know of the people or things housed within. Long ago, this site had once kept and trained the Desert Spiders—a fierce coalition of warriors handpicked by Alabore Ravence himself. But the warriors had fallen out of fashion after Alabore's rule. Now, they were fairytales meant for Ravani children. King Fai had only named the base after them when his daughter, Jumi, had exclaimed that she would one day grow up to be a Desert Spider.

A ring of soldiers stood around the landing pad, their arms crossed across their chests in salute. When the hoverpod docked, Leo shakily rose to his feet. The pain in his head came in waves. In one moment, it grew so gruesome that he felt he would disintegrate on the spot. In another, he could see the world clearly.

Leo gritted his teeth and slowly walked out of the hoverpod, determined not to appear weak before his men. He motioned for the soldiers to be at ease as one walked forward.

"Muftasa," Leo greeted her.

The small woman was dressed in the garb of a solider, and she would have easily passed for one if not for her noodle-armed salute.

"Your Majesty," she said. "Alonjo, Samson. There's something you need to see."

She led them into the dark, quiet halls of Desert Spider. RI agents bowed as they passed. They entered the main room of the largest building, where a wall of holos curved up the domed ceiling. Each holo was a part of a photograph that spanned the length of the room. When Leo saw the image they created, he stopped in his tracks.

The two runes stared back at him.

"I saw this," he whispered.

Muftasa turned sharply, her eyes narrowing. "That's impossible. Our drones just found this fifteen minutes ago."

But Leo shook his head. These were the runes in his dream or hallucination or whatever it was. A wave of nausea swept over him, and he swayed on his feet.

"Saayna," he said through gritted teeth. *Only she can make sense of this.* "Take me to her."

Muftasa studied him for a long moment, but then she nodded to a solider behind them. The soldier pressed a panel, and a chamber opened to their left. "This way."

Leo and his party followed Muftasa into a white, circular room with skylights. Soft shadows slunk down the bare walls. At its center, Saayna sat cross-legged on a floor cushion. She opened her eyes as they entered.

"So you've seen them," she said, a smile in her voice.

A distant roar commenced in Leo's ears. He staggered forward, but his knees buckled and he sank to the floor.

"What are they?" he asked, spots dancing in his eyes.

"Something the Eternal Fire wished for you to see," she said. Her eyes were wide and bright. "You have sat in the flames, tasted their ash. They can call to you any time they please."

Leo licked his lips. His headache thundered.

"But what of the runes? What do they mean?"

The High Priestess looked up, and Leo followed her gaze. He thought he would see what she saw, perhaps a shining emblem of the Phoenix or the heavens themselves, but he saw only the dark underbellies of storm clouds.

"They say, 'The Prophet shall be reborn.'" She fixed him with her dark eyes. "And she will begin her warpath at the Palace."

Any other king would have balked. Any other man would have pleaded for forgiveness. But his father, before he had fallen into madness, had taught Leo how to root out a lie.

Leo heard it in her voice—the slight tremble, the hitched breath. He could see her deception despite his impaired state.

The king pressed his fingers into his eyelids. When he opened them, he saw the imprints of his fingertips, but his vision held steady. Slowly, he breathed. In for a count of four, and out. He always practiced this ritual before he sat in the flames. The Eternal Fire did not need to burn a man to destroy him. It could eat him from within. Leo had seen it happen to his father. The old king had screamed and pulled out his hair on his deathbed. And if the Eternal Fire had shown Leo a vision, it could only mean madness awaited him, too.

Leo let out one more measured breath to calm the hammering in his head.

"Map it," he said, and then louder. "Map the runes. All of them. Join them together and see where they lead."

He heard Saayna inhale sharply, and he smiled. The High Priestess had mapped the first two runes and declared that the Prophet was in the capital. She had sent him on wild shobu chase. *She* had made him kill the girl.

Samson ordered for a holopod and, with the help of Muftasa, began to overlay images of the runes on a map of Ravence. It was only when they stepped back and announced that the task was complete that Leo took his eyes off the High Priestess.

The runes joined together to create a large, smoldering maze that cut through Ravence. And within the labyrinth, there lay no demon, but the Temple of Fire.

Leo stared at the map, the roar in his ears becoming soft and distant.

"The Prophet is a priest," he whispered.

All this time, she had been in his grasp. All this time, the Prophet had grown in the shadow of his throne and in the care of holy men.

He had given her food and shelter, prepared her in the ways of fire. She had watched him perform Ashanta ceremonies knowing one day that the Eternal Fire would claim him and his family.

And he had burned countless innocent girls in his quest to find her.

Leo laughed.

A dry, bitter laugh, full of harsh sounds. Saayna bristled, shifting away from him.

"I've probably met her, prayed with her." He looked at the High Priestess. She was no Prophet. She had no marks, and she burned just as easily as he did.

Still, he ordered for a match. Alonjo brought it, and Leo struck it against the floor. The match flared to life. Without warning, Leo grabbed Saayna's hand.

"What was it you said to me once—that people go astray without their leaders. No? That it is the role of the Prophet to lead us to enlightenment. Yes?" She struggled as he held her hand to the flame, but Leo only tightened his grip. Slowly, he pressed the flame into Saayna's palm. She yelped as there came a soft hiss and the smell of burnt flesh.

"You are the first to burn," he said, his gaze never breaking. "And all the priests you've taught will burn after you. This is your path of enlightenment, Saayna, the path your Prophet will bring—one of madness and destruction."

He tossed the match and stood. Gone was his headache. Adrenaline took its place, along with a surge of hope.

"I will not allow your insanity to endanger this kingdom," he said. "I will burn your priests one by one until I find your Prophet. And then I will bury her in cold stone to end this cycle."

Saayna cradled her hand to her chest, tears pricking the edges of her eyes. Still, when she spoke, her voice rang out loud and clear. "Watch the winds. They don't dance in your favor."

Leo ignored her and regarded Muftasa. "End the search for the girls in the city. We're going to burn the priests."

Muftasa accepted the command with a strained face.

Leo turned on his heel, leaving Saayna in the white room. He swept past the holos of the new runes, past the stone-faced soldiers, for the darkening desert beyond. Once outside, he stopped and stared at the mountains that lay to the west.

His father had warned him about the power of religion—the way it charmed followers to give up their thinking and follow not with their minds but with their hearts. Their weak, malleable hearts.

The High Priestess was wrong. People did not go astray because they had no leader. They succumbed to themselves, to the soft part that wanted to be safe. The part that would rather curl up and sleep in the shadows like a shobu than to rise in the glory of the sun.

He may not be the Prophet, but Leo knew he was stronger. He was the one who could bear the burn of the flames. The only one who could stand in the harsh glare of the sun and still find his way.

17
YASSEN

There once were two lovers: a Yumi and a man. They cared for each other deeply, but their kind would not accept their union. One night, in anguish, the pair met under the stars and cried out their love. So moved were the gods that they turned the lovers into the moons, Chand and Chandhini. "They shall live together in eternity," the gods said, "and give light to those who must meet in the secrecy of night."

—FROM *THE LEGENDS AND MYTHS OF SAYON*

Yassen fell into the rhythm of Palace life. In the mornings, he woke early and ate breakfast with Samson, who would fill him in about the royal family, the status of the grand ball and the interrogations. Through him Yassen learned about Giorna's death.

Apparently, her handler had been too rough; he had used a branding iron to mark her as a traitor, but he had not treated the burn. It had festered and eventually killed her. Samson had been surprised by her sudden death, but Yassen expected it. He understood how Giorna felt. With no home, no people, all a man had left was to die.

"There will be more," he had told Samson.

Samson had turned then. He wore a white silk shirt that opened at the collar, and Yassen caught a glance of the scar that ran down Samson's chest to his upper abdomen.

"Let's hope they'll have quicker deaths," the militant said and smiled.

After breakfast with Samson, Yassen would join Elena and Ferma for morning training. At first, Elena had not allowed him to watch, but after their desert walk, she let him into the gamemaster's box. She still distrusted him, but at least now she did not abhor him. At least not openly.

Elena was proficient with a slingsword as she weaved in and out of Ferma's attacks. She was also excellent in hand-to-hand combat and a crack shot—just like him. But she still could not hold fire. Every time he saw her, a fine coat of ash dusted the patch of skin below her wrist. He wanted to tell her to stop, to tell her nothing sane came from fire, but he knew she would not listen to him. So, he kept quiet.

After morning training, he followed Elena through her slew of meetings with generals, capital officials, policemen, statesmen, bureaucrats, servants, groundskeepers, handmaids, and citizens of Ravence. By the end of the day, Yassen felt as if his ears were bleeding, but Elena handled it all with grace. She smiled when necessary, laughed when appropriate. She softened her voice to address a charity beneficiary and raised it to belittle a general. She knew when to appease and when to rile, how to perfectly add a hint of contempt to rein in a greedy bureaucrat, and how to lower her voice to show deference to the Phoenix.

Through it all, they saw the king sparingly. Leo had little time for his daughter, and his lack of attention showed in Elena's outbursts on the training field. Yassen knew she must have had a particularly difficult conversation with her father when she threatened to pull out Ferma's quills and stab them into the Yumi's eyes.

Ferma hadn't taken the bait and swung her hair with such force that she cut Elena's slingsword in half.

When Samson pulled Yassen away, Elena asked no questions. They continued their operation of capturing Arohassin agents, and the agents in turn continued to call Yassen a traitor, cursing him to a life worse than death.

Word about the successful operations began to spread, and generals regarded Yassen with less suspicion. Even Ferma nodded at him. But Elena only took the news in silence.

That was just as well. Yassen didn't plan to stay after the coronation, now only three weeks away. With his amnesty, he would leave as soon as she was blessed and spirit away in the commotion that would follow.

Soon, he would only be a memory to her.

But tonight, Yassen wanted to taste freedom early.

After his shift, he took a hovercar into the capital. He parked the unmarked car beneath a highway junction where two homeless women peered out from their sand hovel. A shobu rummaged in a pile of refuse, growling as Yassen approached. He tossed the women three coins and told them to watch the car. The Palace guards knew he was in the city, but if the women stole the car, at least Yassen would have a new story to tell Samson.

Yassen pulled on his hood as it began to rain. He made his way from the flyover to the adjoining street. Music from a club echoed down the alley while a gold cap stood on the corner, crying about the next coming of the Prophet. No one stopped to listen.

Vendors wheeled their carts to the end of the street where hungry patrons awaited eagerly. One cart had a long line that stretched past the corner. As Yassen passed the crowd, he looked over. A Ravani merchant roasted okra on a makeshift grill and served it up with a skewer of kabobs. Yassen's stomach grumbled. He debated on waiting in line but thought better of it. There was still more of the city to see.

As a drizzle dusted the streets, Yassen breathed in the smell of the desert, the musky scent of wet sand and rock. Sandscrapers rose above copper-and-gold chhatris and tiered squares. He recognized a few of the street names. There was still the covered market on Alabore Street with its mosaic ceiling and banyan tree in the center. Long ago, he had sat underneath the tree while his mother haggled for a bag of figs. When the merchant refused to go lower, she had turned on her heel, Yassen following. The next day, he had nicked the figs when the merchant wasn't looking.

Yassen smiled at the memory as he looked into the closed market. The banyan tree shimmered like liquid silver from underneath the skylights.

He continued on, winding through alleys without a set destination. He just knew he couldn't return to the southern outskirts. The memory, though seventeen suns past, still felt raw.

When he came to the corner of Suraat and Sumput, Yassen was surprised to find a shuttered storefront advertising a new lease. Diagonally across the corner, a cropping of jade berry bushes grew below the entrance of the city park.

There, many suns ago, he and Samson had watched people enter the bakery and carry out bundles of honeyed bread and nightdew chocolate. When their hunger grew to pain, Samson had hatched a plan. They waited until the baker went into his back office and the clerk, his daughter, took her break.

Yassen had stolen across the street and entered the shop. He had expected the counter to be empty, but the baker stood behind the glass bins of cinnamon twists and glazed treats.

"What would you like today?" the baker had asked.

Yassen blinked. Out of the corner of his eye, he saw Samson disappear around the corner.

"Um, ten cardamom and nutmeg infused loaves, please," he had said. The baker began to fill a bag with the bread. Yassen watched, his mouth watering. "And two honey muffins," he added.

"Are you having a party?" the baker asked as he took out two muffins from the heated rack.

"No, I—yes, I mean, yes," Yassen had said.

The baker regarded him, but before he could say anything, a scream came from the back of the bakery. The baker spun around, calling his daughter's name. As soon as he had disappeared, Yassen scrambled over the counter and began stuffing bags with loaves, muffins, cinnamon twists and anything he could get his hands on. He heard the baker yell. There came a thump, and then his bald head loomed over him.

"Hey!"

Yassen jumped over the counter and dashed out into the street, the wind singing past his ears as he ran deeper and deeper into the park until he could run no farther. He had collapsed, sucking in air. But his hunger was greater than his exhaustion, and he greedily began to devour a loaf of bread.

He had been so hungry that it wasn't until he had finished his cardamom-spiced loaf that he noticed Samson's absence. He searched the park and eventually found him on a bridge overlooking a sandpit. The bread was cold by then, but Samson had greeted him with a bloody smile and a split eyebrow.

"Looks like you hit the jackpot," he had said.

Yassen peered into the empty store. There were skid marks on the floor where the glass counter had been. Stealing from the bakery had been the first of many transgressions, but, at the time, it hadn't felt like a crime. It felt necessary.

He looked down the street at the unfamiliar neon signs and newly planted trees. Overhead, floating holo billboards advertised companies he had never heard of. A young couple staggered down the street, laughing, their faces red with drink.

Yassen watched them and then looked back at the empty store.

He felt the echo of forgotten suns.

The city had gone on without him, evolving without his supervision. He knew he had no claim on the capital or its ways, but he had been born here in the southern outskirts during the middle of the night. He had been raised by these streets, shaken sand out of his hair after winter sandstorms, strained his neck as he and others watched the Fire Birds take on the Metal Warriors in games of windsnatch.

In a way, he felt betrayed by the changed city. Yet a part of him knew such change was inevitable. He had long ago forsaken this place. He could not expect it to bat an eye at his nostalgia.

The neon signs grew dimmer as Yassen entered the park. The sandpit had been hollowed out. Drunks, vagabonds, and storytellers gathered within its crater. As he walked onto the bridge, the sound of quarreling voices made him pause. Yassen peered down and saw a woman with hair the color of polished bronze standing on top of a broken sand sculpture of King Gorgon.

A small crowd surrounded her. One bearded man with a bull tattooed on his hand argued with a thin teenager still dressed in his school uniform. The woman watched them. She raised her hand, but they paid her no mind.

"Enough," she said as their voices grew louder. "Enough!"

The two men stopped, stricken by the fury in her voice.

"If we continue to argue among ourselves, how will we organize the revolution?" she spat.

"Well, he started it," the Sesharian said.

"This man's head is not screwed on right," the student retorted. "Fucking refugee."

"We *refugees* sweat and toil as much as you. More than you."

"If you want to complain, then just go back to your own damn land! We can carry on this revolution without you."

"Says the boy whose balls haven't dropped."

"I'll have both of your heads lying in a ditch for the silver feathers if you don't shut up," the woman interrupted. The two men looked at each other, as if weighing their options, and eventually fell silent.

"We will never win if we feud," she said. She raised her hand north, where the Palace glimmered like a distant star. "They will devour us like they have countless times before."

She studied the faces in the crowd, her lips curling back into a scowl.

"How many times have King Leo's soldiers marched through these streets to keep peace, when really, they've come to keep us quiet? How many times have his guards killed our brothers and sisters when they spoke up about the state of this kingdom?" she said. "The old king knows his power is slipping. His reign is coming to an end, so he grows crueler. You've heard the rumors of the girls stolen in the night to be burned. The king has gone mad."

A murmur rippled through the crowd. Yassen recognized it—the spark of rebellion, a whisper of justice. He had felt it before, had manipulated emotions of revolution for his own gain, his own survival.

"Ravence is crumbling, and King Leo knows. He sees it before his very eyes but does nothing except kidnap our people under the cowardice of nightfall. But we won't take it anymore," she said. "Because we know the truth. We know the kingdom is old. It was founded upon death and blood—on a myth. The Phoenix is dead. There is no Prophet. A new era has come. An era for new gods and a government led by the people—not by a bloodline."

She paused and looked out at the silent crowd. The air was heavy, tense. Yassen had to give it to her. She knew how to deliver a speech.

"It is time, my friends, for our revolution. This is our chance to stop the bloody cycle of history."

"But they were chosen to rule this land!" someone called out. The crowd pushed an old man to the front. "The Phoenix burned every king's and queen's name in the sand before Alabore. He built us this home."

"If there really was a Phoenix," the woman said, "why did she bless Alabore? What about her Prophet?"

"Because the Prophet's time has not come," the old man garbled. "But they will come, the both of them. You mark my words, the Phoenix will rise from the ashes and Her Prophet will burn us all."

The crowd whispered as the old man licked his dry lips and stared up at the woman. Yassen slipped down the bridge and into the sandpit. Pain slithered down his shoulder to his wrist, but he ignored it. He stood at the edge of the crowd as the woman looked at the sky and the Palace beyond.

"Well, if the Phoenix is real, she'd better hurry because we are here, and we are hungry. This is our home, and we will not let a self-proclaimed Prophet burn us out."

She jumped down from the statue and walked up to the old man. She was at least a foot taller, with the defiant look of a young martyr. Yassen walked around the edge of the crowd to the front as the woman pushed her face into the old man's.

"Your Prophet is no different than that tyrant on the hill," she snarled. "Both wage war on this land without regard for its people." She rose up and this time directed her words to the crowd. "This land is ours to rule and govern as we see fit. And no one, not even some half-forgotten bird, can tell us otherwise."

Cheers and whistles broke out as the woman smirked. The old man shook his head. He grumbled something Yassen could not hear and then pushed his way through the crowd. He began to zip up his jacket and as he passed, Yassen caught a glimpse of a crumpled hat tucked in his breast pocket.

It was the color of gold.

People surrounded the woman, patting her on the back and reaffirming their faith in the rebellion. Yassen watched for a while, but he felt an emptiness within.

Leave it, he wanted to tell her. *Do not lose yourself in these fantasies.* He had seen such dreams bring ruin to their believers. To him.

The Arohassin believed in revolution. They had made him believe that the only way to create change was by destroying the old world order. Yassen did not blame them. He was tired of fire. Tired of its vengeful nature. Tired of continuing to believe in an ancient prophecy that would never be fulfilled.

The only way to change the world was to take back what had been stolen.

The Arohassin decried the Phoenix because She was not real. Alabore Ravence was not a holy figure, but a shrewd general who knew how to manipulate his enemies. And for a long time, Yassen had believed that. When the Arohassin gave him the order to kill, he had followed blindly. But he had come to learn that hypocrisies existed on both sides. And that fire, no matter which side wielded it, was always wild and destructive.

Over the din of the rebels' fevered promises, Yassen heard a sound from above. He looked up to see shadows over the bridge. A face came into a view, and then another. Angry faces with gold caps. He spotted the old man from before. He and the others looked down at the small gathering and sneered. Yassen spotted the glint of a gun.

And then he smelled smoke.

Yassen darted underneath the bridge as the gold caps opened fire. Screams erupted into the night. The gold caps dove into the sandpit as the rebels pulled out their guns. Suddenly, the darkness beneath the bridge erupted with pulses.

Yassen rounded the column of the bridge as a pulse whizzed past him. Another hit the column, spraying stone. Yassen scrambled up the bank of the sandpit. The rain had hardened the sand, and he found purchase. He hauled himself up, instinct and training taking over.

The old man stood on the edge of the pit with his pulse gun. When he saw Yassen, he raised his weapon. Yassen dived forward, tackling him to the ground. They rolled in the sand, struggling, and then Yassen slipped his arm around the man's shoulder and pinned him down.

"Get off of me, Jantari!" he cried.

Yassen froze. *Jantari.* With the acceptance he had slowly won in the Palace, Yassen had almost forgotten his true reality. He still looked like an outsider. His pale eyes were dead giveaway. The man had not heard his voice, his rolling desert accent. To him, he was a stranger. An enemy.

Yassen looked down at the old man, his narrowed eyes, the fury in his brow. He could easily snap the man's neck. Leave his body for his brethren to find. Yassen's left hand shook as he cradled the man's head.

Just a simple twist.

But then more pulse fire erupted in the night. Yassen punched the man on the nose, knocking him unconscious in a spray of blood. He took off into the woods, legs pumping, heart hammering. Bramble cut through his arms and legs but he did not slow.

Sirens began to fill the night when Yassen finally stopped at the western edge of the park. The roar of gunfire still thundered in his ears.

This is the price to pay for revolution. This has always been the price to pay.

Despite himself, Yassen felt his throat constrict. Anger, frustration, and a sense of helplessness squeezed his throat. *They are fools, all of them.*

The way back to the highway junction was cold and dark. By the time he reached the adjoining street, the bars were closed and vendors were gone. Even the homeless women had left their sand hovel, but his hovercar was still there.

Yassen pressed his hand against the door and, once confirming his fingerprints, the door lifted. He sat in the hovercar for a long moment, listening to his ragged breath. The police would catch the gold caps. They would make a show of detaining them, but Yassen knew they would not be punished. Leo was their patron after all. They would be seen as heroes, golden and fierce in their defense of the king.

Yassen shuddered and started the engine. Unlike the night in the desert with Elena, there were no stars underneath the junction, no twin moons with their alabaster glow. Nothing to guide him out. Just his own eyes to feel the path and his bloodied hands to lead the way.

18
ELENA

There is some comfort in the emptiness of the desert.
Here, the past is erased by the wind,
and the future is yet to be written.

—FROM THE DIARIES OF PRIESTESS NOMU OF THE FIRE ORDER

Elena burst into Leo's study.

"You need to stop them," she said. "They're out of control."

Guards scrambled up behind her. Marcus gripped her shoulder, panting.

"Your Majesty, I-I'm sorry, she just barged in."

The king looked up. Headlines detailing the civilian attack in Rani floated around him. Images of the aftermath—the pulse-ridden bodies, the red-stained sand—revolved in a carousel of holos.

"So are you," he said to Elena.

She shook off Marcus and stalked forward. "Your gold caps opened fire in a public place. On innocent people."

"They were rebels," her father said as he brought a holo closer and studied its contents. "Did you notice that they were armed? Preliminary investigations say the guns came from the Arohassin."

"That doesn't matter!" she snapped, and the fury in her voice made him cast away the holos.

His stone eyes fixed on her. "You called them your countrymen."

"This was not what I meant. I called for unity. This, this is destruction."

"You can't call for fire and then blame others when you can't wield it," he said.

"Are you even listening?" she cried. "We have a bloodbath on our hands. On all sides. Civilian, rebel, gold cap—their blood spilled on our sand. This is even worse than last sun's Teranghar bombings."

"And soon it will be over," he said. "Once you're crowned queen, the dust will settle."

"That's bullshit," she said.

"That's power," he responded, and the look in his eyes drained her anger, replacing it with fear. "Everything I do—that they do—is for you. For our throne. Remember that."

Leo's eyes flickered over her, and then he returned to his holos, as if her transgression was no longer worth his time.

"Take her away."

Yassen and Ferma awaited her outside her father's study. When Ferma saw the look on her face, she dismissed Yassen with a whisper. The Yumi trailed Elena to her chambers, waved away the handmaids, and closed the door once they were alone.

Elena sank into a floating ottoman before her vanity. She caught her reflection in the mirror, saw the lines creasing her forehead, the crow's feet around her eyes. This kingdom was aging her. She already felt its grip constrict around her body, squeezing out her youth.

Her hope.

She believed in Ravence, believed that one day it would shed its useless hatred as a desert yuani sheds her old feathers. Spreads her wings anew and launches into the sky. She believed in the dream so much that it hurt—a raw, keen pain in her chest. But her kingdom was crumbling right before her eyes, and it was all her fault. She could not unite them. She could not wield fire. And without the blessing of the Phoenix, she could not lead Ravence to glory.

Ferma sat down across her, folding in her long legs. Her tawny eyes fixed upon Elena.

"I don't know if I can do this," Elena whispered.

"You'll learn," Ferma said back. Her hair tumbled down her shoulders. She touched Elena's hand. "No ruler is perfect in the beginning. Your father wasn't, but he knew how to use others to his advantage. He learned by watching them. And your mother," Ferma said and shook her head. "She taught him the most."

Elena thought of Aahnah: her mess of curls, her eyes the color of dark banyan roots. She would not be here to guide her toward queendom, nor advise her on the secrets of marriage. She was a memory only a few suns from fading. All Elena had left of her was a dusty library and a scroll she had written in.

"Come, let me fix your hair. It's a mess," Ferma coaxed, but Elena shook her head.

"I'd rather do yours. Sit here," she said, and the Yumi obliged. Elena ran her fingers through her long hair—softer than silk, harder than diamond.

Once after Aahnah had died, Elena had slipped out of the castle and into the squalid slums of the outer city. She could not remember how she had gotten there, only that a man had led her back to his home to show her shobu puppies and shut the door on her. She had panicked and kicked him between the legs. She then bolted into the street and ran headfirst into Ferma. The Yumi did not say a word to Elena. She simply walked into the hut, her hair writhing behind her. Elena had watched as her hair pierced the man's body, blood spilling out. When Ferma came back out, not a single drop stained her curls.

Elena began to weave Ferma's hair into a long, thick braid. She hummed as she worked. Ferma sighed and closed her eyes, relaxing her head back against Elena's knee.

"You know, no one has braided my hair in a long time," she murmured.

"Probably because you scare them off."

The Yumi chuckled. "I think you do."

Elena smiled as she twisted another strand into the braid. "I'm pretty sure Samson is intimidated by you."

"Ah, the Sesharian." Ferma gave a lazy, mischievous grin. "How are things going with our famed hero?"

Elena snorted, though she felt her cheeks warm. "Fine. We're going for a ride later."

"The successful Arohassin hunts are winning him favor with the guards and our soldiers," Ferma said. "Looks like his bet on Yassen Knight paid off."

Elena thought back to Yassen standing on top of the dune. The way his pale eyes had met hers as he touched the barrel of the pulse gun. *This isn't just your home. It's mine too.*

She shook the memory away, focused instead on finishing the braid. "When I become queen, I want you to retire," she began. "You deserve the rest—"

"I'd rather you throw me into quicksand," Ferma said, eyes still closed.

"I was going to say you deserve rest before I promote you to be my Astra," she said, tugging on the braid harder than necessary. Ferma winced.

"Easy." Her eyes fluttered open, and she looked up at Elena. "Astra, eh?"

"I could think of no one else," Elena said.

"But I would better serve you as your Spear than a coddled bureaucrat," Ferma said. She pulled away from Elena and turned to face her. "You have Samson. As your king, he'll be your closest confidant. That's the way it works."

"It doesn't have to be that way, though," Elena said.

"Shutting out Samson will only weaken your reign. And he's a man. It'll bruise his ego. He'll start to plot against you from the shadows."

Elena scoffed. "Now you're being dramatic."

"I'm being realistic." Ferma drew up. Her thick braid snaked down her shoulder. "You have a strong ally in Samson. *Use him.*"

"But I need *you*," she said and took Ferma's hands into her own. "You're my strongest ally."

"I'm growing old, Elena," the Yumi said and gave a soft smile. "I will serve you until my last breath, but it will come sooner than Samson's."

"As my Astra, you won't have to put yourself in the line of fire," she insisted. "It'll be a cushy job, and you'll have servants to see to your every need."

"There is no cushy job in Ravence."

"Just think about it, Ferma."

The Yumi sighed. She gave a slow nod, but Elena could see the sorrow in her eyes. "I'll think about it."

Samson and Elena rode north into the desert, the sunset painting the sky in brushstrokes of red and pink.

Her mare fought the lead, eager to run across the dunes. Elena gave her more rein, and they took off. She crouched in her stirrups, sand stinging her skin and the wind singing in her ears. She closed her eyes and breathed in the desert, letting its wildness fill the spaces between her bones.

They climbed up a rock face, and Elena opened her eyes. She slowed her horse and sat back in her saddle. Pebbles tumbled off the precipice. Beneath them, a deep valley stretched across the desert like an unhealed scar.

She heard the clatter of hooves and turned to see the rest of her party. The guards spread out as Samson trotted up beside her.

"You're a fast rider," he panted. "Even gave me quite the run."

But Elena had sensed that Samson had held back. He had the form of a strong rider, but he had allowed her to take the lead. She wondered what else he was merely *allowing* her to do.

"Do you know this valley?" she asked.

He peered over the cliffside. "Looks like the rest."

"You'll need to know everything about this desert if you're to be my king," she said. The smile fell from his face, and Elena hopped off her mare. "Come."

They descended into the valley. Unlike Yassen, Samson trudged through the dune. He left a trail, one that an enemy tracker or yeseri could follow. Ferma had insisted she would learn from Samson, but she had more to teach him.

When they came to the valley floor, Elena stopped. The rock walls towered above them. No flowers nor desert fruit grew within the crevices. Here, the sun did not shine; the air crept with a slick coolness.

"This is Alabore's Tear," she said. "This is where he met the Phoenix."

"Don't you think this place is too dark for the Holy Bird?"

"Fire burns brightest in the darkness," she returned.

Samson walked forward, craning his neck. She watched him take it all in: the cold sand, the weathered rock, the tough bramble.

"Have you ever seen anything like this?" she asked.

When he turned back to her, his mouth was a thin line. "Once."

He held out his arm, and she took it. They neared a skorrir bush, and its buds shrank back as they approached. Elena pointed.

"These are helpful markers," she said. "You can tell if something has passed before you."

"We have something like that in Seshar," Samson said wistfully. He studied the skorrir bush, but Elena could tell by the distant look in his eyes that he was gazing upon his homeland.

"Have you gone back to Seshar? Would Farin allow it?"

Beneath her hand, she felt his forearm tense. "I don't want to go back, not yet," he said. "There's so much I want to do here before returning."

"Like what?"

He did not answer. A pensive look grew on his face as they walked. Long shadows crawled up the red walls, and a long, heavy silence hung in the air. Elena was about to suggest they return to their mounts when Samson spoke.

"I was born under Jantar's rule," he said, his voice hoarse. "By then, they had executed all the noble families on Seshar except mine. They were afraid that my mother, a priestess, would set the evil eye on them. The metalmen aren't the superstitious type, but my mother could make you believe in anything."

"I suppose you get your allure from her then."

He gave a wry smile, but his eyes remained dark. "When I was eleven suns, she knew we were running out of time. They were coming for us. So she sent me a dream.

"I dreamt of a deep fissure in a desert," he said. "Darkness covered the path, but at the very end, there was a light. An ember. It was so small that a breeze would extinguish it. I ran toward it, but before I could reach it, I woke up."

"You think your mother sent you to Alabore's Tear?" Elena asked.

Samson surveyed the valley. "I think she meant to show me that there is a fire I must seek and protect. It could be Seshar. It could be Ravence, perhaps even Jantar. It could even be you," he said with a wink. "But don't they say that dreams of fire lead to madness?"

Elena kept quiet. They stopped before a long crevice, one that began from the valley floor and sprouted up across the entire length of the wall. A million tiny cracks splintered from the scar. Gazing upon it, Elena was reminded of gulmohar tree, dead and bare in the winter.

"What happened to your family?" she asked after a few moments. "Does this have a name too?"

She shook her head. "None that I know."

Samson stared at the crevice. He leaned forward, and she thought he was going to reach out and touch the wall when he disentangled his arm from hers and turned around.

"We should start heading back," he muttered.

"If you won't tell me about your family, tell me about Yassen," she said, trying to sound nonchalant. "When did you meet him?"

"In Ravence, stealing the same piece of bread." He shot her a glance, but if he sensed something amiss, he made no mention of it. "After my parents died, I ended up in Ravence. It's a long story. I found this bakery and was about to swipe a loaf when Yassen grabbed the same one. We fought over it, but Yassen let go. He was smart. Because a second later, the baker came out and grabbed me.

"Back then, they burned thieves, even children. He dragged me into the street to summon a silver feather when Yassen threw a pot of boiling tea into his face. After that we ran." Samson stopped and looked up at the sliver of orange sky. "You know, it was on a day a lot like this."

They trekked up the valley. Guards brought forward their horses, and Elena jumped on. Samson did not. She waited for him, but he continued standing on the edge of the rock, looking down into the dark valley.

"What is it?" she asked.

"There's so much about Ravence I don't know."

"You'll learn."

He stood there for a moment longer and then turned back to her. "You still don't trust Yassen. Do you?"

"How can you?"

Samson came up to her. He stroked her mare's head, spoke soft words in a language Elena did not understand. "Because despite everything, I think back to that kid who saved me. Because I owe my life to him."

Elena nudged her horse and turned away from Samson. Without waiting for him, she dug her heels into her mare and galloped toward the Palace.

When Elena reached the Palace, she called the gamemaster and strode into the control room before her gamesuit was even prepped.

"Your Majesty, y-you're early," the gamemaster stammered and bowed.

Elena slipped on her gamesuit and stepped into the pod. It hummed, and her suit molded to her shape. When Elena stepped out, she felt the heightened strength of her body: the coiled muscles in her legs, the elasticity in her arms. It was such a shame that gamesuits could not function outside the field. Soldiers in gamesuits would end wars more quickly.

"You can leave," she said to the gamemaster and Ferma. Yassen was gone on another hunt. "Just turn on the field before you go."

"You want to train alone?" the Yumi asked.

Elena nodded as the gamemaster turned dials on the control panel. The blue lotus lights of the field turned on, and the black sand began to swirl. Elena grabbed a slingsword from the rack. She balanced it in her hand, checking its weight and trigger mechanism before belting it to her hip.

"I need to clear my mind," she said.

Ferma opened her mouth to retort, but Elena held up her hand. "Fine. If you want to be useful, make a list of all the victims of last night's capital shooting. I want to honor their families."

The Yumi nodded slowly, her hair curling around her shoulders. Elena could tell that her Spear wanted to stay and supervise her training, but she wanted to give Ferma more administrative tasks. If the Yumi was to become her Astra, Elena needed to train *her*.

"As you wish." Ferma bowed, the gamemaster following suit. "I'll post guards at the door."

"Thank you." Elena watched them go. When the door shut behind them, she exited the glass box and descended the stairs that led to the field. The black sand vibrated underneath her feet.

Elena crouched down as the lights dimmed. A counter sounded through the chamber.

"Three, two, one."

The lights blazed, and the sand rose. It solidified into a large spiked wall twice her height. Without warning, the spikes shot forward, racing straight toward Elena.

She drew her slingsword and slashed down a shard. It fell in a spray of sand. Another whistled by her ear. Elena ducked and weaved through the attack, her movements smooth and practiced, her feet light. She sliced another and cut through one that threatened to rip out her eye. Elena advanced forward, the slingsword hilt slick in her hand. Sweat trickled down her face, but she did not mind.

She fell into a trance, into the primal physicality of her body. She did not think; she acted.

Lunge.

Duck.

Spin.

Advance.

Her body moved to its own accord, and for one splendid moment, Elena felt attuned to something higher. Forget the gods and the rebels. Here was something she was good at. Here was something she could control.

Elena ran toward the wall, but before she could reach it, the sand collapsed. She coughed as dirt and dust clotted the air. The ground rumbled as the sand shifted. A low hiss began to creep across the field. Elena held her slingsword in front of her, slowly turning to sense the next direction of the attack.

It came from below.

The sand grabbed her feet, sucked her down into a rippling pool of quicksand. Elena grunted, trying to twist out of its grasp, but she only sank deeper.

"The more you struggle, the faster you'll sink."

Her head snapped up. There, standing in the glass box, was Yassen.

"What are you doing here?" she growled.

"Relax your legs and shoot out your blade. You can pull yourself out that way."

She glanced at her sword and then up at the blue lights. The sand gurgled, swallowing her up to her waist.

Cursing, Elena raised her sword and pulled the trigger. The blade shot out and embedded into the ceiling. She tugged, but it held. With a grunt, she pulled herself up, climbing the steel rope that connected the projectile blade to the hilt. The sand hissed, squeezing her legs, but Elena put one hand over the other, her muscles screaming as she pulled herself out of the pool. As soon as she escaped, the blue lights flashed, and the sand froze.

The round was over.

She sighed and let go. She landed on her feet, but her knees buckled and she fell. Elena groaned and rolled onto her back. She stared up at the lotus lights, but a shadow fell over her. Frowning, she craned her neck. Yassen stared down at her, a rare smile playing across his face.

"You've never dealt with quicksand. Have you?"

"Oh, shut it."

She pushed herself into a sitting position. Yassen offered his hand, and then she noticed the slingsword tucked into his belt.

"Did you have to use that on your hunt?"

"No," he said, hauling her up. "Pulse guns are much faster."

"Amateur," she said. "Guns are for cowards. Swords show the mark of a true fighter."

"Oh?" Yassen looked down at his hip. He wore no gamesuit, but after a moment's debate, he drew out his slingsword, the blade glinting in the blue light. "Then show me."

Elena paused. Her legs felt like lead and her arms weak as Cyleon balsa. But she saw the look in Yassen's eyes, the determination and the curiosity, and she thought back to their first duel.

"Alright," she said. "But this time, don't just roll over like a shobu. I might get your other cheek."

They crouched at opposite ends of the field. The gamemaster had only programmed one round, so no timer blared over the intercoms. The sand was as still as the desert on a summer night. Elena met Yassen's gaze. He nodded.

They both charged forward. With a snarl, Elena raised her slingsword for an overhead strike. Yassen brought up his weapon, and their blades clashed with a screech. Without missing a beat, Elena stepped back and lifted her slingsword. Yassen cut up for a parry, falling for the feint. Grinning, she sidestepped and wheeled down, the tip of her blade nicking Yassen's shin. He yelped and hopped back.

Elena lunged, using her momentum to knee him in the liver. Yassen stumbled but quickly regained his footing, spinning out of her reach. He swept aside her advance and parried the next.

The clang of their slingswords thundered through the field. Elena could feel herself beginning to tire as he continued to fend off her cuts. Her arms shook, and her shoulders began to cramp. As if sensing her fatigue, Yassen flicked aside her strike and then lunged, his shoulder ramming into her chest.

She gasped, the impact knocking the air out of her. She scrambled back, bringing up her slingsword, but Yassen easily hit her wrist with the flat plane of his blade, knocking her sword from her hand. Her eyes widened. He rushed forward, his blade arcing up, and Elena saw her opening.

She spun down and around, sweeping her leg out as she had seen Ferma do so many times before, and clipped Yassen across his ankles. He fell, his slingsword clattering to the ground. Elena snatched it and jumped on top of him, pinning him down as she raised his own blade to his throat.

"Peace," she said, panting.

This close, she saw a bead of sweat run down the side of his forehead and into his hairline. Yassen looked up, his eyes clear and wide.

"Peace," he whispered.

She realized then that he had let her win; that he would always let her win. The opening, though not a rookie mistake, was preventable. Yassen had offered it, knowing that a skilled fighter like her would notice.

Elena suddenly felt aware of how sharp his hips felt against her legs. She pushed to her feet and offered her hand. He took it, and she helped him stand. A thin line of red marked his throat where the slingsword had kissed his skin. Yassen saw her looking and touched it.

"It'll heal," he said.

Elena hobbled into her room, feeling as if sand was lodged between her bones. She sank into the warm bath Diya had drawn up for her and soaked in the tub until her toes shriveled like dates. When she closed her eyes, she saw Yassen's pale eyes looking up at her.

It'll heal.

Diya brought her a robe, and then Elena dismissed her handmaid with a soft goodnight. When she was gone, Elena opened the doors to her balcony. A cool wind rustled the curtains. The air felt charged, and she looked up at the burdened sky. Another storm was due.

Elena grabbed a glass orb and took it to the fire crackling in the hearth. As tired as she was, she could not rest. Not now. Carefully, she dipped the orb into the fire and scooped up a flame.

The flame flickered but held steady.

Holding the orb out in front of her, she took the scroll from her desk and descended into her garden. By now, the seven forms and their directions were ingrained in her mind. She dreamed of flowing through them like the wind over the dunes. Effortless.

Lotuses drifted in the stone basin of the fountain. She set the orb on the lip of the fountain and unrolled the scroll. In the distance, lightning flashed through the grey clouds, but Elena heard no thunder.

She took a deep breath and sank into the first pose. The Warrior.

The path of fire is dangerous. Tread it with care.

Her muscles ached. Elena bit back a groan as she concentrated on her pose. She held out her arms, palms outstretched. Sweeping her right leg, she shifted her weight into the second form.

The Desert Sparrow.

Sweat beaded on her forehead despite the cool night. Elena bit her lip as she balanced on her right foot, her left tucked behind her right thigh, her arms folded behind her like a resting sparrow. The fire hissed in its confines.

Empty your mind. See nothing but the fire—for that is all that matters, the scroll instructed.

Elena stared at the flame until she could see its shape beneath her eyes. She unfolded her arms, raising them above her head like wings. The fire sighed and then lengthened. She unlocked her leg to move into the third pose, but she moved too quickly. She lost her balance and stumbled back. The flame sputtered and died.

Cursing, she took the orb and went back to the hearth. Once more, she dipped the orb in the fire and withdrew a single flame. Back at the fountain, she resumed the pose but lost her balance. The flame left behind a thin trail of smoke. She tried again.

And again.

A light sheen of sweat covered her face, and her robe felt slick against her skin as she balanced on one leg. With a deep breath, Elena lifted her arms above her head. The flame curled. Slowly, she unwound her limbs, and the fire grew. She sank into the third pose.

The Lotus.

She splayed out her fingers like a flower as she sank back into her heels. The flame pulsed. A strand of her hair fell before her left eye, but Elena ignored it. Her gaze never wavering, she spun, arms out, chest high—and the flame twisted with her. It expanded, beating against its glass prison.

Think of the brightest light you've ever seen, the scroll said of this form.

Elena thought of the Eternal Fire, the way it spat and crackled as if alive. The way it swooned when the priests chanted. She concentrated not on its form, but on its life. The heat it gave. The power it granted.

Her hands like lotuses, she moved toward the fire. She imagined it breaking through the glass and dancing in her palm, but as she approached, the flame exploded. The orb shattered, glass shards cutting into her outstretched arms.

Elena shrieked.

The fire swelled, licking the air. She lunged toward the fountain, plunging her hands in. She began to splash the fire with water, but it only rose higher. She jumped in the basin and kicked the water onto the flames until finally, they sputtered and died.

A dark patch of ash lay where the fire had once been. Elena sank into the bowl of the fountain, water spilling over her shoulders. Thick, red drops of her blood swirled within the stone basin. She stared at the ring of ash, and a low sound began at the back of her throat.

It was somewhere between a laugh and a sob.

19
LEO

Swindlers run with sand in their veins.

—A RAVANI PROVERB

Leo arrived early to watch the burning of the priests. He stood in a grove of banyan trees that grew a hundred paces behind the Temple. In the middle of the grove, a singular gulmohar tree held court. Its fiery red leaves danced in the breeze as the priests trudged in. He watched them shiver in their thin, orange robes.

When all the priests had filtered in, Leo turned to his Spear.

"Make sure none of them leave," he ordered. He then strode out of the grove, his long black tunic fluttering behind him.

Leo entered the dark, cool halls of the Temple. As he approached the Seat, the air grew warmer. The shadows waned, and then he entered the large, circular room where the Eternal Fire roared in greeting. It beat against the air, its flames snapping like whips. Saayna kneeled below the dais, gathering ash in a brass urn. When Leo came up beside her, she straightened but did not look his way.

"The Phoenix shall judge you harshly for this," the High Priestess said. Her voice was a mere whisper over the crackle of the Fire. She wore no shackles this time. Golden robes wrapped around her shoulders and waist, and firelight played across her high cheekbones, giving her an almost regal appearance.

"She is the god of vengeance," he replied. "I would think less of Her if She didn't."

Leo walked up the dais as Saayna watched. He had brought her because customs were still customs. As High Priestess, she would need to oversee his last Ashanta ceremony. And as king, he needed to receive the blessings of the heavens for his last ceremony with Elena.

The Eternal Fire growled, its heat buffeting against his face. Leo did not waver. He dipped his hands into the Fire. Heat prickled up his wrist, but he was used to the pain.

He was to commit the highest treason against the heavens. His soul would be eternally whipped and burned in all the seven hells. But all of this was for Elena. For their throne. If the Prophet was allowed to rise, she would destroy everything that he and his ancestors had built. And he would not allow that, no matter what it meant for him and his soul.

The king withdrew a flame in his right palm. He returned to the grove, Saayna trailing after. They stood before the priests. The Order had not seen their High Priestess in weeks, and they regarded her warily, as if they knew she was the cause of their suffering.

"Is this everyone?" he asked.

Saayna nodded.

"Check the tunnels," he said to Marcus. "Make sure none of them are hiding."

The Spear barked orders for a group of his men to search the tunnels beneath the Temple. Alonjo surveyed the priests and then bent toward Leo.

"I count forty-eight, but there should be fifty," the Astra whispered. "The High Priestess accounts for one, but what of the other?"

Leo studied the nervous faces before him. "The young boy," he said, and he thought back to the priest with the runes burned on his back. "He must be dead."

Saayna watched wordlessly. A soft rain began to fall. The trees shielded the priests and the royal party, but Leo felt a raindrop slip beneath his collar. He fought back a shiver.

When his men returned, Marcus turned to the king. "The tunnels are empty, Your Majesty."

Leo nodded. A sour, acrid taste filled his mouth. He had not slept nor eaten well since his vision in the desert. Nightmares plagued his sleep, and when he awoke in the morning, he saw shadows of twisted trees stretching across his bedroom walls. Yet when he blinked, they vanished.

The heavens were challenging him, waiting to see if he would crumble. Leo stepped forward as the trees rustled and the rain whispered against the leaves. The flame hissed in his palm.

Well, let the heavens see. Let them laugh after today.

"I have called you all here to search for the truth," he said. His eyes traveled over the orange-robed priests. "The Prophet comes, and I believe she is one of you."

He watched their reactions. Some gasped, others stood still, and a few looked down at their hands; he zeroed in on these priests.

"You. The one with a face like a ruined turnip. Come here."

The priestess looked at him and then at the others. But when Leo did not avert his gaze, she stepped forward.

"Your Majesty," she said in a frail voice and bowed. He noticed the star-shaped birthmark on her cheek. This was the girl from before, the one who had watched over the burnt, dead priest.

"Give me your hand," he said.

The priestess looked at Saayna, but her leader said nothing. She stood, stoic, her mouth set and eyes fixed upon the horizon.

Leo took the priestess's outstretched palm and guided it to the flame. Her hand shook slightly.

"Are you the Prophet?" he asked, searching her eyes.

"N-no."

"Prove it," he said and forced her hand into the flame.

The priestess yelped and tried to pull her arm away, but Leo gripped her wrist and held her hand until he saw her skin blacken. Only then did he release her.

The priestess stumbled back. She cradled her hand to her belly. Her shoulders shook, but she did not weep. Saayna stepped forward and placed her hands on the girl's shoulders.

"You have done your duty," she said and kissed her three fingers before placing them on the priestess's forehead. "The Phoenix's Light shines upon you."

The priestess's lower lip trembled, yet she bowed and retreated. Leo thought he saw a tear fall to the ground, but it could have just as easily been the rain.

He motioned for the next priestess to step forward. And the next, and the next. They came, one after the other, a silent procession of bowed heads and neatly wrapped orange robes. He held their hands over the flame, and to Leo's growing dismay, they all burned.

When the last priestess shambled back to the crowd, cradling her hand to her chest, Leo turned sharply to Saayna. His voice cut through the air, dripping with venom.

"You've lied to me," he snarled. "Where is the Prophet? Where are you hiding her?"

When the High Priestess made no move to answer, Leo felt his anger grow cold, calculating. The flame danced in his hand. Slowly, he turned back to the priests, and the flame lengthened, eager.

"I intend to burn all of you," he announced, his voice charged and smoldering. "I intend to burn you until I find this Prophet. But, if you are here, Prophet, I am giving you the chance to step forward. Announce yourself, and I will spare your brethren. If you don't, I will burn them all alive. Priestesses and priests alike. And then you will sweep away their ashes."

There was no sound other than the patter of raindrops against the long banyan leaves. Leo scrutinized every face, but no one came forward. The flame swooned. Before him, the smoke from the Eternal Fire twisted into the grey sky.

"So be it."

He nodded, and his guards stepped forward. They formed a ring around the priests as they pulled torches from their belts. One by one, the guards struck matches and ignited the torches. Fire blossomed around Leo. The flames hissed against the rain, but they held.

Marcus stalked forward and grabbed one priest by the nape of his neck. He cried out, scratching Marcus's arms, but the Spear kicked him and forced the priest to his knees. The torch crackled. Slowly, Marcus forced the priest's face into the flame. He screamed as his eyelashes started to smoke.

The priests bolted then. They pushed against the ring of guards. Some screamed, others begged. One priestess shrieked as a guard grabbed her by the hair and swung her down. She tried to claw away, but the guard wrapped his hand around her ankle like a vise and dragged her back. She screeched as her robes caught fire.

A few priests managed to get through the ring and ran down the mountainside. Marcus turned to Leo, who nodded.

"I want wet swords," the king said.

The Spear unsheathed his slingsword and roared out the order. The whistle of thirty slingswords and the smell of burnt flesh filled the grove. Leo watched a priestess stumble as a blade ripped through her backside. Her body crumpled and rolled into the tree line.

One priest turned, a wild, desperate look twisting his face. He charged toward Leo, but Marcus stepped in front of his king and struck his attacker down. He yanked the priest up so that his eyes met Leo's.

"Do you know what happens to those who try to hurt their king?" Leo asked softly.

The priest shuddered.

Leo closed his hands, smothering the flame. A pang shot up his arms, and when he opened his palms, a ring of ash marked where the fire had died. He took the bloodied slingsword from Marcus.

"Your Majesty," Alonjo said, stepping forward, but Leo waved him away.

The king never bloodied his hands. He left that for his Spear and his servants. But the heavens were watching. They had openly sent out their challenge, and Leo wanted them to pay.

He placed the edge of the blade against the priest's neck. The man closed his eyes, whispering a prayer, and then Leo slashed down with a snarl. Blood sprayed across the ground. Thick, warm drops splattered across Leo's face and his black coat. The priest's head rolled to the side. His eyes stared up at the sky, wide and sightless.

Leo dropped the slingsword. His body suddenly shook, and he gripped his knees. Blood stained his shoes.

Let them see. He straightened. *Let them know that I won't cower.* He unbuttoned his coat and shook out the ceremonial robes he wore underneath, clean and unblemished.

"Do you see, Saayna?" he asked.

The High Priestess stared at the horizon, but her eyes were strained as if she held back tears. She clenched her fists so tightly that her knuckles bleached to a bone-white.

"Their death is not on my hands," he said. "They die because of you. All the blood that has been spilled today, and all the blood that will spill after, is because you held your tongue."

Finally, she turned. Finally, she met his eyes.

"I am merely doing my duty, as you are doing yours," she said.

Through the trees, Leo spotted a black dot on the horizon. A hoverpod. Elena was early.

"Clean this up," he said to Marcus, but he saw his Spear pause. "What is it?"

"The men, Your Majesty, they're beginning to grow squeamish. There are still twenty or so priests left—"

"Then get the Yumi," he snarled. "Make her do what the men cannot."

Marcus bowed his head, his voice small. "As you wish, Your Majesty."

Alonjo picked up the slingsword and wiped it clean with his handkerchief. "We will still need enough priests for the ceremony. Seven to be precise. Shall I lock up the rest in the tunnels?"

Leo nodded and then held out his hand to Saayna, palm outstretched, the ring of ash dark against his olive skin.

"Come," he said to the High Priestess. "Let us do our duty."

20
YASSEN

A sadness resides deep within these walls.
A hollow truth made more crude as the centuries pass. When
discovered, it shall chase away one's peace,
and their life shall never be the same.

—FROM *THE PROPHECY OF THE PHOENIX*, TRANSCRIBED INTO
WRITTEN WORD BY THE FIRST PRIESTS OF THE FIRE ORDER

Yassen blinked sleep from his eyes as the hoverpod flew across the desert toward the Agnee Range. Clouds pregnant with storm lumbered along the horizon. He felt a tightness in his arm, but temples always made him uneasy.

Up front, by the curved windows, Elena stood with Samson. She was dressed in her gold ceremonial garb with a long lehenga and embroidered blouse. The thin sunrays that managed to peek through the heavy clouds highlighted the lily-of-pearls woven in her hair. Samson said something that made her laugh. Yassen tried not to stare as Samson leaned closer and whispered something into her ear. His hand found hers, and Yassen turned away.

The mountains rose, and thick trees older than the kingdom itself reached up to greet them. The hoverpod skimmed over their boughs. The last time Yassen had been to the Temple was the day he met the Arohassin. He and Samson had taken a pod to the Temple for the Fire

Festival. During the flight, devotees had chattered excitedly about the fire ceremonies and ash blessings, but Yassen and Samson did not pay attention.

They had only come for the food.

Yassen remembered scarfing down sweetened lemon rice and cloud biscuits until he felt too sick to move. Samson had to drag him out of the Temple. Yassen had hobbled forward, feeling as if he was going to vomit. That was when he saw him—the tall man with the dark eyes. His brown skin stretched across his face like tough leather, like every burn victim. His eyes met Yassen's; there was a familiarity in them, a mix of grief and anger that Yassen held in his own.

"What are you two doing stealing from the Temple?" the man had asked, pointing to their pockets stuffed with cloud biscuits.

"The Phoenix wouldn't want us to go hungry," Samson had replied glibly.

As the tall man peered down at them, Yassen felt his stomach twist. He vomited right on the stranger's shoes.

The man did not try to get out of the way. He had simply looked down at his shoes and then at Yassen. Samson's face was frozen in horror. Yassen had tried to apologize, but the words lodged in his throat.

Finally, the man moved. He had calmly shaken off half-digested remnants of rice and banyan leaf. He looked between Yassen and Samson, his eyes grazing their skin like a whip. Yassen felt his breath hitch. Suddenly, the man grabbed Samson by the neck and dragged him forward. Samson protested, trying to twist out of the man's grasp, but the man said nothing as he led them down the stone steps to the statue of the Phoenix perched along the mountain's edge.

When they had reached the platform, the man released Samson. A fountain lay beneath the Phoenix, but the water in its basin remained still.

"Do you know what that is?" the man asked.

"Are you trying to kill me?" Samson shrieked. "It's a holy day!"

The man turned to Yassen, and his dark eyes bore into him. "Can you tell me?"

"It's the Phoenix," Yassen said, wiping vomit from his chin.

"What is it really?"

Yassen gazed up at the grey statue. It had grown discolored, with spots of moss blooming around its base. Only the eyes of the Phoenix remained bright. The builder had fashioned red mirrors in the Phoenix's eyes, and Yassen saw his reflection staring back at him. Small and dark.

"A man," Yassen had answered.

The stranger had smiled. "There is only what we men make for ourselves." He held out his hand. "I'm Akaros."

The hoverpod descended and docked on the stone ledge beneath the stairs. They walked out as a soft rain fell. Yassen breathed in clean mountain air and something more acrid. He stopped. He could recognize the smell of burnt flesh from anywhere. Overhead, smoke from the Eternal Fire curled up to meet the grey heavens. His arm ached. The king's guards lined the staircase, and as they ascended, Yassen noted frayed sleeves, rumpled jackets, and the occasional scuffed boots. A struggle had happened here.

The High Priestess and the king came to greet them at the landing. If there had been an attack, they gave no sign of it. Elena went to them with Samson by her side, but when Yassen followed, Ferma grabbed his arm. He tried not to wince as she pulled him aside.

"The king asked me to stay after the ceremony," the Spear said. "You'll escort Elena back to Palace Hill. I'll send a squad of guards for extra security." She gripped his elbow, her nails digging into his sleeve. "Watch the sands, Yassen. You'll have to be there for Elena when I'm not."

She released his arm. Yassen straightened his sleeve, hiding the mark on his wrist.

"I'm taloned, Ferma. Don't worry."

They returned to the others. The High Priestess held out a branch of red fyerian flowers and dusted both Elena's and the king's shoulders. After a moment's pause, she did the same to Samson.

"Come," she said, "the Holy Bird awaits."

As she pulled her hand back, Yassen spotted something dark on her wrist, but Saayna folded her hands into her robes and led them into the Temple.

The hall to the Temple's center lay dark and quiet, but as they neared, Yassen could hear the Fire's crackle and hiss. It sounded like a battlefield with the snaps and pops of pulse fire. The air grew warmer, but Yassen felt as if the heat grew from within him, eating his bones and boiling his blood. They turned the corner, and the Eternal Fire roared and lashed at the domed ceiling, its heat hitting Yassen square in the chest.

He backed into the wall, clutching his right arm. The pain returned with a vengeance, as if a dozen needles pierced his skin.

"Are you alright?" Ferma asked.

Yassen nodded. The Eternal Fire was confined to a pit, but it seemed as if it was ready to pounce. The Fire swelled, its flames splitting into forking tongues that licked the air.

He could barely see the raised dais within its center. A few priests stood beside the steps leading to the raised platform, but even they seemed to linger an arm's length away.

"Mother's Gold," he whispered. "How is Elena supposed to sit in there?"

Leo bowed to the Eternal Fire, and then he took Elena's hand. Together, they walked up the stone steps. The Fire swallowed them immediately, but Yassen could see their shadows dancing along the dais. The High Priestess waved her hand, and the priests sat in a semicircle around the pit. Alonjo and Samson joined the priests. The militant leaned toward the Fire. Yassen recognized the look in his friend's eyes. The depth in his stare. It was the face of a man who recognized power and gave himself willingly to it.

A sharp jolt of pain shot up his arm, and Yassen gripped the stone wall. The Eternal Fire hissed and lengthened. For a moment, the flames parted, and Yassen saw Elena looking straight at him. The Fire chased the light from her eyes.

"Kneel," Ferma hissed.

Yassen sank to his knees as the priests began to chant. The Fire crackled, but as their voices rose, it wavered. Listened. The flames withdrew, caving inwards as the High Priestess stepped back.

He could no longer see Elena. Only a trembling shadow.

The flames curled as the priests chanted and threw white ash into the pit. The air grew thick with smoke and incense. Yassen licked his lips, his mouth dry.

"O' Bearer of Hope, we are Your servants," the High Priestess sang. Her voice was clear and beautiful, rising over the din of the Fire. "We will guard Your interests, protect Your lands. We will walk the Agnee-path and find succor at its end."

The High Priestess threw dried marigold petals into the pit, and the Eternal Fire soared up like the wings of a bird, golden and free. Yassen spotted Elena on the dais, her brow furrowed and her mouth set in a grim line. Leo sat calmly beside her, his face stoic and cool.

"We will feed Your followers, give strength to the weak. And when enemies dare to steal Your power, we will destroy their seats."

The Eternal Fire hissed. It flared upward, beating against the ceiling, and then plunged down toward the dais.

Ferma shot to her feet. Even the priests sucked in their breath, their chant faltering. Light pulsed like waves from the Fire's core, but neither Elena nor Leo yielded. Yassen saw their faint, fluctuating shadows. The Fire roared, enraged, its light growing blindingly bright, its heat searing the skin beneath his eyelids, and still, Yassen kept his eyes on Elena. Her flickering form. He felt that if he took his eyes off her, she would vanish.

Suddenly, her shadow rose, and Elena emerged from the flames, coughing. She managed to stumble down the steps and lurch past the priests to the adjoining chamber. The High Priestess continued to chant, but Yassen could sense her disappointment in the inflection of her voice.

The flames growled, yet Leo remained.

"I should check on Elena," Ferma began, but Yassen held her back.

"She wouldn't want you to."

The Yumi kneeled, and they both stared into the Fire as it swooned to the rhythm of the chants. Slow and hypnotic. Yassen blinked, his head light. Slowly, the world began to ebb away. The priests' song became a distant drone as shadows pressed along the corners of his eyes.

The Fire reared up and swallowed him.

Heat pressed into Yassen's bones, but it did not suffocate him. Not this time.

As he stood within the Fire, Yassen felt the pain in his arm drain away. It found the ache hidden deep in his heart. He saw the faces of his mother and father in the flames, the faces of the boys he had befriended and lost in the Arohassin. He saw the suns of loneliness, of anger, of hate and misfortune. And he felt the Fire cleanse it away. It washed him as if he were reborn. Soft and new, unknowing in the ways of men.

The flames parted to reveal the bottom of the pit. Yassen saw a dark red feather—a feather not of this world, ancient and pure. He felt it give the Fire power, succor. And he felt the feather run through him, pull him, call him to the deep darkness that lay beyond this world.

Ferma squeezed his shoulder, and Yassen sat up.

"You fainted," she said as he rubbed his eyes. "And you look pale—I mean, paler than usual."

Yassen looked around the chamber. It was empty—only the Eternal Fire remained, sighing. The Ashanta ceremony must have calmed it.

"Where's Elena?" he asked, his voice hoarse.

"With the High Priestess," Ferma said with a small frown. "She almost made it."

"And the king?"

"He's with her as well. He sat until the Fire had calmed down," she said and hesitated. "Elena's right. The king needs to teach her the way of Agneepath if she is to become queen."

But she's learning on her own, he wanted to say but held his tongue. Though Elena knew the mechanics of fire, she was no wielder. He supposed he should feel vindicated. The Arohassin had been right—the Ravani were not the true wielders of the Fire. Their throne was a lie built on a decaying religion—but he only felt pity for Elena. Pity that her father could carry out their family name and not her.

"She still has time," he said.

"The Fire will choose her," Ferma said, though her eyes told a different story. "Let's go. They should be out front."

"I'll join you in a bit," he said. "I want to pray."

The Yumi regarded him, her tawny eyes glowing in the light of the flames.

"I thought those in the Arohassin didn't pray," she said.

"I was Ravani before I joined the Arohassin," he said, "and I'm still Ravani."

Ferma studied him for a moment and then nodded. "Hurry. Before you change faith."

He gave a small, rueful smile as the Spear disappeared down the dark corridor.

Slowly, Yassen walked up to the pit. He did not dare go up to the dais. The Eternal Fire was quiet now, but he knew it would only be a matter of time before it snapped.

The flames purred. The vision of the feather came again. Without thinking, Yassen held out his arm, his right one, the burnt one. A single flame rose, like a beast raising its head at the sound of prey. It uncoiled and sniffed the air. Yassen felt time slow and the seconds stretch as the flame slowly slithered closer until it was only mere inches from his hand.

The Fire snarled and exploded, heat striking his face. He stumbled back, coughing. A figure stood on the other edge of the pit. He recognized the high cheekbones and dark, determined eyes as Elena spun and cupped her hands. The Fire hissed again.

"Wait!" he cried out.

He ran to her just as she called a flame. It curled within her cupped hands, and a grin split across her face. Her eyes met his, and Elena opened her mouth to say something when the flame suddenly elongated and spiraled down her arm, singing her skin. She screamed and staggered back.

Yassen grabbed her hand, beating back the flame with his sleeve. Elena flung the flame back into the pit as the Fire roared and smashed down. They both fell back. The inferno swelled, eating shadow and air. Elena grabbed his arm and yanked him to his feet, pushing him forward until they stumbled into the corridor.

The Eternal Fire roared behind them.

They gulped in the cool air of the hallway. Yassen gripped his knees. His body buzzed as if the heat of the Fire was inside of him, but he knew it was only the adrenaline.

Elena pushed past him without speaking. Her long hair tumbled down her shoulders as she ran down the corridor, the sound of her footsteps slowly receding. Yassen stood there a moment longer, waiting for his heart to calm, for the buzz to seep out of his body, but it gave no signs of leaving. Finally, he hobbled out.

Rain dusted his cheeks, and Yassen sighed in relief. Out of the corner of his eye, he saw Elena stride past the guards and down the steps. Ferma hustled after her.

"What did you do to piss her off?"

He turned to see Samson. Smoke writhed from his lips as he drew on a long, black pipe.

"I thought you stopped smoking ganshi," Yassen said.

"I use it sometimes to calm my nerves," Samson said. "Looks like you need it too." He handed the pipe to Yassen, who raised it to his lips and slowly drew in the sweet, narcotic taste of moonspun ganshi. Yassen exhaled; a thin wisp of smoke twisted and dissipated in the air.

"Better?" Samson asked, eyeing him. Yassen nodded. "Good."

They stood in silence, watching the clouds darken and the guards shift their feet. The rain fell steadily now and gave the mountain an eerie glow. Below the lip of the cliff, Yassen caught a flash of Elena's gold skirts.

"Interesting thing, fire," Samson said. "It both destroys and gives life. Cleanses, yet leaves ash in its wake. Do you remember the last time we were here together?"

"We met Akaros," Yassen began.

"And then everything changed," Samson finished. He chuckled, smoke puffing out. "Funny, isn't it? That our journey with the Arohassin started in the holiest of places."

"Maybe it's not as holy as we think."

"Maybe." Samson took one long pull and then dumped out ash from his pipe. "The world's changing, Cass. If we're not quick enough, we'll be stranded."

He gripped Yassen's shoulder and squeezed. Yassen watched him walk down the Temple steps and then descend the staircase Elena had taken, his coat fluttering behind him. Maybe he meant to console his fiancée, or at least pretend to do so, but Yassen wondered if he went down those steps to visit the statue of the Phoenix.

Yassen hugged his arm to his side. It ached again, but this time, the pain was sharp, more precise. He thought of the Fire, and the deep, ancient pull he felt toward its core. It may have been a hallucination, but the sensation was too visceral to be imagined. A truth lay within the flames, a truth that predated him and the very steps he stood upon.

And it was growing impatient.

Yassen glanced back down the dark corridor. In the sound of the falling rain and the emptiness before him, he thought he heard the Fire cackle.

21
ELENA

Oh, dear lady, why do you look so pale? You glow like the sun,
both from within and without, selfless, like the honey
a mother drips into her child's dream.

—FROM *THE ODYSSEY OF GOROMOUNT: A PLAY*

Elena dipped her trembling hands into the basin of the fountain. The water cooled her skin, but when she withdrew, her hands still shook. The statue of the Phoenix rose above her, and she could see her reflection in its red eyes.

Elena plunged her hands back into the cold water, her fingers slowly turning numb. She breathed in deeply to still her thundering heart, but it did not calm. It beat harshly, her blood pounding in her veins.

Useless. She was so useless. Elena heard footsteps, and she quickly turned, hiding her hands behind her back.

"Are you alright?" Ferma asked. Ash and sweat streaked the Yumi's face, but she looked steady. Grounded.

"I'm fine," Elena said. "I just needed some fresh air."

"You did better this time. You almost had it."

"Almost isn't good enough."

She needed practice, not meetings fretting over the details of the Fire Festival and her coronation. She needed to be alone in the desert, to lose herself in its dunes, to feel its breath against her skin. She needed time.

The Phoenix stared down at her with hard, unflinching eyes.

Curse this bird. Curse it and its useless traditions.

What god used violence to rule and conquer? What god used fire to bring justice? Elena felt a deep, sudden hatred toward the Phoenix and its Temple that rose above her, so still and calm against the backdrop of the towering mountains. Did the Phoenix not know how many people had killed and bled to capture Her Fire? Did She not understand how easily Sayonai fell to Her tune of purity and so-called truth? Elena wanted to drive a blade into those red eyes, to shatter the mirrors that reflected only her and nothing higher. She wanted to weep.

Hot tears rose to her eyes in frustration, but Elena fought them. She would not cry here. She would not give the Phoenix that victory.

"I thought you were down here."

She looked up to see Samson descending the steps.

"Leave us, Ferma," he ordered.

Elena saw the Yumi bristle and her hair begin to curl. No one commanded Ferma other than her and her father.

Elena touched the Spear's elbow. "It's alright."

Ferma hesitated and then whispered in Elena's ear. "I have to stay behind," she said. "Yassen and the guards will be with you, but watch yourself." She gripped Elena's shoulder. "And don't fret. You'll find a way. You always do."

Elena tried to smile convincingly. She squeezed Ferma's hand and watched her vanish up the stone staircase.

Samson stood beside her and examined the statue.

"Needs to be cleaned. Doesn't it?" He pointed at marks left from birds and other creatures of the mountain. "I swear these priests are getting lazier." He glanced at her and softened his voice. "I heard your father say how proud he was to see you sit in the flames for so long."

"Bullshit."

"The High Priestess confirmed it. She was impressed."

"No, she's disappointed," Elena said, recalling Saayna's soft, solemn words after she had retreated from the flames: *The only way to rule is by holding the fire. Your hands will know the truth, and you will answer to it.*

"No Ravani can rule without fire," Elena said after a moment.

"Well, I wouldn't say it's too late," Samson replied. "I read that Queen Jumi only managed to sit in the Fire on the day of her coronation."

Elena stayed quiet. The numbness in her hands began to ebb away, replaced with tiny prickles of heat traveling up her palms.

"I should get going," she murmured.

"You know, the Arohassin once instructed me to shoot an innocent woman in the back," Samson said. He stared up at the Phoenix and its sharp, red eyes. "I couldn't do it. They beat me the next day. A hundred and fifty lashes. Real old school.

"The pain was horrid. I couldn't sit or stand. I lay on my stomach for two weeks wallowing in misery and self-pity. I had nightmares that made me question if I had made the right choice. Maybe I should have just shot the girl. But by the time the two weeks were over and the bandages came off, I knew I had made the right decision."

He looked down, his dark blue eyes set straight on hers.

"Sometimes, the moments that define us are the moments in which we spare ourselves. They force us to examine who we truly are and what we stand for." He reached behind her and gently took her hands. He uncurled her fists and traced her darkened skin. "Don't lose hope. Perhaps this is the moment when you decide what you need rather than what you seek."

She squeezed his hand.

"Thank you," she whispered.

He smiled and kissed her darkened fingertips. "I'll see you back at the Palace, yes?"

She nodded, and Samson gave a low bow. She brushed past him, descending the steps quickly. As she neared the hoverpod landing, Elena looked up. Samson stood beneath the Phoenix, gazing into the still fountain.

She wondered what he saw in his reflection.

"The hoverpod is ready to take you back to the Palace, Your Highness." Elena turned at the sound of Yassen's voice and found him standing before her, clear-eyed and covered in ash.

"Let's stop in the capital," she said. "I need some time away from, well, everything."

He began to protest but then stopped. His eyes traveled to her burnt palms.

"Alright."

They entered the hoverpod, and Elena settled into her seat. She sighed and closed her eyes. The hoverpod hummed, and they rose into the grey sky. Beneath them, the Temple grew smaller.

Yassen offered her a cup of tea and sank into the seat beside her.

"Did the Fire burn you too?" she asked.

"A bit," he said, his face a mask.

She wanted to ask for his hand, to see if he had been burned, but then she remembered he already had. He did not need to relive that pain again. Elena watched smoke escape from the Temple and coil toward the heavens, ash on her lips.

Elena had no particular destination in mind when they reached Rani. She told the royal chauffeur to just drive and the guards to follow. The buildings rose and fell beyond her window as they glided through the spiraling streets.

Yassen seemed to be asleep in the seat beside her, the blue light of the control board throwing shadows on his face, but Elena could tell by his breathing that he was awake, listening. She smoothed a wrinkle on her lehenga when the car stopped.

Yassen shot up, and Elena smiled to herself.

"What is it?" he asked the driver.

"The motorcade stopped up ahead, sir. I think the festivities have begun."

Yassen cursed under his breath and reached for the door panel.

"Leave it," she said. "I'm sure it's nothing."

"It looks like some kind of parade, Your Highness," the driver said. "The Birdsong."

Elena craned her neck to see balloons of red and gold through the sunroof. A soft drizzle dusted the streets. She could hear the steady beat of dhols in the distance.

"I forgot," she muttered. The Birdsong marked the unofficial prelude of the Fire Festival. It was supposed to be a small affair, with the first day of the Festival starting next week, but no citizen of Rani knew how to celebrate things quietly.

"It wasn't supposed to come down Desert Row," Yassen said. She glanced at him, surprised to see him so agitated.

"Take us down some other street, Maro," she said, and before Yassen could object, added, "The others will follow us."

"No, it won't be safe," Yassen said, but Maro already turned the nodes on the control panel, and the hovercar swiveled.

"Wait," Yassen said. He withdrew his holopod and sent out a flurry of messages to the guards. He opened a map of Rani and scrutinized the crisscrossed streets. She saw him highlight a path and then stiffen.

"What?" she asked.

"I think we'll need to head toward the southern outskirts to drive around this," he said.

"Anything wrong with that?"

He shook his head, his face tight. "I-I just haven't been there in a while. Haven't gotten the chance to do recon."

"Send some guards to scout the area then," she said to Maro. He nodded and sent the orders.

Elena leaned back in her seat, watching as Yassen sat upright, all pretense of sleep gone. Sure enough, the other cars had turned, and their silver party began to circumvent the parade route. Towering sandscrapers and embellished chhatris slowly gave way to smooth adobe walls. Gone were the cramped bazaars and beggar children chasing after beacons of wealth. Here, small, modest homes and neat gardens hedged with sandstone lined the streets.

Elena pressed her head against the window. Raindrops curved down the glass, but the sun had broken out, and the sky was awash in orange.

She could still hear the High Priestess's chants and the crackle of the Eternal Fire along with the soft hiss of the shadows. Yassen's shout as he had beaten the flames on her hand. She glanced at him. He sat oddly erect, his face pinched. When he saw her looking, Yassen turned back to the window.

"What's wrong?" she asked. They had been driving for nearly thirty minutes now and had reached the slums. Dilapidated homes with tin roofs and mismatched brick hunched beside the broken road.

"This used to be my block," Yassen said, but his voice wasn't really there. He wasn't really there. She could already see him sinking away, retreating from avenues of memories.

"Then we must stop," she said. "Maro!"

The hovercar slowed, as did their train.

"Come, you have to show me where you grew up," she said.

At first, Yassen did not move. His face was still in the shadow of the sinking sun. Yet, she could tell that something had changed. She could feel it in the air. Was it regret she heard in his voice? She wanted to see his pain. To unearth his past. To know all there was to know of Yassen Knight.

"I'm getting out," she announced. The door swung up like the wing of a bird and closed softly behind her. As the guards joined her, she knew Yassen would follow.

The street was strangely empty. No urchin or beggar stood on the corner, no gold cap prophesied about the next coming of the Prophet.

"What's the name of this place?" she asked the guard on her right.

"Wren," Yassen answered. If there had been any pain or regret in his voice previously, Elena must have imagined it. His face was slack, his gait graceful and clean. He came up beside her and nodded at the uneven brick walls and the shuttered windows. "A quiet place."

"How did such a subdued place produce such a misguided man?" she asked.

"A lot of things can happen in slums," he said. "Maybe you'd understand if you had been here a couple of suns ago."

He ordered the guards to fan out. The ones who had been sent to recon the area reported that nothing was amiss. They had ordered the citizens to stay in their homes.

"Good," Yassen said as he scanned the horizon. He turned back to Elena. "A short walk should do. And then we need to head back to Palace Hill."

"Maybe." She pulled her dupatta over her head and swept back her black curls. "But first you have to show me around."

Yassen nodded and motioned for the guards. They formed a ring around Elena and Yassen as they walked.

"This place looks a bit different now," Yassen said. "The house on the corner there used to be a store owned by a Sesharian family. I was friends with their son, a boy named Roldan."

"A friend? You?" she asked.

"I wasn't corrupted then," he said with a small smile.

She skirted a puddle as they drew up to a playground with fluorescent colors and dry grass.

"This park wasn't here either," he said.

"What was here before then?"

"Just a stretch of sand."

Elena watched him closely, but there was no inflection in his voice,
no change in his demeanor. The guards closed around them. The sun
bounced off the tin roofs of the homes, washing them with a soft pink
hue. The falling rain glistened like tiny crystals.

She rarely took walks like this. She rarely played in playgrounds
or abandoned fields. There was always someone lingering, a guard or
a nanny, ready to swoop in at any sign of trouble or mischief.

She had tried to escape. Once, when Ferma had fallen asleep, Elena
had slipped out her bedroom window and climbed down an adjacent
pipe. It had taken them hours to find her. She had hidden beneath the
raised roots of a weeping tree in a garden, giggling to herself as she
watched the guards and Ferma search for her. But as the hours grew
longer and the guards grew more numerous, more worried, Elena felt
afraid. Afraid of becoming invisible, forgotten. Afraid of her parents,
who had come tearing through the garden, a jumble of mortal anxiety
and heavens-given rage.

She had quietly slipped out from beneath the tree and tugged on
her mother's skirt. Relief had flooded Aahnah's face, but the king's
mouth had twisted into a scowl. Elena had cowered behind her mother,
saying nothing as her father cracked down on Ferma.

That was the only time she had seen the Yumi cry.

"Shall we?" Yassen asked, pulling her from her reverie.

They continued down the street, but when they rounded a corner,
Yassen froze. The road ahead was a dead end. Elena looked down the
row of houses, each as unremarkable as the last, until she came upon
a black form at the end of the lane.

"What's that?"

She saw his shoulders roll back, as if he was bracing for what came
next.

"That was my home."

Elena waved the guards off, and they stood on the road, watching
the perimeter as she and Yassen walked up to the ruins. The frame of
the house was still there—crumbled brick and burnt sandstone. There

lay no holoframes, no stuffed animal to mark the presence of a child. Just some overgrown brush and graffiti that spelled *Misfit*.

"Why is it still here?" she said.

"You should know. It's the law," Yassen said. "The home of a criminal is considered evidence. They couldn't destroy it."

Elena nudged a piece of sandstone with her foot, and it crumbled. She shook off the soot. "What happened?"

"A fire."

"I know, but how?"

Yassen didn't answer and walked up to the doorstep. Of all things, the door still stood, sturdy and grim, as if it knew the secrets it must harbor. He bent down and traced the edge of the frame. Overhead, a hoverpod flew in a circle, probably some aerial team the guards had alerted for backup. On its hill, the Palace looked like a large, misplaced beacon.

Elena walked around the house to the backyard. The brick fence, like the door, still stood, though it was pockmarked with holes. Elena bent down and picked up a stone. Something was scrawled along its side. Two letters. R.K.

"There used to be a beaten-up piano, but I suppose it burned too," Yassen said. Elena turned to see that he had followed her into the yard, but he was not looking at her. He gazed upward at the burnished sky. "I wanted to perform all around the world."

"Were you any good?" Elena asked.

"You could say so," he said and then, after a pause, "I played at the Royal Hall when I was seven."

She laughed, the sound breaking through the evening quiet.

"What?"

"It was you! My piano tutor wouldn't stop talking about some musical prodigy he saw at the Hall. He'd hound me to be as good as him—as good as you," she said and looked at Yassen. He couldn't meet her gaze.

"Did you ever see me play?"

Her laughter died down. Elena bounced the stone in her hand, aware of how his voice had changed, ever so slightly, with that question. Was it hope? Remorse? Guilt? And why did it make her feel the same?

"No," she said.

"Funny, just how closely our lives ran together," he whispered.

The thought made her shiver. Elena looked down at the rock in her hand. R.K. She tossed the stone over the fence into the field beyond. Together, they heard it connect with another rock and the resounding click as it separated into various pieces. A part of her wondered what it would have been like if she had met Yassen then. Would he have hated her? Would she have looked down on him as some charity case? Or would he have played her a tune and asked if she could finish it?

"Time to go," Yassen said.

Elena gazed out at the dunes beyond the burnt house, and then turned. Yassen, like always, awaited. He held out his hand to guide her over the bricks, and Elena grabbed it only to tug him closer. Yassen stiffened. She brought his hand to her face and traced his long, spindly fingers. They were slender, deft. A pianist's hand. Elena saw the mark along his wrist and pulled his sleeve down. Yassen yanked his hand back, scowling, but she had caught the glimpse of the burns.

"You can't play anymore. Can you?" she asked.

And just like before, whatever change in his demeanor, whatever glimmer of vulnerability she had seen, was gone. Yassen smoothed down his sleeve and strode away. Elena followed. They said nothing as they got into the hovercar. Yassen held his hands on his lap, one over the other, as if protecting them. Elena leaned back and watched the world blur from unassuming homes to the bustling night streets to, finally, the quiet, winding road leading up to the Palace.

She closed her eyes, recalling the weeping tree in the garden and its dark, warm embrace. The calm she had felt when she sought its hunkering form. When Elena opened her eyes, the car had stopped underneath the ivory entrance of the Palace. The door swung up and Elena turned to Yassen, but his seat was empty.

He was already gone.

22
LEO

Oh Wanderer! What you seek lies within these veins. Look! You carry the story of the world.

—FROM *THE ODYSSEY OF GOROMOUNT: A PLAY*

"I want you to kill the priests," Leo said to Ferma as she bowed before him.

"But, Your Majesty…" she began.

"They've conspired against the throne, and I have burned their names in the sand," he said. "Now go."

The Yumi slowly straightened. Her mouth twisted in distaste, the strands of her hair twisting like serpents, dark and hungry. For a moment, Leo thought she was going to attack him, but then Ferma stepped back.

"As the king wishes," she said, and her voice sounded like branches snapping in half. She did not need to hurt him. He could feel her judgment, sharp as knives, piercing into his stomach.

Her hair slashed through the air, through necks and legs, spilling blood down the mountainside. Where his guards had balked, the Yumi was ruthless and efficient. She quickly butchered twelve priests, leaving only eight. Leo watched as a priestess bolted in his direction, but Ferma whipped around, her hair swinging behind her and slicing into the priestess's back. Her eyes widened as they met Leo's.

He saw her hatred, her pain, but mostly, he saw her fear.

Ferma withdrew her hair, and the priestess sagged forward like a puppet, her eyes, lost and empty, staring upward.

Leo bent down beside the priestess. She was a young woman, no more than twenty-five suns. Elena's age. Gently, he closed her eyes.

Bodies lay everywhere—young, old, woman, man. A wind blew through the mountain, stirring the ends of their bloodied robes. They flapped in the wind like tendrils of dying flames.

As he stared at the heap of bodies, Leo felt something integral leave him. His fear, maybe, his remorse, perhaps, but as he slowly rose to his feet, he knew it wasn't his fear or his remorse, but his humanity.

He would never be forgiven after this. That was all right. The rain would cleanse this mountain and baptize it into something pure. That's what his people did. Like Alabore, they created something holy out of something forsaken. His deed today was but an echo of history. Leo was not the first, and he knew for certain that he would not be the last. Elena may not follow in his footsteps, but her children, his grandchildren, might. And their children. And the ones who came after them. They would repeat the deeds of their ancestors because that's what it took to survive. That's what it took to keep Ravence alive.

"Peace is cruel," his father had once told him. "It dances like sand in the wind and blows out of your reach just when you are about to grasp it."

Leo looked past the flapping robes and to the desert beyond. There, within the dunes, was his home. It had never known peace, not in his father's lifetime or in his. But perhaps Elena might find it. Leo walked past the dead priestess. Elena might enjoy the peace he had killed for.

Leo entered the courtyard housed between the eastern petals of the Temple. Two wings ran along its northern and southern ends: Discipline and Duty. At the end of the wings, small diyas swung in the breeze, their flames fluttering. An ancient gulmohar tree grew at the center of the courtyard. Ferma crouched within its roots, cleaning the blood off her hardened hair with a practiced hand.

"You did well," he said.

The Yumi nodded as the gulmohar branches whistled in the wind like dry bones rattling in a cage. Leo looked up at the bruised sky. The heavens teased him with storms and visions of destruction but only a soft rain fell.

"The remaining seven priests and the High Priestess will be kept under guard," he said, "We must keep appearances."

But even as he said this, the words tasted sour, false. For what were appearances but a mere shade of truth? The High Priestess donned her orange robes, but she was just a puppet for a higher power. The Prophet spoke of bringing ruin upon sinners, but she was a sham, a figurehead who cloaked a harsh reality. The gods were cruel, and the heavens forever out of man's reach.

And him? Leo felt the cold touch of rain on his face. What was he?

Ferma wiped off the last drop of blood and folded the cloth into a perfect red square. "You need to teach Elena," she said. "Her inability to handle fire will only bring more danger."

"You of all people should know the danger that fire brings," he said, and her unspoken name weighed down between them.

Ferma pocketed the cloth and wiped her hands against the roots of the tree. Her hair softened, becoming shiny and sleek. She wound it around her shoulder and stood.

"Then *you* should know what happens when you keep the women in your family in the dark." She bowed, her eyes razing his skin, and brushed past him.

Leo did not watch her leave. He couldn't. It was not the sight of the priests nor the weight of his deeds that threatened to break him. It was her.

Aahnah.

His hands shook, and he felt thick, ugly tears brim in the corners of his eyes. She would have never approved of this. She would have handled it better, been more discreet, taken to her scrolls rather than the sword. If she were here, would she even recognize him? Leo was sure that if he looked back now, he would crumble. Instead, he stared at the gulmohar until his eyes burned and the tears dried and his hands stopped shaking.

He had not told Aahnah about the sacrifice, but she had learned on her own. She had thrown herself into the Fire, and it ate her alive.

He could not let the same madness take Elena, or ever let her feel the same sorrow. She would not feed this insane, hungry Fire. She would remain free of its perfidious grasp.

Drawing a deep breath, Leo wiped his hands on his cloak and entered the Temple.

The Eternal Fire spat out sparks as the Phoenix soared above, Her red eyes glittering. Saayna stood before the flames, her shadow flickering across the charred stones. She turned at the sound of his footsteps. The light of the flames smoothed the wrinkles around her eyes.

"The Prophet isn't here," he said as the Eternal Fire hissed. "Either you've spirited her away, or she has run off."

"You will find her," the High Priestess said. "I have seen it in the flames. But you will not learn her identity in time."

"So you know who she is?"

Despite the carnage outside, Saayna remained composed, her head high. "The Eternal Fire does not reveal its wielder until the last hour. You will know as soon as I do, and by then it will be too late."

Yet, even as she said this, Leo knew she was wrong. He could sense it. His instincts, his tendency to wrench and plot his way through everything, told him that it was not too late. Leo felt a spark fall on his hand, but he did not mind the burn. Saayna would protect her precious Prophet. It was her duty.

"The Prophet abandoned your Order," he said. "She disappeared and let invaders encroach into this desert. Don't you see, Saayna? There was no one to stave off the armies and keep them from murdering each other. Alabore Ravence saved this desert and your people. He brought peace to this land."

"And what have you done?" she countered, her eyes hard, piercing. "What peace have you brought? You and your ancestors have only learned to conquer the Fire. But you have not learned how to love it. To understand it like the Prophet."

Leo watched the Eternal Fire, a dancing conglomeration of death and ruin, life and light. Why did it not strike him down now, after all he had done? Was it merely biding its time? He had spent painstaking hours meditating and treating burns to finally learn that it only took extreme focus and resilience to hold the flames. What was a Prophet to him then? He, who had spent his life dedicated to serving and protecting Ravence?

"I have learned to love my country, and its people," he said.

Saayna's face twisted into a rueful smile. "Love? Is it love when you cut down innocent men and women who have done nothing against you?"

"They held their tongues," he hissed.

"Or, they knew nothing." She shook her head. "You're no king. A king doesn't kill with his bare hands. You're just a common swindler who has tricked everyone into believing you're something more."

The Eternal Fire crackled, as if laughing.

"Sir."

Leo whirled around to see Alonjo standing in the shadows of the corridor.

"There's something you need to see," the Astra said.

Leo turned back to the High Priestess. It took all his willpower to keep his voice level, to not let her see the effects of her rebuke.

"Because we've known each other for many suns, I will let you stay here instead of Desert Spider," he said. "But my guards will remain. And they will cut down your last seven priests if you do not reveal the Prophet to me. You have until Elena's coronation day. Do you understand, Saayna?"

She kissed her three fingers and rested them against his forehead. Her skin felt thin as paper.

"So we the blessed few," she said.

"So we the blessed few," he returned.

Leo followed Alonjo out of the Temple and into the grey, open light. It had stopped raining; feeble strands of sun filtered through a thick mass of clouds. Alonjo led him into the hoverpod to a hub of holos floating above the control board.

"The Arohassin attacked a patrol near the Yoddha base," Alonjo said. "We sustained a few injuries, but the Arohassin left this." He motioned and a holo floated to them. It showed something smoldering in the sand, some great, coiling serpent, but as the image came closer, Leo realized it was no monster. It was the second rune, burned into the dune. The color fell from his face.

"Who has seen this?" he said through pressed lips.

"Only us," Alonjo said, and, indeed, the hoverpod was empty except for them.

"And the soldiers at the base?"

"The Black Scales and few of our officers saw, but they think it's some nonsensical mark of the Arohassin."

Leo stared at the rune smoldering on the dune like a fresh brand on an animal. A sour taste bloomed in his stomach. He could not say why, but something was unnatural about the symbol.

"They know," he said. "They know about the Prophet."

And they left the rune to goad me, he wanted to add. After all their talk of revolution, the Arohassin believed in the Fire Order, in the men and women he had just massacred. He almost laughed. For once, Ravence and the Arohassin agreed on something.

"How did they get there?" he asked. "Did we catch any of them?"

"We believe they camped out in Teranghar and used cruisers to ride the sands. A Black Scale captured one, Your Majesty," Alonjo said, and the holo shifted to show the face of a boy with a hooked nose and small beady eyes. "Goes by the name Moody. A Jantari, only seventeen suns. He's a new recruit."

"That's why they left him behind," Leo muttered. He shifted the holo back to the rune. "Find out what you can and hunt down the others. They mustn't have strayed far."

"Do you suppose they know who she is? The Prophet?"

"No," Leo said at once, but a sliver of doubt made the word sound small. *They couldn't.* If what the High Priestess told him was true, no one knew of the Prophet's identity. No one but the Phoenix. Yet...

Leo peered at the rune. The Arohassin had left black sand in his desert, along the southern border, and the irony did not befall him. They had finally shown their hand, but for what purpose? Had they cracked the rune's meaning? His thoughts raced as the door of the hoverpod opened.

With a quick wave of his hand, Alonjo closed the holos as Marcus and the guards entered.

"What is it?" Alonjo snapped. "Did I not tell you to wait outside?"

"The High Priestess told us to board, sir. She said that the Temple... It," he said and hesitated. When he spoke again, his voice was quiet, strained. "It needs to be cleansed. They want to burn their dead."

Leo looked out the windows to the kneeling dome of the Temple. In a tangle of thorned rakins, he saw an orange robe.

"Leave behind some guards and the Yumi to help," he said. "It's the least we can do."

Silence crept in the hoverpod. Finally the Spear turned and barked out orders. A few guards slunk out of the hoverpod, and Leo saw the dark, ashen look on their faces. He had asked them to commit the unforgivable. Perhaps they cursed his name. Perhaps they cursed themselves, but Leo knew they would remain loyal to their king. The desert bred hard men, and their blood ran thick.

The hoverpod hummed as the doors closed and the remaining guards took their places. The pilot engaged the gears, and they rose into the tormented sky. A northern wind played across the desert. Dunes shifted and melted underneath him, but Leo paid no mind. It was only when they reached the southern border and he saw the rune burned along the face of the dune that he noticed the sand hadn't shifted. It remained perfectly still, while the desert around it rolled with the wind.

They docked in the valley of a dune, and Leo strode out. Marcus and Alonjo moved to join him, but he ordered them to stay back.

A Ravani soldier dressed in a sand-colored combat uniform saluted at his approach.

"Your Majesty," the soldier said, his gold stripes indicating that he was a captain. "The Black Scales have the boy in custody, but he hasn't talked."

"Get out of my way," Leo growled, and the soldier balked. Leo swept past him and walked to the edge of the rune.

The air prickled, as if charged with energy. Leo could hear the familiar hiss of fire. The rune grew darker as he squatted and ran his hand through the blackened sand. It was already beginning to cool. He lumped sand in his hand and watched it spill through his fingers. It fell straight down instead of dancing in the wind. Leo got up and walked along the edges of the rune. It curved up and over the lip of the dune, and he followed it to the other side.

That was when he saw it. Or rather, did not see it. He had stared at the runes for so long that they had burned into his eyes. The second rune, the one that had appeared on the back of the young priest, looked like the eye of a hurricane, a mass of inward lines. The rune before him was also shaped like a storm, but along its outer edge, it did not curve inward. Rather, it jutted out in a harsh line. Like an arrow, like a sword.

Leo studied the rune from every angle. *Yes, this one is different.* Did the Arohassin then not know about the prophecy? Were they merely trying to string him along?

"Oi!" he shouted at the captain still standing at the base of the dune. The soldier jumped. "Where's the boy?"

"Well, sir, there's an issue there," the captain said. He paused, tasting the wind. "The Black Scales, they took the boy. They won't let us have him."

"The Black Scales serve Ravence now," Leo said.

"Yes, but there have been some administrative concerns and mishaps—"

"Take me to them," Leo said. He walked right down the middle of the rune, scattering sand across the desert's burning flesh. It hissed in reply.

The captain straightened and turned, marching forward. Instead of heading toward Yoddha, they slipped into the valley to the makeshift base of Samson's Black Scales. Behind a barbed fence, soldiers milled in and out of neatly ordered tents and barracks. Leo spotted no refuse, no discarded bottles. He had always heard of the Black Scales' efficiency, their rigid honor code, but he was still amazed by the sight before him. In less than a month, they had created a new base, one more streamlined and cleaner than any Ravani encampment. He realized with bitterness how much he had underestimated Samson.

They arrived at a gate flanked by two soldiers. The men scowled at the Ravani soldier, but when they saw Leo, their scowls slackened.

"Your Majesty," they said and saluted.

"Let me see the boy," he said.

"Our orders are to keep the gates locked until Commander Chandi has finished interrogating the boy," one soldier said.

"You serve Ravence now," he said. "You serve *me.*"

The Black Scale hesitated, but his partner spoke up.

"We apologize, sir, but our orders are orders. No one is to see the captured personnel."

"Do you know who you're talking to?" the Ravani soldier seethed, but Leo held up his hand.

He looked at the Black Scale, and his voice was chillingly soft, devoid of inflection. "Move aside, soldier. I've already killed many men today."

The Black Scales glanced at each other. An unspoken message flitted between them, and then one soldier stepped back and pressed his hand on a screen. The gates of the base rolled back. A Black Scale stepped forward, indicating for them to follow. Other soldiers stopped and stared at Leo and his gold, ceremonial robes.

None bowed.

The soldier took them past the tents to a small adobe hut.

"Who's in there?" Leo asked.

"The prisoner and Commander Chandi," the Black Scale said. He turned and nodded to the Ravani soldier. "You can stay out here."

He pressed his hand on the door panel, and it slid open. They walked down a short, cramped hall that smelled of dust and sweat. Around the bend, they came to another door. This time, the Black Scale removed a small holopod from his pocket. The sensor scanned it, and they were through.

They entered a white, spotless room divided in half. A boy sat behind a glass screen. His hands were bound while three soldiers, one with their back turned, stood before a glass panel covered in holos and dials.

The two soldiers who stood facing the door snapped to attention.

"What is it?" said the soldier with the turned back.

"The king, Commander."

Slowly, lazily, the soldier turned. Commander Chandi was a tall woman with thick, dark eyes and blue-stained lips. A tattoo crawled up her neck, a skull's hand wrapping around her throat like a savage, horrid necklace. When she saw him looking, she smiled.

"Your Grace," she said.

"It's Your Majesty," Leo corrected.

The commander chuckled, the skull fingers rippling over her throat. "My apologies, Your Majesty."

Behind the glass, Leo saw the boy smile.

"Can he hear me?" Leo asked.

"Yes, sir," Chandi replied.

Leo faced the boy. A tiny smattering of hair grew on his upper lip. Blood sprouted across his chin and dripped into his shirt. His colorless Jantari eyes peered at him behind deep, hooded lids. The boy's smile grew wider.

"We knew you would come," he said.

For a moment, Leo wondered if he had walked into a trap, but Chandi turned a dial and an electric shock ran through the boy, making him shriek and jolt up in his chair. The ends of his hair stood up.

"Why?" Leo said. "Do you have something to tell me?"

When the boy did not answer, Leo's hand found the dial. He turned it, and the boy gasped as pain surged through his body.

"Feels like your muscles are clenching yet ripping all at once. Right?" He notched up the dial. "Almost like a burning. A deep, ruthless burning."

The boy gritted his teeth, but a scream escaped his lips. His body trembled, and his hands curled into fists. Leo watched him writhe in his seat, a sheen of sweat appearing on his skin before Leo turned down the dial. The boy slumped forward.

"Why did the Arohassin leave a rune?" Leo asked. He kept his hand on the dial as the boy looked up at him through bleary eyes.

"We knew you would come," he said again.

Leo stopped himself from turning up the dial.

"They left you behind," he said, changing tactics. "You're dispensable to them, easily thrown away like a stray shobu or an orphan." The boy stiffened.

So he *was* an orphan.

Leo turned off the mic and turned to Chandi. "Let me in."

She had been watching him all this time, a thin, amused smile playing across her lips. "You know, you remind me of him. Our Blue Star." When she saw the quizzical look on his face, her smile widened. "Samson. He's like you. Neither of you would hesitate to pummel a boy."

"I merely want to talk to him," Leo said, his patience wearing thin.

The commander nodded. "Of course."

She pressed a button, and the door to the interrogation chamber opened. Moody looked up as Leo swept in. He towered over the boy, making him crane his neck to see his full height. And then Leo rested his hand on the boy's head. Softly, almost tenderly, Leo cupped his cheek.

"You are unwanted," he said, his eyes boring into Moody. "They discarded you just like your parents did. But in Ravence, you are wanted. You're needed." He gripped the boy's chin, gently yet firmly. "Tell me what I need to know, and I'll see that these men won't kill you."

The boy looked at him with his pale, colorless eyes, eyes just like Yassen's. "I-I don't know," he stammered. "They didn't tell me much."

"Oh, but you do," Leo said. He had seen the shadow of a lie cross the boy's eyes. "You heard something."

Moody gulped. He tried to wrench his face away, but Leo held firm.

"Your time burns, boy," Leo said.

"She's lying to you!" he blurted.

"Who?"

"The one who sees visions in the flames," he said. "That's what they told me! I swear, I don't know her name!"

Leo finally let go. He thought of Saayna standing before the Eternal Fire, the disdainful look in her eyes. At least *that* was not a lie. He strode out of the room, the door sliding shut behind him with a click of finality.

"Throw him into a sandpit," he said to Chandi.

The commander nodded, her blue lips curling into a wry grin. "My men will see you out," she said. "As for the ones at the gate, I apologize for their insolence. They seem to have forgotten who they report to."

Leo accepted her salute and followed the Black Scale, but he was no fool. Double meanings and lies threaded through Chandi's words. Samson may have forfeited his command of the Black Scales to the Ravani, but their hearts still bled for him.

Leo burst out of the building, surprising the Ravani soldier who scrambled into a salute and scampered after him as he stormed out of the base. Clouds thickened in the heavens. The rune appeared as a dark, ruined mass, a blemish in the desert. Alonjo awaited him on the hoverpod's ramp. When he saw the king's face, he turned to his guards and quickly ordered them in. He led Leo to the private pod in the back as they lifted off.

"I've been a fool, Alonjo," Leo said once they were alone. "The runes. They were wrong. She gave us the wrong one."

Alonjo sat down with a sigh. He appeared to pick his words carefully. "Perhaps there is a reason she misled us."

Leo ground his teeth, his knuckles turning white. Raw fury roiled through him, fresh and hot. Suddenly, he understood why the Eternal Fire raged so often. He wanted to burn something, too.

"She wants to protect the Prophet," Leo said.

"Yet she doesn't know the Prophet's identity," Alonjo said. "She clings to her belief because she knows that no matter what we do, we won't be able to stop the Prophet. I will always follow you, Your Majesty, but," he said and paused to lick his lips, "I do not think we can stop the coming of the Prophet. It is inevitable. Perhaps we should then consider the return of the Phoenix. A way to assuage Her wrath."

Leo gave a dry, bitter laugh.

"You too, Alonjo?" he said and shook his head. "Damn."

His Astra gave a small smile and looked down at his wrinkled hands. "We're growing old, Leo," he said. "Don't you think it's time to ask for forgiveness?"

Leo thought of Alabore and what he had seen before building Ravence—a desolate stretch of desert underneath the pale moons. A haven for his people. A chance for peace.

He would not let Alabore's dream burn.

"There's no time for redemption," he said.

"Your Majesty—"

"I am not going to throw my hands up!" he snapped. "This is *my* kingdom. *My* desert. My people have fought for it, slaved for it. This Prophet has no claim to this land. She gave it up when she disappeared from this world. And by heavens," he growled, "I will not let her take it."

23
ELENA

The art of the slingsword is not easy to master.
It demands suns of practice, diligence, and failure.
For one can only master the slingsword when
they understand the sting of its blade.

—FROM CHAPTER 14 OF *THE GREAT HISTORY OF SAYON*

Elena swung her slingsword, but Samson parried her attack and moved to her left. She followed him as the black sand shifted beneath her feet. The blue lights flashed. She feinted right and whirled as a column of sand erupted between them. Samson grinned, using the distraction to retreat behind another column.

"Not taloned enough to face me?" she cried out.

She waited for the sand to still before darting forward, weaving through the columns. In her peripheral vision, she spotted a flutter of movement. She whipped around, pressing the trigger of her slingsword. Its blade shot out.

Samson jumped, the sling narrowly missing his shoulder and lodging into a column in a spray of sand. He disappeared behind another column as she retracted her blade. She tensed, listening for the whisper of sand, the rush of air, but no sound came.

Slowly, Elena stalked forward. Sweat coated her upper lip. *Why does he hide?* She was used to fighting head on, used to seeing her opponent's eyes catch her own before she slashed her blade down. But Samson was different. She had heard the rumors of his remarkable swordsmanship, his swift and silent attacks. Goosebumps traveled up her arms as Elena rounded another column.

Still, she saw nothing. It was as if he had disappeared as effortlessly as a shadow.

The blue lights flashed again, and the sand rumbled beneath her feet. The columns began to crumble. Elena dodged a falling mass of sand when she felt a cold breath stir the hair on her neck. She turned and nearly yelped. Samson stood directly behind her; she hadn't even heard him approach.

A smile crept across his face. He was so close that she could see the dark depths of his eyes, deep blue like the uncharted seas.

"You were saying?"

It was if his words had melted the ice lodged between her joints. Elena reacted, revealing the dagger hidden between her shoulder blades with a flourish of her hips. He took a step back, surprised, but it was too late. The tip of her blade pricked the bottom of his chin.

"Peace," she offered.

His chest heaved as he looked into her eyes. "Peace."

"End of round," the gamemaster called out. The blue lights hummed, and the sand stilled.

"A queen with a blade up her sleeve. Or should I say her back?" Samson shook his head. "And I almost had you."

Elena stepped away, unease slithering down her chest. It unnerved her that she hadn't heard Samson's approach. Usually, she could read the sands. Hear the whispers of its subtle shifts. She glanced at Samson, masking her disquiet with a smile.

"Don't pout," she said. "Shall we go again?"

He grinned. "Of course."

It had been Samson's idea that they start their morning with training, and she was grateful for the distraction. Despite the preparations of the Fire Festival and the celebrations in the Palace, she could not shake off the weight of her failure. The hiss of the Eternal Fire still haunted her. Last night, she awoke from nightmares of burning. Her handmaid had left a glass of cold, honeyed milk on her bedside table, but even that could not wash away the taste of ash in Elena's mouth.

Elena brushed back a loose strand of hair.

"One more time then," she said.

They had been at this for nearly two hours. Sweat streaked down Samson's face, but he flashed her a smile. Amusement glimmered in his eyes as he crossed to his end of the field.

Elena returned to her spot and crouched into her opening stance—blade out, palm forward. She glanced up at the control room where Ferma watched. The Yumi gave her a curt nod. She had been quiet this morning. Elena had meant to ask her Spear if something was amiss, but then she had received Samson's invitation.

Yassen walked up to the window beside Ferma. He had not reported to Elena this morning. When she had inquired, Ferma had told her that he was out hunting. Elena did not need to ask what or whom.

Even from this distance, she could see the shadows beneath his eyes. She wondered if he too dreamt of the Eternal Fire, but the gamemaster's voice rang out and Elena turned her attention back to her opponent.

The blue lights flashed, and the sand swelled. The ground suddenly erupted, the sand rising like a wave. Elena squatted, riding it out. Samson pulled the trigger, his blade shooting out and parting the crest. She crashed and rolled, shooting to her feet, but Samson was faster. He rushed forward, slicing down as she parried.

Samson turned for the counterattack. Again, she parried. He advanced; she retreated. She lunged; he dodged. They fell into a rhythm with blades singing, and despite the sting of sand and taste of ash, Elena smiled.

"Not bad," she said between blows. At least this time, he met her head on.

Samson feinted right, but she anticipated his move and blocked his overhead strike.

"You know, we really should finalize the guest list for the ball at some point," he said as he pressed down against her sword.

She grinned, her arms shaking as she held her own blade inches from her face. "Why not now?"

She brought her foot around and twisted from beneath his slingsword. Samson sidestepped, suddenly bringing his sword down to her leg, but she parried and forced him to retreat.

"Who's first?"

"Well, there's the Humber family from Rasbakan," he said, whirling behind her to avoid her attack.

"And the Kairos family from Magar," she said, whipping around. Her blade arced through the air as Samson slashed and parried.

"The ambassador from Cyleon already accepted the invitation, but sends her regrets that their royal family can't join."

"Must be because you broke the young queen's heart," she said, sliding her blade down to catch his hand, but Samson snapped out of her reach.

"Well, she was no warrior." He advanced but then switched hands. His blade missed her by a finger's breadth.

"The desert could do her some good," she grunted.

"There's also the Jantari family," he said. Their swords connected, and he pushed against her blade. "We've gotten Farin's attention now with the Black Scales on the southern border. If we invite him, he'll come."

She shook her head as he inched her back, her feet sliding in the sand. "He won't come."

"He will," Samson said. "Farin never could resist the sweetness of the desert."

He turned then, blade flashing, and cut down. Elena brought up her sword again, but her arm buckled under the force of the blow and she fell back.

"Besides, I have a gift to return to him," he said, grinning at her stumble. "A map."

Out of the corner of her eye, Elena saw Yassen start. He stepped forward, pressing his hand against the glass. His eyes met hers, and he opened his mouth to say something, but Samson shot forward and brought his sword down with such force that he knocked her slingsword from her hand. Stunned, Elena backpedaled, but Samson was quicker. The tip of his slingsword hovered inches from her throat.

"Peace," he said.

Only then did she realize what Yassen was trying to say: *Watch out.*

"Peace," she muttered.

Samson withdrew his blade and straightened. "So what do you think? Will you take a look at the invitation I've drawn up?"

She nodded, afraid that if she spoke, her voice would sound weak.

The doors to the field opened, revealing Ferma and Yassen.

"How'd the hunt go?" Samson called out as they approached.

"We got two more this time," Yassen said.

He looked paler than usual, and Elena could see blue veins spider underneath his eyes. His cheeks sank in, highlighting the sharp edges of his cheekbones. As Yassen withdrew a small metal flame from his pocket, she noticed the marks on his wrist.

"It's all in there," he said, handing the device to Samson.

Samson stared at the metal flame for a moment and then up at Yassen. "Perhaps you should rest, Yassen. You look like death."

"I'm fine."

"The map," she said suddenly. "What is it?"

They both looked at her, and then Samson gave a slow shrug. "A map of ancient Jantari tunnels. King Farin gifted it to me when I built Casear Lunar, but, alas, I'm afraid it's of no use. Most of the tunnels are caved in."

She would have believed him, but she saw the furtive look in her guard's eyes. The map meant something to Yassen.

"Returning a gift while extending an invitation will hardly set us in King Farin's good graces," she said.

"Trust me, darling. I think Farin would like to see that map again." Samson smiled, and she bristled.

Ferma stepped forward.

"Your swords, please," she said, but Elena, her eyes still on Samson, tightened her grip on her slingsword's handle.

"I'd like to see this map," she said. "Send it with the invitation, and I'll sign once I review them both."

"We have little time," Samson said. "You have to appear in Rani for the Fire Festival, and then we need to finalize the song list and dance procession of the ball—"

"Darling," Elena said, her smile not meeting her eyes, "you never refuse a queen."

Maurilis, Samson's top aide, brought the map to her study. Elena slowly unrolled the scroll as the Sesharian watched.

"You can go," she said without looking up. "And on your way out, send my guard in."

"Which one?"

"The one who's too proud to admit he's sick," she said and looked up at him.

Maurilis gave a short bow, and she heard the door slide open. She looked back at the scroll as she heard Yassen's footsteps.

"You'd better start explaining why you wanted to see this map," she said, running her fingers over the corners of the parchment.

"Did you ask for it on my behalf?" he asked.

She did not know how to answer, so she said nothing. She gestured for him to sit, but Yassen remained standing.

"Samson's right. Most of those tunnels no longer exist," he said.

She studied the sprawling maze before her. A network of lines crisscrossed beneath the Sona Range. Some were marked in red, others blue. Most of the tunnels ran north to south, but a small patch in the center and southern corner of the range ran from east to west. She pointed at that section. "This is below Casear Lunar. Correct?"

"Yes."

She pursed her lips and traced her finger along a tunnel that started at Samson's palace and ran upward to the middle of the mountain range. There, more lines splintered from a central point. Silver stars indicated the locations of mines. She tapped the map and then looked up at Yassen.

"What does this map mean to you?"

He hesitated. For a moment, Elena thought he would turn away, but then he sat down. He folded his hands, his sleeve riding up. The marks on his wrist had darkened to a deep, boiling purple.

"My father was Jantari," he said. "He used to live in a small mountain town where we would go hunting. But one day, he disappeared. I think it's because he discovered a tunnel and found something he shouldn't have."

"What did he find?"

"I don't know," Yassen said quietly. "But whatever it was, he died for it."

Silence sank between them. Across the room, the fireplace crackled. Elena smoothed the map, her hands shaking.

Funny, she thought. *We both hold grudges.*

She knew what it meant to lose a parent to an idea, a concept. She knew of the hole they left behind, the deep emptiness. Sometimes, she still dreamed of Aahnah. She wanted to tell him of her grief, but her tongue lodged in her throat.

"Did you join Samson just so you could find this map and discover the cause of your father's death?" she asked, finally breaking the quiet.

"No," Yassen said, his tone too heavy to be dishonest. He looked up at her. "I just want to be free. Of the Arohassin. Of you. Of this country."

She felt a pang of guilt and looked away; she knew he could not be free. When she became queen, he would burn. She would see to it. She had vowed it. But now she...

Elena carefully rolled up the map and handed it to Yassen.

"Hopefully this will help you," she said.

Yassen took the map, and she spotted the marks on his wrist again. "And look out for that arm," she said.

Yassen pulled down his sleeve as he slipped out his holopod. He ran it over the map, scanning it. When he was done, he handed the map back to Elena. "You don't need to help me."

"I know," she said. "Go before I change my mind."

The door closed softly behind him. Elena let out a deep breath. He was right. She did not need to help him. Of all people, he deserved her wrath. Yet, she could no longer conjure her fury. Perhaps this was why she could not handle the Eternal Fire. It seemed to demand a ruthless hate, a rage that knew no end. Her father had learned how to sustain his anger, but she could not see herself living such a life. Ruling with fear, letting her supporters kill without consequence—it filled her with disgust.

Ravence would never know peace if it continued to devour its dissenters. It would not become the shining beacon Alabore had envisioned if she allowed herself to be consumed by the Fire.

Elena leaned forward and rested her elbows on her desk. A piece of wood split in the fireplace, showering the floor with a spray of sparks. She watched the flames bend, her blackened fingertips itching.

24
YASSEN

At some point, we must all grieve for our old selves.

—FROM THE INTRODUCTION OF *THE GREAT HISTORY OF SAYON*

Yassen stalked through the Palace courtyards, unable to sleep. The night air felt sharp and cold after the rain. Storm clouds still hugged the horizon, but here on Palace Hill, the heavens spilled open. Tiny stars shone in the dark like uncut gems. His holopod lay tucked in his jacket, but Yassen did not withdraw it.

The courtyard he entered was one of the smaller ones in the back of the Palace. A white path, gleaming with inlaid lights, led to a large banyan tree. The tree stood in the middle of a wide basin carved out of red desert stone. Moonflowers floated in its still water, their pale petals curled inward.

Yassen paced underneath the banyan tree. Few people frequented this courtyard, and the servants who did hurried through with a quick nod in his direction. Though they no longer regarded him with disgust, the servants did not exactly offer him kind words.

A dark shape broke from the canopy with a squawk, and Yassen looked up. He watched it ascend and circle over the tree, hovering for a moment before dashing off into the night.

Sighing, Yassen sat on the lip of the stone basin. He hugged his arm to his side. It felt heavier than before, as if someone had tied lead weights around his elbow and wrist. His entire arm had darkened to an angry purple. The welts had blackened, and some were filled with pus. When he had tried to break one open, pain had shot through his arm.

He knew, eventually, he would have to cut his arm off. He could already smell the rot. The Arohassin had been right. What was a one-armed soldier other than a liability in the field?

Yassen used his left hand to withdraw the holopod. He scanned his thumb, and the map materialized before him. He saw the patch of tunnels beneath Casear Lunar and followed the path Elena had traced. In the middle of the range, he spotted a black dot. Zooming in, he identified it as Samson's base, the training grounds for his Black Scales. Yassen swiped to the north where his father's cabin was tucked in the upper mountain range, surrounded by mines.

He remembered the drone of the machines and the rumble of the mountain.

"Jantar always knows how to disturb a man's peace," his father had said.

Ekaant Knight worked in the mines and only came to visit Yassen and his mother during his short rest periods. Once, when Yassen and his mother had managed to obtain a Jantari visa to stay with him, he had told them about something he had seen in the mountain.

"A metal so fine it could cut through steel," Ekaant had whispered. He promised to bring Yassen a piece of this special ore, but when he returned from the mine, he had made no mention of it. Instead, he had hurried Yassen and his mother back to Ravence and told them to stay there until he sent word for them to return.

That was nearly eighteen suns ago. Yassen had not seen him since.

A breeze licked his sleeve, and Yassen shivered. A sudden wave of homesickness swept through his stomach. That, and the familiar feeling of being torn between two homes. He had not returned to the cabin since his father's death. Like the remnants of his burnt home in Ravence, it housed too many memories. Memories of the boy he had been—free and decent. A boy who would be ashamed of the man he was now.

He had never learned what his father had found, yet here lay his chance. He could go back to the mountains and find that ore. Find why his father had disappeared. Yassen zoomed in to the mines surrounding the cabin, but his hand wavered. For a part of him knew the Jantari had killed him. Ekaant Knight had always been a careful man, private in his affairs. He never spoke of the horrors of the mines, not until that day he told them about his discovery. That day, Ekaant Knight had told everyone, and Yassen had a hunch it had killed him.

He closed the holopod. Perhaps Samson had already discovered the cabin. Perhaps the Jantari had destroyed it. That would save him the misery of conversing with its ghosts. Perhaps, when this was all over, he would go neither to Jantar nor Ravence but out across the sea to the uncharted lands, to a new home.

Yassen shoved the holopod back into his coat at the sound of footsteps. A shadow stretched across the white path.

"Oh, I didn't realize this spot was taken," Ferma said.

"It's alright," he said, patting the lip of the fountain next to him. "There's plenty of room."

She hesitated but did not depart. Yassen could make out the high curve of her forehead, the elegant bridge of her nose as she stood half-cloaked in shadows. The ends of her hair writhed in the slight breeze.

"So," he said, "what's keeping you up?"

"Nothing," she replied, a bit too quickly. He smiled at the terseness in her voice.

"Sounds like you can't sleep either."

"Most of the Palace can't," she said. "We have a coronation to see through."

"And Arohassin to catch, *and* a festival to celebrate, *and* an angry fire to calm, *and*—"

"What's your point?" she asked, annoyance flashing across her face.

Yassen looked up at the moonless sky. "If you keep worrying about all the things to do, you'll run yourself to ruin."

She gave a low snort, and Yassen turned to her.

"What?" he said.

"Nothing. You just reminded me of someone I used to know."

She sat down beside him and withdrew a flask. Yassen watched her take a long, desperate gulp.

"Rough day?"

She wiped her lips. Her eyes, often bright, looked drained. Tired.

She took another swig and then another. She tipped back the flask until nothing was left and then threw it down, watching it bounce and skitter down the stone path.

"Ferma," he began.

"I've done a terrible thing," she whispered.

He looked at her. "We all do terrible things."

The Yumi made a sound caught between a laugh and a sob. "You would know."

He waited for her laughter to die off. He knew it would. Alcohol, drugs, distractions—they only lasted for a moment. Guilt always lurked at the edges, waiting to pounce.

Ferma's smile faded. She looked up at the sky, the shadows carving out harsh lines along her eyes and mouth.

"What did you do?"

For a moment, she said nothing. She just looked up at the night sky full of clouds and unshapely stars. When she finally spoke, her voice sounded flat, devoid of life, as if it came from far away.

"I killed the priests," she said. "The king ordered me to, and so I did."

Yassen felt his stomach drop, but he forced his voice to stay steady. "Why?"

"I don't know," she said, and her voice sounded so small. "I never question my king."

Don't ask questions. Wasn't that what he had told himself during assignments? When they sent him the name and location, he never asked *who* he was to murder, nor *why*. He merely did what he was told because he was a good solider. The Arohassin had trained him like a shobu, and he became their warrior. No assignment had been too difficult, no kill too dubious.

"Imagine a house," his old mentor Akaros had once said. "Imagine a house with emotions as rooms. One room for sadness. One room for guilt. Another for pain. Let the emotion consume that room, but that room only. And when you're done experiencing that emotion, shut the door. Lock it, and step away."

It had been hard to do at first. To let nothingness take over and drain away his morality. It felt unnatural, like forcing oneself to be a hermit, devoid of outside contact for weeks. But Yassen had been a quick learner.

He would look into the snake's venom-colored eyes as it wound its way inside of him, hissing of his guilt. He saw it, and then he would slowly close the door. Shut it in. Step away.

"Then don't allow yourself to start questioning," he said. He bent forward and picked up the flask. "Questioning will do you no good."

She blinked. "Is that what you tell yourself?"

"Yes," he said. He felt the familiar rattle in his chest, but he pushed it away. He could not be fazed, not when he was so close to the end.

"If you allow yourself to regret, you'll freeze," he said. "And when that happens, you become useless. The only thing left to do then is to die. So either you move on, or you go quietly off into the seven hells."

He stood up and handed her the flask. "Stop feeling sorry for yourself. We're all going to burn anyway."

He turned to go, but she gripped his arm. Her eyes bore into him.

"But I killed them," she said, her voice breaking. "The Fire Order. The holy ones. He gave the order, and I killed them. I even cleaned up their blood afterward. I didn't stop to ask why. I-I should have—"

Gently, he pried off her fingers and folded her hand.

"Don't worry," he said. "If you burn, I'll keep you company."

She shuddered and pulled her hand away.

25
ELENA

Fire gives both life and abandonment. It reveals your true friends yet lets your enemies lie in its shadows. One should be wary of fire and the things it grows.

—FROM THE DIARIES OF PRIESTESS NOMU OF THE FIRE ORDER

Agneepath netrun. Fijjin a noor.

The path of fire is dangerous. Tread it with care.

Elena furrowed her brow, sweat dripping down her nose as she focused on the single flame in the bowl before her. The scroll lay open on the lip of the fountain. The night's breeze cooled the sweat on her cheeks as she sank into the first pose.

The Warrior.

Her toe traced a half-circle across the ground. Seamlessly, she whirled, dipping her head and executing the follow-through. The flame sighed.

She balanced on her right foot, raising her arms behind her like the wings of a desert sparrow. The flame slowly tugged left. She moved her hands to the right, and it followed. Elena unwound her legs and transitioned into the next form of the dance—palms outstretched, mind clear.

The Lotus.

Think of the brightest light you've ever seen, the scroll said of this form.

Previously, she had thought of the Eternal Fire, and the flame had exploded. She had been wrong then. The Fire was not a bright light. It was a source of rage. Destruction.

Elena blinked fiercely as sweat dripped into her eye. If the Fire was not the answer, she had to think of something else. Something whole. She thought of her mother, but the memory of her was already fading. Her father was more of a dark cloud than a source of light. And then her thoughts landed on Ferma.

Yes, Ferma will do.

Elena thought of the Yumi's prickling hair, the grace in her stride, the depth of her tawny, cat-like eyes, and the way she moved so smoothly in combat.

The flame grew.

She called upon her childhood memories—the times when she hid in the garden and Ferma pretended she didn't already know where she was hiding. Elena would watch her underneath the banyan leaves, holding her breath. And then Ferma would pop up behind her, scaring her into a fit of giggles.

The flame rose in response.

Elena licked her lips and curled a finger. The flame bowed.

Still thinking of Ferma, Elena whirled and transitioned into the next pose. She spread out her feet, held up her arm as if reaching for the stars.

The Spider.

Like the desert spider, the Fire sees all, the scroll said.

She envisioned the ancient Desert Spider warriors, and she pictured Ferma in their ranks. Tall and proud, her hair dancing in the wind. She saw the Yumi traversing the dunes and hunting down enemies of the desert.

Elena bowed her head and swept up her leg, her foot touching the back of her head.

The Tree.

Fire is steadfast and eternal. Root yourself in its heat and the truth it carries.

She thought of the desert on a summer day. How heat shimmered over the dunes in golden waves; how she hopped over hot stones in the courtyard to get to the covered path. Heat could be soft as a mother's kiss, as mean as the sun's glare. It operated in dualities, yet Elena rose to greet it like a flower. She drank it in, opened her heart, and let it blossom.

The flame hissed and grew.

She unwound her leg, opened her arms, and spun, hair flying as the flame elongated and flickered. She came to a stop and rose on her toes, wrapping her arms around her body and twisting into the Snake.

There are those who fear fire, and there are those who learn to possess it, control it, and make it theirs, the scroll said.

Her mother had thrown herself into the Eternal Fire because she loved it. Her father held fire because he needed it. But Elena? She balanced on her toes, her eyes trained on the flame as it danced with the night breeze.

She would control it.

The flame began to crawl out of the bowl. Its tip flickered, tasting the air. Elena glanced at the scroll for the last form, but the drawing was faded, and she saw no translation of the ancient language. She hesitated, her balance wavering. The flame reached forward and slithered up her forearms, roping her hands together.

Elena froze. Suddenly, the memory of the Eternal Fire rushed back to her. The pain. The smell of burnt flesh.

The flame began to move further up her arm, touching the inside of her elbow. Her skin prickled. There came a soft hiss as it singed her hair. Elena tried to hold still as the flame began to explore her body. It grew even larger, wrapping around her chest, underneath her breasts, traveling down her slim waist to her knees.

"Concentrate," she whispered.

The flame constricted. Elena gasped as its heat sank into her bones.

Fire will test you, the scroll had said of the first form. *Be strong like the desert. Steady, yet always shifting.*

Elena let out a low, shaky breath. Slowly, she struggled against her fiery bonds, wincing as the flames sank deeper into her skin. Pain lanced up her arms, her legs, but Elena reassumed the first form of the dance—the Warrior. The fiery rope slackened. She moved into the second form, and it began to uncurl. The flame licked her ear as if it could hear the throb of her vein underneath, the secrets hidden in her heartbeat. Elena shoved out her fist, and it retreated.

Without thinking, she spun, slashing her arm down. The flame burst on the stone path in a shower of ash.

Elena stared at the small, black pile.

What have I done?

The sudden urge, the *disgust* of fire, had come over her, and she had shirked off the flame as if it were vermin. Guilt and frustration roiled through her. Elena blinked back hot, angry tears, the glassy red eyes of the Phoenix flashing in her mind.

Damn that stupid bird.

"Do you plan to train here?" a voice came from behind.

Elena spun around, fists raised, and saw Ferma descending the steps into her garden.

"It's the only place I can be alone," she said.

Ferma shook her head. Her eyes looked dull, but, then again, they all had been sleeping less.

"Where've you been?" Elena asked.

"Sobering up," Ferma replied. She straightened. "I had a momentary lapse and drank too much. I'm alright now."

Elena blinked. *Ferma drinking?* She had never heard of such a thing.

"Are you sure you're alright?"

"I have a better place for us to train," Ferma said. Her hair writhed behind her. "Come."

Faint starlight illuminated the stone arches as they walked through the grand central courtyard. Thick ironwood trees with ivory trunks and pale, pink flowers rustled in the breeze. In the middle of the courtyard, a gulmohar loomed over a single, gas-lit flame. It flickered, beating away the night shadows.

They turned past the courtyard and entered the rear wings of the Palace. Here, the hallways were tall and ornate but with fewer paintings and stone lattice work. Above them, on the arched ceiling, the red feather insignia of the Palace guards glowed with inlaid lighting.

Ferma moved swiftly, her hair rippling behind her as they rounded a corner and entered a rear tower. They stepped onto a stone platform, and Ferma pulled down a lever.

"Where are we going?" Elena asked. She could not remember the last time she had been in this part of the Palace.

The platform docked, and they entered a narrow, dark hall.

"This way," Ferma said. Red strips of light illuminated their path. Several doors lined the hallway, the names of the guards floating before each room.

They came to a plain, wooden door at the end of the hall. This one had no name, no design. Ferma pressed her hand against the touchpad, and the locks clicked and spun. They entered a room as big as Elena's foyer.

Training pads lay across every inch of the floor while a dozen or so mirrors lined the ceiling and walls. A small corridor connected the main room to a kitchen fashioned out of black desert stone. A simple cot was tucked next to the stove.

"Is this... where you sleep?" Elena asked. It occurred to her that despite knowing Ferma all her life, she had never seen her quarters.

"Don't sound too surprised," the Yumi said. She clapped her hands, and holostrips shed red light across the room. The mirrors engaged, holos sprouting up on their reflective surfaces. "Sometimes I prefer to train here than with the other guards."

Elena circled the mirrors. A dozen of her reflections stared back. "But how?"

Ferma motioned to a dark mass in the corner, and Elena recognized the shapeshifting black sand of the training arena. It formed the shape of a man. The air buzzed and twin scissors of electric light appeared in the training dummy's hands.

"Is that a Junhni 2000?" Elena said. "I thought they were put out of production."

"I snagged one before they switched them for the Almanys," Ferma said. She smiled at the dummy as if it were an old friend. "This one is named Macho."

Elena laughed. There came a hum, and the training mats split open to reveal a deep pit with a tiny flame.

"If your father can't teach you, we'll have to learn ourselves," Ferma said. She gave a grim smile, and Elena returned it.

She suddenly felt self-conscious and looked down at her blackened fingertips. She had only ever practiced the fire dance alone.

"How much did you see?" she asked softly.

"Enough," her guard said. "We need to work on your form. Your Warrior pose needs to be deeper."

With a flick of her hair, she knocked Elena to the ground. "See? Your center is off balance."

Elena rubbed her back, groaning. "Maybe we should do this another time. How about tomorrow morning? After you bring me the list of the affected families from the park shooting."

"I already have the list," Ferma said as she circled her. The Yumi's hair prickled, the ends sharpening. She looked like a cougar slowly stalking its prey.

Elena rose to her feet with a wary look.

"Feet wide," Ferma said and grabbed her by the waist. She tapped Elena's legs, motioning for her to widen her stance. "You need to be strong, like a tree. Rooted to the ground. Immovable like a rock." Ferma sank into her heels, feet wide, shoulders back. "See?"

Elena mirrored the movement, her twelve reflections following suit.

Ferma touched her back. "Straighter."

Elena nodded, though she could already feel her legs beginning to shake. "About the list—"

"No matter what I do, don't move," Ferma instructed as she approached the training dummy. "You're a tree—a banyan tree. Beautiful and steady."

She pressed her hand on the mirror beside the dummy. A holo materialized, and Ferma tapped in a few commands. The dummy spun to life, its scissor hands flashing.

It threw a lightning-like blast toward Elena's head. She bit back a yelp as she felt the wind of its passing brush against her ear. It sent another charge, this one right between her legs, barely grazing her lower thigh. It almost threw her off, but Elena gripped the mats with her toes, her eyes set on her reflections in the mirrors.

The dummy moved closer and then shattered into a pool of sand. Elena looked down, just as shards of sand whizzed upward. She gasped, losing balance, tottering.

"Focus!" Ferma snapped.

Elena centered her weight and sank back down into her feet. Her whole body trembled. She thought back to the scroll and how it told her to be as still as the dunes on a hot summer day.

The pool of sand rumbled, and more shards flew toward her. This time, Elena kept her eyes on the mirrors. She did not waver. Her legs shook, but she stared at her reflections until she could no longer feel her legs nor the weaponized sand grazing her body.

"That's enough," Ferma said, but Elena kept on.

In the mirrors, she saw the flame swoon. She thrust her hands out, one palm out, the other curled into a fist, and beckoned for the flame. It listened. It shot straight into her fists, making Ferma jump back, but Elena cupped the flame in her hands, holding it steady.

"Holy Bird Above," Ferma whispered.

Elena managed a smile even as the small blaze peeled the skin of her palms. Ferma noticed the smoke, her eyes widening.

"Let it go," she said.

But the flame only strengthened, and her hands began to throb. "I can't," Elena whispered.

"Elena," the Yumi began.

Suddenly, the flame hissed and shot toward the mirrors. Her reflections turned, and as the glass shattered, Elena saw herself: ashen and alone, her hands dark and trembling, crumble.

Ferma sprang and grabbed a mat and leapt on the flame, suffocating it. The blaze hissed, its pain ripping through Elena. She cried out, falling to her knees.

"Stop it," she gasped.

But Ferma pressed down harder, and the flame gave one last gasp before dying in a gush of ash.

They stared at each other in the silence that came after. Amongst the shattered glass, Elena saw her own doubt reflected in the Yumi's eyes.

"I can do it," she said. "I know I can. I just need more time."

Ferma stood slowly. Glass snapped as she kneeled down and took Elena's burnt hands into her own.

"You will no longer practice this dance," she said. "I forbid it."

"No." Elena ripped her hands out of Ferma's grasp. "This is the only way I can learn."

"You're going to kill yourself if you continue," the Yumi said. "And then what? Who will rule Ravence? Leo? The king's gone mad—"

"What do you mean?" Elena asked, but Ferma looked away, regret flashing across her face.

"Nothing," she muttered. "Forget it. Let's get you cleaned up and into bed."

"You speak to me like I'm still a child."

"That's because you still act like one sometimes."

"I'm not giving up," Elena said, rolling back her shoulders. "I won't. If I can't hold the Fire without being burned, I can't become queen. I have to do this, Ferma. You of all people should understand."

"I'm sick and tired of you and your father telling me what I should or shouldn't understand," the Yumi snapped, and Elena recoiled. Shock spread across her face.

"Ferma," she whispered.

But the Yumi stood, her hair twisting behind her.

"Can't you see, Elena?" she said. "Every time someone from your family touched fire, they went mad. It happened to your grandfather, your mother. The king is already losing his grasp, and then it'll be you. Do you want that? An eternity of suffering?"

"I want Ravence," Elena said, "and if I have to walk through fire to get it, I will."

"If you believe that, you truly are a fool," the Yumi said. Her words cut like a whip, and Elena looked away.

The glass threw back their shattered reflections a million times over.

26
LEO

"Peace," the land rumbled.
"Change," the sky whispered.
"Destiny," the fire hissed.

—FROM *THE LEGENDS AND MYTHS OF SAYON*

Leo tapped the concrete table before him, the bitter taste of sand still in his mouth. After learning of Saayna's deceit, he had wanted to rush back to the Temple. He had wanted to hold her remaining priests over the Fire until she cowered and told him the truth.

But Alonjo had advised against it, arguing that killing the priests and the High Priestess before the coronation would only bring trouble.

"Citizens will question the legitimacy of Elena's reign if she is not properly inducted by the Order," the Astra had said.

Grudgingly, Leo had found himself in agreement. The Order was a crucial part of the coronation. The High Priestess bestowed the blessings of the Eternal Fire onto the next monarch, who then promised to lead Ravence into another glorious generation. A divine ruler was nothing without her god.

Everywhere he turned, the Phoenix lay in wait. Her fiery grasp reached every part of his kingdom, his history. He despised Her, yet he could not rule his kingdom without Her.

The coronation was now less than two weeks away, and the Prophet was still free. As he sat at his desk, studying the runes, Leo no longer felt rage. Instead, a cold resolve had hardened in its place like the desert's diamond-backed serpent.

Alonjo arrived carrying a tray, and Leo watched him pour tea into gem-encrusted cups. The surrounding fire crackled softly. Alonjo offered a cup to Leo.

"To Ravence and her dream," he said.

"To Ravence," Leo returned.

The tea scalded his tongue, but he swallowed it without complaint. Alonjo sighed and sank back in his seat. His eyebrows drooped past the corners of his eyes, giving him a sleepy, dazed look.

"I suppose there is only one thing left to do," he said, his voice heavy.

Leo nodded. He enlarged the holos of the runes. The burning symbol left by the Arohassin glared at him. Spreading out his hands, Leo brought up a topographical map of Ravence with all her dunes and canyons. He looked at Alonjo over the peaks of the Agnee Range.

"After we plot these runes, we'll know the truth," Leo said.

I hope.

He overlaid the first sign, the feather of the Phoenix, onto the map. It stretched across Ravence like a long scar. He then took the second rune—the one left by the Arohassin, the inward storm with an arrow's end—and planted it over the feather. It swept across the valleys and dunes, the eye of the storm settling on the capital.

Leo waved his hand, and the third symbol floated over the others. The leafless banyan tree. He placed it on top of the others, noting how its bare branches brushed the tips of the Agnee mountains while its trunk split the desert in half. Leo called for the last sign, but then he hesitated.

This rune was simple—a circle with a dot in the middle. He had never seen it before in his texts, or, if he had, he overlooked it for its mundanity. Yet, it was the final piece to the puzzle.

Leo motioned for the holo. Together, he and Alonjo watched it sink onto the map of Ravence. Its circumference cut perfectly through the southern canyons and western mountains, ringing the trunk of the banyan tree and the stem of the feather.

Apart, the runes looked nonsensical. Together, they created a maze that would lead to the truth.

Leo let out a deep breath and leaned forward. The maze's path began at the southwestern corner of Ravence, deep within the Agnee Range. He followed it across Magar and the southern canyons, straight through Teranghar and up north. The path skirted around Rani, pierced straight through the deep desert like a Desert Spider's arrow, and then curved inward to its destination.

Palace Hill.

Leo blinked. He traced the path again and again, but it always ended at Palace Hill. His Palace.

The king sank into his chair in disbelief. He looked at Alonjo, trying to find words, and saw that his Astra was just as speechless.

All this time, the Prophet walked within the walls of his home. All this time, she had watched him run around like a fool. He wondered if she had laughed as he burned innocent men and women, or if she felt some ounce of guilt. Did a fiery heart like hers even know of guilt? Or did she believe that sacrifice was just a means to an end?

"The Prophet," Alonjo said finally, "is *here*?"

Leo gripped the arms of his chair so hard it left imprints of its carved pattern on his skin. His first thought went to Elena. If this labyrinth was true, she could be the Prophet, yet his daughter could not hold fire. Her handmaids reported no strange marks. Ferma was too old, and he had never heard of a Yumi wielding fire. Perhaps it was a servant then, one who prayed at the shrine within the Palace. However, Alonjo and Marcus always kept a close eye on the servants and would report if anything was amiss.

Leo let out a slow, shaky breath. There was no use for madness. He had to keep a steady head if he wanted to find the Prophet. He had to be ruthless.

"I have to become the man I wanted my father to be," he said in a soft whisper.

His eyes met Alonjo's. "Start a search through the Palace. Look for any man or woman with strange marks. Do it quietly though. The coronation is almost upon us, and Elena must not know." He swept his hand across his desk, and the holos dissipated in sparks of blue. "And bring Saayna here. I need to know what else she's hiding."

"Men and women, Your Majesty? I thought the Prophet—"

"The Prophet could be anyone at this point," he snapped. "If Saayna lied about these runes, she could have lied about the gender of the Prophet."

Alonjo looked down at his hands.

"Your Majesty, we are running a fool's errand," he said. "We are burning our people to find a grain of sand in the desert. The Prophet will rise no matter what we do." He looked up. His drooping eyebrows looked longer, his face tired and drawn. "We must repent."

"Alonjo," Leo sighed. He knew his Astra meant no harm. All these suns, Alonjo had never wavered, but Leo would not allow him this moment of weakness. "What is done cannot be altered. We must continue."

"But, sir—"

He held up his hand, silencing Alonjo. "Send for Saayna. I will await her at the shrine."

He stood and the Astra made to follow, but Leo waved him off.

"I need to be alone."

The fire purred as he swept out of his study. The guards bowed. Leo ordered them not to accompany him as he walked through his Palace. The hallway that led to his study was quiet. He could hear the sound of his footsteps echo and stretch across the stone walls. He made his way past the royal quarters toward the main chambers.

All this time, he had been too busy chasing runes and false words to notice the change around him. The Palace was abuzz with excitement for its new queen. He heard it in the whispers of the servants as they hung garlands of golden marigolds and crimson roses. They lit incense bowls of sandalwood and washed the marble hallways with rosewater. Guards wore freshly starched uniforms and lined their eyes with kohl.

Leo passed the kitchens where cooks prepared feasts of roast lamb garnished with spiced pomegranate, buttered bread stuffed with cottage cheese and crushed pistachio nuts, and steamed rice with candied almonds and cashews. Their assistants carried barrels of aged desert wine and honeyed whiskey. For the first time this week, Leo's stomach rumbled. He had lost his appetite since the massacre, but now he wouldn't mind a plate of sweetmeats.

He turned, entering the main courtyard. The sky, for once, was unblemished and lay open for him, wide and blue. He watched servants sweep away sand left behind from last night's sandstorm. It was part of their dance with the desert. It raged, they acquiesced. They built, and the desert watched. Leo had learned long ago that he could not win against this horrid, beautiful landscape. He only hoped that when the time came, he would not falter. He hoped that at least Elena could achieve what he could not.

At his approach, the servants bowed and stopped sweeping.

"You," he said to a young servant with an ash mark on her forehead. "Tell me—has the shrine been cleaned?"

"Yes, Your Majesty," she said, not meeting his eyes. "It was cleaned as of this morning."

"Good," he said. "Instruct others not to wander there. I want to pray in peace."

"Yes, Your Majesty," she said. "May the Holy Bird answer your prayers."

She shut off her ears for me long ago, he wanted to say, but Leo held his tongue. He motioned for the servants to resume their task.

The sun felt warm against his shoulders as he strolled through the garden. The main courtyard stretched several yards, full of thick banyan and blooming ironwood trees; their pink flowers created a rich, heady scent. In the middle of the plaza, a lone flame hissed. Leo avoided it. He'd had his fill of fire to last a lifetime.

After the library, the main courtyard had been Aahnah's favorite part of the Palace. She would sometimes take her reading and sit at the stone bench beneath the smallest banyan tree. Leo came to that bench and sat down.

He listened to the sound of the feathered brooms sweeping against the stone path. Overhead, a desert hawk shrieked. Leo felt something crawl within his stomach, and his throat tightened. When he opened his eyes, he saw the wide blue expanse of the sky. The hawk flew in a lazy circle above the trees. He wondered what Aahnah might have pondered over as she sat beneath these leaves. Had she already been taken by madness then, or had she seen the world with clarity? His fingers curled under the lip of the stone bench. He wished she was here now. He wished it so hard that it hurt.

"Father?"

Leo turned to see Elena with her guards trailing behind her. She wore a long, marigold dress that exposed her muscular arms and the delicate curve of her neck. Lotus petals were woven through her long curls, and she wore her mother's ring on her right hand. As Leo looked at her, he felt a small warmth of pride. Despite all his failings as a father, his daughter had grown into a strong, beautiful woman. And Aahnah would be proud of this.

"What are you doing here alone?" she asked, looking around. "Where are your guards?"

"Can I not walk through my Palace without guards nipping at my heels?" He made room next to him on the bench. "Come, sit with me."

Elena sat, smoothing out her silk skirt. Her jade earrings glowed in the warm sunlight.

"You're to make an appearance at the Fire Festival tomorrow," he said. "How do you feel?"

She shrugged. "It's just another day, Father."

"One of your last as princess," he said and gazed around the courtyard at the rustling banyan trees and cloudless sky. "Take it all in. Once you're queen, you'll rarely find peace."

She looked down at her hands. "You deal with it just fine."

"At times," he said, and he wondered if she could hear the strain in his voice, the weight of suns. "I'm glad you'll have a partner by your side, though."

"Samson is satisfactory," she said, and Leo smiled. Like him, she rarely gave compliments.

"Did you know he secured King Farin? The Jantari are coming to the ball," she said.

"Holy Bird Above," he muttered.

The Jantari were a nefarious lot. They smiled with their teeth, but their pale eyes held no mirth. He had tried to create a truce with Farin, but the treaties had all fallen through because the word of a Jantari crumbled like sand in the wind. Once, they had come close to peace along Ravence's southern border. Farin had agreed to pull back if Ravence allowed his emissaries safe passage through the desert. Leo had agreed, but at the last moment, the emissaries disappeared. Farin cried foul play and continued his petty proxy wars. Muftasa had later discovered that the emissaries were alive and well—so well that they feasted with the king in his castle. Leo had no choice but to reinforce the southern wall. The border had remained tense ever since, erupting every now and then with guerrilla warfare and subterfuge.

"At least his appearance will pause the fighting in the south," she said. "If only for a moment."

"Maybe your future king can convince his friend to stop it altogether."

"Maybe he'll win them over with Dragon's tits," she said, and they laughed. The sound surprised the hawk above, who cawed and spiraled out of view.

Elena watched it go, her smile slowly unraveling. "Will you come to the Fire Festival with me?"

"I can't. I have to meet with Saayna about the coronation ceremony."

She nodded, her lips pressed into a thin line. "You and your Fire," she said. "You hold it more dearly than any of us."

No.

He wanted to tell her that he was lying, that the real reason he sought Saayna was to pull out her lies until his hands bled. He wanted to tell her that the Phoenix was a vengeful god and that fire was just its cruel serpent. He wanted to tell her that he had made a mistake. While he had fooled everyone about his devotion to the Eternal Fire, he had misled her in the process. He had driven her further away than he had expected, and he could only blame himself for the distance between them.

He wanted to tell her, but he could not.

Because he feared what she might do with the truth.

"I wish you luck," he said and kissed her forehead. "You will look like the queen you've grown to become. The people shall adore and follow you blindly."

She fiddled with Aahnah's ring. Her eyes, Aahnah's eyes, grew dark and hard.

"Blind devotion leads to endless murder," she said. "The gold caps—"

"Don't ruin a good moment," he said and stood. He kissed his three fingers and rested them on her forehead. "So we the blessed few."

He left before she could comment on the tremble in his voice.

The shrine room was empty and cool. Leo relished the shadows that crept along the corners of the room. The golden ceiling reflected the warm glow of the fire that burned in the center. Floor cushions formed a ring around the pit of the fire. Leo sat and listened to the crackle of flames and the hiss of sparks. On the far wall, the Phoenix watched him. Artisans had carved Her likeness out of stone. They threaded Her wings with gold and adorned Her eyes with rubies found deep within the Agnee Range. Leo lit an incense stick, and the smell of sandalwood permeated the room. He set the incense in a lotus-shaped holder and closed his eyes.

Meditation had not initially come easily to Leo, but after decades of practice, he found the act as simple as drawing breath. He exhaled and sank his weight down so that his feet rooted to the stone, which then rooted to Palace Hill and the desert beyond. He saw his worries flit before him, from Elena's coronation to Saayna's lies. He observed them and then he let them go. With each exhale, he sank deeper. With each inhale, he felt his consciousness slowly untether from his body.

He became adrift. He knew nothing but darkness, a clean, black slate where the world had no beginning nor end. Rather, it was a single, present moment—an entity that existed within him, an entity that would disappear as soon as he opened his eyes.

At once, he was nothing.

At once, he was everything.

He was the desert and the mountains, the valleys and the canyons. He existed in the space between the stars, within a grain of sand, a part of the banyan leaf that struggled and broke in the wind.

He was the sun that beat down from the heavens; he was the twin moons that helped Alabore build his kingdom.

He was Leo, the king of Ravence, the son of Ramandra, grandson of Kishi.

He was a part of history, and he was creating history.

A hand touched his hand, and somewhere far within him, Leo was cognizant of a voice—a woman's voice. He traveled to the sound, treading shadows, and when he opened his eyes, he saw Saayna sitting before him.

"Forgive me for interrupting," she said. "You looked deep within meditation. Did you find anything?"

He looked at the fire. Its hiss had been distant; now, it filled his ears.

"I found some peace," he said.

Saayna folded her hands in her lap. Her long hair was held back by an ivory comb. The fire reached out toward her but did not touch her.

"You asked for me," she said. "I suppose I know why."

"You have misled me from the very beginning, Saayna," he said, choosing his words carefully. "But I'm not angry. I understand why." He opened his palm, revealing the ring of ash left by the Eternal Fire. "We both have someone we want to protect."

Saayna dipped her head. He knew she would not divulge the identity of the Prophet if he raged. She would deflect his anger. To win her over, he had to atone. Repent. After all these suns, he had learned that the best way to cull fanatics was to beat them at their own game—to show reverence.

He lifted his eyes to the Phoenix.

"The Phoenix protects Her Fire, like the Prophet protects Her image," he said. "You protect the Prophet, and I protect my kingdom against her." He gave a slow, measured laugh. "Perhaps then that is the true way to serve. We must give our lives in order to protect the ones we love. We burn so that they may live. But in the act of burning we become purified by the love we gave them."

He looked down and met her eyes in the light of the dancing flames.

"But what has that love gotten you, Saayna?" he asked. "The blood of your brothers and sisters is on your hands. They burned because you held your secret. Tell me, do you dream of their screams at night like I do?"

The High Priestess broke from his gaze and stared into the fire. The dancing shadows made her face a war zone, flickering between regret and piety. Yet when she finally spoke, her voice was unwavering, full of strength that only the faithful could possess.

"I never expected the runes to point to the Temple, but I had suspected the possibility. I put my brethren at risk. I know this. But it is our duty to protect the Fire and Her Prophet. We swore an oath. We gave our blood. There is no higher honor."

"You changed the second rune," he said, his voice low and sharp. "You somehow altered the burn on the young priest's back. Why?"

The fire sighed out sparks. They danced in the air and then spiraled downward, dusting his hair and hands. A spark caught on Saayna's chin, and she raised her hand to touch it.

"As above, so below," she murmured.

Leo leaned forward, his voice a deadly whisper. "Is it because the Prophet isn't a woman but a man? Is that it? Will a man of the desert burn down my kingdom?"

She finally met his gaze, the glow of the fire curving around her chin. For a moment, her eyes almost looked golden, and Leo understood that he had arrived at the truth.

"You wished it was you," he said and laughed. "You wished the Prophet was another woman, another priest, just like the sixth had been. But it's not. It's a man, and you already know it's not me."

Saayna turned back to the flames, a look of sorrow crossing her face. "The Prophet can never be the same man twice."

Leo stood. The flames hissed, retreating. He had been right. Saayna had lied to him, but he had found the wrong lie. Her simple brutality, altering the rune on the priest's back, had sent him on a bloody path he could not hope to return from.

"Seek forgiveness," she said. "Repent now, and the Holy Bird might give you reprieve in the afterlife."

Overhead, the Phoenix watched. Her red eyes glittered with the harshness of fire, with its cunning shadows and white, hot glare.

"Oh, Saayna," he snarled. "It's much too late for that."

27
ELENA

*Beware of the Black Hawk of Death. Its golden eyes see
the passing of our world into the next.*

—FROM *THE LEGENDS AND MYTHS OF SAYON*

Elena raised her arms as Diya wrapped an amber sari around her hips and then up over her shoulder, revealing the delicate curve of her waist. The handmaid withdrew a golden brooch set with rubies and pinned the fabric right below Elena's shoulder blade. With a delicate flick of her wrist, she draped the sari down Elena's arm, the fabric floating and then falling like the wings of a desert eagle.

Elena touched her neck. The necklace, a delicate array of gold and diamond insets, was a gift from Samson. Its singular jade teardrop rested just above her breasts.

Diya smoothed back her hair and clipped on the matching earrings. "Beautiful," she said.

Elena did not return her smile. Her hands felt hot. She had an urge to seize the necklace, to burn and mold the gold and jade into something new, something more free.

She sighed, her breath dragging in her chest.

Ferma had come earlier in the morning but had not said a word to her. The Yumi's eyes looked tired and strained. She spoke only with the handmaid. At one point, she had glanced over at Elena, who pretended to busy herself with a set of bangles. When Elena looked up again, Ferma had slipped out. Still, she could feel the Spear's presence outside her door like a cloud's shadow over a dune.

"The Spear wanted me to give this to you," Diya said as she tidied the flaps of the sari into symmetrical folds. From her pocket, she withdrew a holopod. "She said it has the list of names you were looking for."

Elena took it. "Thank you," she murmured. "Will you bring me some tea, Diya?"

She watched the handmaid's reflection recede in the mirror. When she was alone, Elena reached inside the drawer of her vanity and withdrew the scroll. The delicate paper rustled against her fingertips. The corners curled up. Slowly, Elena traced the dancer as she progressed through the seven forms.

Empty your mind. See nothing but the fire, for that is all that matters.

She ran her hands over the words, allowing them to sink in and take root in her mind. She wondered of the scroll's author; if she had a name, a family. Perhaps the author was the dancer. Perhaps this was a map of her life.

Elena ran her fingers down the length of the parchment to its bottom edge. Gently, she smoothed down the curled corner, revealing the penciled flower and her mother's initials. A.M. A remnant of a stranger.

"Your Highness," Diya said as she carried in a tray of tea and cloud cookies. Elena quickly rolled up the scroll and slipped it underneath the sash of her sari as Diya set down the tray.

"Thank you, Diya," Elena said.

She sat back as Diya took a stone bowl and filled it with rosehip oil. The handmaid withdrew a chip of sandalwood from her waistband and set it aflame with a match. The wood began to smoke, and Diya slipped off the clutch that held Elena's hair.

Elena breathed in the smell of sandalwood and jasmine as Diya carefully lifted her hair and let the steam warm her neck. Layers of smoke coiled around her, tickling her ears. She stared at her reflection in the mirror. She looked like a dragon. Horrid. Powerful. A deadly queen who knew how to quell rebellion and rule her people. But as Diya added more sandalwood into the stone bowl, Elena understood that the reflection was only a mirage.

She had survived the desert. She could withstand its heat, its silence, but when it came to fire and its insidious hiss, she was outmatched.

Elena looked down at her hands, at her blackened fingertips. The end of the scroll rustled against her elbow. She was just as powerless as before, except now she had burns to show for it. Alabore had not built this kingdom in a day. He had toiled for it, night after night, guided by the moons and the Phoenix. Yet, hadn't she toiled also?

A flicker of doubt slithered through her chest, sly and nefarious. Elena stared at her reflection and remembered the shattered mirrors in Ferma's room. What if she was not meant to be queen?

"There," Diya said. She sealed the bowl, suffocating the smoke. Her hands brushed Elena's neck as she began to braid her hair, but Elena waved her off.

"Let's leave it down," she said. "And tell the guards to prep the hoverpod. I'm ready."

Diya bowed and slipped out of the room. Stray tendrils of smoke flitted across the mirror, and Elena leaned forward to blow them away. The scroll shifted beneath her sari at the movement, threatening to fall out. She carefully removed it and was about to tuck it into the waistband of her petticoat when she saw the curled corner again. A.M, and the jasmine. Aahnah's favorite flower. Elena glanced at the writhing smoke, and suddenly, it clicked.

Jasmine.

The Jasmine.

The old woman who ran the tea shop, the place where she had danced in search of the love of her people, in search of the love of herself and who she was becoming.

Jasmine is a woman.

Elena rubbed the corner of the scroll between her fingers, the ink darkening her fingertips. She could be wrong. This flower could just be a random drawing, a thoughtless doodle. Perhaps Aahnah had been sitting in the garden, reading beside a jasmine bush when she drew this...

Or perhaps she had been in the tea shop.

Elena's mind raced as she stood, smoke sinking down her shoulders. Other than books, her mother had had a great love for tea. Elena had never seen her reading without a cup in hand. Perhaps then her mother knew of this old tea shop. Perhaps the old shop owner knew of this scroll. Perhaps all was not lost. The door opened, and Yassen and Ferma stood waiting.

"The hoverpod is here," Ferma announced.

Like Yassen, she was dressed in crimson, her uniform freshly pressed. Gold ringed her neck and spiraled down her arms. Her hair, threaded with bands of Ravani crystals, rippled down her shoulders. When she moved, they glinted in the light.

She looked beautiful.

She looked monstrous.

"Then let's go," Elena said and tucked the scroll in her sari.

Firecrackers ripped through the air as plumes of colored smoke danced across the sky. The smoke twisted, forming the shapes of animals: the yellow shobu, the blue dragon, the green vesathri, and the red bird. Along the street, performers beat drums and people popped bottles and waved golden flags.

Elena sat underneath a pavilion as her float made its way through Alabore's Passage. Before her, columns of soldiers dressed in red and gold marched down the main road, carrying banners of the kingdom as crowds whistled and hooted. The city police struggled to keep them behind the glass barriers. Elena watched as a guard beat back a gold cap who ripped off his shirt, revealing a newly inked feather on his chest.

"For the queen!" he screamed.

She wanted to hold her face in her hands, but she looked forward. Beside her, Yassen gave a soft snort.

"You want to rule a people like this?" he asked.

"They are mine," she muttered.

Curtains roped around the columns of the pavilion. From her vantage point, Elena saw snipers along the rooftops. She smelled spiced street food and the sweet smoke of cured meats. Further down the road, she observed a child wave a red ribbon that curled and unfurled like the tongue of a flame.

Everywhere, people cheered. Everywhere, people roared. The generals had informed her of her high approval rating after her speech, but

Elena had not expected this. The voices of the Ravani rolled through her, swept her up, and made her feel sick.

I am a fraud, she thought. *I cannot hold fire, yet they cheer for me.*

Diya brought her an iced drink garnished with crushed rose petals. Elena thanked her, her eyes traveling to Ferma, who stood at the edge of the float watching the crowd. Muftasa had also warned of protestors; she saw one, his face painted white, projecting a holo with a feather snapped in half.

"Out with the tyrants!" he yelled.

The policeman who stood by the barrier raised his baton and swatted the man's holo.

Elena glanced up at Yassen. "I need you to do something for me." She took a sip, rolling crushed ice in her mouth, and then set down the glass. "After I make my speech at the White Lotus, I need you to sneak me away."

His mouth hardened. "Are you trying to get me killed?"

"Not yet," she said, her eyes on Ferma's back.

He followed her gaze. "Why not Ferma?"

"She would disapprove."

"Rightly so."

"But you, my sweet Knight, like to break the rules," she said and looked at him.

He did not avert his gaze, but she saw him lean back as if wanting to. A new roar went through the crowd as the artisans lit up their rockets. They cut through the air with a high whistle and then exploded in an array of colors. The sparks flung out and then sucked back in, forming the wings of their Holy Bird. It soared down the street before exploding once more.

Still, his eyes did not leave hers.

"Where do you want to go?" he asked.

She smiled. "An old teashop in Radhia's Bazaar. There's an old friend I'd like to meet."

"Can't it wait?"

"No," she said and felt the scroll beneath her sari. Her hands itched. "I need to go today."

He turned and scanned the crowd. She saw him take in the guards, the police and the soldiers, the crowds raving mad along the street.

"It would be impossible," he said finally.

"Yet," she said, knowing that when he looked out at the crowd, he had already found a way.

"Yet it's good you asked me," he said slowly. The feather on his breast glistened in the sun. He withdrew his holopod, tapped something she could not see, and pursed his lips. When the pod pinged, he stared at it for a long moment, as if considering.

"Well?"

He turned to her, his voice low. "After your speech, we'll bring you back to the float, and the handmaids will close the curtains. There will be a guard change then. I just checked the schedule. We can slip out, get lost in the crowd."

"My dress—people will recognize me."

Yassen looked past her where Diya stood by the curtains, dressed in a plain, linen cloak. "We can fix that."

She turned back to face the crowd. She raised her arm, and they clapped and cheered, beaming. Ferma glanced back at her. Her tawny eyes glowed in the summer heat. Elena smiled, waving. The soldiers twirled their pulse guns above their heads, the blur of silver like moonflowers opening at midnight. Someone began a song, and she heard parts of the crowd catch on until they all began to sing.

"We are the chosen,
   the ones led by Alabore the Great.
We gave our hearts to the desert,
   and our mother swept us in.
Her sweet long curves,
   the dips of her valleys
   the heat of her flames
gave us a home, a home we say,
   to tend and call our own."

Elena hummed along with them, but she did not sing.

The Passage curved and led to the White Lotus, a large lotus-shaped sculpture sitting directly in the heart of the city, within a luscious, circular garden. At the center of the flower, a fire burned. It hissed as the crowd cheered along the roundabout. Soldiers formed a security perimeter and then turned inward, saluting as the float came to rest.

Elena stood, exchanging a look with Yassen as they descended her float. Ferma led her to a podium at the base of the White Lotus. Journalists and their camera crews shot to their feet as she approached, shouting and clamoring for her attention. Hovercams flashed, and her image was broadcast across every holo in the city.

She smiled, allowing it to reach the corners of her eyes. When she reached the podium, she held up her hand, and the city lit up with the chorus of thousands. Proud and strong. She let them roar, knowing that every nation, from Pagua to Jantar, was watching her.

Slowly, Elena lowered her hand to her heart, and the crowd hushed. Ferma stood beneath the podium and caught her eyes. She gave an encouraging nod.

"My fellow countrymen," Elena said, "today we celebrate a Fire Festival like no other. For this sun, you will have a new queen."

Cheers and hoots rumbled through the city center, spreading throughout the capital like the tremors of a heart. In the holos above her, Elena saw herself—tall and golden, dressed in regality and grace. At that moment, the sun filtered through the sandscrapers, and the White Lotus was basked in gold. Her necklace shone with the brilliance of stars. She understood then why Samson had chosen it.

"You will have a king trained in the ways of the sword. Already, our southern border is stronger than ever, thanks to the joint operations of our armed forces and the Black Scales," she said and was met by disjointed sounds of approval. Elena remembered the beggar and his scowl as he called her a Sesharian. She leaned forward, gripping the podium. "But, my countrymen, we will not have peace. Not when we kill our own in the sanctuaries of our parks."

She stared at the journalists, at the hovercams, at the crowd in the distance. "We will not have peace if we burn our own names in the sand."

A disquiet fell over the square. Below her, the reporters whispered and scribbled notes in their holopods. She waited until she had their attention once more and then withdrew the holopod Diya had given her earlier.

"In last week's killings, we have seventeen dead Ravani. Seventeen. Shall I read their names out for you?" She opened the pod, and a holo emerged with a list of names. "Ajax Rathore, Jasleen Kumari, Kazenia Bo, Hassan Ruim, Huna Vi, Ramila Neuri, Uday Vyseria, Tia Givan, Anthosh Biswan, Yemani Nour—"

She stopped suddenly, her eyes sharp and hard. "Shall I go on? Or does hearing their names make it more real? Does knowing who they are make us realize our loss?"

She closed the holo, and her voice echoed down the streets of Ravence. "As queen, I will try the men who opened fire on these innocent civilians. Today, Ravence will know justice. Today, I will burn *their* names in the sand." She looked up at the clear blue sky. "By the Phoenix's Fire, I swear this to you."

She descended from the podium in silence. The crowd did not cheer. Not even the journalists spoke up. All stared at her as she strode down the pathway of the garden, the Lotus fire crackling behind her. It was only when she reached her float that the people of Ravence awoke from their shock.

At first, it was a quiet sound, weak and hesitant. But once it started, it began to grow until it bloomed in pockets of cheers and stunned applause, in circles of admiration and approval, in wordless nods and the squeezing of hands. Because if there was one thing Elena knew, it was the nature of her people. A people brought together by a dream for peace, by the fiery hand of justice. She had laid down her sword. Whether or not they agreed with her, a Ravani would respect that.

Elena climbed back onto the float, and the handmaids closed the curtains of the pavilion, obscuring the public's view.

Yassen motioned to the back, where a small private chamber was sectioned off by thick red curtains. As she passed him, he muttered quickly: "That was a brave thing to do."

She stopped. His eyes flickered over her, and he looked as if he was about to say something else when he turned away. "Go, change. We've got little time."

Wordlessly, Elena ducked inside.

Diya helped her change into a plain, linen cloak and then draped the ceremonial sari over her own head, hiding her face. The heat pressed around them, and Elena blew sweat off her upper lip.

"Thank you, Diya," she said. Diya nodded, her hands shaking.

"You ready?" Yassen's voice sounded faint from outside the thick curtains.

Elena squeezed Diya's hand and slipped out. She ducked her head as the trumpets sounded, announcing the end of the parade. Soon, hovercars would arrive to take her back to the Palace, where her father was probably seething. At this, Elena smiled—a genuine one.

Yassen pushed her through the curtains. He hopped down and held out his arm to help her as the new guards strode up.

"How was the shift, Knight?" one of the guards asked.

Elena felt him stiffen, but then she stepped out of the float and stood behind Yassen.

"It's too hot," her guard said. "Her Highness is in the changing room catching her breath. Diya here is going to fetch some fresh ice. In the meantime, don't bother her—and keep Ferma away. I think they had a fight."

The guard chuckled. "Only the princess would dare to get on the bad side of a Yumi."

"You couldn't get on any side of her," another guard said.

They laughed, and one clapped Yassen on the shoulder. Elena saw him wince.

"Did you take a peep, Knight? I'm sure you saw something through the curtains."

Color rose on her face, and she dipped her head as Yassen straightened.

"Just keep the Yumi away."

He saluted and drew past them. Elena followed, hiding her face. They walked quickly as the guards grumbled something about the Yumi and justice. Yassen led her to the perimeter line, where soldiers stood with their pulse guns. He nodded at one, saying something about ice for their queen, and they drew back. They did not give her a second glance.

With the parade over, the crowd mingled along the road. Many were drunk on whiskey and desert wine. Some whispered about the speech while others laughed and pushed, pointing at the soldiers' banners flapping in the wind. A gold cap warbled off-key.

"Justice in the sweet, harsh dunes," he sang.

Elena sidestepped him as he wobbled. A friend helped him up, but then the man doubled over and vomited. Elena wrinkled her nose, pushing deeper into the crowd. She followed Yassen's tall frame, his head bobbing over others. When they reached a corner, he stopped to allow a hovercar to pass as she drew up beside him.

"A peep, huh?" she said, and he looked at her, surprised. "Were you looking?"

"What, no!"

"The guards—"

"They joke—"

"But you—"

"Come on," he said and tugged her down a side alley.

Colored powder stained the stones. Ahead, a boy flung crimson powder at a young girl, who squealed and ran, red flying from her hair. They passed an open restaurant where the waiter popped a bottle, and the people at the table laughed and raised their glasses to catch the spray. A hovercar beeped, and Elena slunk along the wall to let it pass.

"This way," Yassen said, ducking into another alley.

Elena pulled the cloak closer as she followed him. She wondered if Ferma had caught on by now. She must have. The Yumi probably sent guards to track them down; Elena imagined Ferma stalking through the streets, her hair prickling behind her.

Elena ducked as two gold caps hoisted up dried azuri branches. The smell of ash permeated the streets. Already, the city began to build large fire pits for the coronation. She spotted one in the middle of a square where gold caps piled azuriwood on high, the white branches clawing the air as if to escape their fiery fate.

Along windows and storefronts, she saw holos for the coronation, proclamations of success and glory. Tourists who came for the festival marveled and took photos of the streets.

Elena pushed past them. Out of the corner of her eye, she saw Yassen swipe a holo away, its blue dust dispersing into the afternoon. She smiled.

They came up to another alley. This one was so narrow that Yassen had to walk sideways to get through, his back and chest touching the two walls. Elena waited for him to pass before she followed.

They turned a corner and moved down another road before they finally arrived at the square. Jasmine's Tea Garden stood, dark and awaiting. But as Elena followed Yassen, he froze.

Two guards crept out from under the awning. Yassen held up his hands as they raised their guns.

"Where is the queen?" one growled.

Before he could answer, Elena pushed past him, drawing back her hood so that they saw her face.

"Lower your guns," she said.

After a tense, hesitant moment, they did.

The square was empty of urchins, merchants, and even stray sho-bus. Elena glanced around and saw the Palace guards hiding in the corners, in the shade of the sun. The hilt of their slingswords glinted above their waists.

The dark awning of the teashop opened before her. Elena sighed, knowing who waited inside.

Ferma sat at a table with a fresh pot of tea. She looked up as Elena entered, and her tawny eyes met the princess's.

"They almost shot Diya for helping you sneak away."

"She did nothing wrong," Elena replied, sitting across from Ferma.

The table was small, yet the distance between them seemed to stretch for miles. Elena folded her hands before her as the old teashop owner appeared from behind the counter. Her hair, thick and grey, was combed into a long braid that trailed down her arm as she bowed.

"Your Highness," she said.

"I need to speak to you, Jasmine," Elena said and looked at Ferma, "in private."

The Yumi regarded her for a moment and then stood. "You know, your actions today could have cost many lives," she said. "Diya's, Yassen's, mine—imagine the chaos if something had happened to you."

"Enough, Ferma," Elena said, not looking at her. "Let's talk about this later. We're safe now."

But Ferma only shook her head, the ends of her hair writhing like angry snakes. Without a word, she brushed past Yassen and walked out. He glanced at Elena, regret crossing his face.

"Don't take too long," he said and followed Ferma.

"Would you like some tea?" Jasmine asked when they were alone.

"No, please sit," Elena said. She studied the network of wrinkles that sprouted across the old woman's face. A filmy look obscured her brown eyes, making them pale, grey. Had she been younger, Jasmine would have had eyes like her own.

Eyes like her mother's.

Jasmine sat down. The pot of tea steamed between them. Elena leaned forward, reaching across the table and wrapping her hands around the old woman's.

"I know of you," she said. "You were my mother's friend. Weren't you?"

"Ah, so you know," Jasmine said with a soft smile. "How did you find out?"

"I discovered an old scroll of my mother's," she said. Jasmine's hands stiffened, but Elena held them tighter. "She left an odd note on it—a drawing really. It was a flower, a jasmine, and for the longest time, that's what I thought it was, just a flower. But it's you. Isn't it?"

Jasmine lowered her eyes. "We were dear, old friends," she whispered.

"Did she ever tell you of the contents of this particular scroll?" Elena asked, letting go to withdraw the ancient parchment from her cloak. She set it down between them.

The old woman stared at it but made no move to touch it.

"Yes," she said finally. She looked up, past Elena, to the small window of light pooling in from the door. "Your mother and I grew up in the same neighborhood. We studied together until university. She was so bright. She wandered through the world with a profound sense of curiosity and a yearning for knowledge that humbled everyone. And she was kind. Sweet. When you talked to her, you felt the world slip away. You felt that you mattered simply because she was listening to you."

Elena scoffed but did not interrupt. The woman Jasmine spoke of was not her mother. Aahnah had never paid attention to her. She was lost within her books, her flowers, the world she had constructed for herself.

"Everyone noticed her, including your father," Jasmine continued. "I'm sure you know this, but they met at university. He consumed every part of her—from her mind to her heart and the very time she had. As she grew closer to him, she grew further from me. We had a row. She said I was jealous, and I called her a fool." Jasmine shook her head. "I never received an invitation to the wedding. And once your mother was behind the Palace walls, I couldn't reach her. It wasn't until she came here into this shop and sat down in front of me just like you, that we spoke again."

"When was this?" Elena asked, her voice hollow.

"You must have been three suns. She had changed then, Aahnah. Grown more pale. But when we began to reminisce about the old days, she became the girl I remembered. Do you know that her favorite sport was windsnatch? She would steal out of the Palace, and I'd brew a fresh pot of tea and bake cloud cookies before we watched the game here. She loved the Fire Birds."

Elena stared at Jasmine, who smiled to herself. Elena could not picture Aahnah, the woman who sang to her flowers, as Jasmine's Aahnah, a woman who intently watched players knock opponents from their wind-gliders to the molten ground below.

"But what about the scroll?" Elena asked. She tapped it. "When did she show this to you?"

Jasmine did not answer right away. Instead, she got up slowly, the scrape of her chair filling the empty café. Without a word, she disappeared into the back of the shop. Elena waited. She drummed her fingers against the scroll. A minute passed, then two, then five, then seven. Elena began to get up from her seat when the old woman reemerged carrying a metal tin.

"Here it is," she said. She hobbled over and set it down beside the scroll. She wiped off sand and dust, making Elena cough, and opened the box.

Inside were two papers carefully folded into small squares. Jasmine delicately picked one up with two fingers. Slowly, she unfolded the paper and set it before Elena.

Elena peered at the tiny scrawl, her heart hammering.

There was a drawing of a woman in a wide stance. She held her arms out before her, one hand curled into a fist with the other flat and open.

The seventh form: the Goddess. Become the fire, the light, for the entirety of the world.

And then, at the bottom: *Give it love. It is as alive as me and you.*

Elena looked up, her eyes wide. "What is this?"

"I think you know."

She looked back down and unrolled the scroll with trembling fingers. She took the parchment and held it to the final, faded form. The lines bled into each other, and Elena gasped.

It was the final form.

"Your mother gave this to me to keep safe," Jasmine said. She gazed at Elena, and there was a dark, hard look in her eyes. "She didn't trust your father with this, and I hope you understand the gravity of her decision."

She opened Elena's other hand and set the second paper square in her palm. Elena stared at it. If it was supposed to hold the weight of the world, it did not. It felt like nothing.

"What is it?" she asked.

"A letter. Something that will keep you safe during the time of reckoning," Jasmine answered.

More riddles! Elena shook her head. Her hand closed around the parchment.

"What else did my mother know?" she asked. "What did she learn after all that time in the library?"

"Oh, child," Jasmine said. This time, she was the one who wrapped her hands around Elena's. "Your mother came across something horrible. Deeply horrible. But she would not tell me about it. She just said that upon learning it, it changed everything. She went back to the library to find more texts, but then there was the Ashanta ceremony and," Jasmine's voice faltered.

"And then she died," Elena whispered.

Jasmine's eyes grew duller as tears blurred them. She merely nodded.

Elena sank back in her seat. A sense of sickening dread filled her, and a question emerged in her mind, one that made the warmth leave her body.

Did she jump into the flames to hide what she knew? Or was she forced to?

Elena stared at her hands, stunned. She could not find it in herself to move. The only person who could influence Aahnah had been her father. *Did he...*

She felt her throat go dry. She did not believe it, of course not, but... Elena shuddered. She could not deny her father's ruthlessness. His burning desire to rule. A Ravani never allowed a person to come in the way of his kingdom. It was one of the first lessons Elena had learned as a child. A Ravani held true to the throne. A Ravani was her kingdom, and nothing else.

She stood up abruptly. "I have to go." She rolled up the scroll, hiding it and the letter underneath her cloak. "Thank you."

"I'm sorry I could not tell you more," the old woman said, but Elena was already moving for the door.

She stumbled into the square, blinking furiously in the harsh sunlight. People, sounds, the city—they all seemed so far away. *How has this come to be, this treachery?* She wanted to wail. To rage. She wanted to drag her father to the Eternal Fire and shake the truth out of him. Elena swayed on her feet.

Out of the corner of her eye, she saw Yassen. He looked up from where he leaned against the wall, but he did not meet her eyes. He looked straight past her, and horror swept across his face.

Elena turned just as the sound of pulse fire ripped through the air. She fell on her hands. Screams erupted through the square. A guard toppled over, blood blossoming from the hole in his head.

Her guards shouted out orders, but her ears were ringing, and she could not hear them.

Someone grabbed her arm, and Elena gasped. Ferma loomed over her, screaming, but Elena could not hear, she could only watch her lips move.

Ferma jolted her to her feet and pushed her. Suddenly, Elena was running. Her legs moved on their own accord as if her body realized what her mind could not—*run*. She ran down a side street, Ferma sprinting ahead with Yassen and two guards bringing up the rear. More pulse fire split the air, and Elena saw a woman on a terrace cry out, her body slumping over the railing and tumbling to the ground.

"Move, move!" Ferma barked.

Elena ran. Her chest beat wildly and her hair came loose as they rounded a corner and dashed into the open market. A hoverpod had already docked. Pulses ripped along rooftops as her guards returned fire. But then came a bright flash and a loud smack, and the air exploded. Elena hurtled forward. She fell to her knees, biting down on her tongue. A ringing filled her ears, blood and dirt in her mouth. The blast had torn down a building to her left, and a fine dust coated the air.

She looked up. The hoverpod still stood. Ahead, she saw Ferma rise to her feet, her hair sharpening and raking the sky. Elena clawed the ground, found purchase, and lurched to her feet.

A gun sounded. She felt the pulse graze her cheek, heard its whisper at her ear, and saw it race through the market and rip into Ferma's chest.

She saw the Yumi's eyes widen. The surprise. Everything was in slow motion, like a dream. The blood sprouting from Ferma's chest. Her hands scraping the air. Her body, her hair, Ferma, falling.

Falling.

A scream burst from Elena, but it sounded as if it came from another creature. And then the world was spinning. A sniper on the roof fell. An urchin lay squashed underneath a fallen wall. Blood spilled down the side of his head, his eyes wide open and his mouth frozen in a silent cry.

Someone pushed her, but her legs were lead, and she stumbled, almost falling. But then there was Yassen, yelling, shouting *move! Move!* Then he pulled her, nearly ripping her arm out of her socket as her guards returned fire and they dashed into the pod. The door closed and then they were airborne, shooting straight into the sky like a comet, like a meteor, except this time it was the other way around. They headed for the heavens, not down to Ravence.

Elena gasped. She clutched Yassen's arm. Everywhere, she trembled. Suddenly, her feet could no longer bear her weight and she sank, taking Yassen with her. He was telling her something, something about the Palace, her father, and she turned to him. Somewhere deep in her mind, she registered that his eye was bleeding and then realized it was blood from her shoulder. She must have been shot, but she felt no pain.

Everything felt so distant. Everyone swam. Who took off her cloak? Was that a medic wrapping treated cloth around her shoulder? Someone pushed something into her mouth. It tasted bitter yet sweet. Elena gulped it down, and then the shadows that crept along the edges of her vision grew longer. She was on her side. People were shouting. Her hands lay in front of her and there, in her palm, was the folded letter. Someone had given it to her. It winked at her as her eyes fluttered and she sank, willingly, into the deep, forgiving darkness.

28
LEO

When the Phoenix rises, the sky will burn. Dunes shall unravel, mountains shall shake, and valleys shall fill with the bones of generations past. She shall rise from the flames, and She will seek Her Prophet.

—FROM *THE PROPHECY OF THE PHOENIX*, TRANSCRIBED INTO WRITTEN WORD BY THE FIRST PRIESTS OF THE FIRE ORDER

"Anything?" Leo asked.

Marcus shook his head. "No, Your Majesty. They're all clean."

Leo rested his chin in his hands, his head heavy. All morning, Marcus and his men had searched the servants for strange marks under the ruse of an outbreak. Leo had come up with the idea. He had instructed Marcus to round up the Palace men because a "sickness" was spreading in the city—one that left black marks on the victim's body.

"The servants will call it an omen," Alonjo said. "That a so-called sickness descended into the Palace before the coronation."

"The Prophet brings plagues," Leo snapped. He turned back to Marcus. "Have you sworn the servants to secrecy?"

"Yes, sir, but I expect some will tell their family members," the Spear said.

"Well, if they're clean, they'll have nothing to suspect," Leo said. "Inform them that the disease is mild, but that we can't risk infecting

Elena." He waved away the servants' holos before him and drew up the guards' profiles. "Search your men next, Marcus. The Prophet could be anyone."

"Sir," Marcus said and then hesitated. He looked at his hands. "I don't believe any of my men are the Prophet. They're Ravani. But the new men who've come in..." he said and trailed off. Slowly, he met Leo's gaze. "They might be worth searching."

"Do you dare accuse your future king of smuggling in the Prophet?" Alonjo said.

Marcus shook his head. "I mean no harm, sir. But the runes appeared after Samson and his men arrived. Perhaps the Black Scales are the omen."

"Or it could be coincidence," Alonjo began, but Leo silenced him with a look.

"There are no coincidences when it concerns the Prophet," he said and thought back to his vision in the desert. He had seen the runes before they had been burned in the sand. The Eternal Fire was warning him, taunting him. "Fine. I'll speak with Samson, but search your men, Marcus. No one shall be overlooked."

Marcus bowed. At the door, he paused.

"Your Highness," he said, and Leo looked up, meeting his kohl-rimmed eyes. "What if the Prophet does not know that he is the one? What if his power lies dormant? What if... he's you?"

Leo did not smile. In his stomach, he felt the cold serpent coil within itself. "Then we have all committed sins for naught," he said. Stone filled his veins, the crevices between his muscles. "Send for Samson."

The fire around the room whispered when Samson arrived. He stood at the door, his eyes traveling over the flames and the mosaic floor before resting on Leo. He bowed.

"Your Majesty," he said. "Alonjo."

"I flew to our southern border recently and had the opportunity to meet a peculiar commander of yours," Leo said.

"Ah." Samson shifted his feet, crossing his arms behind his back. "You mean Chandi. She's harmless."

"She's insubordinate," Leo growled. He thought of her dark eyes, her skull necklace. "Your Black Scales wouldn't let me, their king, go through the gates. They insisted that your Commander Chandi did not share her prisoners."

"Chandi can be a bit possessive—"

"I cannot have your men defying me," Leo said, his voice slicing through the room like a blade through sand. "They've sworn their allegiance to Ravence. If they cannot even pretend to stick to their words, what use are they to me?" His eyes met Samson's. "What use are *you* to me?"

The fire hissed. Samson stared at him, as if shocked, and then nodded slowly.

"I suppose my men do not recognize the true king." He held up his right hand and spread out his fingers. "But I've taken the Desert Oath. And as long as you are king, I'm beholden to it."

Leo rounded his desk. Sunlight spilled in from the skylights, warming the crest on the marbled floor. He stopped at its edge, Samson across from him. Silence wedged between them, as solid as the Agnee mountains. Leo expected Samson to fidget, but his future son-in-law stood tall, his face carefully composed.

He knows why he's really here.

"Saayna lied," Leo said, and the crackle of the fire filled the space between his words. "The Prophet is in the Palace."

Samson closed his hand. He did not look alarmed. "Do you know her identity?"

"The Prophet is a man," Leo answered, but Samson showed no hint of surprise. "I've searched the servants and the guards. All who remain are you and your men."

Again, Samson nodded. "I see."

His composure annoyed Leo. He wanted to see some reaction—a twitch of an eyebrow, a downturn of the lip, a slackness in the jaw—but Samson did not yield. He would make a brutal king.

"Come," Leo said.

Samson followed him to the edge of the room. The fire that had listened calmly now grew at their approach. Leo felt its heat buffet his face. He held out his hand and, without hesitation, Samson opened his palm, his signet ring glinting. Leo took his hand and held it over the fire. The flames grew and brushed the back of Samson's knuckles.

Leo pushed down; the flames bit into Samson's flesh. The militant sucked air through his teeth, grimacing as the stench of burnt hair filled their nostrils. Leo held both of their hands over the fire until his own arm began to smart. Only then did he withdraw.

Samson cradled his fist to his chest. His fingernails blackened at the tip, and a bruised patch of skin began to worm above his wrist. His family ring pulsed with the heat of the flames.

"Aloe will help with the burn," Leo said and then added, "Son."

Delicately, Samson pulled off his ring and slipped it onto his other hand. "Do you plan to burn down this whole kingdom to find the Prophet?" he asked, his voice barely a whisper over the hiss of the flames.

"I won't have to if he comes forward," Leo said. "This Prophet is a coward. He hides while people die in his name."

Alonjo drew up beside them and held out a damp towel. Samson took it and wrapped it around his hand, concealing the burn but not the smell of burnt flesh.

"I assure you, none of my men are the Prophet," he said as he knotted the ends of the towel. He met Leo's gaze then, and there was a gravity in his eyes, a depth that belied his charming demeanor to reveal something more dangerous underneath. "You run a fool's errand."

"There's the shobu's bite," Leo said with a mirthless smile. "And here I thought you would always roll over to please me."

"You jeopardize our rule," Samson said. "How can Elena and I begin to rebuild the kingdom if you leave us nothing but ash?"

"Don't worry. I'm sure your Jantari king can lend you some metal." Leo waved his hand and the flames fell back, purring. "If the Prophet rises, there will be no kingdom for any of us to rule."

"You don't know that," Samson whispered.

"Oh, but I do," Leo said, his voice piercing the crackle of the flames. "There will be no mercy under the rule of the Prophet. He and his Phoenix will lay waste to Ravence, and they will not stop there. Jantar, Cyleon, Nbru, the islands, they'll all fall. We will enter a war that men cannot win. The last Prophet made Ravence into these dunes. Can you imagine all of Sayon as one big, barren desert? How long do you think we'll last if we aren't burned already? Half a sun, maybe more if we're smart. And then what? He'll pick us off like carrion, burn us in the name of his vengeful god."

Leo unwrapped the towel and touched the burn on the back of Samson's hand. "This is the small price we must pay to avoid war. A few misdeeds for a greater future," he said and looked into the younger man's eyes. "So you will search your men with my Spear, and you will report to me if you want this kingdom."

Samson dropped his arm, the towel wilting in his hand.

Leo returned to his desk as Alonjo guided Samson out. A cloud passed overhead, and sunlight seeped out of the room. It suddenly felt cooler. The shadows lengthened, cutting across the marble floor like sharpened slingswords.

Leo touched the necklace underneath his clothes, the jade bird above his chest. Aahnah's bird. Of all people, she might have understood. Or all people, she knew the meaning of sacrifice.

The day she had jumped into the Eternal Fire, she had told him something odd, something that came to him now as the heavens opened and rain drummed against the skylights.

"I think the desert forgets easily," she had said as she donned her ceremonial robes for the Ashanta ceremony.

"Forgets what?" he had asked, but she only mumbled to herself, falling back into her nonsensical world.

He had only meant to protect her. The day of his coronation, the Eternal Fire had demanded a sacrifice, but he, selfish and young, had refused. He could not imagine a life without Aahnah. She knew how to root out his faults and iron them into something stronger, better. When they used to lie together at night, she would trace his eyebrows, smoothing out the tension in his brow.

He closed his eyes and imagined her face. Drew it line by line, as if by doing so, he could conjure her before him. The perfect arch of her brows. The deep, brown eyes. The birthmark hidden behind her ear, at the edge of her skull. He rubbed his thumb against her necklace. What was it that she would always say to him?

"The dead and the living are full of fear."

Oh, he was afraid. Afraid of what would happen should he fail: the intense fury of the Prophet and the Eternal Fire, the rupture of his kingdom, the death of his daughter. He could feel his fears eating the edges of his mind, racing toward him.

Seek forgiveness.

That's what they all told him—Saayna, Alonjo, Marcus—but they did not know the cost of forgiveness. The dagger it wrenches into one's heart. Forgiveness required vulnerability, an admission of his faults. It required him to bare his chest to the world and allow others to dig into his flesh. But he did not need forgiveness. Aahnah was dead. What he sought now was power—power to protect Elena and shield this desert from its merciless master.

The rain fell harder, yet as Leo looked up, the sky was afire. A bright, living red ringed with pink—Aahnah's favorite type of sunset.

A message popped up on the glass panel of his desk as Alonjo returned. The Astra wore a pinched expression, but Leo did not question him as he turned to see his Spear in the holo.

"Your Majesty," Marcus said and then hesitated.

"What is it? Have you found him?" Leo asked, but the look on Marcus's face made his stomach clench and his heart skid.

"There's been an attack in the capital," the Spear said. "We believe it was an attempt on Elena's life. We—"

"Is she alive?" he gasped.

"Yes, sir," Marcus replied.

Leo collapsed into his seat. His heart hammered in his chest, and the relief that washed over him seeped away like a fast-fading sunset.

"Her Highness is already on her way to the Palace in a hoverpod," Marcus continued. "She should arrive in seven minutes. We suspect the Arohassin are behind the attack."

"Yassen Knight," Leo said, his voice rising. "Where is he?"

"He's with Her Highness," Marcus said. "It appears, according to initial reports, that he was the one who saved the heir."

Leo's head snapped up. "What?"

"Those are the initial reports, sir," the Spear said. "We've had casualties, both Palace and civilian. Some of Her Highness's guards died in an explosion. The Yumi, Ferma, was killed on the spot."

"Holy Bird Above," Alonjo whispered.

Leo stared at Marcus's floating image. *Ferma dead, Yassen Knight alive. It makes no sense. And for him to save her...*

"Seven minutes you said?"

"Yes, sir," Marcus said, and Leo shot to his feet.

The passage from his office to his chambers rumbled open. He strode through, past the polished halls and overflowing kitchens, through the main courtyard and Aahnah's banyan tree, his heart fluttering in his chest like a caged bird. *How in the heavens did the Arohassin get past capital security? Past Samson's own men?* He heard a hum and saw a black dot on the horizon—the hoverpod.

He began to jog and then run. Aahnah's necklace jostled against his chest as he sprinted through the halls, past gaping servants and guards. Leo thought of the image he created—a king so full of fear, so aware of his own mortality.

He burst through the gates and onto the landing platform that jutted out behind the Palace, along the cliff of the hill. He saw a team of medics huddled against the rain. They jumped and bowed. Guards lined the platform, and there was Marcus, ordering his men to surround their king.

"Your Majesty!" Alonjo said as he ran up behind him. Sweat beaded on his forehead.

The hoverpod appeared through the burning sky, and its descent seemed to take an eternity as Leo watched it dock and its ramp slowly unfold before bloodied guards stumbled through. He craned his neck to see over the heads of his guards.

And then he spotted her. That dark mess of curls. Leo pushed past the guards, the medics, Alonjo, Marcus, all of them, and saw Yassen supporting her, helping her down the ramp, pushing her forward. Her eyes fluttered to Leo.

"Elena!" he cried and drew her into his arms. He squeezed her tightly and felt blood on his clothes and his face, but he did not care.

Elena. His daughter. His heir.

She was alive.

Elena made a soft, rasping sound.

"Yes?"

Her eyes locked on him. Her words were faint, barely above a whisper.

"Ferma," she breathed. "What happened to her?"

But then a team of medics rushed in and unhooked him from her. Leo watched, heart thundering, as they eased her onto a hoverbed, undid the wrapping on her wounds and sedated her. He watched her go.

"They got Ferma," a voice said behind him, and Leo turned to see Yassen. His eye was bleeding.

"You," Leo said. Yassen flinched and took a step back. "You saved her. Why?"

Yassen looked past him to Elena's fading form.

"Ravani or not," he whispered, "the desert does not claim me as its own. I am only what I am."

A medic came up to Yassen, fussing about his eye, his shoulder, the blood, but Yassen waved him off. He bowed to Leo and followed his daughter. Leo watched him leave, watched the medics guide the hoverbed into the Palace, watched Marcus dip his head to say something to Alonjo. A second hoverpod docked, and more medics rushed in. Leo could only stare at the steady stream of bloodied men, his hands stiff by his sides.

Standing there, at the edge of the platform, he had never felt so small.

So powerless.

29
ELENA

The Yumi, above all else, are loyal warriors.

—FROM CHAPTER 16 OF *THE GREAT HISTORY OF SAYON*

The royal doctor wrapped her shoulder with clean gauze and pulled. Elena winced. The pulse had only grazed her shoulder, drawing blood but ripping no flesh.

He said she was lucky. Elena tried to laugh, but the sound caught in her throat and came out more like a mewl.

The clean white walls of the infirmary blinded her. She was in a small private room, but through the window of the door, she caught glimpses of a hallway filled with bloodied guards and harried medics.

The doctor, satisfied with his work, clipped the gauze.

"The stitches will heal, but you'll have a scar," he said.

She nodded. She felt weightless, as if she could float away at any moment.

The doctor withdrew glass vials and a syringe from a cabinet by the door.

"For the pain," he said.

The needle pierced her skin, but Elena did not even feel its prick. She felt detached from her body, as if she were watching herself from afar. Distantly, she noted that she still held her mother's letter in a clenched fist.

"You might feel drowsy," he said.

Her tongue felt swollen and clumsy. Her lips would not move. She heard a knock, and Yassen entered.

"How is she?" he asked.

Her blood caked his cheek and chest. His sleeve was torn at the elbow, and she saw his purple, rotting flesh.

"Shocked, but Her Highness has been graced by the Holy Bird Above. She will recover," the doctor said and pointed at Yassen's arm.

"Have they seen your arm?"

"It's fine."

"It's purple."

But Yassen shook his head as he withdrew his holopod. "Other guards need more attention. Besides, we need to inform the king and Samson. They'll need us for a debrief."

The doctor gathered the empty vials and the syringe. He dropped them in a heated bin and turned on the burner; a warm glow spread along the white walls. He then offered Yassen a bottle of pills.

"Tell Her Highness's handmaid to give her this every night for the next two nights, but no more. The coronation is nearly upon us, and we can't have her groggy."

Elena blinked. Somewhere in her mind, she registered that they were speaking about her. She wanted to tell them that she couldn't take the medicine—that the ball was tomorrow, and she needed to practice her dance with Samson, but her mind and lips veered in different directions. She sagged forward, whimpering. Yassen caught her and gently pushed her back into the bed.

"You need rest," he said.

He leaned over, adjusting her pillow, and she smelled death on his shoulder—a sickly, sweet smell that reminded her of overripe grapes left out in the sun. The doctor dimmed the lights. Shadows stretched along the walls, and Yassen pulled away.

You're dying, she thought.

The shadows came down the walls and into her eyes. They washed over her and pulled her down. She was sinking. Her body felt heavy as shadows piled on like layers of sand, like the dunes shifting and growing, burying her alive. Her eyelids fluttered. Yassen grew smaller.

Don't leave, she wanted to say, but he was already gone.

Elena awoke to a cool hand pressing against her forehead. She moaned, and the hand moved away.

"Your Highness."

It was Diya's voice.

She heard a rustle of fabric and felt Diya rise from the bed. Elena opened her eyes, one by one, blinking away sleep. She was back in her room. A bowl of iced water sat on her bedside table along with the small square of a letter. A breeze stirred the curtains, and she smelled iron.

Diya returned to her side, cradling a bowl of soup in her lap. She stirred its murky contents, raised the spoon, and held it to Elena's lips.

"Drink," she ordered.

Elena drank. The soup stung her tongue, but its warmth seeped down her throat and fanned out across her chest. Suddenly, hunger pressed against the sides of her stomach. She grabbed the bowl and raised it to her lips. Diya watched as she desperately slurped, wiping away drops that dribbled down Elena's chin with a kerchief.

"I can get more," she offered.

Elena shook her head and wiped her lips with the back of her hand. She gazed around her room and was struck by its emptiness.

"Where's Ferma?" she asked.

Diya took the bowl from her hands and set down the tray. She gently cupped Elena's hands in hers.

"Your Highness, Ferma is dead."

Elena stared at her. "No."

But Diya squeezed her hands, her voice soft, eyes wide and sympathetic. "She fought bravely."

And then the memories flooded Elena: the burning square, the crushed boy, blood blooming across Ferma's chest like a carnation. Ferma, her Ferma, falling.

Grief stung Elena's throat, her eyes, her nose. The pain felt enormous, intense; it pierced into her chest like a finely tuned slingsword, cutting down, down, down. Her stomach clenched, and Elena crumpled.

Diya held her as she sobbed, her cries like that of an animal, a desert yuani stranded in the dunes with wings torn from a storm. Her stomach burned. Her shoulder ached. She clung onto Diya because if she let go, she would become unmoored, lost in a deep black ether of grief.

What had been Ferma's last words?

You truly are a fool.

And Elena felt like one. She was a fool for going off into the city without her guards, without Ferma. Because of her Ferma was dead.

Slowly, her grief blackened into rage. She detached herself from Diya and rose, swaying on her feet. Her hands prickled. Her face felt hot, and she felt a sudden desire to *burn*, to destroy, to create a hole in this world to compensate for the hole it had drilled in her.

The fire in the hearth flashed. Elena reached for the flames. They reared back, as if afraid, but she ripped one off as if breaking a limb. The flame pulsed in her hand. It resisted, but she held on, squeezed, and it coiled around her fist.

Burn. She wanted everything to burn.

The images of the dancer flashed in her mind as Elena sank low into her heels. This time, she did not falter. This time, she knew every part of the dance as if it had always been known to her.

The Warrior.

She squatted low, feeling heat build up in her legs and then thrust out. The curtains were the first to light. The fire leapt onto the thin blue silk, eating, laughing. She spread out her arms like the desert sparrow, and the flames jumped onto the floating ottoman. She heard a loud pop as it deflated, sagging to the ground.

She whipped around. The flames soared as Diya screamed, rushing out into the foyer. Elena guided the flames onto her bed. The sheets peeled away like the decaying petals of a lotus.

The Spider, the Tree, the Snake, she flowed through the forms, her anger—her grief—building power. The flames cackled. They rushed past her like eager shobus as she descended into her garden. She set them upon the banyans, and the air filled with smoke. Sparrows cried out as they fled from their homes. She watched them go, and her hunger grew stronger.

The water in the fountain began to boil as the flames swelled. They latched onto an ironwood and tore it apart, split it right down the middle to reveal its white, fragile flesh. Elena heard Diya begging for her to stop, but the flames were louder. They crooned to her.

Burn, they cried. They wanted everything to burn.

Elena closed her eyes, concentrating. A flame grew in her hand, and she willed it to elongate, to strengthen, to strike. She saw the last form of the dance, saw the coiled muscles of the dancer and the heat in her veins. As she crouched back and raised her hand, lifting her fiery spear like a warrior, like a goddess, Elena felt something unlock within her—a spark that flared up her spine.

She felt the power of fire course through her veins, and it tasted delicious.

Elena threw the spear of flame, and the fountain shattered in an explosion of stone and dust. The boiling water splashed out, hissing. Flames burst through, hopping from stone to stone, setting everything ablaze.

And Elena wielded them. She swept her hands, and the flames turned. She beckoned, and they listened. When she pulled her hands in, they surrounded her but did not burn her; their heat licked her face like the kiss of a lover, a mother, a friend.

Elena held out her hand, and a flame curled around her wrist.

This is what it meant to be powerful.

This is what the Phoenix must feel like.

"Elena!"

She turned and saw her father at the balcony. Guards tripped down the burning stairs. They made to grab her, but her fire would not have it. The flames screeched and plunged toward them.

"Stop! Stop!" Leo cried out.

And then he was running toward her, and the flames were cackling, waiting, but he tore through them as if they were nothing but air. He grabbed her hand, pulled her to him. She gasped. The flames cried out and fell inward, bearing down on both of them, but she swept her other hand and they dissipated, turning to ash that rained into her eyes.

Leo held her tightly, whispering. She had not heard him over the song of the flames, but now, in its aftermath, she heard him.

"Don't," he choked. "Don't turn into her."

They gave her stronger medicine afterward, and Elena drifted between dreams of burning flesh and dying women. She awoke in fits, slick with sweat, and Diya would place a cold towel on her head and hush her back to sleep.

When her fever finally broke, Elena awoke alone. She sat up slowly. They had brought her into a guest bedroom, where a mirror stood across from the bed.

Elena caught her reflection. Dark rings circled her eyes. Her lips, dry and pale, were cracked like a desert that had seen no rain. Her skin still smelled like the burning banyan leaves.

With a soft groan, she stood. The floor felt cool, and her toes curled. She heard a soft knock as the door opened.

"You're awake," Samson said, entering the chamber.

She felt too tired to smooth down her hair. "I am."

"Should I call for tea?" he asked, and she nodded.

He turned and whispered to someone outside, but she could not see who. Samson closed the door and gestured toward the seating area.

She sank down, resting her head against the back of her chair.

"How do you feel?"

"Like I've been dragged through the desert," she croaked, her throat dry.

Diya arrived carrying a pot of tea and glazed cups. Samson poured the tea, his hands swift and precise, and then handed the cup to her. She held it close to her chest but did not drink.

"Try it," he encouraged. "It's a gift from the visiting lords of Cyleon."

"I thought no members of the royal family were coming," she said.

"They still paid tribute," he said and raised his cup, "to the Burning Queen."

A smile cracked across her lips, but it shriveled as she looked out the window to the grey storm clouds. At the sky not yet ready to give.

"The garden," she began, but then Samson lowered his cup. He reached inside his pocket and withdrew a yellowed square of paper. The letter.

"I found this in your room, after we put out the fires," he said. He laid the letter down on the table, and she stared at it.

"Did you read it?" she asked.

"No."

She studied him, searching for a sign of a lie, but her vision was still foggy from the medicine.

She reached across and picked up the letter. "I thought this would have been the first to burn."

"Fire knows its brethren," he said. She turned to him, and he held out his hand. There, right below his knuckles, was a faded, red burn. "A souvenir from your father."

"What did you do?"

"Nothing," he said and looked at her. "Your father believes the Prophet is in the Palace, and he's burning every man to root him out."

She set down her cup and folded her hands in her lap to stop them from trembling.

"How can you be sure that the Prophet is here?"

"There were runes," Samson said and withdrew a holopod. He opened it and four images fanned out. She did not recognize the strange marks, but Samson pointed them out one by one: "The first two were burned onto the back of a priest. Supposedly they say, 'Daughter of Fire,' but Saayna misled us. The Prophet is a man. The other two runes appeared in the desert, and they mean rebirth or something of the like."

"But Palace Hill?"

Samson swiped away the holos and brought up a new one. It was a map of Ravence, overlaid with the runes—imprisoned within a tumultuous maze. Samson leaned forward and touched Palace Hill, the center of the labyrinth.

"They lead here," he said.

She stared at the labyrinth and the monster that lay within. Her mind reeled as she tried to grasp its meaning, but her thoughts felt distant, dream-like. She tried to form a plausible answer, but she was only full of questions.

The Prophet. *Here?* Had he laughed when she burned down the garden, or had he recognized her as his own? Had he seen her strength?

Her sorrow?

"Leo killed the priests, you know," Samson said. "He left the necessary number needed for the coronation... He made Ferma do it."

Ferma's name sent a fresh pang of grief through Elena; she clenched the letter in her hands.

"That's why she looked so defeated," she whispered and recalled the dull, haunted look in the Yumi's eyes. "Where, where is she now? Where's her body?"

"I'm sorry," Samson said, his voice soft. "They had to cremate her while you were asleep. So her soul would not tarry."

Elena bit her lip, blinking back tears. "May the skies guide her."

"May the skies guide her," Samson returned, and a silence descended between them. After a moment, Samson sighed, rubbing his hands together.

"Your father has to be stopped, Elena," he said. "He's going to burn down this kingdom before we even get the chance to rule it."

Elena thought back to Ferma amongst the shattered mirrors, the way she had clutched her hand.

The king's gone mad, she had said.

"One thing I can't figure out," Samson continued, "is why. Why all the reckless killing? When the Prophet comes, none of this will matter in the end. Those priests, the girl, they died for nothing."

"The girl?" she asked. She saw him pause and saw the regret flash in his eyes before he looked down at his hands.

"Before we knew the Prophet was in the Palace, we looked for young girls in the city," he said, his word heavy, flat. "Saayna told us the Prophet was a young girl in Rani, and Muftasa found one. A pyromaniac with hair of starlight. A girl barely twelve suns. Leo killed her."

He looked up at her, and his blue eyes turned a shade darker. "Her name was Ynez."

"Stop," she pleaded. She could take no more. "Please."

Samson stood. He tucked the holopod and its ruinous map back into his coat.

"The attack in Rani paused the search in the Palace, but believe me, after seeing what you did to the garden, Leo won't stop until he has the Prophet's head at your feet," he said. "He thinks you're damned because you learned how to hold fire."

I don't just hold it. I wield it, she thought, but her tongue would not move. Samson bent down and placed a kiss on her crown.

"Rest up. We still have a ball to host," he said.

After the door closed, she sank her face into her hands and then recoiled. Her hands *burned*. Ash rimmed her nails.

She was damned.

The guests began to arrive three nights later in a long procession of hovercars that trailed up the Palace Hill drive. At the doorsteps of the Palace, servants bowed and escorted the dignitaries in. There were diplomats, lords, ministers, generals, and royal heads of state. The ladies wore lavish dresses with long trains or heavy cloaks threaded with gold. Some wore tall feathers woven through their hair while the daring ones wore tailored suits of lightning thread. When they passed, the air gave off a burnt, metallic scent.

Lords wore sharply creased coats with their family crests shining above their breasts. Generals donned their brass and gelled their hair into neat side parts while the kings and queens glittered amongst them. They did not need loud ornaments or fancy dresses. They had their crowns.

Elena watched as Leo set the Ravani crown on his head. In the dark halls behind the ballroom, the Featherstone glowed. He wore a rich ivory kurta with intricate golden embellishments around the collar and cuffs. Over his breast, the Phoenix spread Her wings.

Leo glanced at Elena, and she saw just how much he had aged in the few days since the attack. Deep lines ran across his forehead and brow. His cheeks sank in and his eyes, usually a steel-grey, had dulled to worn metal.

He reached across and adjusted the simple gold band around Elena's head. His fingers brushed her ears, hovering over the earrings.

"These are Aahnah's," he said.

She touched them, feeling the groove of the wings. They were jade birds caught in mid-flight, with gold in their eyes and beaks. They matched the necklace Leo always wore, the necklace her mother had gifted him.

"I thought she would like it if I wore them."

Leo drew back his hand. "Yes, she would have," he said, his voice strained.

Servants bustled by, carrying large bouquets of flowers and last-minute arrangements. Elena could hear the excited chatter of their guests through the doors. Today, all of Sayon gathered to see her, the young queen-to-be, the heir who would bring fresh life to Ravence.

They had liked her before, but now they loved her. Her speech had thrown off royalists, but after the attack in the capital, her approval ratings had shot to the heavens.

"There's nothing like a national crisis to band a country together," her father had told her.

He had not commented on her speech.

Elena smoothed out the layers of sheer tulle of her long red dress. The gown revealed her smooth brown shoulders and her lithe arms. Diya had rubbed her down with almond oil until her brown skin shone like gold. Around her neck, she wore a heavy necklace shaped like the Phoenix—a Ravani heirloom passed down from Queen Jumi. The bird's head nestled in the dip of her right clavicle; its wings fanned out across her bare chest and curved toward her ears. From afar, it looked more like a golden tattoo than a piece of jewelry. Jumi had swapped the Phoenix's traditional ruby eyes for emeralds, and Elena preferred it this way. They matched her mother's earrings.

"I assume you reminded your guard to stay out of sight," Leo said, and she nodded.

"Yassen will keep to his rooms," she said. She had instructed him to stay in his wing; the world still did not know that the Palace had employed an assassin of his rank. If their guests caught wind, she would begin her reign with more enemies than friends. Yassen had, after all, targeted or killed members of Sayon's elite, relatives of royal families who now graced their halls. And she had heard of Yassen's mistake with the Verani king. The old man was here now, drinking her wine and flirting with the young princes of Mandur.

"Your king is late," Leo muttered, and, as if on cue, Samson appeared at the other end of the hall.

He wore a long black velvet coat that brushed his ankles as he approached them. The coat stretched across his broad chest and shoulders, tracing the pattern of muscles that lay underneath. A thick gold band of Agnee gems curled around his neck. He wore kohl, and it brought out the darkness of his eyes against his raven-black hair. When he reached her, she could smell the rich musk of mutherwood—a mountain smell.

Samson kissed the back of her hand and straightened, his smile smooth and easy. "You look beautiful."

"So do you," she said. He laughed, the sound of it lifting the shadows in the hall.

"Watch out for the vultures," Leo said, and he looked at Samson. "Especially the ones across our borders."

"Of course," Samson said glibly, but she saw his smile falter. He turned to her and held out his hand. "Shall we?"

Elena looked between the two of them—her father and her fiancé, her past and her future—and she suddenly pined for Ferma. She wished the Yumi was here now, holding her hand, escorting her into the ballroom with her hair prickling behind them. It felt wrong to enter this next stage of life without Ferma.

Violins sounded, indicating their entrance. She mustered a smile and took Samson's hand. "Let's give them a show."

Leo led the way as they climbed the stairs, coming to a door that opened upon a landing overlooking the ballroom. The guards lowered their slingswords, and a royal melody hushed the crowd. Samson squeezed her hand. Through the doors, she heard the muffled voice of the announcer.

"All bow to the King of Fire, Son of Alabore, the Divine Grace of Desert and Sky, His Majesty, Leo Malhari Ravence."

The doors swung open, revealing the grand hall. Long curtains of roses cascaded down the gold shimmering walls, and the ballroom smelled full of life, of promise. Chandeliers floated along the ceilings, each more impressive than the last. Tipsy guests danced on the main floor, crushing fallen petals as they spun. Servants dressed in crisp white coats with gold lotuses on their lapels served glasses full of honeyed wine and spiced whiskey. Along the far wall of the ballroom, hungry guests milled over tables filled with roast lamb, seared ham garnished with candied pomegranates, and platters full of desert sweets.

The king stepped onto the landing, and the guests applauded, raising their glasses. Despite the attacks, despite all the death that he had caused, Leo stood tall. Elena admired and hated him for it. He knew how to rule, and he would never show weakness to these people.

Leo raised his gloved hand, and the applause died down.

"Friends," he said, his voice filling the space of the large ballroom. "Thank you for coming. Together, we shall herald a new age of Ravence, a new dawn brought by a queen of sand and fire. So please, raise your glasses for the blood of Alabore, the Thirty-First Ruler of Fire, my daughter, Elena Aadya Ravence."

And Elena stepped forward into the gaze of the hundreds gathered below. She heard them gasp, clap, and shout out toasts as she stood smiling, beaming, hoping they did not see the broken girl beneath.

She raised her hand, beckoning, and Samson drew up beside her.

"My future king," she said as Samson looped his arm around her waist. They waved and smiled, and the world ate it up.

The guests stared as she descended the marble staircase. The lords from Teranghar were the first to approach. They bowed low and kissed her hand. Next came the ambassador from Cyleon, who presented her with moonspun flowers that blossomed at her touch. The princess of Nbru dipped her head but smiled coquettishly at Samson. Wherever they went, people crowded around them. They laughed, doling out praises in hopes of getting into her good graces.

Their words are sweet now, but how long until they sour? she thought as the Verani king continued on and on about how he hoped Ravence would open its southern borders for Verani trade. As she listened, her thoughts turned to Yassen. How close had he come to killing this king? Had he put a gun to his head? Or had he used a poisoned dagger? Had he felt the same disgust she did as he looked upon the king's wide face, with his baby cheeks and thick beard?

"In due time, Bormani," her father cut in, finally ending the Verani king's long speech. Leo smiled and gripped his shoulder. "Let the young ones dance now. Eh?"

Elena smiled, relieved, but before she could head for the ballroom floor, she felt Samson stiffen beside her. She turned, looking up at him, and followed his gaze. There, walking toward them, was the Jantari king.

"Leo," Farin said. His voice came as a wispy rattle as air pushed through the metalwork of his neck. He was not a tall man, yet he was square in the shoulders with a large block of a forehead. He was dressed in Jantari blue—a deep, vivid color that mirrored the mountains of Jantar's eastern borders—and wore the silver emblem of a horned mohanti on his chest. His green metallic eye swiveled across the room, taking in the floating chandeliers, as the pale, colorless one set on Elena. "Charming place."

It had been almost a year since Elena had seen this half-metal man face to face. She had accompanied her father to meet Farin at the southern border, during a truce that did not last more than a week. After the emissaries' ruse, Farin had accused Leo of smuggling ore out of Jantar and into his kingdom. Her father had denied it. Troops had assembled on Jantar's border. War would have broken out if Leo hadn't requested the meeting.

Elena still remembered the gleam on Farin's face as they discussed the parameters of the treaty. The metal king, on the last day, had torn it apart, claiming subterfuge. He had only reinforced her distrust of Jantari metal. It was fickle, wild, uneven to the touch. Yet somehow the Jantari were able to meld it into engines and skyscrapers and hovertrains.

"Farin," Leo said, not bothering to hide the distaste in his voice. "You've lost some weight. Hopefully your diet isn't too strict."

"Nonsense. What are pounds if not the result of delight, hmm?" Farin said and looked at Samson. "This chap and I have often challenged each other in drinking games, and I swear he lets me win."

Samson grinned and waved over a servant carrying glasses full of desert wine. "Not tonight, Farin. I'm going to drink you into the ground."

Farin laughed, a dry, grinding sound. "Only if Her Highness drinks with me."

Elena plastered on a smile as she took a glass and handed it to Farin. Before, his metal eye used to unnerve her. Now, after the attack, after Ferma's murder, she felt empty of fear.

Everything—including the centuries-old hatred between Ravence and Jantar—felt trivial in the face of death.

"Let us drink to our new friendship," she said.

"Here, here," Farin said. He drank with calculated ease, his iron lips working to suck in the wine and distribute it to his tubes. It was a wet, noisy process. Elena abhorred it, but she did her best to hide her disgust.

The Jantari were metal freaks. Farin's ancestor, Queen Rhea, was the first to start the tradition. She sacrificed half of her body to boast of Jantar's superior metalsmiths. She had ordered the royal engineers to build a body more capable than flesh, and with each generation the gears became more advanced. The tradition belonged only to the royal family, luckily, or else Elena would have had to deal with a half-metal army along her borders. She supposed she shouldn't be too appalled by Farin. The Ravani sacrificed to fire, the Jantari to steel. Different gods, but with the same vein of fanaticism.

"Thank you for coming," she said.

"Thank your future king," Farin said. He set down an empty glass and belched. A gear hissed and then began to hum. "He's a dear old friend."

"I brought us together because I'd like my friends to coexist peacefully with my family," Samson said. He had only taken a sip from his wine. "This is a new era for Ravence, which means a new era for Jantar. Perhaps we can finally bring peace to this holy land."

Farin snorted. "Since when did this land ever know of peace?"

Ravence would know peace if the Jantari didn't wage petty battles, Elena thought, but held her tongue.

"My condolences to you, Your Highness. I heard that your old Spear passed in the attack," Farin said, his metallic eye examining her.

The mention of Ferma twisted a dagger in her stomach, but Elena would not let him see her grief.

"Thank you," she said, offering him a courteous smile. "But her death was not in vain. The Arohassin will answer for their crimes."

"They're a rotten lot," Farin said.

Elena looked at Samson, who remained still, his face carefully blank. She had heard of Farin's cruelty toward insurgents. He forgave no one, not even the smallest of informants. He dragged them to prison, tortured them, and then melted iron onto their heads until their skulls collapsed. Farin's ancestor had done so to Elena's great-great-great-great-great grandfather during the Five Desert Wars. It was a point in history of which Leo had never failed to remind her.

"Which is why I have brought us together today," Samson said. "The Arohassin are not just Ravence's problem. They're a plague on Sayon herself. They've grown bolder. This week they targeted Ravence, but who knows which kingdom they'll target next. Jantar? Cyleon? Pagua? We have credible sources," he said and glanced at Elena, "that tell us of rogues operating in both Ravence and Jantar *right this second*. We're haggling over the southern border while they rot us from within. Perhaps if we join—"

"There are more Arohassin in Ravence than Jantar," Farin said, his eye swiveling to Leo. "A three-to-one ratio, I hear."

"I think your information is mistaken," Leo said. Elena saw a slight muscle work in his jaw. "You have the island colonies. I've heard the Arohassin love to recruit sea rats."

"Gentleman," Samson said. His voice was firm yet with a subtle edge. "The Arohassin are a problem. We can agree on that. And we can only squash them, once and forever, by working together."

"Ah, but if we are to join forces, the Black Scales should withdraw from the southern border," Farin said.

"Absolutely not," Leo said.

"It would be a measure of confidence," Farin drawled.

"One that should be paid in kind," Elena said. She knew that the metal king was only goading her, waiting for her to lose her composure and lash out; to give a reason for another generation of hate. But Farin's words were just ash to a fire—inconsequential.

Leo had always warned her of instigators like him. They were just as foul as the gold caps.

"My queen is right," Samson said, nodding at Elena. "If we withdraw my Black Scales from the southern border, who is to say a trigger-happy Jantari won't shoot?" His gaze turned to Farin. "Everyone is watching Ravence. And if all eyes are turned to the desert, they're also watching Jantar."

"The older, brighter cousin," Farin said.

Elena laughed, a sharp, harsh sound that cut through the air. She raised her glass, smiling widely as she stared Farin down.

"I think Ravence is more capable than you think," she said.

Farin's gaze did not waver, but his smile did. He could no doubt sense the threat veiled beneath her words.

"Enjoy your dance, young ones," he said, and he bowed, gears whizzing and whining the brutal song of a body forced into mutation.

Leo nodded at her. "Go. It is your night."

Elena took Samson's hand and led him to the ballroom floor. Other couples acknowledged them with a curtsy, making space for them. When they reached the middle of the floor, she turned to Samson.

"It was a mistake inviting Farin," she whispered as the quartet began a new piece.

"He's not that bad. You just need to know how to work him," Samson said and took her hand. He placed the other on the small of her back and drew her close. She could smell cologne on his collar, see a flake of stray kohl on the top of his cheek.

"By 'work,' do you mean get him drunk?"

The violins rose, and they twirled. They fell into rhythm with the waltz, their feet skipping over the floor as marigolds revolved on the ceiling and shed their heady scent. Samson spun her, and her skirt flared like the petals of a blossoming lotus.

"It's serious work," he said as she turned back into him.

They wove through the other couples. Samson held out his hand, and she dipped underneath his arm. She twirled behind him, her hand slinking across the small of his back as he drew her back in.

"Am I to marry a drunk?" she asked.

"No, but as the first decree of our reign, we will order for barrels and barrels of wine. Mountains of it," he grinned. They swayed, and his hand dropped back down to her waist. "And we'll ship them out to Farin so he and his metal friends will drown in it."

She bit back a smile. "Attack by wine is your master plan?"

"The most refined type of subterfuge," he said, and this time she actually laughed. It surprised her. After Ferma's death, she had not thought it possible to laugh again. She still didn't. But Samson smiled, and his voice was gentle as the violins slowed.

"We will make this kingdom great, Elena," he said. "That is my promise to you."

The violins quieted. The air grew still as the dancing couples broke away.

"I know," she whispered, parting from him.

After their dance, the royal couple mingled with their guests again. Elena forced a smile as they continued to kiss her hands, shower her with gifts, and laugh boisterously at Samson's jokes. Her cheeks hurt from forcing pleasantries. When she found a moment, she excused herself and made her way across the ballroom, the train of her dress rustling behind her.

She returned to the hall behind the ballroom. A few servants lingered behind the hall's columns, likely taking a break from serving her guests. Elena dismissed them with a wave of her hand. When she was alone, she slumped against the wall and closed her eyes, drinking in the cool darkness and savoring its still, muted silence.

She had a lifetime of balls, war rooms, and festivals ahead of her. Yet, she had only *this* moment. *This* breath.

A gnawing sensation grew in her chest, and Elena knew it was her grief. In the emptiness of this hall, she felt it as keenly as a burn. Her nose prickled. A heavy weight pulled down her chest, her shoulders, threatening to sink her like a pebble in quicksand. She clenched her fists, her throat tight. She could not cry. Ferma would not want this. Ferma would want her to bear a fresh face and return to the ballroom with grace.

"Elena."

She did not open her eyes right away. She inhaled deeply and slowly uncurled her fists. To her left, she could sense him move closer.

Elena finally opened her eyes and turned to her father. In the low light, the lines in his face looked more pronounced, cutting deeper into his flesh.

"Are you alright?" he asked.

"Yes." She pushed herself from the wall and forced herself to stand straight. "I just needed a moment."

"I—" he began and then sighed. "I'm sorry. About Ferma. I know how close you were to her."

"Samson told me something interesting the other day," she said quickly to hide the tremor in her voice. "He told me that Ferma executed the priests on your order. He says you've gone mad chasing after the Prophet."

"Elena—"

"I'm putting a stop this," she said, her eyes boring into him. "There will be no more hunts, no more killing. Can't you see? I can *wield* fire now. I have to protect my kingdom from madmen, including you."

"You don't know how to control fire," he said. "It's dangerous. The Prophet is dangerous. If he rises, he'll burn us alive."

"He'll burn you," she said. "Not me. I'm not the one who killed his priests."

"The Prophet knows no mercy."

"That's where you're wrong, Father," she said. As she stepped toward him, she imagined Ferma, her hair rising and her face as fierce as a storm wind. "I understand fire in a way that you never will. The Prophet knows, and he will honor me. Fire knows its brethren."

Leo shook his head. "Now *you* sound like a madman."

"And you sound like a murderer."

He flinched, as if the words had physically struck him.

"Elena—"

She pushed past him, away from the ballroom, away from the fake smiles and cloying laughter. The pain in her chest doubled. Grief was a double-edged sword from which they both drew blood.

30
YASSEN

Forever and forever, farewell, dear friend.
May the moons and the stars bless our parting.

—FROM *THE ODYSSEY OF GOROMOUNT: A PLAY*

It had been easy to steal out of the Palace during the ball. All the guards and servants attended to the guests, so Yassen slipped out from the servant's side entrance. Around the front of the Palace, he watched hovercars pull up the long drive. Lords, ambassadors, ministers, and bureaucrats spilled out. Despite the attack in Rani, they still came with their glittering jewels and painted smiles. Even the neighboring monarchs weren't thrown off by security concerns. For them, this was a night to take stock of the Ravani kingdom—to see how far it had fallen and how brutally it would rise.

Yassen threw on his hood and tried to ignore the ache that traveled up his right arm. With each passing day, his skin grew darker. The burns had turned from a bruised purple to the black of a crow's wing, the color of rot. The markings had begun to inch up his wrist to his fingers. He would need to treat it, and soon. With his left hand, Yassen found the holopod in his pocket. He squeezed it for good measure.

He had received a message on his holopod earlier in the day.

Honey muffin.

Nothing else. Seconds after he opened the message, the holo dispersed in blue dust, but its meaning had been clear enough.

Yassen began to make his way to his hovercar when he saw a familiar face. The Verani king stepped out of his car, his belly straining against the confines of his blazer. Yassen froze. The king sniffed the air with distaste as Palace servants bowed. Behind him, the Verani queen, a petite woman with eyes the color of amethysts, scowled.

They both wore leather, despite the desert heat. The king said something, and the queen shook her head, fanning herself. Yassen sucked in his breath as they entered, and only exhaled when they were out of sight. Then, he slipped out from the shadows and got in his car.

Yassen sped into the city as it began to drizzle. He veered down the flyover, speeding through side streets until he came to a narrow alleyway. At its end, two shobus tussled over a scrap of meat. They looked up as Yassen killed the headlights. He leaned down in his seat, ran his fingers along the soft leather, and found the tracking device—a small black square with a tiny blinking light. Yassen detached it from its holder and got out of the car.

The shobus growled.

"Easy, boys," he said. His hand found the gun tucked underneath his cloak. It was his father's gun, a silver pistol of genuine iron and steel. The police were conducting pulse sweeps, using sensors to locate the heat of unregistered pulse guns. His outdated firearm would go undetected.

Yassen wrapped his hand around the holster as he backed away from the shobus.

"Easy."

One shobu barked, taking a few steps forward, but then stopped, its twin tails flicking. Yassen slipped out of the alley, walking quickly. A child in rags stood at the corner, and when he held out his hand, palm outstretched, Yassen dropped the tracking device along with two Ravani coppers.

"Stay off of the streets, tonight," he whispered to the boy. "The silver feathers are on their rounds."

The boy blinked, his tiny fingers curling around the coins and the tracker. A small, almost knowing smile touched his ash-streaked face. Yassen turned on his heel and did not look back.

The city was mostly empty. Last week's attack had shaken Rani to its core, and most of the residents—save the orphans and the shobus—hid in their homes after curfew. Yassen sidestepped shards of glass and crumpled petals. In a broken storefront window, a banner from Elena's coronation hung limply.

She had been close to death. Yassen wondered if Elena had realized this as he turned into a narrow alley, walking to an unmarked door at its end. People changed when they saw death's dark face, when they were inches away from its cold grasp. He had. And he had seen it two times already. Each encounter had leached a portion of him, but it had also ignited something—adrenaline and a rush to defy the odds, to defy death itself. Yassen felt it now as he rapped on the door, a simple two-beat knock. The old door swung open, and Yassen stepped in.

The storefront windows were shuttered; shadows filled the old bakery. Yassen recognized the skid marks where the counter once stood, the faint smell of bread jogging his memory. The day came back to him in flashes: Samson's split eyebrow, the girl's shrill scream, bread rolls sweetened with honey and naivety. They had dined like kings that night, wrapped in the bliss of what they did not yet know.

A shadow moved, and Yassen saw a flame flicker. Two scarred hands cupped a lighter. The man bent to light the yron in his mouth; the flame revealed his harsh cheekbones, burned cheeks, and dark eyes. The man inhaled deeply and blew out smoke. It curled like a writhing dragon, and Yassen smelled the sweet scent of narcotics.

"I trust you weren't followed," Akaros said.

"No," Yassen replied.

His old master nodded. Ash sprinkled onto the floor from his yron. "And the Yumi woman?"

"Dead," Yassen said. "They found her body among the wreckage. She managed to nick a few of our men before she died."

"That's a Yumi woman for you," Akaros chuckled. The end of his yron glowed in the dark like a red eye. "It's a good thing you notified us about the change to the teashop. Swift feet, Knight. And the girl?"

"She was only grazed by a pulse," he said, surprised to feel relieved. When he had pushed Elena into the hoverpod, Yassen had seen a deep, animal fear in her eyes. He recognized the look; he had worn it when he first saw death on his mother's burnt face.

"Good," Akaros said. "Then everything is falling into place."

"Our captured men—"

"Sacrificial lambs for slaughter, I'm afraid. They served their purpose."

"So why did you call me?"

"To give you one last task," Akaros said and looked at him. Yassen saw no light reflecting from his eyes. "Now that we've eliminated the Yumi, you're the queen's head guard. Stick with her. When she is crowned, we will strike. Hard. I want you to remain by her side and help her escape down this path," he said as he withdrew a holo-pod. The blue light of the holo illuminated the space and threw long shadows across the former bakery's bare walls. A map of the Agnee Range floated before them with a red, marked path snaking down the mountainside. "Lead her to it. Make it seem safe. And then when the time comes, our boys will pop her off."

His words filled the empty space. They weighed down the shadows, the air, Yassen himself. He supposed he should feel relief. At least they did not ask him to carry out the assassination. He would not have to dirty his hands with Elena's blood. But her blood had already stained him. Her blood still soaked his ruined uniform, the one he could not bear to wash.

Akaros blew out, and tendrils of smoke brushed Yassen's face. "Well?"

Yassen looked at him, a bitter taste filling his mouth. When he had made his plea to the Arohassin, bargained for his life after he had been burned, after he had been deemed expendable, they had given him one last task in exchange for his freedom—to end the Ravani line.

A part of him wished he had run, taken off after his wounds had been treated. He could have even run after the attack in Rani. But the Arohassin were no fools. They would have tracked him down before he reached the sea, before he could escape to Moksh, the land of volcano and debris. He would be miserable there, but he would have been free.

Yet, if he had balked, if he had let Ferma live, it would have been his body lying in the rubble.

Yassen felt Akaros's eyes boring into him. He could not falter. Not now. But the fear in Elena's eyes, the way she had clutched his arm... He could not shake the feeling nor the guilt that stirred in the pit of his stomach.

Shut it out, he thought. *Shut it into a room and never open it again.*

"The girl knows how to hold fire," Yassen said. He forced himself to not break Akaros's gaze. "She found a scroll left by her mother, and now she can wield the flames."

Akaros hissed, the end of his yron flaring. The map and its red path glowered between them.

Yassen reached out and touched the holo. It dispersed into blue dust.

"*If* she's crowned..." he began.

"She must be!" Akaros snarled. A hovercar passed by, and its headlights bled through the slats, revealing his burned skin. He dropped his yron and stamped it out. As Yassen watched the ash scatter across the floor, he wondered what the next owner of this bakery would think of the litter. And then he realized it was no longer a bakery. It was just a building filled with ghosts.

"We can only kill her if she's crowned. That's what will make this siege legitimate. We need to officially end the Ravani line. The Jantari king wants her head at his feet when he sits on the Fire Throne. Wielder or not, she must die," Akaros said, and his eyes met Yassen's. There was an urgency within them, a conviction and, below it all, a deep, troubling fear.

"Is it true then?" Yassen asked softly. "If she can wield fire, do you think she's the Prophet?"

Yassen knew he sounded stupid, but he had to know. All his life, he had abhorred the Phoenix and Her vengeful Fire. All his life, the Arohassin had taught him that the Ravani kingdom was built on a set of lies, of burnt corpses and mindless mantras. There was no Phoenix. The Prophet had only been a mad priestess obsessed with infernos. Ravence was only a desert because warfare had stripped it of its once lush forest. Fire only brought madness, death.

Akaros snorted. "No, she's not," he said flatly. He ground his heel, flattening the yron. "She must have just learned the old fire dance of the Desert Spiders."

"But if she can wield fire, she'll be harder to kill," Yassen said.

"Nothing we can't handle." Though Akaros did not say it, Yassen saw his eyes flit to his arm.

Yassen nodded. He took the holopod from Akaros and slipped it into his cloak. The badge of the Palace guard glimmered on his chest; he had forgotten to take it off.

"And Yassen, give my greetings to Sam," Akaros said.

It wasn't until he had made his way back to the alley, until the door of the hovercar clicked softly beside him, that Yassen realized he did not know of Samson's fate. He knew death awaited Leo and Elena. It was the only way for the revolution to begin. But Sam...

Yassen looked out the curved windows of the hovercar. The shobus were gone. Rain drummed against the glass. He glanced down and saw his badge glinting in the low light. Elena and Samson dead in one stroke—the thought shattered him. It opened a large, black hole that threatened to suck him in, and Yassen did not dare to even think what lay beyond it.

He gripped the edge of the control panel, his knuckles beginning to pale from the effort. *Oh, Sam.* After all these suns, after just reuniting, they would have to part once more. The injustice of it filled Yassen with a sudden, hot rage. Pain jolted up his arm, but he ignored it.

Isn't Ravence enough? Isn't Leo enough? Why do the Arohassin have to claim Samson as well? Samson had given them their due, paid for his penance, and fought his way to his freedom. He had been a beacon for Yassen, a hope for better days. His only friend in the whole world; his only family. Yassen had allowed the Arohassin to take thousands of lives, but he could not let them have Samson's.

Samson must live.

The engine thrummed to life, and Yassen pulled out of the alleyway. The streets were still empty as he weaved through the city. The rain grew harsh, lashing at the glass panes; the world blurred into bleeding strokes of color. Only the Palace remained clear as it stood atop its hill, watching him. He thought of the flashing eyes of the Phoenix, the burn of Her Fire, the way Elena scooped the flames—her look of triumph and determination. And then he remembered how she listened as he told her about music, about the boy he once was, and the way her eyes lingered on him even after he fell into silence.

But she must die. All his suns of training told him this was the way.

The rain lightened as he drew up to the Palace. Yassen parked and nodded at the attendant. He could hear the faint music of violins and the tinkle of laughter as he passed underneath the ballroom windows toward the servant's entrance. Two guards flanked the door in the rain. They stepped forward, and he threw back his hood.

"Men," he said.

"I thought you were inside," the tall guard said, his hand on the hilt of his slingsword. "The king doesn't want anyone seeing you."

"I just wanted to get some fresh air," Yassen replied.

"More hunting?" The other guard grinned, and the scar along his cheek twitched. "Did you bag any Arohassin?"

"Oh, they should've cleared out by now if they know what's coming," the tall guard said. "No one attacks our queen without facing the sword."

Yassen nodded, his face carefully blank. "If I may, gentlemen."

The tall guard tapped a code into the door panel, and it slid open. "Rest well, Knight."

Yassen entered and pulled on his hood again. He skirted the main courtyard where guests strolled underneath the large canopies of the banyan trees. He wondered if Elena was still in the ballroom, dancing among the spinning skirts. He wondered how she hid her grief.

The music and laughter faded as he walked deeper into the Palace. A few servants scurried past, heading for the ballroom, and they nodded at him. When he reached the split of the Palace wings, he stopped. A figure stood in the garden below. He recognized the tumble of curls immediately.

"I thought you were still dancing," he called out, and Elena turned to look up at him.

Moonlight filtered through the canopy and curved down her bare shoulders, dusting the tops of her cheeks, the bridge of her nose. The golden necklace of the Phoenix shone against her brown skin. But her eyes, her eyes were as dark and tumultuous as a desert sky, and they were fixed on him.

Yassen breathed in sharply.

Fuck.

"I came to look for you, but you weren't in your room," she said.

"I went to get some air." He descended into the courtyard and tugged off his hood. He stopped a few paces away from her, the wide trunk of the banyan between them. "Discreetly, of course."

She did not smile. She stood in the moonlight, and it made her look ethereal, distant.

"I should have never forced you to take me to Jasmine," she whispered.

He heard the tremble of grief in her voice. He saw the sorrow in her dark eyes.

He had looked the same when he had seen his mother's charred body after they had cleared the fire. He had thrown up and heaved until there was nothing left within him, until he was as hollowed and empty as the blackened house.

"You can't live with regret," he said for the both of them.

Her earrings tinkled softly as she turned to him. The moonlight and the rain drew long, soft shadows down her face.

"How?" she asked, her voice hoarse.

Her eyes pulled him in, drowned him. He felt the snake rattle in his stomach as she stepped closer, rounding the trunk.

"How did you go on when they died?"

The snake flicked out its tongue, and he felt his heart hitch as it watched, waiting. He licked his lips, his mouth suddenly dry.

"Why did you come looking for me?" he finally managed. "Aren't you needed at the ball?"

"Ferma liked you," she said, and the words cut through him. The snake laughed. "You're one of the few who gained her respect."

He wanted to tell her that he did not need it—their pity nor admiration. They were all fools for trusting him. A bitter taste filled his mouth, and Yassen looked away. His arm felt heavy. The banyan trees rustled in the rain, whispering, and he thought he could hear them tell of his deceit, his treachery.

"You should rest." He stepped back, moving into the shadows of the tree. "Your coronation is in just two days."

"I mean to pardon you as soon as I am queen," she said. She picked her way carefully over the sprawling banyan roots and took his hand, rolling back his sleeve to reveal his blackened wrist, the rotting, bleeding burns. "And I'll call the doctors, the best in the land. They'll treat your arm."

"I'm fine," he interjected and tried to move away, to put the tree between them, but her grip was strong, and her eyes never left his.

"And then you'll be free," she continued as if he had not said a word. She was so close that he could feel her breath on his skin. "But will you stay? Will you help me rebuild what they've destroyed?"

"I can't," he said, and the words dropped like stones, loud and sharp. He tried to sound resolute, to trick himself into believing that he could not stop what was already set in motion. But the snake slithered inside of him, and Yassen felt as bleak and as empty as when he had crouched on the dark street, staring at the remains of his home.

He had made his allegiance. He could not stop a raging desert wind.

He pulled away, tripping on the banyan roots. Cold drops of rain kissed his cheek.

"Trust me," he said. "You won't want me."

31
ELENA

Here comes the queen, the young, frightening queen! Make way,
make way, I say, for the queen has come! Long live the queen!

—FROM *THE ODYSSEY OF GOROMOUNT: A PLAY*

Elena examined the blackened remains of her room and garden. Dawn had not yet breached the horizon, and the air smelled of ash and promise.

Today, she would be crowned queen, but Elena could not muster the joy that she knew she should feel. There was only hollowness accompanied by a sense of despair.

She made her way through her courtyard, stepping carefully. The servants had cleared out most of the mess, but she spotted the ghosts of her rampage: a shattered stone from her fountain, the nub of an ironwood tree, shriveled lotus petals. The charred remains of a banyan raked the blooming sky. She reached up and split off a branch. Dry flakes of soot sprinkled from her hands. Elena sat on what had once been a bench, the broken branch in her lap. Nothing stirred. There was no chirp of a morning dove, nor even the faintest whisper of the wind. There was only her, and the skeletons of the things she had destroyed.

In her anger, she had not recognized her madness, but now, in this silence, she understood. The aftermath of fire. The emptiness it created. Elena looked down at the perfect yellow parchment square in the center of her palm. She turned it over, but there were no markings on the other side. Slowly, Elena unfolded the square, the paper crinkling as she flattened it against her thigh. At the bottom corner of the letter, she spotted her mother's initials. A.M. And beneath that, a faded drawing of a jasmine.

In the dim light of the growing dawn, Elena read her mother's letter.

Elena,

If you have received this letter, then you must know how to wield fire. What a horrible, beautiful responsibility. I am sorry I am not there to guide you.

When you were five suns, you asked me why the desert rages—if there was a reason behind the storms. Do you remember what I told you? For the wind to sing, it must destroy the dunes.

When Alabore built this kingdom, he killed his eldest daughter, his first born. He carved out her chest and buried her heart in the desert. This is how he built Ravence—with blood.

But he did not build Ravence with the help of the Phoenix. The legends say the twin moons helped him, but I have read of a deeper, darker power. I do not know its name, but the writings of Priestess Nomu say it is as old as the Phoenix. This power fed visions to Alabore, and this power led him to the desert and its subsequent madness. It imprisoned the Phoenix in a dark, stony hell, and now the Eternal Fire demands sacrifice for Alabore's sin. Your grandfather sacrificed his youngest brother. Your father refused, but I chose for him. We are stuck in an endless cycle, my love. The Eternal Fire does not rage because it is angry; it rages because it grieves.

Ravence has been built on borrowed time. There will be a day when the Eternal Fire cannot be kept quiet. When the cycle breaks. The Phoenix shall awaken, and She will seek Her Prophet and his friends. You must be one of them.

I know it will be difficult to stand aside and let your kingdom be destroyed by the Phoenix and Her Prophet. Ravence demands loyalty. Blood, above all else. But I pray you will see the light beneath this land—the light that lives in you.

Honor your fire. It is different from the rest. Hone it, love it, and when the time comes, when the Phoenix rises, it will show you the path through the desert.

Forgive me,
A.M.

The letter slipped from Elena's hands. It floated to the ground of cracked stone and charred petals. Elena picked it up, her fingertips staining the paper with soot. She read the letter again and again, mouthing the words until they ran together like a song in her mind.

Sin.

Sacrifice.

Destruction.

My whole kingdom, a lie.

She crumpled the letter, but then smoothed it out again and folded it back into a neat square. Her mother had been a madwoman. The scrolls had filled her mind with delusions. All that reading, all that knowledge that Aahnah had obtained had amounted to nothing. She was dead.

Elena slipped the letter in her pocket and stood. She would throw it into the Eternal Fire. She would watch it burn, and then she would finally be free of her mother's insanity.

Elena returned to the guest room as faint touches of dawn blushed the sky. Diya was already waiting. The princess slipped out of her robe, shivering as the cold morning air touched her flesh. She sat in the bathtub as Diya rubbed her with a paste made of turmeric and sandalwood. She applied it using long banyan leaves that tickled Elena's skin, but the heir sat still, as stoic as a dune on a winter night. She watched as her handmaid turned her skin into gold, and then washed her with cardamom milk and rosewater. Diya squeezed a pea-sized drop of almond oil, and then ran it through Elena's hair, buttering her curls until they shone. It was a ritual the reigning queen would perform on the queen-to-be. But Elena had no mother. She did not even have her guard. Alone in the bathtub, her skin smelling like the desert, Elena only had herself.

After her bath, she dressed slowly, methodically. She donned a thick crimson and gold gown that fell from her shoulders and dragged on the floor. She slipped on necklace after necklace until her neck was weighed down with the wealth of her kingdom. She lined her eyes with kohl like the warriors who defended her borders.

For the final touch, Diya wrapped a white silken belt threaded with pearls and gold around her waist. She stepped back and offered a tremulous smile.

Elena stared at her reflection. She looked beautiful, yet terrifying. The Burning Queen.

The door of her chambers opened, and Elena turned to see Yassen, Samson, and her guards. They bowed deeply.

"It is time, Your Highness," Yassen said.

She cast one last glance at herself in the mirror. This would be the last time she would stand here as Elena. As *only* Elena. The girl who loved to dance and roam the desert, to bicker and argue with her Yumi guard. When she returned, she would be Queen of Ravence, and all the vestiges of childhood would unravel like a scarf in the desert wind. Blown away into the distance.

Elena turned, her bangles chiming softly. In her hand, she palmed the letter and slipped it beneath her silk belt. Samson and three guards carried an intricate velvet tapestry woven with gems of the desert. They held it up, each at a corner, and Elena stepped underneath it. Yassen remained behind her, and they began to walk.

The Palace thrummed with excitement as servants rushed to put together the final touches: sprinkling fresh marigold petals in the hall, draping thick strands of jasmines and desert rose along the windows, scenting the air with incense sticks of sandalwood and lavender.

Guards dressed in white and gold lined the corridor; they bowed as she passed. As she entered the courtyard, servants showered petals upon her. They smiled and sang blessings, raising their hands to welcome the new dawn, but she sensed a quiet unease beneath the joviality. Whispers about the attack and the Arohassin; yet, whenever she turned toward them, the servants fell silent.

Torches flickered along the path to the landing dock. Hovercams flashed as Elena stepped out, her long train dragging petals behind her. Her image was broadcast all over Ravence, all over the world. She was the Burning Queen. The heir of a land of blood and prophecy. May they all bow to her fury.

Her father waited at the end of the dock. He looked regal in his gold and red kurta, with a handspun silk scarf draped sharply down his shoulders. Behind him, his Spear and his Astra were dressed in their ceremonial ivory robes; they bowed as she approached.

The king held out his hand, but all Elena could see was his crown and the red Featherstone glimmering in the morning light.

Today, he would lose his throne to her.

"She would be proud," Leo whispered, and Elena did not know whether he was referring to Ferma or her mother.

The guards and Samson wrapped the velvet tapestry around her shoulders.

"So we the blessed few," they said.

"So we the blessed few," she returned.

Samson bowed and kissed her hand. He was dressed in a gold silk sherwani that shone against his olive skin. Intricate strings of pearls adorned his neck while a white embroidered scarf hung over his shoulder and looped across to his other arm. He looked like a Ravani, like a king.

He would go to the Temple in another hoverpod, for the heir and ruling monarch would go in their own. Still, she wished he could stay as he pulled away.

"You're an inferno, my darling," he whispered.

Leo led her into the hoverpod, and she turned back as the ramp slowly lifted. The servants and Palace guards stood along the dock, waving. Samson winked at her. Yassen gave a slight, imperceptible nod.

Her soon-to-be subjects. Yet, Ferma was not among them.

Elena forced herself to turn away as the ramp closed, shutting her within. The hoverpod rose into the blossoming sky as Palace Hill fell away. They flew west, and Elena looked over the dunes sprawling in the sun to the mountains ridging the kingdom. Her kingdom. The one she would swear to protect, even from the madness of her family.

Leo came up beside her. They stood silently for a moment, watching as the desert unrolled beneath them.

"I know you might not agree with my actions, and that's alright," he said finally. His voice was unusually quiet, pained. "I cannot undo what has already been done. I have made peace with that. But you too will have to make hard decisions. Cruel decisions. You will lose many more loved ones when you take the crown. It is our curse." He turned to her and gripped her shoulders, his eyes boring into her own. "But you must be ruthless, Elena. If you must become a villain, become one. Become whatever Ravence demands, because without you, it will die."

He brought his hand to his chest and clutched her mother's necklace. The jade glimmered in the light of the waking sun.

"Your mother once told me that the only thing that distinguishes a Ravani from others is our ability to sacrifice. To put our kingdom before anyone else. This is what it truly means to lead. To give yourself, and the ones you hold dear, to the kingdom that has already claimed you."

He slowly pulled off the necklace and held it between them. "I was your mother's keeper. Now, you are hers."

He clasped the necklace around her neck. Elena looked down to see her mother's bird, made of cyan jade found only during a summer eclipse, and felt both loss and foreboding. She met her father's eyes. They were the same steel-grey, but they were softer now, more vulnerable.

"You were never her keeper," she said. "She was yours."

Elena cupped the bird to her chest. It felt warm underneath her touch. She thought back to Aahnah and Jasmine, laughing together in the tea shop, sharing secrets. She thought of the women before her mother, the tireless generations of queens. Did they too know of the sacrifice? Or had they known the costs of the throne and accepted them willingly? Had they strode forward, unflinching, like true warriors, like her Spear.

Ferma did not die in vain. Today, she would become queen. Today, she would start her reign. And all the secrets that lurked in the library, her father's office, the hushed rooms of generals, would come to light.

Fire had no room for shadows.

Leo looked down at her. A mixture of pain and pride passed over his face, and he opened his mouth to retort and then seemed to think better of it.

"Take care of it," was all he managed to say.

32
LEO

And thus the Phoenix rose with eyes afire and a cry of vengeance upon Her lips.

—FROM *THE PROPHECY OF THE PHOENIX*,
TRANSLATED INTO WRITTEN WORD
BY THE FIRST PRIESTS OF THE FIRE ORDER

The hoverpod docked on the stone ledge beneath the Temple. A long column of smoke writhed above the cliff like a long, grey serpent. The ramp descended, and Leo led his daughter down.

The smell of ash and incense hung heavily across the mountainside. There were no storm clouds, but the air felt charged. Leo had already ordered for a large swath of guards to sweep through the Agnee Range, but after the attack in the capital, he tripled them. As he ascended the steps, he spotted their white uniforms dotting the mountainside, their pulse guns glinting.

Marcus and Alonjo greeted them at the top of the staircase with a low bow.

"Your Majesty," Alonjo said and then smiled at Elena. "Your Highness. May the sun and the moons shine upon you."

"We've checked the surrounding range at least four times," Marcus informed. "We've found nothing. The area is clean, but I have revolving patrols searching the mountain. If any Arohassin are hiding, we'll root them out and burn them alive."

"What about the tunnels?" Leo asked.

"Clean," Alonjo returned and looked at Marcus. "No Arohassin agents are hiding beneath the mountain," he said, and then, after a pause, "or Prophet."

Leo nodded, glancing at Elena, but her eyes were hard, her mouth resolute. She may hate him now, but she would come around. The Fire Throne robbed the monarch of his idealism, replaced it with cold practicality. She would realize the burdens of the crown, and then she would forgive him.

"And Samson's men?" he inquired.

"So far, they're all clean," Marcus said and looked up as the other Palace hoverpods descended.

Leo watched the pods dock and more guards march out. Samson and Yassen arrived with them; Samson walked ahead, his head high, his shoulders squared while Yassen trailed behind with his head bowed. There was a heaviness in his step, and Leo noticed how his right arm hung limply by his side.

"What's wrong with him?" Leo asked, nodding at Yassen.

"His arm is infected." He turned at the sound of Elena's voice and saw that she too was observing the men. There was a softness in her brow, a deepening in her eyes. "I've ordered for the royal surgeon to be on standby when we get back. She can treat Yassen's arm."

Leo looked from her to Yassen. A dark worry bloomed in the pit of his stomach.

"How bad is it?" He forced his voice to stay nonchalant.

"She'll likely have to cut it off," Elena said, and she must have caught his underlying meaning because she turned to him then. "Don't worry. He's not your Prophet. He burns. I've seen it."

"I'll take your word for it," he said, but when she turned away, he nodded at Marcus. His Spear nodded back.

When he finally climbed the steps, Samson greeted Elena, kissing her cheek.

"Your Highness, Your Majesty."

Leo pressed his hand on Samson's head, blessing him. The young man looked like a king from every angle, with his broad shoulders and kohl-lined eyes. The gold caps would fawn over him. The people would croon at his feet, but Leo could still not get over the way the boy moved, the way his vowels curved—the fact that he was not desert-born.

"Come," Leo said, and he took Elena's hand as they walked toward the Temple.

He glanced back and saw Marcus block Yassen's path and whisper something in his ear. Yassen faltered. The Spear gripped his arm and led him away from the Temple.

Samson followed his gaze. "Where are they taking him?" he whispered to Leo.

Leo said nothing as they crossed the landing to the Temple's gate, where Saayna stood waiting. She pressed her palms together, bowing deeply.

Leo and Elena returned the gesture. The High Priestess held out a fistful of lotus petals, and Leo took them.

"So we the blessed few," she intoned.

"So we the blessed few," Leo and Elena returned together.

They followed the High Priestess into the Temple, the stone floor growing warmer underneath their feet. Though they walked together, Leo noted Elena was a step ahead. She was eager; never mind her pace, he could see it in her eyes. She saw her kingdom glimmering before her, and Leo recognized her hunger. After all, he had felt the same on his coronation day.

A wall of heat hit Leo as he entered the Seat. It was if stepping into a furnace, but it was different this time. There was an urgency to the blaze. It pushed against the walls, chasing shadows, and Leo was surprised to feel a bead of sweat roll down his forehead.

The Eternal Fire licked the air as if it knew what was to come, the flesh it would eat. Forty suns ago, in this room, at the eve of his crowning, his father had told Leo about the price to rule Ravence—a loved one's life willingly given.

"It is the burden each heir must bear," he had said.

At the time, Leo had not grasped its meaning. He had refused, and Aahnah had suffered for it. But as they came before the Fire, Leo held his tongue. If the Prophet's rise was inevitable, there was no need for a sacrifice. Why waste a life when the Prophet was so near? He walked in the Palace halls, hidden in plain sight. It was only a matter of time before Leo would find him. He would kill the Prophet with his own hands. Offer his bones to the Fire, and put an end to this vicious cycle of sacrifice.

Elena strode forward, tall and proud. Today, they would remake history. Today, she would take the power of the Eternal Fire, but she would not bend to its fiery whip. She would reign without the loss and heartbreak that he'd had to bear.

Leo stared into the Fire, felt its heat singe the tip of his nose, but he did not balk.

The remaining seven priests rose from their seats around the pit. Each held a fistful of freshly plucked lotus petals.

"Come, blood of Alabore," they sang. "Come and seek blessings from the source of all life, the Fire of the one true ruler. Come and share Her benediction with our people."

The priests came forward and, one by one, deposited their lotus petals in their hands. "So we the blessed few."

"So we the blessed few," Leo whispered.

It would be the last time he uttered these words as king.

As the guards took position along the walls, Leo could not help but feel a pang of regret. He had aged so quickly, and Elena had grown so fast. He glanced at his daughter, with her head held high and an intense look in her eyes. She was the spitting image of him, yet Leo was dismayed by it. He had hoped, in some way, for things to change. Perhaps he could have bequeathed her with a better kingdom, one that was more forgiving and pliant. Perhaps he could have tried harder to rid their home of its dissenters. Perhaps he could have been kinder.

The Eternal Fire snapped, and the statue of the Phoenix soared in Her eternal glory. Leo closed his eyes and let the heat wash over him. He hoped it would cleanse him of his sins, but he knew that was wishful thinking. Some sins were too heavy to burn. Elena would have to bear his burden, as he had borne his father's, and he had his father's, and so on. That was the Ravani way.

Leo opened his eyes and cast some petals into the pit. He watched them curl and burn. The Eternal Fire hissed, and tendrils of flames touched his wrist. He stepped back as the priests began to chant, a low, hypnotic drone that reminded him of a rumbling desert wind. Out of the corner of his eye, he saw Marcus take up position by the eastern wall. Leo turned to him, and Marcus shook his head. On the other side of the room, Yassen Knight stood, clutching his right arm, a bruise darkening his lower lip.

I will find him. Leo looked up at the golden Phoenix. *Wherever Your Prophet is, I will find him.*

Samson and Alonjo knelt with the priests as he, Elena, and Saayna walked up the steps to the dais. The Eternal Fire surrounded them, snapping at the ceiling. Its heat beat against his face, and Leo suddenly remembered how the Eternal Fire had lashed out at him and burned his leg during his crowning. The white-hot pain. He squeezed Elena's hand as the High Priestess blew into a conch horn.

Together, they knelt as the Fire snarled.

"Great One," Saayna sang above its crackles, "we come to serve You. To uphold peace in the holy land." She spread her hands out wide and flung spark powder into the pit below them. The Eternal Fire shot up. Heat buffeted Leo, but he ground his knees into the stone floor and pressed his hands together. "We ask You to bless the new bearer of Your Kingdom. To lead her down the Agneepath."

Leo threw his remaining lotus petals into the Fire. It ate his offering with relish. He could hear the flames almost hiss in joy. The Phoenix watched from above, wings frozen in forever glory, beak gleaming, eyes raging. Despite himself, Leo shivered. The flames swooned as the High Priestess hummed and the priests chanted.

"From the father, the heirloom of the desert."

Leo bowed as the High Priestess lifted the crown from his head. The Featherstone pulsed almost as if in tune with the dancing flames.

"From the heir, the blood of her youth." And with a silver blade, she pierced Elena's finger. Dark beads of her blood dripped into the Fire.

"From the keeper of the flames, the bone of truth," the High Priestess said, and withdrew a tiny, black bone from her sleeve, throwing it into the flames. The Eternal Fire growled, the heat growing stronger.

"With these offerings, we bring a new dawn to Your kingdom," the High Priestess sang.

The Fire hissed as she lowered the crown onto Elena's brow. Leo scraped ash from the dais floor and cast it upon Elena. She did not cough nor shirk. She simply stared into the flames, her body steeled, her eyes fierce; she was his daughter, and her reign would be long and true. He was sure of it.

"Now, take what is yours, Daughter of Fire, and rise as Elena Aadya Ravence, Queen of Ravence," the High Priestess sang, and Elena extended her hand toward the pit. The flames curled around her hand, but she did not tremble. She withdrew a single flame and rose.

"Rise, Queen Elena," the priests sang.

The priests threw ash upon the dais, their voices low and guttural as the Eternal Fire grew. Leo still kneeled and looked to his daughter. The Fire silhouetted her shoulders and the high dome of her head. She needed to give the command for him to rise. But as Leo waited, Elena took the conch horn from the High Priestess. In her other hand, she cupped the flame.

"Call the new dawn of your reign," Saayna said.

"I will walk the Agneepath," Elena said, and blew into the ivory horn.

The sound, steady and strong, filled the chamber, dancing down the corridor to meet the open sky. It vibrated through Leo, stirring him with the hope—the pure, innocent hope—of a kingdom long and true, a kingdom in which every man could find peace. Yet the song also rattled his bones. It made him feel small and insignificant. Weak.

The Eternal Fire roared, and Leo looked up. The flames arched over him, and, in them, he thought he saw the faces they had taken, the lives they had claimed. He saw Elena, blowing the horn, and then a loud blast ripped the air and threw him onto his stomach.

Leo gasped. Blood burst down his nose. Pain splintered up his neck. For a moment, he lay dazed as the walls shook. The rumbling grew louder, and he realized it was not rumbling, but the sound of steady explosions and pulse fire. His kingdom. His home.

Leo struggled to his feet, his mouth tasting of blood and ash, as the flames grew longer, larger. Saayna lay crumpled on the steps of the dais, but Elena stood, the horn still in her hand, the flame in the other. She turned to him, her eyes wide. Above them, the Eternal Fire laughed. Leo reached for her, but then the mountain shook and the ground tilted, and he saw Elena screaming.

And then he was falling, falling, the Fire rushing to claim him.

33
ELENA

When the Phoenix rises, the Holy Fire will lay claim to the sinners. The desert will eat its transgressors. Only the true shall survive. Only the blessed few shall be forgiven.

—FROM *THE PROPHECY OF THE PHOENIX*,
TRANSLATED INTO WRITTEN WORD
BY THE FIRST PRIESTS OF THE FIRE ORDER

Elena lunged to grab Leo, but the Fire pushed her back with such force that she tumbled down the dais, landing on her back. The crown clattered across the floor. The flame in her hand leapt back into the pit, and the Eternal Fire hissed. She watched it rise and scrape the high ceiling. She saw their faces: her grandfather's youngest brother, her mother, Leo. The sacrifices for Alabore's sin. She saw them open their mouths and wail as the Eternal Fire growled and beat against the ceiling.

Deep rumbles shook the Temple, and Elena scrambled to her knees. The priests shrieked as the Eternal Fire grew; one tried to open the entrance of the tunnels, but the Fire surged, blocking his path. It lashed out and grabbed the priest by the arm and sucked him into its fiery pit. Saayna swayed to her feet, blood trickling down from a gash in her ear. She clawed at Elena's head and tugged upon her collar, yelling at her to *get up, to run, move girl, move!*

But Elena could not look away from the Eternal Fire. It sang and danced. Curled and swooned. Her father was in there, trapped within the inferno, screaming as the Fire raged. Vomit pushed up her throat.

Saayna tugged at her arm, and Elena stumbled to her feet. They made for the corridor. Stone and ash rained down on them, the air thick with smoke. The High Priestess clutched her wrist, pulling her forward, and they ran out into the smoke-filled sky, so dense and grey that Elena began coughing at once. Explosions erupted down the mountainside, and the ground heaved beneath her. Elena teetered.

Pulse fire sparked through the smoke as loud snaps pierced the air.

The trees! They were falling. Down the mountainside, she saw the great forest of her ancestors flatten as if a large hand had crushed it beneath its palm.

"The Fire, it knows," the High Priestess gasped, and Elena looked to the sky. All she could see was ash.

The High Priestess grabbed her chin, and Elena winced as her nails dug into her skin.

"The Prophet, he shall rise, but only in the next life," she crooned. Her voice was a mix of a wail and a cry of elation. "Together, he and the Phoenix will cleanse the land of our sins."

There came a great groan; flames surged out of the Temple and cascaded down the mountain. Elena threw herself off the steps, but Saayna was not so lucky. The Fire engulfed her as she screamed. She lurched to the side, flaring like a torch, and ran for the thicket of trees bordering the Temple.

"Saayna!" Elena screamed. She whipped around, her heart bubbling up her throat. "Sam! Marcus!"

The Fire snapped and lunged for Elena, but she jumped, running for the staircase. She took the stairs two at a time as the Temple moaned behind her. Her right foot missed a step, and Elena skidded, slamming right into Yassen. He yelped, and they both landed on their knees. Elena bit back a cry of pain, and Yassen clutched his arm. In the dancing light of the flames, she thought she saw the marks on his arm elongate and twist, but then she blinked, and the moment was gone.

"Run," she croaked.

The Eternal Fire lashed at the air, swelling with power. Without a word, Yassen took her hand, but then the sound of a great crack whipped down the mountainside. Together, they turned. The Temple trembled on the cliff above them, as if resisting the beast within, but then it sighed, finally relenting. One by one, the great wings of the Temple, Truth, Perseverance, Courage, Faith, Discipline, Duty, Honor, and Rebirth, snapped off of the center dome, as if the gods were plucking petals from a flower.

They tumbled down the cliff, crashing into the forest below. A wave of rubble and dust rose where the Temple once stood, and it roared down the staircase.

Without thinking, Elena grabbed Yassen and pressed him to the wall, using her body to protect his as the wave tore over them. She gasped, digging her face into his collar. Dust and plaster stuck to her skin, her hair, her clothes. Yassen gripped her tightly, but when the onslaught of stone and debris subsided, she noticed he was shaking. His right arm hung limply; she smelled its rot.

"Can you run?" she asked.

He nodded. His skin was pallid, his cheeks sunken in with a bruise blooming beneath his lip. Yet when he pulled her to her feet, she sensed strength in his grip.

"We need to head for the forest," he said, coughing. "We're exposed up here."

She tensed, as if somehow a fighter jet would appear out of the smoke to gun them down. "The hoverpods—"

"They're gone," he said. "I think the Arohassin snuck through the tunnels and took them out."

"No," she whispered. All around her, she heard the laughter of the Fire, and her people's cries for mercy. She heard screams, commands, and the dying wails of injured soldiers. She heard the deep groans of the forest and the rumble of the shaking mountain. She heard her kingdom crumbling.

"I have to stop it. I have to stop the Fire," she said and looked down at her hands, but her fingers trembled. "I can wield it, redirect it away from the forest—"

"For once, you have to be a coward," he said and gripped her hand. "*Run*."

They ran down the staircase that she had ascended countless times. They ran as men howled and died around her. They ran as the Fire devoured the last parts of the Temple and began to pick its way down the staircase. She could feel its heat nipping at her heels. Elena ducked as a stray leg of a statue flew past her head. Her heavy robes dragged against the stairs, slowing her. She grabbed for the gold clasps and tried to undo them, but her hands were shaking. She grunted in frustration and yanked. The clasps popped off, and she tossed the robes off the staircase, watching as they plummeted down the cliffside like crippled wings.

Slowly, the landing pad beneath the staircase came into view. Elena gasped. Yassen was right. There were no hoverpods. Only the mangled bodies of men.

She spotted legs twisted at unnatural angles, bodies with heads bashed in. From faraway, they looked like broken toys, snapped and bent by cruel gods. The Fire roared around her, picking up speed, the flames tumbling toward the landing dock like eager children.

Elena sprinted, her heart pounding in her chest. She had to get there before the Fire. She had to stop it. Twenty steps, fourteen, ten—

Something shot through the air and then clattered across the landing. Before Elena could discern it, Yassen screamed, *"Grenade!"* but it was too late.

Debris and limbs exploded in the air, and Elena felt the grenade's heat sear her face as she tried to stop. She fell forward, rolling across the landing. Dirt and rock hit her face and filled her mouth. She flung out her arms, trying to hold on to something, but she only grasped air and fell off the edge.

Elena tumbled down the mountainside, bramble cutting through her clothes. The heavens and the land rolled into one incohesive blur. The mountain was melting. She was melting. Elena gasped and tried to grab a root of a banyan when she skipped forward and hit, hard, onto a ledge. She nearly fell over, but then she flung her arm out and found a jutting stone. Straining, she pulled herself up and saw the heavens falling.

Torrents of fire washed down the mountainside like great red waterfalls of wrath. Below, clouds from the initial explosions dotted the forest. Pulse shots tore through the trees. *The Arohassin. It could only be them.* Anger and despair filled her as she lay stranded on her meager ledge. Elena tried to stand, but the mountain rumbled again, and she fell to her knees. She looked up to see the fountain of the Phoenix jutting out of the cliff face, and she saw a small figure. He was clinging to the statue, climbing on top of it, and even from this distance, Elena recognized the broad shoulders and the steady hands.

"Sam!" she called out.

His head whipped at the sound, and as he turned, an avalanche of flames ripped down the steps and launched upon him.

"No!" she cried. But she had no time to grieve, for the Fire had finally found her. It slithered down the mountain, its hiss filling her ears. It knew her. It knew her fears, her fate, and in its blaze, Elena saw their faces again.

Jump—she had to jump.

Elena flung herself off the ledge. For a moment, she was suspended in the air, the mountain beneath her, smoke above, and then she plunged down, wind rushing past her ears, ash filling her lungs, the forest dark and awaiting.

34
YASSEN

Do not run, wanderer. Arrive.

—FROM *THE ODYSSEY OF GOROMOUNT: A PLAY*

The Fire was everywhere.

It singed his arm, filled his lungs, blinded him. Yassen wheezed, clawing his way back to his feet. The grenade had knocked him down, and he spat out blood. It sizzled even before it hit the ground.

Behind him, the inferno swelled. It tumbled down the staircase, gaining speed. Yassen scrambled down the remaining stairs, hugging his arm to his body as dots swam in front of his eyes.

Air, he needed air.

"Elena!" he croaked.

But the dead around him gave no answer. He stumbled across severed limbs and broken legs, panic filling his chest, thick and sharp like barbed wire. Yassen looked down and saw a burst of white smoke from an explosive. Pulse fire lit up the forest below. He needed to head west like Akaros had shown him, to the path where the Arohassin assassins lay hidden, but the Fire roared toward him. Yassen ran forward, but there was nothing beyond the landing; nothing but the burning forest. He skidded, nearly falling off the edge when he saw a flash of dark curls.

"Elena!"

But she did not hear him over the din of the inferno. She leapt off the ledge—hair flying, skirts flaring around her—and plunged into the forest below.

He did not even hesitate.

He jumped after her.

The wind roared in his ears, heat searing his skin. The tops of the trees glinted like spears as he hurtled toward them. Yassen braced himself, knees bent, head curled, but the branches met his body too fast. He crashed through the canopy, leaves and branches clawing at his face and skin. Pain lanced up his arm. He tried to stop himself from falling farther, tried to kick out his legs and grab a tree limb with his good arm, but the mountain heaved from another blast and the trees swayed as he smacked into the ground.

Yassen gasped. He lay staring at the burning sky in shock. Blood filled his mouth. But adrenaline, training, and the pain that splintered up his arm wrenched him awake and pushed him to his feet. Yassen grimaced, sucking air between his teeth.

He could not die here on this mountain. Not when he was so close.

He stumbled through the dark forest. Here, the air was cooler, but the smoke lay on top of the canopy like a thick cloud, slowly suffocating everything within. Yassen felt for his old pistol and found it still wedged in the band around his thigh. He pulled it out and clicked back the safety.

"Elena!" he called.

The sound of distant pulse fire answered him. He crept through the underbrush, searching every shadow, every crevice.

"Elena!"

He followed a trail of broken branches and wilted leaves as the pulse fire grew closer. He coughed, his chest burning. A branch snapped to his right, and Yassen whirled, finger on the trigger; then he spotted the soiled edge of a skirt.

Elena lay crumpled within the roots of a massive banyan. It was the only banyan in a thicket of pine, and it was almost as if it was protecting her, the long vines curling around her in an embrace. Blood trickled from her nose, staining the Phoenix necklace wrapped around her neck.

Yassen fell to his knees. He tugged off the necklace and hurled it to the side as he felt for her pulse and gasped in relief to feel a thrum of life.

"Ferma?" She lifted her head, bleary brown eyes looking up at him.

"I don't have the hair," Yassen said, regret lacing his voice. "Can you stand?"

She licked her cracked lips, her tongue curling at the taste of blood, but she nodded. He helped her to her feet.

"Did you break anything?"

"No," she whispered and looked at him. "You?"

Pain stabbed through his arm, but he shook his head. "There's an escape route Marcus mapped in case of an attack. We need to get there."

She nodded, blinking groggily. Yassen led the way, pistol out. The ground was high and uneven with thick leaves that slapped his face. He tried his best to pick his way through the bramble, but another explosion shook the mountain. He teetered, and then Elena yelped and knocked into him, and they both tumbled down.

This time, the fall was shorter, meaner. Jagged rocks cut across his skin, scraping his knees and elbows. Yassen hit the forest floor and moaned as pain shot through his arm and shoulder. It almost made him faint.

"Get up," Elena rasped beside him. "Get up."

He lifted his head. Her dark brown eyes met his, and he was shocked to see how steady they were, how clear.

She slowly pushed to her knees. He noticed fresh blood spotting her shoulder, but she did not seem to be aware of her wound. This time, she helped him stand. She picked up his pistol and handed it to him. When his fingers brushed hers, she touched the black mark on his palm.

"Did you know that the Arohassin would attack today?" she asked softly, her eyes boring into him.

Yes.

He was to lead her to her death, to deliver her head to the Jantari king. He would bring destruction upon the people who had forsaken him, watch their bodies ignite like torches in the war to come. And then he would be free. He would finally leave this desert and its ghosts behind.

Yassen felt a stirring in his stomach—the cold grip of the snake as it flicked out its tongue. Smoke stung his chest, his throat, his eyes. He knew that in the capital, the remaining Arohassin agents and their allies struck coordinated attacks. Fire would lay waste to Rani and Palace Hill. The Ravani would consider it to be the coming of the Phoenix when really, fire brought destruction. Ruin. *To be forgiven, one must be burned.* Wasn't that what they said? But he knew the pain of burning. He knew the metallic stench of charred flesh. He knew that to burn was to live with a cruel knowledge that, no matter how hard he tried, he would never truly be forgiven, even if he was free.

A desert yuani shrieked in the canopy, and Yassen spun around to see a man raising his pulse gun in the brush behind them. Instinctively, Yassen seized his pistol and shot, once, twice, hitting the man square in the chest.

The man fell back with a cry, his weapon falling into a thicket of bramble. The yuani took to the air in a rush of squawks and golden wings. Calmly, Elena strode forward and picked up the pulse gun as Yassen stared at the blood blossoming across the man's chest. He recognized the metal serpent, the mark of the Arohassin, to the right of the man's bullet wound. It glared at him, dark and knowing. Yassen looked at the pistol in his hand; horror slowly leached the air from his lungs.

Yassen staggered back. The Arohassin would recognize the bullets of his gun. They would know of his betrayal, accidental or not. They would never forgive him. He would never have his freedom.

But he had known this. Hadn't he?

"Th-the Arohassin," he stuttered, "they're all over this place. They'll pick us off."

"You knew," she said, and he saw the betrayal in her eyes, the deep, shattering hurt. She stepped back, raising the pulse gun.

He did not move. He did not even lift his pistol in return.

"Do it," he whispered. "Be done with me."

She flicked on the pulse gun, its barrel warming to life with a blue light. As he stared her down, Yassen felt an odd clarity. This was an appropriate end to a cursed life. All his friends and family were dead. No one was left to remember him. The world would continue on, as cruel and apathetic as it always had been. His death would make no difference.

Yassen closed his eyes, but instead of sweet darkness, he felt the snake in his stomach rattle and hiss. He knew if he died, Elena would not survive. The Arohassin would find her and bring her head to the Jantari king. She would never master her fire. She would never bring unity to Ravence. She would never pin him down in the field, so close that he could feel her breath on his skin. He would never be able to let her win again.

Yassen opened his eyes and met her gaze.

"If you kill me now, you won't make it off this mountain," he said softly. "I am your only ally left. And the Arohassin are here. They will hunt you down. I know where they are, and if we move fast, there's a chance we can get out alive."

He watched her calculate the danger, her finger curling around the trigger, her face a war of emotions. The desire to both believe him and to shoot him flashed in her eyes. She tried to mask her indecision, but he knew every inch and curve of her face, every tremble of her lip. Hers was a face he had been forced to study but had grown to know as if it were his own. He knew of the way her chin jutted when she spoke defiantly; the way her nose scrunched when drinking whiskey; the way her eyes crinkled when she laughed. If there was one thing Yassen could claim, it was this: that even in the darkness of death, he would know her.

The pulse gun whined, and the blue light slowly faded. A look of hollow acceptance drained her face.

"You traitor," she whispered.

"This way," he said.

He headed east. She could easily shoot him, easily slice his body in half with a single pulse, but he knew she would follow.

Ash coated the forest. Panicked squawks filled the canopy as more birds took flight. He heard the crunch of leaves and felt her at his side.

"This way leads to the desert," she muttered.

"Yes," he said. He inhaled sharply as his arm throbbed.

Elena clenched the handle of the pulse gun, her knuckles white. Without another word, she strode past him. Thick brush blocked their path, but she stomped through it, a grim sureness in her step. She knew the desert; she knew where they were headed. Amidst all this chaos, all this madness, the dunes were a beacon. A vestige of a home that was beginning to shatter.

They trekked through the forest, keeping to the shadows. The pulse fire had strangely fallen silent, and though Yassen knew it was because most of the assassins were on the western path, he still held his pistol at the ready. Distantly, he heard the snaps and pops of burning trees. His chest itched, and he fought down a cough when suddenly there came a rustle in the canopy. He held out his hand to stop Elena, and they both looked up to see a black figure flit between the branches. Before the assassin could shoot, Yassen raised his pistol. His bullet ripped through the leaves and hit the man in the back of the head. His body plummeted to the ground.

Out of the corner of his right eye, Yassen spotted another assassin, but Elena was quicker. Her pulse sliced through the forest, and the man fell in a spray of blood. The air exploded with pulse fire, and Yassen shoved Elena behind a tree. They huddled behind the trunk as the assassins returned fire. Branches splintered and crashed above them. Yassen winced, his ears ringing. Elena scrambled back as a pulse hit the tree, leaving a deep wedge in the wood.

"There are too many!" he shouted. He could tell from the direction and frequency of the pulses that the assassins were steadily advancing toward them.

Elena cocked her gun, but even she seemed to recognize their situation. Slowly, she tucked the pulse gun into her skirts, placed her hands on the ground, and closed her eyes.

"What are you doing?" he asked as the forest groaned.

He heard a low hiss, a soft, slithering sound that traveled up his spine. Though he could not see it, Yassen felt it in his bones. Its prickling heat. Its deep hunger. The fire came at once, rushing from behind them in a red wave of destruction. It tore through the forest, snapping leaves and stones, but skirted their tree.

Elena stood. The ground rumbled again, but she did not lose her footing. She darted forward with her arm outstretched, and the flames followed. He yelled at her to stop, but his voice caught in his throat. Heat pressed around him. Yassen raised his gun, shooting to give her cover, as Elena raised her hands above her head. She slashed down, and the inferno ripped through the trees like a stampede. The assassins screamed, their voices piercing the air.

"Come on!" She sliced her hand down, and the flames bowed to create a path. "Let's go!"

He lurched to his feet as the fire tumbled forward, eager and unchained. Elena ran in front, guiding the blaze. Yassen shot the assassins in the trees, watching as their bodies fell into the hungry flames. The smell of burning men sickened him, but he forced himself to look straight ahead and follow her.

They finally came into a clearing, and Elena doubled over, hands on her knees. Her shoulders shook. The flames coiled, burning along the edges of the clearing to create a protective perimeter.

Yassen panted, his chest tight. He could see the desert ahead of them, the rolling dunes free of fire. Elena shuddered. He took off his belt sash and offered it to her.

"Here."

Her fingers brushed his soot-covered palm. She swayed, the sash limp in her hand, and he held out his arm to steady her.

"I, I burned them," she said, her voice hollow. But there was a look in her eyes, the same look Leo and Samson had worn at the Ashanta ceremony—reverent, with the unconscious stir of desire. It was a look of the powerful, and it made him shiver to think what else she could do with fire.

"Yassen," she said, "why are you still here?"

"Because I have nowhere else to go," he said.

Her face twisted like the flames, and her voice broke. "Neither do I."

They slipped further into the forest, leaving the Temple and the past behind. The sky was a deep, boiling red, as if the sun had burst. The inferno crept with them, shielding them from harm and delivering them from the crumbling mountain to the quiet desert. Sand began to line their boots. The dunes awaited, stoic and still as if nothing had changed. When they reached the desert edge, Yassen raised his eyes to the smoke-filled heavens.

The litany came unprompted to his lips.

"Ash begets ash. Heavens burn to reveal the truth. May the sinners be forgiven, and the pretenders see their doom."

It was a chant recited at the end of the Fire Festival, but there was no big parade, no city bursting with color. Here, there was only the dry, barren land.

"And thus justice shall bloom," she whispered.

THE DAWN OF THE KINGDOM OF RAVENCE

—AS TOLD IN THE DIARIES OF PRIESTESS NOMU

Alabore Ravence was a small man. He barely reached the shoulder of a horse, but he walked as if he knew how to ride one. He was five feet and one inch tall. He liked to give special emphasis to the one inch because a man of simply five feet was a disappointment to his family. He had a weather-beaten face and pockmarks down his cheeks, but his eyes were dark and sharp, older than they seemed, as if he knew all along that his meager hut and rusty sword were beneath his destined social station.

He had a conviction about him, so deep and true that it gathered newcomers and travelers like moths to a flame. In that sleepy, unknown village, Alabore Ravence gathered a following of men and women who heard his impassioned sermons of a better life, of a greater future. They all sighed in agreement. Among them were his family: his wife, taller than him, and two daughters. They looked like timid birds next to his broad, masculine stance, but only a fool would believe they were as shy as they seemed.

Alabore Ravence's two daughters, Jodhaa and Sandhana, bore the elegant grace of their mother and the hard, ruthless stance of their father. They were quick-witted and sharp of tongue. They could dance circles around a trained swordsman while they followed the beat of dhols. They could shoot arrows with their eyes closed and open them to find a poor lark spasming on the ground. They were their father's fiercest warriors, and he took them on a secret rendezvous.

The night before, Alabore Ravence had a vision that told him his time had come. It showed him an unforgiving land and an ancient flame; the blood of men soaking into the sand while the sky was afire; and him, standing within it all.

He knew then of his destiny.

They traveled at night from their sleepy, unknown village deep within the Parvata Mountains. They rode on the backs of emus, giant birds with golden beaks and feathers of steel (sadly, the last one was killed in the First Desert War). They rode for fifty nights until they reached the edge of the monstrous desert. It had once been a forest, but fire and belief had burned it to the arid landscape before them. Even in the cold light of the twin moons, they could see that the immovable dunes were giant, stoic mountains.

Alabore Ravence stood before them, his dark eyes taking in all the curves and ridges and valleys of the silent space. After a long moment, he turned back to his daughters, who knew immediately that something about the endless terrain of sand had changed him.

"We will build our kingdom here," he said. "We will work with the moons and slowly gain friendship from the sun. We will forge the bricks of the palace ourselves, and they will all come."

"But, Father," Sandhana asked, "how can you be sure?"

"Because I will get the Eternal Fire," he said, and they realized that it was not the desert that captivated him but the silent mass beyond. In the darkness below the horizon, they saw the ghostly shape of the mountains. Jodhaa whispered to her sister that she saw a light, a tiny glimmer, but a light nonetheless in that mass of darkness.

"You can't get the flame," Jodhaa said, but Alabore Ravence gave a cold, hard smile, an expression she had never seen him wear before.

"I know of a way," he said.

And so it began. Alabore Ravence's ardent followers trekked out to that unforgiving sea of sand, buoyed by his speeches of prophecy and destiny. He preached until his throat was sore and his face red, but his voice never left him. They worked in the cloak of the night, in the steady gaze of the twin moons that Alabore Ravence had already befriended in his dreams. That portion of the year, the nights were long and cool. As kings and queens fought against sandstorms and heatstroke to get across the land and into the dark mountains, Alabore Ravence and his followers worked continuously, untouched. Even his daughters could not believe their good luck.

But Alabore Ravence knew better. He had seen in his vision how the world would unfold for him. He knew this was the easy part, that the moons would protect him. The real challenge would come when the city he built could no longer be ignored, and the sun would take notice. The mountains beyond would take notice.

When that day finally came, Alabore Ravence took his two daughters into the heart of the desert. Like before, they traveled at night. His daughters did not believe he knew where the heart of the desert lay, but as the night stretched on and their father sank deeper into his silence, they knew not to question him. Finally, as dawn glimmered on the horizon, they stopped.

"Are we to build sand hovels here?" Sandhana asked. The air was already beginning to warm. A solitary bead of sweat rolled down Alabore Ravence's forehead.

"Close your eyes," he told them.

His daughters obeyed. He watched as the sun drew their shadows on the ground. He knew what he had to do. The vision had shown him how to acquire this desolate land and its flame. But for the first time in his life, Alabore Ravence hesitated. The sun glared. As quietly as he could, Alabore Ravence drew his sword. He closed his eyes and saw his kingdom and brought his sword down.

Jodhaa shrieked as the limp body of her sister fell to the ground. Her blood rapidly stained the sand, hissing. Thin strings of steam rose around her body. Jodhaa stared in horror as her father plunged his sword straight through her sister's chest and withdrew her heart. It was oddly shaped and small. Alabore Ravence kneeled and, with his own bare hands, buried his daughter's heart, and the sword that viciously claimed it.

"This is the heart of the desert."

And as he spoke, the light within the dark mountains that Jodhaa had seen grew brighter. Stronger. Higher. A plume of smoke steadily rose from the mountain, and it was then that Alabore Ravence and his daughter knew the deed was done.

The Phoenix came to them in a shower of light that singed their skin. Jodhaa cried, hiding her face, but Alabore Ravence did not balk. He spread out his hands, stained by the dark blood of his daughter.

"This is the heart I give to you."

The Phoenix flapped Her wings, Her voice rising from the dunes, vibrating through his bones until he was full of song.

"So you shall have mine," She sang.

The desert rumbled. The dunes undulated, and the sky burned and filled with smoke. The cries of the warring kings and queens amplified as the Eternal Fire within the mountains roared and burnished the heavens. Despite it all, Alabore Ravence stood tall.

"This will be the Ravani Kingdom," he said.

And so it was.

Within months, the kingdom arose. Some fanatics say the desert itself helped, but scholars believe sandstorms wiped out any opposition, leaving Alabore Ravence and his followers to build in peace.

The Kingdom of Ravence was built three hundred suns ago, with Alabore Ravence as the founding king. He lived a long, successful life, forging a flourishing kingdom in the middle of a desert. Under his reign, the desert finally saw peace.

He ordered the image of the Phoenix to be etched onto the Ravani flag, for She had sent him his vision. After his death, he was succeeded by his only daughter, who wore an eternally haggard expression. But Jodhaa too reigned with a steady, forceful hand.

For on that fateful day when her sister died, Alabore Ravence had turned to his daughter and allayed her grief.

"The heavens will forgive us. Every one of us deserves to be forgiven."

Note: The page after this has been torn out. There is hesitancy in Priestess Nomu's prose. Is it because she came to know the truth? That the Kingdom of Ravence was built not on the power of the Phoenix, but through a darker, eviler god? I shall resume my studies after searching the libraries at the Temple. For now, Elena weeps for plums. I must attend to her. —A.M.

35
ELENA

The night when Alabore Ravence built his kingdom, it is said that men feasted on starlight. For it was Alabore Ravence who brought the heavens closer to Sayon, who brought the power and mystique of the Phoenix into a real, solid hearth. The desert may be unforgiving, but it was spun from stardust, and to stardust it will go.

—FROM *THE LEGENDS AND MYTHS OF SAYON*

They had traveled the desert for two days, and the smoke had not let up. It wrapped around the dunes like a sheet over a corpse. They trekked north, where there were no cities and no people. The northern Ravani desert was dry and barren, full of shadowed canyons and brittle plants. Sandstorms often rose out of thin air, and they could rage for hours. Elena watched the dark horizon for the telltale whirl of sand, but no storms came. It was as if the wind held its breath.

Elena blinked, her eyes heavy. Her palms still smarted, pulsing with heat, but she was too exhausted to summon fire. Her pulse gun had run dry, and she had tossed it into the dunes, along with her heavy jewelry. She kept only her mother's necklace, tucked beneath her blouse.

Flames flickered in the distant mountains, the bright sparks eerily silent in the desert stillness. Her kingdom was under attack, yet here she was, stranded in the unforgiving dunes.

She had waited for the army. She had waited for Ravani hoverpods or scouts on cruisers to scour the desert for her, but no one came. Not the generals, not the Black Scales, not even the Palace guards. It could only mean one of two things: they didn't think she had survived or Ravence had already fallen.

She slipped down a dune, sand spilling before her. *Swish, sip, swish, swoon.* Elena tried to move lightly, fluidly, but she was tired. She turned to see Yassen trailing behind her. He moved slowly, ploddingly, leaning to the right as if his arm was weighing him down.

Swish, sip, swish, swoon.

Blood caked her shoulder where her stiches had ruptured, but Elena only felt the steady pressure of the sand beneath her and the rhythm of her feet.

Swish, sip, swish, swoon.

The smoke coiled tighter, slowly squeezing her chest.

Swish, sip, swish, swoon.

She wondered what had become of her Palace. Had the Arohassin burned down the throne? Or did they sit upon it now, laughing like jackals? Did they notice the flowers hovering along the ceiling? Would they tend to them? She had wanted to get rid of the marigolds when she became queen, but her father had always loved them. The memory of him sitting on the throne, the crown on his head, her mother's necklace around his neck, suddenly opened a well of grief within Elena. She tried to block it, but that was as useless as trying to stop a summer monsoon.

Leo was dead, as was Ferma, and likely Samson. Her entire world, shattered over the course of a single day. Was this how her father had felt when Aahnah died? Had he felt the same pain as she did, or had he felt relief? Relief to be free of her mother's madness?

Elena swallowed, her throat as raw and dry as the land around her. Leo had betrayed her. His hunt for the Prophet had blinded him to the true value of Ravence—the blessed few. The Phoenix had blessed Alabore Ravence to lead the holy land. That was why they wore Her feather in their crown. Had her father forgotten his duty? Was he so hungry for power that he thought he could surpass the heavens? Elena shook her head. Anger, confusion, and pain threatened to rip her throat. But the dagger of sorrow felt even more acute—so sharp that it cut through all other emotions and spilled them into the sand until an aching hollowness filled her chest.

Her father was dead. Her kingdom was burning.

She was the last Ravani.

"Where can we find water?" Yassen croaked behind her.

His voice pulled her from her reverie. She paused on a stone slab overlooking a valley. Tall pillars of sandstone lined the valley edge, scraping against the thick smoke. Yassen slumped against a boulder, wincing.

Elena ran her tongue over her cracked lips. "Maybe we can find a skorrir."

"We don't have a knife to cut off its branches."

"We can use a stone." She fell to her knees, searching the uneven ground. Her knee knocked into something sharp, and she hissed. Gingerly, she drew back and found a stone with a pointed edge, no bigger than her palm. She rose and held it out to Yassen.

Pain flickered across his face as he turned to her. "That's too small."

She chucked it, and they watched the rock skip into the valley. Elena walked around the pillars, her torn skirts trailing behind her. Pebbles crunched underneath her thin juttis, and she winced as one dug into her heel. She began to pull off her shoe when a low rumble echoed through the valley. Sand shifted across the floor. The rumble gradually turned into a buzz that reverberated off the boulders.

Elena hobbled back to Yassen as tiny lights pinpricked the night across the valley.

The scouts!

She began to raise her hand when he grabbed her.

"Wha—"

He shoved her behind a pillar. When she tried to turn back, he pushed her forward.

"Would you quit push—"

But Yassen held his finger to her lips.

"We're exposed here," he whispered.

He motioned for her to follow, and they weaved through the pillars alongside the valley edge. They scrambled up a boulder hidden between two pillars and watched as the lights in the distance grew bigger. Shapes moved within the valley, but Elena could not make them out. She turned to Yassen and saw the color drain from his face.

"What is it?" she asked.

He did not answer. He did not need to, for she heard it then—the whine of a cruiser.

A soldier on a cruiser crested the stone slab where they had once stood. The cruiser's metal hull shone in the night with an uncanny glow, and she spotted a winged ox on its side. The soldier turned, studying the shadows. A long, jagged blade with the butt of a gun hung down his side.

Elena breathed in sharply. Only the Jantari carried zeemirs.

Yassen gripped her hand and tugged. They sidled down the boulder as the soldier slowly drew closer. For a moment, Elena thought he would jump off his cruiser and search the pillars, but then he turned and sped off to the south. To Rani.

Her hand tightened around Yassen's.

"The city," she whispered.

They crawled back up the boulder, and Elena finally understood what had been there all along—the Jantari army. After the scout, more cruisers zipped out of the valley, heading toward the capital. The cavalry came next: men dressed in navy, their zeemirs glinting in the darkness. Soldiers on metalboards and motor-slicers flanked the formation, their faces as rigid as stone. Tanks brought up the rear. She watched as they crushed the scraggly brush that grew within the valley.

As they passed, the buzz grew louder, closer. Elena stilled as two large metal hovertanks came into view. Thick and blocky, they obstructed her view of the desert beyond. Three soldiers stood in the armored cockpit of each hull. The blue light of holos outlined their gaunt features while thick metal cables latched on either side of their temples. They moved in unison, as if they were one body.

When they were finally gone, Elena let out a shaky breath. Her heart hammered in her chest, so loudly she could hear the blood pulsing in her ears.

"Jantar," she said, and the very word overwhelmed her. The Jantari were marching through her desert. Farin had moved past mutilating his own body to turning his men into machines. He finally brought the war her father had always feared. But Leo was not here to stop them. There was only her.

"We should get moving," Yassen said. They crawled down the boulder, but when he walked forward, she did not follow.

"Did you know?" her voice was a whisper, thin and fragile.

He stopped, his back to her.

Slowly, she raised her eyes. "You knew about the Arohassin, but did you know about the Jantari? That they were coming like this?"

He turned around, and the regret in his eyes broke something inside of her.

She jumped on him. Slapped him hard, his neck whipping to the side, an angry red mark blooming on his cheek. She beat him with her fists, kicking, tearing.

"How. Could. You!" She rained punch after punch, landing in the soft spots that she knew would hurt him: his belly, his cheeks, his chest. She should have killed him on the mountain. She should have shot him that night in the desert. She should have burned him the moment he stepped into the throne room.

He had watched her train with Ferma, watched as she and Samson announced their engagement. He had watched Saayna rest the crown on her head, and the Fire take her father. He had watched it all, knowing what would come next.

When her fist slammed into his right arm, Yassen's eyes widened, but he did not cry out. He took it wordlessly. And his silence drained her anger. It felt like hitting a dummy in the training arena. And the look in his eyes—his pain, his grief—she slowly felt her fury simmer and die. Her shoulders slumped, and her fists fell softly against his chest.

"How could you?" she gasped, sagging against him.

"I'm sorry," he whispered. Blood spilled down from his broken lip. His good hand curled over hers. "I'm sorry. I wish I hadn't."

She shook her head. She felt suddenly tired and alone and useless, all at once.

"I couldn't let you die on that mountain," Yassen said. "I couldn't deliver your head to the Jantari king. I'm sorry. I'm sorry." His voice fell, and she met his eyes.

A part of her urged to leave him. To part ways then and there—to trek off into the dunes without a backward glance.

But then what? Where would she go? Who would help her? All her life, there'd always been someone: Ferma, her father, her guards. Despite her escapades, they had kept a vigilant watch. They had died for her, but they did not die so that her head would rest at Farin's feet. They died so that she could become queen.

And now, Yassen was the only one left standing by her side. He could have left her to die on the mountain. He could have abandoned her.

Elena bit her lip, overwhelmed. He had betrayed her. He had betrayed himself. What a pair they made: the runaway queen and the traitor.

She slipped her hand out of his, heat pulsing from her palm.

"We should get moving," she said, defeated.

"Elena, I," he said and paused. He sighed, looking down at his hands, the blackened and the pale, and finally met her gaze. "I know a place where you can be safe. It's a small cabin, a safe house in the Sona Range. They'll never suspect us hiding in Jantar. You can rest there. Heal."

"How can I save my kingdom from Jantar?"

"Don't you see?" he said, and she thought she heard his voice crack. "You are what's left of this kingdom. If you die, so does Ravence. It can't go on without you. And you can't go on hiding in the desert."

She wanted to tell him that *she* could not go on living without her desert, but he was right. There was no capital to return to. The Ravani army was disorganized. Samson's men were likely in disarray without him. Teranghar, Magar, and Iktara were too far. Rasbakan, the closest port, was probably sacked.

Even if she tried to reach the Black Scales or the generals, the Jantari or the Arohassin would find her first. They would parade her through the streets, and then they would melt metal onto her head. She would die like her ancestors in the Five Desert Wars.

Elena looked down at her feet, at the sand underneath her toes. Without Leo, she was fatherless. And without her desert, she was motherless.

She was just another orphan wandering through the dunes.

"There's something else." He reached into his jacket, pulled out the holopod from within his inner pocket. It was dented and scuffed, but when he scanned his thumb, it opened. Elena recognized the map of the tunnels Samson had given her. "Samson has a training base in the middle of the range. There are still some Black Scales left there, I think.

We can't get to the base directly, but if we go to the cabin, there's a possibility we can take the tunnels from there."

"I thought Samson pulled out all of his troops from Jantar," she said.

"Do you really believe that?" he asked, and she looked away.

"I don't know who to believe anymore."

"You can believe me."

She laughed, sharp and cruel. "That's rich."

"Now you know everything," he said, spreading his hands, "I have no more secrets left to keep. I took the Desert Oath, and you may think that I've broken it, but I haven't. You're the kingdom now. I'm still willing to give my blood for you. Here." He pressed his pistol into her palm and took a step back. "If you don't trust me, then shoot me. This might be your last chance."

She stared at the gun in her hand. It was heavier than a pulse gun, the trigger more curved. She could shoot him and leave his body to rot for the vultures. Perhaps she might feel relief, vindication. She could live in the desert, like she had before, and wait for help. But the absolute conviction in his eyes, and the thought of wandering the dunes alone, without a kingdom or a hearth waiting for her, made Elena hesitate. She shook her head. "I don't need your gun. I need your word. The desert words." Her eyes met his. "Prove it. Swear it."

Yassen sank to his knees, his face grim, resolute. A low wind finally stirred the dunes as he pressed his palms to her feet, his voice steady and clear as the desert whispered with him.

"The queen is the protector of the flame, and I its servant. Together, we shall give our blood to this land. I swear it or burn my name in the sand."

"So it is thus sealed," she whispered, and Yassen rose to his feet. They looked out at the horizon. There was nothing ahead of them but Jantar. Nothing behind them but sand.

36
YASSEN

*There is no hard line between the servant
and the sinner. There is only a soft blur, a delicate edge
in which a man can lose himself.*

—FROM THE DIARIES OF PRIESTESS NOMU OF THE FIRE ORDER

They slept during the day and walked at night. They applied wet skorrir leaves to their wounds, and ate what berries they could find. Yassen forgot his thirst. He forgot what hunger felt like, for it had become a constant pain, a relentless numbness. When they stopped to rest, he tried to work some feeling into his right arm, but the smell of rot drove fear into his body. His entire hand had blackened, and he was too scared to even peel back his sleeve.

Yassen could feel the decay slowly spreading through his shoulder. Elena often glanced at his arm, but she had said nothing of it. They both knew, and they were both too afraid to admit it.

He had to cut off his arm, or he would die.

A week since passing the Jantari army, they stopped at a shallow canyon in the eastern desert that had once held a river. The rock bed was dry, with skorrir bushes hugging the wash. The landscape had begun to change, the dunes shrinking and giving way to harsh canyons and low valleys. Stars pockmarked the sky, silent and cold. Yassen could no longer see the forest, but he imagined the fire wrapping around the mountain like a dark, lumbering beast scourging the world of its sins. He wondered if Samson had burned too.

Guilt slithered in his stomach. He had betrayed them all: Samson, Ferma, the other Palace guards. If they saw him now aiding their queen, would they forgive him? Yassen stared at the horizon until his eyes smarted. The mountain was behind him. Dead or alive, Samson would have wanted him to aid Elena, to protect her.

"What good is the past, Cass, if it's only meant to make us feel like shit?" Samson had once asked him.

"It tells us who we are," he had replied.

"Or who we shouldn't become," Samson had whispered back.

"The Jantari base is just north of here," Elena said. Wind tussled her wild curls, and for a moment she resembled a Yumi, hair writhing, eyes steely, a face so angular that it cut right through him. "If we head further into the desert, we can go up and around."

Yassen squinted, studying the shadowed faces of the rocks. He had no idea where they were, but he trusted Elena's judgment. She navigated through the desert without hesitation, cutting through valleys, following the curves in ways he never thought possible. When they had been on the cruiser, riding out the storm, he had attributed her aptitude to luck. But now he understood that Elena's connection to the desert ran much deeper than he or the Arohassin had ever imagined.

The Arohassin. Heavens, they must be livid—or dead. Yassen wondered if Akaros had already found the wounded assassins, if he recognized his bullets and his treachery. Or perhaps the Eternal Fire had burned all the evidence.

The Arohassin would be looking for him. He knew that. They were careful, methodical, and ruthless—just like he had been.

Fresh pain coiled around his right arm, and Yassen grimaced. His fingers curled inward like a frozen claw, and, try as he might, he could not move them. Maybe this was his penance. Maybe this was his way to redemption—a limb for all the destruction he had caused.

He watched as Elena climbed a boulder. She reached the top and paused, her figure silhouetted in the grey smoke. For the Arohassin, she was the vestige of a crumbling kingdom, an old order of fanatics and martyrs, but for him... She looked back, shouted. The distance ate up her words, but he knew what he had to do.

For him, she was the way forward.

Gritting his teeth, Yassen hobbled after her. Slowly, using his left arm and his body, he climbed up the rockface. Elena reached out to him and hauled him onto the summit.

"Thanks," he said breathlessly, but she immediately shushed him.

She turned to the north. Without saying a word, she slipped her hand behind her back and pointed to the right and then down. Curled her fist once, twice. He recognized the Ravani cavalry code.

Danger, two miles to the north.

Yassen scanned the outcroppings beyond the canyon, but he saw nothing. He felt exposed, bare.

She curled her fist again and then opened her hand. *Wait.*

She jumped down, scaling up the other edge of the canyon. Yassen hesitated only for a moment before following. He climbed onto a ledge that opened toward the northeast. Slowly, like a man shaking off the ghosts of a dream, he saw what Elena had seen. The trail of dust and sand rising from the north, toward them.

After a few moments, he saw the cruiser enter the far edge of the basin. It must not have spotted them as it drove through the riverbed, making its way east. Its way home.

Elena slunk down the ledge.

Moving closer, she motioned with her hand.

Yassen slipped out his pistol as she swung underneath the ledge, heading for the riverbed. He steadied the butt of the gun against the rocks and waited. If he timed it right, he could hit the scout right as he passed below.

Yassen considered what they would do if they captured the scout. They could interrogate him to find out the access points into Jantar. Maybe he could even wear the man's uniform and pose as a soldier. But they would have to kill him, of this there was no doubt.

The cruiser grew closer, and Yassen heard its steady hum as it spit pebbles in its wake. Below, Elena crouched behind skorrir bushes, and he emptied his mind. Breathed in. Rested his finger in the curve of the trigger.

One, two, three.

The hum grew louder.

Easy now.

Four, five.

The cruiser neared, but then Elena turned, waving her hands, shouting. The scout whipped around. And Yassen realized it wasn't a scout at all, but a young boy who stared up at him in horror. He tried to right his cruiser, but he lost control; it skidded and spun, slamming into the skorrir bushes.

Yassen cursed as Elena ran to the boy. He did not put his gun away even as he saw her pulling the boy out of the bramble.

"Drop him!" he shouted.

She looked up into the barrel of his gun as she helped the boy stand. "Stand down, Yassen."

But Yassen trained his gun on the boy. He looked fourteen or fifteen suns, with a mole on his nose and a smattering of pimples across his cheeks. Old enough to be an initiate of the Arohassin, older than he had been.

"Step away from him," Yassen said.

The boy shirked back, but Elena held on to his arm. She glared at Yassen.

"He's just a kid," she said.

"Kids can be dangerous, too," he said and looked into the boy's eyes. They were pale and colorless, just like his. "What are you doing out here? Can't you see that there's a war?"

The boy looked between Yassen and Elena. A small visor hung askew from his neck. His clothes were covered in dirt and frayed at the edges.

Fear and confusion spread across his face as he stammered: "I-I was out here, c-camping when I saw the army. I tried to get out, but a storm hit me and I b-barely got out."

Yassen knew he was lying. He could see it in the way the boy tensed his shoulders, the way his eyes darted to the back compartment of the cruiser.

"What's in the cruiser?" he demanded. When the boy did not answer, he edged closer. "What's in there?"

"N-nothing," the boy said, holding up his hands, but Elena was quicker, twisting his arms behind his back, forcing him to the ground as Yassen opened the compartment.

It was full of sawed-off branches of skorrir bushes and red desert berries. A forager's case. A poor boy's livelihood.

A means to survive.

Yassen pulled back his hand as if he had been cut. He knew this kind of desperation. He had done the same: sneaked under the cloak of night into gardens, bakeries, and the desert itself to find morsels of sustenance, something to drown out the deep, inescapable pain of hunger and loneliness.

"Don't you know it's illegal to forage in the desert?" he scolded, but he put away his gun. Gently, he loosened Elena's grip and helped the boy to his feet.

The boy wet his lips. His eyes darted to the cruiser and then back to them.

"I-I only meant to take a little," he said.

"You missed the best ones," Elena said. "There are violet lilliberries that grow underneath the sand of a skorrir bush. Tastes like shobu shit, but three can fill you for a week."

"Wh—" the boy began, but as he looked at Elena, a vague sense of recognition grew in his eyes. "Why are you telling me this?"

Yassen saw the boy's eyes widen as understanding finally dawned on him. A look of surprise and horror twisted his face, and he shot forward, but Yassen grabbed him and pushed him down into the sand.

"Easy," Yassen said as the boy struggled. "We just need your help. We won't hurt you. I promise."

When the boy finally stilled, Yassen let him sit up.

"If you help us, we won't turn you in for stealing this cruiser and taking berries from Her Majesty's desert," Yassen said.

"It's not the Ravani's desert," the boy spat.

"It's not the Jantari's either," Yassen said. "It belongs to the Phoenix and Her Prophet. But if we stay here any longer, the soldiers will find us. So help us, and we'll help you."

"Everyone thinks you're dead," the boy said to Elena. "I saw it in my holos before the storm broke my receptor."

"Let's keep it that way," Yassen said. "Help us get into Jantar, and we won't kill you."

"They've invaded Ravence," the boy continued, looking up at Elena. "It's all Jantar now, the city, the desert, and soon the southern cities. They're fighting back, your people. Even The Landless King's army is defending your southern border, but he's dead too."

"Samson's dead?" Yassen said, his voice hitching.

Deep down, he had known it, yet a part of him had hoped that Samson survived. Just like he had survived after defecting from the Arohassin. Samson was a fighter. He could claw and scrounge his way through anything.

Yassen dug his hand into the ground. *Damn this desert. Damn this forsaken land. Damn its fire.* He curled his hand into a fist and felt the roughness of the sand. *Damn it all.*

"Get us into Jantar, or he'll kill you now," Elena said.

The boy turned to Yassen, his brow furrowing as he took in Yassen's pale eyes, his golden hair. "Aren't you Jantari?"

Yassen flinched. "No," he said roughly as he felt Elena staring at him. "I'm Ravani."

The boy stood slowly. Elena motioned, and they pulled the cruiser out of the bramble. She swept off the thorns and hopped on, patting the seat in front of her.

"Any trick and I'll know," Elena said. "The desert will know."

Yassen sat behind Elena as the boy slid into the front seat. He revved the engine, and they shot forward, leaving the canyon behind them. Instead of heading east, the boy banked south. They went over a ridge of burnt stone and skirted a sandpit that hissed as they passed.

Yassen kept his eyes trained on the horizon in search of some scout but none came. The boy led them into a valley and stopped in its bowl. He hopped off, heading toward a boulder the size of a winged ox. Yassen tensed, but Elena rested her hand on his knee.

"Wait," she said.

They watched the boy disappear behind the boulder. Shortly after, the rocks rumbled and the boulder shook off sand as it edged a few feet to the left, revealing a passage just big enough for the cruiser.

The boy jogged back to them.

"So the Jantari built tunnels too," Elena mused as he hopped back on. "How many are there?"

"More than you know."

He turned the control dial, and they sped into the darkened tunnel. A few seconds later, the boulder groaned as it rolled back into place. The tunnel was long and narrow, and Yassen ducked as they swerved right, barely missing a hanging shard. They rode for hours, following twisting tunnels that held no markings before the darkness lightened, and Yassen saw a pinpoint of light above them. The boy slowed the cruiser and stopped underneath the opening. Yassen could make out rusted rungs leading up to the tiny pinprick of light.

"We have to climb," the boy said.

"Where does it lead?" Elena asked.

"Just inside Jantar, to the shacks," the boy said.

"The shacks?"

"It's where urchins like him live," Yassen said, and he saw the boy stiffen. "Don't worry. We have them in Ravence too."

"Let's get moving then," Elena said, and she prodded the boy forward. "You go first."

The boy glared at Yassen but went to the ladder. He jumped, catching the rung, and pulled himself up. He climbed like a spider, and Yassen thought of how poor boys like him—boys who relied on their wits and their cunning to survive—were easy fodder for the Arohassin. The group promised that he'd never again experience hunger, nor pain. Instead, they promised revenge and power, a means to take back what had been so ruthlessly snatched away. They weaved their tale so seamlessly that Yassen had fallen for it long before he recognized the lie.

Yassen followed the boy, with Elena close behind. His right arm hung uselessly as he wormed his way up the ladder, dragging his body up the rungs. The boy was nearly at the top, but he stopped and looked down.

"When we get up there, you have to be quiet, alright? Everyone will still be asleep in their shacks."

"You have our word," Elena said.

Yassen only nodded as the boy began climbing again. With a grunt, Yassen neared the top, and the boy slid back the grate and scrambled out. A patch of orange, muted sky stared down at them. The boy helped Yassen up, and then they pulled out Elena. The urchin locked the latch back into place and motioned for them to follow.

The shacks were small, lopsided, made of scrap metal, tin, and anything else a beggar could find. While Ravence's slums were low, brick structures, Jantari slums were built in stacks, with metal fire escapes clawing down the side. Every window was barred, and a metal sign of the winged ox hung before every door.

The boy was right; everyone was asleep, and the streets were empty. But the shanty town looked outlandish in the reddish haze. It was too quiet, as if the strange sky had descended, wrapped around the homes, and trapped all sounds within. Everywhere Yassen turned, that same orange silence greeted him. Without thinking, he reached for his pistol, but Elena's hand grazed his back. He turned to her and saw the unspoken question in her eyes.

What do we do with the boy?

He glanced at the urchin and then back at her, closing and opening his fist.

Wait.

They followed the boy as they crept through narrow alleyways. Lights trapped in metal cubes illuminated their path. Everywhere, Yassen spotted the infamous silver Jantari steel, but it did not gleam. The orange sky blocked the sun, giving their eyes reprieve for once. They rounded a corner and walked down a sloping side street until they came to an intersection. The boy stopped.

"The main road is just off to the right," he said. "Follow it, and you'll find a hovertrain platform ahead. Take it."

"Why are you helping us?" Elena asked, and the urchin smiled wryly.

"Don't have much of a choice. Do I?"

"The desert is a fickle place, and it's changing. Be careful," she said.

"Once we expand our cities, there won't be a desert to return to," he said. "Soon, this slum will be a part of the metal. We can finally become city folk and conquer the desert."

Yassen saw a muscle work in Elena's jaw as she reached for the boy and squeezed his hand.

"Just be careful," she said.

The boy yanked his hand away and disappeared back the way they came.

Elena watched him go, and then she turned to Yassen. Her eyes were dark, her mouth a thin line.

"You know what to do," she whispered.

Yassen nodded. "Just stay out of sight," he said. "I'll find you."

It did not take him long to spot the boy. He crept along the side of the alley with the easy, sloping gait of an urchin who knew his street. Yassen followed, feet quick and light like a cat, like a shadow. When the boy turned, he looked back and caught sight of Yassen. Instantly, he took off. Yassen chased him down the alley, pulling out his gun as the boy scrambled up brass steps. He stumbled, opening his mouth to howl for help, but Yassen pounced on him.

He clamped his hand over the boy's mouth. The boy beat his hands against his arm, clawed his face, but Yassen squeezed harder. The urchin kicked, his entire body flailing, fighting to survive. Tears slipped down his cheeks as his pale, colorless eyes met Yassen's.

They were so like his own. It made Yassen balk.

He thought of the fleeing prisoner, the look of horror on his face before Yassen had gunned him down. His hand trembled. He had told Samson then that there had been no choice. They had to shoot the prisoners or meet the firing squad themselves. But Samson had just stared at him, eyes wide with pain and disappointment.

The urchin kicked. Yassen could feel him scream against his palm.

He couldn't.

This wasn't survival. It was desperation.

Yassen released the boy. He fell back, wheezing against the steps.

"We were never here," Yassen muttered. He leaned down and snapped off the visor around the boy's neck. "Don't say a word to anyone."

The urchin nodded, gulping in air. Yassen could already see the hate bubble beneath the boy's film of tears, but he turned before he could change his mind.

Yassen weaved past the quiet shanties silhouetted against the burdened sky. Shame burned in his chest. Maybe he should have killed the boy. Urchins like him died in shanties like this every day. It was the way of the desert, a land already thick with blood. But he was just a boy, a boy with no name, a boy who pickpocketed and scavenged the streets for his next meal. How could he take a life from someone who mirrored his own?

Yassen looked down at his hands. Maybe he had lost his edge. Maybe he wasn't taloned, just like Samson had feared. Or maybe he was just beginning to cut himself some slack. Offer himself a glimmer of forgiveness.

He followed the road to the hovertrain station, an open-air platform on the edge of the slum. It was empty. Holos hovered above him, headlines flashing. A crystal monitor embedded within a pillar of brass informed Yassen that the train for the morning labor shift had already passed.

He strode along the edge of the platform, searching for Elena. On his left was a short, rectangular track where a hovertrain would dock. The Claws, curved metal fixtures that locked and charged the train, bordered the track. Their buzz filled the morning quiet.

He found Elena huddled beside the ticket booth. It was powered down, with no attendant on the glass screen. Slowly, he sank down beside her.

"They took Casear Lunar," she said, pointing to the holo above the booth.

News streams showed Jantari forces ransacking Samson's garden, overturning the very tables where he and Samson had sat nearly a month and half prior, reminiscing about their childhood. It felt like a lifetime ago.

"The Ravani royal family has been assassinated by the Arohassin," a reporter said in a clipped voice. "Reports detail that Samson Kytuu aided the terrorists in the usurpation of the Ravani government. King Farin has officially declared war against the Arohassin and the Black Scales. He has invoked his claim over Ravence in the absence of the reigning government. Hail Farin. May our brass prove unyielding against the instigators."

Yassen stared, stunned. The holos shifted to show footage of Jantari soldiers marching across Ravence's southern borders. Missiles fired. The red wall fell in a blast of stone. Blood drained from his face as he watched the Jantari lay out the dead bodies of Ravani and Black Scale soldiers in neat, orderly lines.

"That fucking pig," Elena seethed, and sparks flitted from her hands. "He marches into my kingdom, pretending to be the hero? Pretending that *he* has claim over the desert?" she spat, her eyes flashing. "I'll have his head. I'll melt his metal body and throw it into the Eternal Fire."

Yassen clenched his fist to stop it from shaking. From what he knew, Farin had agreed to make Ravence a tributary state, with the Arohassin at the helm. He had never expected this. And to indict Samson... Rage bubbled in his chest, thick and hot. If he could wield fire like Elena, he would burn down Jantar just for that.

"We need to take a train to the mountains," he said, fighting to keep his voice under control, to be logical. There was nothing they could do now. "It'll take us three days. I still have my holopod. I can buy us tickets."

Elena turned to him, her eyes reading what he guarded.

"What happened with the boy?"

"Look, the next train is in fifteen minutes," he said, nodding toward the monitor. He forced himself to not look at the newscast. "It should be less crowded than the morning trains. We'll need a disguise though—something ordinary." He handed her the urchin's visor. "Use this for now."

"Is this the boy's?"

He tried to keep his face as stoic as possible, his voice level. "We don't have much time."

"Did you kill him?" she asked, and when he said nothing, she scoffed. "Holy Bird Above, you didn't do it."

"You don't understand," he said. She couldn't. All her life, the difficult decisions had never fallen onto her. She never had to second-guess. Shooting hidden assassins in the forest was entirely different from aiming your pistol point-black at a young boy whose face constricted with terror. "I gave him a good scare. He won't talk."

"Of course he'll talk! He'll talk just to spite you."

"Then let's get moving," he said. "Your father wouldn't like if we stayed here."

"You speak as if he's still alive," she said, her jaw hardening. "Leo died and brought Ravence down with him."

"You think Leo would let Ravence fall if he were still alive? It'd still have a fighting chance with him at the helm," he spat.

She laughed, a short barking sound that held no mirth. "Ravence fell because of King Leo, and that's how it will go down in history. You don't understand what he's done, Yassen—the crimes he's committed against the Phoenix. The lies he fabricated, the ones he made me believe as truth." She shook her head. "*You* don't understand what it means to build your life upon falsehoods."

Oh, but he did. All his life, he had lived with varying identities, fake personas, disguises. Sometimes he was a businessman who dealt in cane sugar, or a fisherman living along the Hyuku River. He lived lives big and small, none of which were true to his own. He could never be the simple boy who loved to play the piano, the boy who dreamed of competing in windsnatch, the boy who lived in the burnt house at the end of the lane.

"Let's just get to the cabin," he said.

They sat in silence as they stared out at the empty platform. Sand swirled and danced in the wind. Yassen rested his head against the wall and glanced at Elena. Her eyes were dark, brooding, but he sensed her sadness, her misery. They were both orphans now. At least they both understood that pain.

The air screeched with the approach of the hovertrain. They saw it fly in from the distance as the Claws buzzed and leaned back. The hovertrain slowly lowered onto the track, and the Claws hissed and latched on to its sides. Steam whizzed out.

Elena pulled back her hair and slipped on the visor. She got up without another word.

Yassen rose, his steps heavy as he boarded the train. The car, like he had suspected, was empty.

He pressed his holopod on the scanner beside the door and purchased two tickets for the Sona Range. He pocketed the pod and sat across from Elena. She did not look at him.

Guilt and frustration cut through Yassen. He tried to find the words to break the silence, but then the Claws buzzed and unlatched. With a groan, the hovertrain rose and hurtled east, leaving the orange sky and the desert behind.

37
ELENA

Distance makes the heart grow fonder, but what of the eyes?
Do they show the sorrow of our parting?

—FROM A SAYONAI FOLKLORE BALLAD

Elena watched the desert give way to deep forests and metal buildings. They left the orange silence behind them, the hovertrain zipping past bronze skyscrapers and metal bridges. She had never been in a hovertrain before, let alone one in Jantar. It was so... unremarkable. The purple lights clashed with the plastic, grey seats. Panels on the wall advertised the latest skin creams. Their compartment smelled stale, like old banana chips.

Yassen sat across from her, staring out the window. They had said little to each other since their argument on the platform. She was still furious that he hadn't killed the boy and still furious over his betrayal. She wondered if he missed Samson and Ferma as much as she did.

Sometimes, when she looked at Yassen, Elena was filled with disgust. But pity would soon follow. They were both stranded, alone and unmoored. What else could two broken people do, other than use their broken parts to mend their wounds?

Elena sighed and rested her head against the curved window. The trip to the Sona Range would take three days by hovertrain, and they had already stopped twice. Only two passengers had boarded during their last stop. One was a young woman with hair like honey and eyes of steel; the other a younger boy, possibly her son. He slumped into her, his face pressed against her stomach, his mouth slightly parted. The mother shifted the boy and rested his head in her lap. She looked up and saw Elena staring. She smiled, but Elena quickly looked away.

The hovertrain sighed as it began its third descent. They looped past a large sign that read "Welcome to Monora," and then turned into a platform full of people. Elena tensed. Yassen stood, studying the crowd as they pulled into the station. The Claws buzzed and latched on to the train. Steam hissed out of its engines. She turned to Yassen as he scrubbed the dried blood from his lip with the back of his hand. He had since discarded his Palace badge, and the spot above his chest looked dark and empty without it.

"Wait here and save me a seat," he said.

"But, there are so many people," she said under her breath, glancing at the sleeping mother and child. "What if someone recognizes us?"

"I know how to shake a tail."

The purple haloscent light that lined the tube blinked, and a robotic voice announced that they had arrived in Monora.

"I'll be back," Yassen said, and he strode through the doors.

Passengers rushed in, fighting for seats. They carried a rancid smell; for a moment, Elena thought they were day-workers bringing the scent of the city, but then she saw the look on their faces, and she realized it was fear. She twisted in her seat to catch a glimpse of Yassen, but he was already lost in the crowd. Faces of reporters floated along the platform. She could not hear them, but she froze when she saw the headlines.

The Arohassin have claimed Palace Hill.

Someone tapped her shoulder, and Elena turned to a man with a green visor and pudgy cheeks.

"Is this seat taken?"

She nodded, spreading her arm on the seat beside her. "My friend just jumped out, but he's coming back."

The man scowled. Another worker, dressed in black slacks, bumped into him.

"Grab a seat," the worker said.

"Girl said it's taken," the man snapped.

"Hey, lady, you can't save seats," the worker said. He winced as someone poked him in the side. "It's too crowded for that shit."

"I-I—" Elena stammered. Where was Yassen?

The man glowered as the worker pushed into him. "Leave her alone."

"I'm just saying, there's an open spot—"

"She said it's for her friend—"

"—too hot for this mess," the worker finished. He jostled forward, teetering as the hovertrain hissed.

"One minute until departure," the robotic voice intoned.

"Hey, back up," the man growled.

"Lady, I've been on my feet all day," the worker said, his red visor flashing. "Can you move on over—"

"I *said* back up—"

"I'm just talking to the girl—"

"Is there a problem?" Yassen's voice cut through the air, silencing the two men.

Elena whipped around to see Yassen push up to their seats. His face was hidden behind a visor, his dirty clothes hidden beneath a new cloak.

The worker straightened as the man with pudgy cheeks shook his head.

"We don't want no trouble. There's already enough coming our way," the man grumbled.

"You can't save seats," the worker said indignantly. He scowled at Elena, but Yassen forced himself in front of her.

"There isn't any rule against saving seats," Yassen said. He stood a head taller than the worker, and the man seemed to consider this before shaking his head and mumbling something about his legs. He moved away in search of an unclaimed seat.

The Claws unlatched, and the hovertrain took to the sky. Elena sighed as Yassen sank into the seat beside her. The sign of Monora winked goodbye as they hurtled past, gaining speed. The sun broke through, and for a moment it was if the city was on fire, each bronze building lighting up like forks of a flame. She tightened her visor as Yassen handed her a folded leather jacket.

"So you'll look less like a beggar," he said.

She snorted. "It'll take more than that," she said and gestured to her ripped skirts. "Diya would have a heart attack."

"And Ferma would've muscled you into a gamesuit," he said, and, despite herself, Elena managed a smile.

He reached back into his cloak to withdraw two bundles of pound cakes and spiced chicken wrapped in bhakri.

"Here, I found these at the station café."

"And the jackets?"

"I may have nicked it out of someone's luggage when they weren't looking," he winked.

"Thanks," she said, and paused. "Thanks for handling that too."

He nodded as she bit into the pound cake, savoring its sweet, vanilla aftertaste and licking the brown sugar that stuck to her lips. Yassen split the bhakri and offered half to her. She took it as they zoomed past the outskirts of the city for the deeper country beyond.

The hovertrain docked, and the crowd spilled out. Elena spotted the worker trip down the platform. He had untucked his shirt, and it rumpled behind him like a stunted tail. The pudgy-faced man stalked past him, muttering to himself. Along the platform, newscasts of the war clogged the holos. She saw images of the burning mountain, crumpled sandscrapers, and the steady approach of the metal army. Ravence was under attack, and here she was running away from it. She wanted to go back, to fight, to set the silver hulls of the Jantari army afire. Her entire training screamed for her to do so. Elena gripped the edge of her seat as the hovertrain hissed and rose to the sky again. But she could not take on an entire army by herself. She was no Prophet.

Sunlight poured into their empty compartment. Yassen groaned as he stretched out his legs.

"Skies above." He grimaced as he pulled off his visor, which left an angry red mark across his face. "What?" he said, when he saw her staring.

"The cabin in the Sona Range, was it your family's?" she asked.

"My father's."

"Is it still there?"

"Yes, although it's been many suns since I've been back," he said, his voice dampened by regret.

Yassen reached into his cloak and withdrew his holopod. He opened the map of the tunnels underneath the mountains.

"He taught me how to navigate the tunnels. One leads right up to the cabin, but we'll need to rent brennis to get there. They're more surefooted than horses, and they can carry a heavy load of supplies." He moved to pocket the pod, but then hesitated. The holo flickered in his hand. "My father told me once that tunnels underneath mountains are only made to harbor secrets. He wasn't wrong." Sunlight cut across his face, deepening the grooves beneath his eyes. "The Jantari are hiding something beneath their mountains. We have to be careful."

She thought of the tunnels underneath the Temple—the priests who lived within them and the secrets they held. And then there were the tunnels underneath Palace Hill, the ones that led to the Royal Library and the capital. Poor, rich, royal—everyone had their secrets, and everyone buried them deep within Sayon.

"You told me your father found something," she said. "Are you going to track it down?"

For a long moment, Yassen said nothing. The hovertrain hummed as it sped across the sky. With each passing minute, she grew further away from her desert. Her home. With each passing moment, he drew closer to the remnants of his past. She wondered what ghosts awaited him, what scars she would find burned into the mountainside.

When Yassen finally spoke, his voice was quiet, steady. Full of power like the songs of the priests.

"The past is binding, but I want to break it," he said. "If we carry the burdens of our fathers, we'll never know what it means to be free."

The sun was beginning to set, and its raw edges warmed the corners of their compartment. Yassen leaned his head back and closed his eyes. For once, he became clear to her: a solid man rather than a ghost. He was neither assassin nor traitor—just a man carving his own path in a life bound by fate.

Just like her.

The hovertrain began to slow as they neared their connection. Elena smoothed the wrinkles in her skirt and zipped up her leather jacket. The sunset began to ebb away, and the horizon lined with gold. She stood, hovering over Yassen.

"You're still a coward for running away from the truth," she said, but her voice was gentle.

"Maybe," he said, and in the shadows of the fading sun, she saw him smile. "But at least I'll live."

Elena drew her jacket tighter to fight off the chill. Although the sun had set, people still milled around the platform. News of the war had delayed several hovertrains, their connection included. Elena huddled underneath a steel pillar, studying the faces of the people she had been bred to distrust. She spotted a young girl with a lopsided smile; an old man with eyebrows thicker than a sandstorm; a woman who paced across the platform, talking rapidly into a headset glued to her ear.

They were, in short, far more mundane than she had imagined.

All her life, she had been taught to abhor the Jantari. Her father called them zeemir-slinging oppressors, bent on robbing Sayon of her riches and turning her people into machines. But here, she saw only men and women tired after a long day of work, tensing at every new war-ridden headline. Mothers and fathers impatient to get home and wrap their arms around their family to make sure they were safe.

War was meant to demonize the other side. To make the enemy less than yourself. After all, it was far easier to shoot down a Jantari soldier if he was considered a metal devil. At times, Elena had dreamed of bringing the southern border disputes to an end by staging a full-force military campaign. She had wanted to bring peace to Ravence. To be considered a hero for vanquishing their enemy. But as Elena watched the young girl complain to her mother, and the old man droop his head in sleep, she saw them for what they were—a people as Sayonai as her own.

"Here," Yassen said, breaking her reverie.

Elena turned as he handed her a hot cup of tea from the vendor at the end of the platform. She cradled it between her hands, letting its heat chase away the chill of the evening. Yassen leaned against the pillar, sighing.

"The train should be here by now."

She began to tell him that their train had been delayed by another hour when a gasp rippled across the platform. Elena turned as the holos flashed. A brief headline warned viewers of gruesome content, and then it was replaced by a video.

Elena instantly recognized Alabore's Passage, the route of her parade.

The buildings, once adorned by marigolds and streamers, lay in shambles. Walls were missing or blown out. Ripped orange banners and debris littered the streets. But it was not the smoke or the ruined buildings that made Elena's blood still.

It was the body.

A tank rolled across the fallen banners, dragging a blackened form behind it. Though most of the corpse was burned, Elena could tell that it once had been a tall man. It wore long red robes that dragged across the broken ground. Soldiers dressed in black, with the silver snake of the Arohassin, marched beside the tank. Their faces were streaked with ash, but their eyes burned with conviction as they shouted: "Long live the king."

The video cut to the White Lotus, where she had once stood on the platform and burned the names of gold caps into the sand. The Arohassin soldiers looped a rope around the neck of the corpse. They climbed up the stone lotus sculpture, pulling the body. At the top, they tied the end of the rope to one of the petals and then flung the corpse over. It bounced, swaying in the air. Its eyes, bloodied and swollen, bulged as the fire beneath licked its bare, blackened feet.

A soldier brandished the Ravani flag and threw it into the flames. He turned to the camera in mock salute.

"Long live the king."

And then it hit Elena.

She made a sound, something caught between a squeal and a scream. People turned. Yassen draped his arm around her shoulder and pulled her close, burying her face in his chest. She tried to pull away, but he only held her tighter.

"My fath—"

"It's not him," he whispered fiercely in her ear. "There's no way they could have fished him out of the Eternal Fire."

But the body, the robes. It was her father. They dragged him through the streets like a criminal, like an animal. She struggled against him.

"Elena, think," he pleaded. "If that really is Leo, then where is the crown? They were in the same room. How could they have found his body but not the crown?"

She slumped into him. He was right. She had lost the crown at the same time the Eternal Fire had claimed her father. The body the Arohassin paraded down the streets was merely a decoy, a beggar whose dream of becoming a king had finally come true.

When she stopped struggling, he finally let her go. Elena pulled away and drew in a deep, long breath, but her throat hitched. How dare they dishonor the Ravani king? How dare they even *think* to desecrate his body?

The video ended, and a reporter appeared within the holos.

"King Farin has issued a statement. All Ravani within Jantar must report to the authorities," he said nonchalantly, as if he were talking about the weather and not people. "If you do not report willingly, you shall be detained. Find your nearest hovertrain station and report to the police. Do not bring your belongings."

A murmur rippled through the platform. The girl with the lopsided smile hid herself within her mother's skirts. The old man snorted, his mouth twisted in disdain. Workers glanced furtively at each other, at her, and for once Elena felt grateful for her awful visor.

Yassen gestured. "Let's move to the other side of the platform."

Elena turned but saw a man heading straight for them. He was dressed in black, with a winged ox across his chest. A Jantari policeman. She pretended that she had not seen him, but he blocked their path.

"I need to see some identification," he demanded.

At the other edge of the platform, Elena saw more police officers sauntering through the crowd. The crowd split away, revealing those who hid within. She saw a policeman shout at a young man. When he did not produce a holo, the officer grabbed him by the back of his neck and kicked him down. Someone screamed as the policeman ground his foot into the young man's head. Elena stiffened, but then Yassen stepped forward and held out his holopod.

"The name's Cassian Newman," he said to the policeman.

Across the platform, the officer clasped cuffs around the young man's wrists. Dragged him behind a pillar as his colleagues rounded up others.

"You're from Nbru?" the policeman asked as he scrutinized Yassen's holo. His eyebrows furrowed. "Says here that you arrived nearly a month and a half ago. Why'd you leave?"

"Work," Yassen replied. At once, she recognized the change in his accent. Gone were the heavy, rolling sounds of the desert, replaced by the high, lilting tones of the Nbruian. He gave a bashful smile, and his voice lowered like the servants in the Palace. "Jantar gives better coin."

"Take off your visor," the officer demanded, and Yassen slowly unclipped his, revealing his colorless eyes. "You're a Jantari?"

"My father was," Yassen replied with a tight-lipped smile.

The office snorted. "And her?" He looked at Elena, and she saw him take in her long curls, her dark brown skin. "Where's her passport?"

"My, uh, wife forgot it at home," Yassen said, and she shot him a look. "We're sorry. We rushed out when we heard the war declaration. My poor mother-in-law, may the Mountain bless her soul, has a frail heart. She lives across the city. We just want to check in on her."

You're talking too much, she thought, but she held her tongue.

"Tough luck," the officer growled. He pointed at Elena. "Without holos, I can't let her pass. Come with me, miss."

Elena bristled, but Yassen stepped in front of her. He slipped something into the officer's pocket.

"Sometimes we forget things when we're worried," he whispered.

The officer's upper lip curled back in a sneer. "Are you trying to bribe me?"

"No," Yassen said, his voice calm and serene. "Just paying my deference to the guards of Jantar."

The officer considered this. Finally, he patted his pocket and nodded.

"Next time, bring your pod. We can't have Ravani mingling with our people," he said. "Hail Farin."

He strode past them, heading for the next man unfortunate enough to catch his attention. Elena let out a shaky breath.

"They're rounding us up." She shook her head. Anger flashed through her—a keen, sudden pain, like needles piercing through her fingertips. She had to protect her people. With her fire, she could burn down every Jantari policeman and Arohassin soldier. With her fire, she would hang them from the rafters.

Yassen must have recognized the look in her eyes because he touched her arm as heat rolled off her. He did not flinch.

"Easy now," he said, glancing around them. "Remember why you're here."

She forced herself to nod. A hissing sound grew in her ears, and she knew at once that it was the fire within her begging to be unleashed.

To rage.

To burn.

In time, she told it.

She flexed her hand, and a wisp of a flame, a tiny little thing, danced and died in her palm.

They arrived at the Sona Range at dawn of the third day. On the train, Elena had snagged a scarf left by a passenger and used it to hide her dark, curly hair. Officers, luckily, had not combed the hovertrains once they boarded. They only searched the platforms for traveling Ravani, and Elena shuddered to think what was happening to her countrymen.

The sky bled in drops of rust and carmine as their hovertrain neared the mountains. Like most of Jantar, the mountains glinted unnaturally. Small patches of snow dotted the peaks in sharp contrast to the blue and red pines, but what drew Elena's attention were the rigs. Massive, metal conglomerations hugged the mountainside like ugly beetles. The mine's four legs embedded deep within the mountain. In the middle, two pressurized glass pipes acted as elevator tubes. One was used to send Sesharians deep into the mountain; the other to retrieve carts filled with the raw ore of Sayon. Elena was both impressed by the sheer might of the mines and repulsed by the way they gutted the land of its value.

The Jantari did not respect the ridges and dips of their landscape, as her father had once told her. They built and mined without pausing to consider their effect on the land. At least her people knew how to coexist with the desert, to learn its shapes and curves. At least the Ravani knew when to give and when to beg.

Her thoughts turned to the nameless boy at the edge of the desert. He would talk. Perhaps he had already alerted the authorities, maybe even gotten some coin if he was smart. She should have killed him herself. She should have seen the act through—for Ravence. Everything she did, everything she knew she had to do, was for its deserts.

She longed for her home. So much so that her ache felt more intense than hunger, more fervent than prayer.

But was it enough to kill a boy? Elena swallowed. She did not know.

Yassen stirred and rolled onto his back. He was laid out across the seats, asleep. The pale sun outlined the bridge of his nose, the high plane of his forehead, softening him.

She had forgotten just how Jantari he looked, with his colorless eyes and pale skin. Even the boy had mistaken Yassen for one, and she remembered how the name had made him flinch, as if stung. If she had not known better, she would've thought metal ran through his veins, not sand. But Elena admonished herself. Equating identity with appearances never created the whole picture.

Elena got up and slowly sat beside Yassen. His lips were slightly parted, his long lashes dusting the tops of his cheeks. Age lines crinkled along his eyes, but the sunlight made him appear as if he were in repose. As if he'd found peace beyond this world.

The hovertrain descended to a stop. The Claws latched on as Elena glanced up to see another empty platform. When she looked back down, she saw that Yassen was awake, that he'd been awake all this time, and his pale eyes stared up at her. The doors swished open. She felt a cold blast of air, smelled the fresh tinge of pine and the acidity of metal, but she did not turn away.

Slowly, Yassen reached up. His fingers brushed her cheek, and she stilled. He ran his thumb along her cheekbone and then gently withdrew, holding up his thumb to reveal a thin eyelash, her eyelash.

"Make a wish," he whispered.

She looked down at him, her breath caught in her chest. A wish? She almost laughed. What would a wish do in a place like this? But he did not break her gaze, and she could not tear herself away.

"I wish for us to survive," she said, and blew. The eyelash fluttered and disappeared.

He reached up, and for a moment she thought he meant to touch her cheek again, but he only pointed out of the curved windows.

"There," he said, and she turned to see the vivid shades of the thick, lush forest. No rigs had infiltrated this part of the mountain. At least not yet. "The safe house."

"How will we get there?" she asked.

"With brenni." His pale eyes found hers again. "Are you still up for this?"

She nodded, and he slowly sat up with a soft groan. He cradled his arm to his chest, and she saw a flash of bruised skin.

"Are you in pain?

"Always," he said.

"Your hand," she started, but he waved her off.

"Let's go before the train leaves."

They deboarded and walked down the empty platform. An old merchant wrapped in fyrra fur sat behind a rickety stall. His coat made Elena envious as she shivered against the mountain chill.

"Looking to escape the city, eh?" the merchant called out as they neared. His plastic visor bobbed as he spoke.

"Mountain air is good for any man," Yassen said, "but I admit we're poorly packed." He pointed at the musty shelves behind the merchant. "Got any furs back there?"

"Oh, just two," he said.

"Perfect, we'll take them," Yassen said and pulled out his holopod.

The man scanned the pod and handed them two heavy coats. Elena pulled hers on; it was too big, but she hugged it close to her body to trap whatever warmth she had left.

"Thank you," she murmured.

"Watch out for the autumn snaps, mera," the merchant said. "There's been talk of brush fire, but the season's already changing. I blame the war."

"We'll keep an eye out," Yassen said. "Is there a place nearby where we can find a nice hot meal? Or brenni?"

"Follow the road," the merchant drawled. "You'll find the handler along it. Oh, and tighten them visors. The mines been flashing lately, and they blinded a poor girl just last week. They're doing the same to those poor Ravani. Soldiers will be here any day now to collect the ore, so best stay out of their way, or else they'll recruit you." He laughed.

Elena's stomach tightened as she recalled the lumbering hulls in the desert. The soldiers with their zeemirs. Light bounced harshly off the dunes; Jantari's fickle metal would only worsen the effects.

"Do you know when the soldiers will be here?" she asked.

"Oh, in a few days' time. Shouldn't be too long now," the merchant said.

"And where—"

"I'm sorry, she has a thing for soldiers," Yassen said, squeezing her arm. "Down the road you said?"

"Yes, the handler's the one with the brass and durian-colored front."

Yassen thanked the merchant as he nudged Elena forward. His hand pressed into the small of her back, and he did not remove it until they were well out of earshot.

"We have to stop them," she hissed.

"No," he said. "We can't stop an entire army."

"But we can slow it down! You heard what he said. They're going to use the ore for weapons. Do you remember those tanks? Can you imagine what hundreds of them could do to the Ravani army, to Samson's army? At least help Samson's men."

"I'll help Samson more by keeping you out of sight," he said firmly. She had never seen him look so focused and distraught at the same time. "You have to pick your battles."

Ferma had said the same. How annoyingly similar they were.

Elena kicked up gravel as they followed the road. It was almost three miles long, and by the time they reached the town, the sun was high in the sky. Elena shook out a stone from her shoe as they stood on a corner. Tiny metal shops and glass storefronts lined the street. Purple haloscent lights guided hovercars that hummed past merchants sleeping behind their stalls. She spotted a metalsmith hammering thin slices of steel into a sleek wooden board. There were no urchins, no street dancers. It was so subdued compared to Ravence's bustling streets.

Elena spotted a storefront of brass and durian and pointed it out to Yassen. They slipped inside. A tiny, empty desk sat at the front while two doors behind it opened to a covered pasture filled with pine needles and brenni. Elena walked around the desk to the pasture. One brenni raised its furry head at her approach. It brayed, alerting the woman raking out muck.

When she spotted Elena and Yassen, the woman dropped her rake and hurried over.

"Mounting a ride?" she asked.

"Just two," Elena said.

"For how long?"

"A month," Yassen said and lifted his holopod. "And we'll need feed for them, too."

"Of course," the woman said.

Elena watched as she slipped rope halters on two brenni and led them out. She saddled them and swung heavy bags of feed onto their backs. One of the creatures stared at Elena with buttery eyes, and flicked her long, drooping ears. They were not as elegant as Ravani horses, but they would have to do.

"Thank you," Yassen said and took their leads. The woman smiled, color rising to her face. Elena could not help but notice how she beamed at Yassen, how her eyes lingered on him.

"Bring them back before the two new moons, mero," she said to Yassen.

Elena took a brenni's lead. It nuzzled her shoulder, soft and warm, yet it smelled of a forest so unlike her own.

"Wait here for a moment," Yassen said when they were back out.

He crossed the street and disappeared into a storefront. Elena rocked on her feet. The visor itched the bridge of her nose, and she wished to tear it off. She longed for Rani. Here, the buildings and the mountains reflected the harsh gaze of the sun, and Elena felt a strange disquiet as she stood alone. It was a whispering feeling, a slippery one. A premonition perhaps, or the knowledge that what lay ahead was uncharted territory—a long, twisting path that she had no hope of controlling.

Yassen jogged back carrying bundles. He stuffed them into the saddle bags and handed her a package of wrapped meat.

"How were you able to buy all of this?" she asked, examining the food.

"Suns of saving and insurance," he said, lifting another pack onto the brenni.

"Insurance?"

"It pays to take out powerful people." He tightened his brenni's girth as it snorted. "Shall we?"

He gave her a leg up, and she swung onto the saddle. The brenni shifted, straining at the bit, but then became still under her touch. It wasn't quite like a horse, but it felt solid. Sturdy.

Yassen hopped on and nudged his brenni forward. When they reached the forest road, he twisted in his saddle and looked at her.

"I need you to make me a promise," he said. He took off his visor, his eyes boring into hers. "You have to give me your word that you will do everything I say. If I tell you to hide, you hide. If I tell you to run, you run—even if you have a clear shot. There will be no time to argue. This land may not be as rough as Ravence, but it has its harsh edges, and I know them better than you."

"And what if I have to leave you behind?"

"Then you'll leave me behind," he said, and his words fell like stones. It saddened her. Yassen was all that she had left of Ravence.

"Then make sure you keep up," she said and spurred her brenni on.

38
YASSEN

Everything points north, even death.

—A RAVANI PROVERB

Yassen remembered the amethyst pine with the ivory trunk. It hunkered on the edge of the mountainside like a squalid banshee—a sordidly welcoming sight.

"We're almost there," he called out to Elena.

They were already three hours into their journey. Yassen had taken off his coat as the day grew warmer, but now, as they wandered deeper into the forest, he wished he had kept it on. A chill crept through the pines, cold and slippery. His brenni shifted nervously, but he steered it beyond the tree.

Yassen hadn't been in the mountain for many suns, yet he still remembered the path to his father's cabin. There was the tall sapling with its blue needles; there, the cliffside that resembled the aging face of a king. Yassen kicked his brenni, and it hopped over a fallen log covered with dry leaves and dust from the mines above.

If what the merchant said was true, the Jantari soldiers would be here soon to collect their precious ore. They would most likely go straight to the mines without searching the mountain; after all, they were deep within their own territory. They had little reason to suspect danger. Yassen still made sure to cover their tracks when he could. He guided their brennis over pine roots and weaved them through creeks, where it would be harder to find their prints.

He nudged his mount through a narrow slit between two trees. He spotted a flutter of blue above, and Yassen looked up to see the faint edges of a mountain lark.

"Stay still," he said, and out of the corner of his eye, he saw Elena rein her mount to a stop.

He jumped out of the saddle and landed softly on a carpet of pine needles. Black neverwood branches clawed out from beneath the underbrush, reaching for him. The mountain lark called out.

Two notes.

"You hear that?" he said softly to Elena. "Two notes mean no danger."

"What about one?"

"It means you run."

He stepped in the pockets between roots and came to stand before a long retherin pine. It was an old master of the forest; its velvet blue trunk was wider than three grown men, and its tawny leaves were thick and heavy despite the summer heat.

Slowly, Yassen sank down to study its roots. They spanned the forest floor, a vast network that led to the very base of the mountain. His father had taught him that the roots of a tree were a map that linked the land together—from its valleys to its summits—and that to understand it, he need only to observe. To truly *see*.

Yassen traced one root that led to the trunk. The bark felt soft, supple even. He followed it diagonally until he found the knot, the pear-shaped bulge that his father had pointed out to him ages ago, and he pressed it.

The wood splintered with a whisper.

The leaves rustled behind him, and the neverwood separated to reveal stone steps that descended beneath the mountain.

"Mother's Gold," Elena whispered. "How did you do that?"

"It pays to get out of Ravence every once in a while," he said and hopped back on his brenni. He squeezed his calves, and his steed trotted forward with Elena following.

The old tunnel veered steeply into the mountain, but their steeds were sure of foot. With a groan, the entrance closed, and they were submerged in darkness. Yassen's hand tightened around the reins. He wished they had some sort of light, but he would have to rely on memory now. His eyes gradually adjusted, and he saw that the staircase led to a ledge, and that a deep abyss plunged down just beyond it. Yassen stopped his brenni, twisting in the saddle to get his bearings. It came back slowly, piecemeal, like the glowing embers of a campfire: his father leading him across the narrow ridge, through the obsidian rocks that had scared him as a child, and up until he could smell the rotten leaves.

"This way," he said.

The bowels of the mountain glinted despite a lack of light. Unlike the mining tunnels that burrowed deep within the Sona Range, this one had not been made for miners. It was wider, taller, the walls still rough. When Yassen had asked his father who had created this tunnel, his father had merely shrugged.

"Does it matter?" he had asked.

He made Yassen memorize the tunnels that connected the mines, the cabin, and the foothills of the mountain, but he refused to let him explore the ones that led to the middle of the range.

"Stick only to this path," he had said.

As they trotted forward, Yassen recognized an oblong obsidian rock that rose on their left. It leaned forward like an old hunchback on the verge of losing his balance. Raw ore glinted within his body. Suddenly, the mountain rumbled. His brenni neighed as dust and dirt rained down.

"They're drilling," Elena said, and though her voice was barely above a whisper, it echoed through the chamber. "I thought you said there were no rigs in this part of the mountain."

"There aren't, but they're close. You can feel the drills everywhere."

Something scuttled between the rocks, and his brenni reared. Yassen squeezed his knees to steady it, speaking softly as his hand dropped to his hip.

They heard a growl. It bounced off the rocks and filled the chamber with a deep, guttural boom. His steed bucked and tossed its head. Yassen fought for control just as they heard another snarl, closer this time, and he saw a flash of something black—something deeper than the darkness—slither down the rocks. A chill crept down his shoulder and into his burnt arm. Elena's brenni chortled and bucked; she pulled on the reins, but her brenni shot forward, shoving past Yassen and his mount. It ran up the tunnel with breathtaking speed, spraying rocks in its wake.

At the sound of its sister's flight, Yassen's brenni sprang forward. He pulled on the reins, pain jolting up his arm, but his steed frothed at the bit. Yassen threw one last look over his shoulder. The black shape sprang into the abyss, and his hand twitched, as if stung.

Yassen cried out at the sudden pain, but then his brenni vaulted forward, screeching. Up ahead, he saw the fork in the path. East and west. Where had his father taken him?

"Left, go left!" he yelled.

Elena struggled, her brenni fighting her every step of the way, but she ripped off her visor and slapped it against its hide. The brenni yelped and swung left.

The path began to ascend. Yassen could smell the forest above. The scent crawled over the rocks as the darkness began to lighten into a muted grey. The path widened, and Yassen urged his brenni on until he was side by side with Elena; he flung out his right hand to grab her brenni's bridle. Perhaps it was the sweet, rotten odor of his hand, or the sight of his blackened fingers reaching for its eyes, but Elena's brenni shrieked and skidded to a stop. She gasped, grabbing her mount's mane to steady herself. Yassen's steed suddenly halted as well, almost flinging him over its neck.

Above, pockets of sunset peeked through a crumbling stone roof. Roots cracked through the surface, crawling into the chamber. Yassen dismounted, and a white-hot flash of pain shot through his arm. He stumbled forward like a drunk, blinded by agony.

"Yassen?" Elena called.

He sagged against the wall. Her voice seemed to come from the bottom of the mountain. He gritted his teeth, forcing himself to breathe.

One, two, three, count dammit.

One, two, three.

One, two, three.

He breathed out. When he opened his eyes, he felt a little less sick although he could taste some of the wrapped meat pushing back up his throat. With his good arm, he felt the rough wall. He followed it until he found the smooth rock—the false rock—and pushed it. The stone ceiling hinged open; rotten leaves and dirt fell in, burying them neck-deep in forest litter.

Yassen coughed, pulling himself up. His brenni popped its head out. It snorted in disapproval, but easily climbed onto the steady ground, shaking leaves from its drooping ears. Elena's hand shot up, and Yassen pulled her out.

"Why weren't there steps for this one?" she huffed as she pulled pine needles and molorian leaves from her hair.

"Patterns are dangerous," Yassen said as her brenni jumped out of the debris.

He grabbed its reins. The words came unbidden to his lips.

"Jo leh aasher."

Bless the ones who carry.

It was an old Ravani chant, one that his mother had taught him, yet the sound of the ancient language calmed the brenni. It gave a soft snort and nuzzled his shoulder. He stroked its ears.

"Is that it?" Elena said, pointing to a slanting structure within the trees.

Yassen turned to see his father's cabin. Fashioned out of molorian wood, it stood on top of a hill between two thick retherin pines. Reflective panels on the roof warded off the sun. The door, black and heavy, with a golden phoenix knocker nailed across its top, glowered in the distance.

Yassen climbed the stairs to the cabin, every step bringing back torn and faded memories. He had been seven suns the last time he had visited. It was the week before his father's death. They had gone hunting. It was an ancient sport, but his father was that way—traditional, slow to change. That was until he died and left Yassen and his mother alone to pick up the frayed pieces and make peace with the secrets he left behind.

The phoenix glinted as Yassen stepped onto the landing. Its eyes opened, a laser beaming out. It scanned Yassen's eyes, face, veins and heart. It traveled down the length of his body and then up to pause on his arm. Yassen lifted his left hand. The laser followed.

"Are you supposed to do something?" Elena said.

It was the same question he had asked his father, and Yassen did the same that his father had done. He reached forward and closed the phoenix's eyes.

Even man needed time away from the gods.

The door swung open, and they stepped across the threshold. It was not a large cabin, yet it seemed to hold the span of lifetimes. There was the modest, wooden furniture covered with colorful blankets that his mother had chosen; the fireplace of grey stone and flecks of Ravani gold that his father had built; the tea set that he had stolen from Radhia's Bazaar, resting on the kitchen counter in the back. Sunlight streamed in through the window, brushing the dusty hourglass and cups.

Yassen had never believed in ghosts, yet they were all he found: the ghost of his mother, father, and the boy he had once been. They crowded the room.

Waiting.

Watching.

Yassen whimpered, his knees suddenly weak. Elena helped him into a chair before the fireplace. In the corner of the mantel, he spotted the initials he had carved when his father wasn't looking. Of course, his father had found out. Laughing, he had carved his own next to Yassen's.

Y.K. E.K.

Yassen Knight.

Ekaant Knight.

His father had taught him how to fight; his mother had shown him how to think. When he would come to the cabin, Yassen had been comforted with the knowledge that he was worth something, that he was loved. Back then, the mountain had been his playground, the cabin his haven. He was free to be whoever he wanted, free to dream, to aspire, *to be something*.

Yet here he was, broken, useless. He had not become the man he had dreamed he would be. He had not even become the assassin he had trained to be.

In the end, he had amounted to nothing.

Yassen's chest constricted, heat prickling up his spine. He was too stunned to move, too harrowed to speak. Elena squeezed his shoulder and straightened.

"Let me handle this."

He watched as Elena tied up the brennis, gave them their feed, filled the pantry with food and set the water to boil. He watched her as if he were looking through a foggy window, adrift. She must have noticed him staring—she noticed everything—yet she said nothing. She was silent through her work, and when she set the tea on the molorian coffee table, she was soft—not in the fragile sort of way, but in the receiving kind. As if she too could sense the ghosts in the room.

"Here."

Yassen stared at the tea but made no move to pick it up. His good hand shook; the other curled inward like a frozen, black claw. He knew if he picked up the cup, he would spill all of its contents.

The sun sank behind the mountain, and darkness crept from the corners of the room. Elena rose and touched the panel beside the door. One by one, the lights in the cabin lit up.

Finally, Yassen found the strength to speak.

"Nothing has changed in here," he said, his voice thin and frail. "Yet everything has."

"The living need to change," Elena said as she sat back down. She poured his cold tea back into the pot. "Only the dead can remain untouched."

Yassen gave a dry, caustic laugh. "I think I've changed too much."

"Maybe." She reached forward and took his blackened arm, resting his hand in her lap. Slowly, she traced the lines in his palm, the bruises that ringed his wrist. Her touch was warm, gentle. "But you're still Yassen Knight. That has not changed. And you're alive, despite everything."

"Elena," he whispered.

She met his gaze. "You told me that if I keep living, then Ravence cannot truly die. You're the same. You carry your family with you, their stories. As long as you keep breathing, they live."

She was right, but a part of him thought his transformation was too extreme. It felt strange to be back in a home after spending so many suns away from it. The cabin had stayed the same, trapped in time like an old photograph while he had altered drastically.

Yet, Yassen recognized parts of himself in the inscription in the mantel, in the frayed corners of his favorite blue blanket, in the teacup he had chipped when running past the kitchen counter. They brought back memories, and within each memory, a story.

If a man was just a tapestry of the characters he donned, his was the most unusual of all. He had been a boy who dreamt of pianos and windsnatch, an assassin who sold his brethren without batting an eye.

He was a traitor who turned on his country, and a servant who saved his queen. These stories were all a part of him.

They *were* him.

Perhaps, then, the boy he had been, the man he wanted to be, was still here, still within him.

Waiting.

Later, when Elena retired to the inner bedroom and he lay on the sofa, awake, Yassen remembered a story his father had told him.

It was the story of Goromount, the fabled traveler who crossed the Ahi Sea after his home had been destroyed by the gods. Goromount traveled using the stars with ancient instruments called telescopes and star charts. He followed them without knowing where they would lead him.

"Why?" Yassen had asked his father. "What if they just led him to another ruined land?"

"Belief, Yass," his father had said. "He believed that though the gods were savage in their fury, they were also kind in their mercy. If they destroyed all the land and all its creatures, then the gods would have no one to worship them. They would truly be forgotten."

At first, Yassen had not understood the story, but now, as he stared up at the ceiling, listening to the creaks in the floorboards and the whistle of the wind, he understood some of it. Goromount had been an orphan just like him. He had lost everything, but then he had gathered the pieces that had remained and had traveled in search of a home to make them whole again.

Yassen wondered if Goromount, when he built a new shelter on a foreign land, had created it in the image of his homeland. Or had he stared at his new home and declared it free of the past? Something entirely new—a fireplace free of inscriptions.

He heard a sound, and Yassen sat up, his hand reaching for the gun on the coffee table. He listened, his muscles tensed. The noise came again, but this time it was low, mournful.

He stood and followed it to the end of the hall. His bare toes curled against the cold wood. The sound came from behind the closed bedroom door, and he then realized it was Elena. She was sobbing.

Yassen moved to open the door but then hesitated. Maybe he should leave her be. Maybe she wouldn't like it if he saw her cry. But Yassen remembered how he had felt the nights soon after he became an orphan. The rawness in his throat. The crushing loneliness in his heart. It was if someone had cut a hole in his chest, sucked everything out, and left him without so much a goodbye.

Finally, he knocked on the door. "Elena?"

The noise stopped. He pressed his ear against the dark wood, listening. She did not reply, but she also did not tell him to leave.

He cracked open the door and peeked in. She was lying on her side, her back to him. She did not turn as he sat down on the edge of the bed. He felt her grief; it was as palpable in the dark as a thick, humid night. And he also knew he could not alleviate it. It was a pain that only the bearer could hold, a pain that only the bearer could absolve.

The sheets rustled as Elena slid her hand across the bed, her face still turned away.

Without saying a word, he took her hand and squeezed. Her fingers curled in his.

He would stay here all night.

He would stay for as long as she needed.

39
YASSEN

Rest thy weary head, wanderer,
for you have found the honey of life—freedom.

—FROM *THE ODYSSEY OF GOROMOUNT: A PLAY*

Yassen dreamed of an avalanche of fire roaring down the Agnee mountainside, eating everything in its wake. He stood at the bottom, frozen. When the inferno engulfed him, he did not feel its heat—only white-hot shards of pain.

The pain grew until it climbed his arm and wrenched him awake. Yassen gasped, clutching his elbow. For a moment, he did not know his bearings, but then he recognized the wooden paneling of the bedroom.

His childhood cabin, and the ghosts that came with it.

He sat up with a groan. His right arm dragged across the sheet like a log. A pool of sweat bloomed across his chest. Gingerly, he unwrapped the blanket caught between his legs and stood. His vision swam. Yassen leaned against the bedpost, forcing himself to breathe, to recall his training, to make his heart calm. He was safe. There was no fire. He heard the clatter of pots, the thrum of the stove coming to life. Elena was in the cabin; Elena was safe.

Slowly, Yassen opened his eyes. Slowly, he made his way to the kitchen.

Elena flipped the hourglass. Her eyes were red and swollen, but she smiled as he walked in.

"Tea?"

He nodded and edged closer to the window. The mountains lay quiet. The miners had not yet started their drilling, and for a brief moment Yassen saw the mountains for what they really were: giant, intimidating, and gentle. Serene. He saw the tall pines rake the pale, morning sky. A mountain lark flitted between the canopies, calling.

He had always loved their songs as a boy. When he came to the cabin with his parents, the first thing he would do was run into the trees, armed with a seeing glass, and find a quiet spot. There, he'd watch the treetops for the telltale flutter of blue and listen for the bird's two or three-note song. Afterward, when he and his mother returned to Ravence and his father to the mines, Yassen would play the birdsong on the piano, relying on memory to coax out the tune. No matter how hard he tried, it had never been quite the same.

Yassen drummed his fingers against the windowsill. A ghost of a melody whispered along the edges of his mind, and he began to hum. He could not remember the lyrics—or even the song's name. He only remembered that the tune belonged to an old Sayonai ballad about lovers so morose they became the moons. A melancholy song yet, familiar and warm.

"What's that song you're humming?"

He turned around as Elena spun the hourglass and poured tea into their cups. Her hair cascaded down her shoulders like a dark, tumbling waterfall, like the fire in his dream, and it rippled as she set his mug before him.

"Just some story about morbid love." He nodded toward the window. "Remember how I told you about the mountain lark? They're good scouts. Three notes mean you have no one near you, two means they're getting closer, and one means you'd better start running."

"Or shooting," she quipped.

Yassen began to pick up his cup when his right arm seized. His muscles locked with such excruciating intensity that he stumbled, leaning against the counter.

"When was the last time a medic saw your arm?"

"Months," he said through gritted teeth.

Elena set down her mug and took his hand. Carefully, she peeled back his sleeve to reveal blackened skin as dark as the bowels of the mountain. A sweet, sickly odor rose from his rotting flesh.

"You'll have to amputate it."

He pulled down his sleeve. "Once we get to the Black Scales, I will."

"Yassen," she said and pursed her lips. She did not need to say it. He knew already what she thought.

"We'll get there. Remember, you made a wish, and I heard the wishes of queens are as true as gold."

"Mother's Gold," she said with a wry smile, realizing the pun. It was a Ravani curse, but it was also an idiom that meant a queen's gold was as good as her word.

He returned the smile, but it quickly fell from his lips as he slid out his holopod and set it on the kitchen counter between them. The map of the tunnels materialized.

"We can't stay here for long. I say we rest for a few days and then start heading toward the Black Scales." With his good hand, he zoomed in on the red tunnels that snaked down from the northern range. "We're here. These tunnels lead down to the middle to," he pointed at the black dot above a crisscross of red lines, "Samson's base."

"Why are they red?"

"Because they're not safe."

Elena leaned closer, scrutinizing the hovering dots and tunnels that twisted like snakes. "So you're saying you don't know if this will work."

"No, I…" Yassen paused. He glanced around the cabin, and his eyes rested on the fireplace. "I think my father took these tunnels. He found something in the middle of the mountains, and it got him killed."

He remembered his father gripping his shoulder, the excitement in his voice, the gleam in his eyes.

"'A metal so fine it could cut through steel,'" Yassen whispered, his voice hollow. He felt the ghosts rustle, as if they too could sense his distress. "I think the tunnels still work. The Jantari would have made sure of it."

"But the Black Scales are right there," Elena said. "How? Why would the Jantari let them stay if they're sitting on top of valuable resources?"

Yassen remembered how Samson had watched him carefully as he had unrolled the map. The look he had exchanged with Maurilis.

Had Samson known about the cabin? Did he know what lay beneath the mountains?

"I'm not sure," he admitted. He wanted to believe that Samson knew nothing to allow grace toward his friend.

"So your father may have found something the Jantari want to keep secret. But then he disappeared, and the Sesharians replaced him in the mines," Elena mused. She looked at him, hesitating. "Was he—"

"Like me? An agent?" he said and shook his head. "Impossible."

But in truth, Yassen knew little about his father. He remembered how his hands had always felt rough, his fingernails lined with dirt, but he did not know if Ekaant Knight used those hands for darker deeds.

His father had been a man of few words. He was tall and strong, built like an ox with deep-set, colorless eyes. Yet, when he laughed, it was as if warmth suddenly filled the room, spreading across Yassen's chest. Yassen would count down the days until he returned to the cabin. His mother would lapse into long stretches of muted silence after these visits. In what would be their last trip to the Sona Range, she had stayed in bed with a headache while he and his father set off to hunt. When they had returned, she was still in bed. Wordless. It was as if she had known what his father had told him.

A metal so fine it could cut through steel.

"You're filling that boy's head with fantasies, and yours too," he later heard his mother say to Ekaant.

"If I can sell some of that ore, Rani, then that boy won't grow up poor. He won't be like us."

Yet, Yassen *had* become like his father. Tall and quiet, quick to produce a gun. Ekaant had taught him how to shoot, how to listen for the warning note in a morning lark's song, how to slow his heartbeat to near stillness as they waited for a stag. Ekaant had taught him how to survive.

I'm here, he wanted to say. *Look at me for what I am.*

A drone suddenly rumbled through the forest; they looked out the window to see a hoverpod graze the tops of the trees as it headed for the rigs on the other side of the mountain. More hoverpods followed. Yassen counted three, but he knew there would be more.

"They're here already," Elena said in a drained voice.

A brenni neighed, and Yassen heard the mountain lark respond with its three notes. At least the soldiers hadn't found their cabin yet.

Yassen cradled his arm. Its smell was beginning to dizzy him.

"It's alright," he said, wincing. "They won't find the cabin, and we'll be gone by the time they do."

Elena rubbed her hands together. The air sizzled softly, and Yassen saw sparks dance between her fingertips.

"Hey," he said, touching her elbow. Her eyes met his. "We'll be okay. Promise."

She did not smile. "I don't like promises."

She brushed past him, shrugging on her coat. The door slid open, and she paused in the threshold.

"I'm going to get wood for the fireplace," she said and stalked off before he could tell her they couldn't burn a fire.

The door slid closed, and Yassen sighed. The cabin fell eerily quiet, and he stood there for a moment, taking in how sunlight slanted in through the windows and dusted the frayed Ravani rug. Once, he had sat on that rug while his father told him old hunting stories or Goromount's travels. He had listened, enraptured. Lost in the beauty of tales he could never spin. What a dark world he had descended into. Yassen felt it closing in on him now as he looked down at his clawed hand.

He went to the closet in the hallway and pulled out the surgical kit his father had left. Injuries were common in the mines. Once, Ekaant had nearly drilled a hole in his foot, but instead of hopping to the doctor, he had taught Yassen how to stitch up the wound.

Yassen pulled off his shirt in the bathroom, breathing in sharply as he took stock of his arm. It had entirely blackened, with a ring of purple around his elbow. Lacerations sliced across his forearm, while the welts on his upper arm had swollen and ruptured. Dried dirt caked the raised grooves of his skin. Yassen pulled a small towel off the rack and balled it into his mouth. Then, soaking a cloth with the whiskey his father stored beneath the bathroom sink, he began.

Every time he touched his bruised skin, Yassen wanted to scream. Tears pricked his eyes. His toes curled within his boots as he slowly washed away the dirt and grime. Drops of murky brown blood dripped into the sink. He gritted his teeth, the towel in his mouth damp with saliva. Yassen spat it out, grabbed another clean towel, and shoved it in. When he was done cleaning, he grabbed a needle and surgical thread. He poured whiskey over them and sanitized the wound before inserting the needle.

Yassen nearly fainted. His knees went weak, and he slumped forward. Blood and dirt swirled within the sink.

Come on, he urged himself. *Come on.*

He blinked fiercely and carefully threaded the needle through a cut on his forearm. His fingers trembled as he stitched, but whenever he got too dizzy, Yassen thought of the journey ahead of him, the work that had to be done, and he found the fortitude to continue.

He tied off the stitch, snipping off the excess thread when the bathroom door opened. Elena stood in the doorway, her eyes wide.

"*What* are you doing?"

"Mhhm mm," he said through the towel in his mouth.

"What?"

He pulled it out, gasping. "Can't you see?"

"Sit down," she commanded, and when he didn't move, she placed her hand on his left shoulder, forcing him onto the toilet seat.

She took the tissue forceps and needle, her lip slightly curling.

"You're a stubborn idiot. You know that?" she said as she cleaned her hands. She examined his arm, but there was no disgust in her eyes, only a resolute sternness, like the steady gaze of a medic.

"How many people have you stitched up?" he asked.

"Ferma made me volunteer at an army hospital on the southern border," she muttered as she threaded a new needle. "I've treated soldiers with wounds worse than this."

"Really?" He gasped as she pierced his skin, jerking his arm back, but Elena held firmly, her hands sure and steady.

"Quit squirming," she said, handing him the bottle of whiskey, "and drink."

Yassen hesitated. He never drank, but the pain in his arm made him toss back his head and take a long swig. A mistake. The whiskey burned his throat and his nose. Yassen coughed as Elena knotted the thread.

"Easy there, yeseri," she said.

He stared at her, bleary-eyed.

"I think I'll need something stronger," he rasped.

But they had nothing stronger, and after an hour of gritting his teeth and fainting twice, Yassen slumped into the wall as Elena cleaned off the last welt.

"There," she said and stepped back, surveying her work. "That should patch you up for the next few days."

He could only nod, his eyes closed and forehead damp with sweat. It was a lie, and they both knew it. The stitches might prevent further infection, but the rot had already spread through his arm. The sooner they got to the Black Scales, the better.

Elena closed the kit and leaned against the doorframe, crossing her arms. She was silent, and he could feel the weight of her gaze. When she finally spoke, her voice was soft, quiet.

"Thank you," she said.

He lifted his head, his brow furrowing. "For what?"

"For staying last night," she whispered. She bit her lip, her hands hugging her sides. She opened her mouth to speak again, but no sound came out.

"It's alright," he said gently. "Grief is like that."

She looked at him, her eyes bright with tears and a tremulous smile tugging her lips. "The song," she gasped. "That's it! 'Grief is like that, my love, but the stars are here, and they will lend us their eyes.'"

"'So that we may gaze upon each other when we are apart,'" he finished.

They stared at each other for a moment and then looked away. Yassen stood, blood beating in his ears as he reached for his shirt. It was lined with dirt and sand from the desert, and he hesitated.

"The closet," he muttered and slid past Elena in the doorway. In the hallway closet, he found his father's old shirts folded neatly into two stacks. Beating away the dust, he pulled one on. It smelled of iron and pine, just like Ekaant.

Yassen strode back into the kitchen, where Elena brewed a fresh cup of tea.

"It fits perfectly," she said.

He glanced at the pile of logs sitting beside the fireplace. "Elena—"

"I found an axe in the shed behind the cabin. It was a bit rusty, but it worked well," she said as she crossed the room, carrying their mugs. She set them on the coffee table and patted the seat across from her. "Sit."

He sank down. Wisps of steam danced in the air as Elena drew her knees to her chest.

"I have a proposition—" she began.

"Skies above," he muttered.

"—that can benefit us both," she said, her eyes narrowing. "The soldiers are already here. They'll transport the ore to their factories, create weapons and heavens knows what. According to your map, we have three mines east and north of us. I say we blow them up. Jantari ore is highly combustible, and I have fire," she said. "The fires will distract the soldiers, and we can escape through the tunnels."

He stared at her, aghast. "You could blow up the entire mountainside, Elena. Think about the towns below! We wouldn't be able to get out alive."

"We will—just like we did in the Agnee mountains," she said, her mouth a thin line. "You saw those tanks out in the desert. Imagine what else the Jantari will create with their fickle metal. Imagine all the Ravani they'll kill."

"I don't care about the soldiers. I care about getting you safely to the Black Scales," he said.

She sat back, as if considering this. The cabin trembled slightly as the drilling began, the air reverberating. Mountain larks took to the sky. Yassen watched them flutter by the window.

"The Arohassin—are you sure they don't know about this place?" she asked after a while.

He shook his head. "I haven't been here since I was seven suns. They wouldn't know of it."

"How can you be sure?"

"I just know," he said firmly. Maybe it was foolish of him to believe that the Arohassin had overlooked this small cabin, but he knew their ways. He had never uttered a word about this place. He had ignored it since Ekaant's death because he could not bear exploring the woods without him. The man he barely saw, the man who made his mother cry, the man who had taught him everything to survive.

"Why did you join the Arohassin?" The sudden directness of her question took him aback.

"You've read my holo."

"I want to hear it from you."

"I—" he began and looked around. He felt a sudden change in the room, a drop in temperature as the ghosts grew nearer.

"I—" he said again. The words felt heavy, yet there they sat, right within his grasp. Memories of the house fire and his mother's burnt body flitted in his mind.

"I was an orphan," he said finally. "My parents were both dead, and I had no one else. The streets of Ravence aren't kind to urchins. The Arohassin seemed kinder. At least they had hot food and a bed."

"So you went because you were hungry?"

He shot her a look. "I didn't know who they really were, not at first. They just made us do odd jobs like deliver a holopod to someone or stake out some corner. Sometimes they made us stand out there during winter nights, but I didn't care. It took my mind off things," he said, and he saw the ghosts flicker. Death had visited him at an early age. He had expected it to be cold and cruel, and it had been. But now, after being a victim and facilitator, Yassen knew death was far more than that. It was a transition—a note scribbled in the desert. Vanishing with the brush of the wind.

"Samson told me about the training they gave you," she said. "About the fleeing prisoners. How that was the first test."

When he said nothing, she continued. "He told me you shot your man, and he didn't. He said it changed you."

"They knew what I was," he said bitterly. The stakeouts had evolved into tracking a man in a crowd and reporting his whereabouts. Hot food turned into money if he could find a traitor. A warm bed twisted into long sermons about power and the decaying foundation of divine rule. Yassen had regarded those sermons with aloofness, listening only because he was forced to. But when they had placed a gun in his hand... He remembered lying beneath neverwood bushes with his father. Stilling his breath. Watching dew form on the tips of grass as they waited for the stag. "They said if we didn't shoot, they would kill us. They made it so it was either us or them. And that's what it became—a battle between us and them."

"Them?" she asked, and he looked at her.

"People like you."

With his left arm, he pulled his gun from his waistband and set it on the table. The silver barrel glinted.

"I thought if I practiced their technique, I could deal with the pain," he said. "They taught us how to shut off parts of ourselves, to lock emotions in a room and leave them there. I didn't care what I did. I just wanted to forget the pain of losing my family."

"And you felt no remorse?"

"I did. All the time. But I only hated myself more," he said. He did not know why he was talking so much. Maybe it was the whiskey, but he could feel a growing pressure in his chest, an urge to speak and not stop. The house of emotions he had built was tumbling down, like a sandcastle toppled by a wave. "So I worked harder. I trained, I fought, I meditated. I even let Akaros starve me just so I could block out the world. And they loved me for it. I became the best because I refused to give in to regret. Nothing fazed me. Fear passed through me but could not linger. I was master of myself.

"Akaros told Sam and me that we were different—more alert than the others, cleverer. I don't know if that was true, but it worked. I finally had someone who saw me. Who taught me how to handle my grief."

"So why did you leave?"

Yassen stopped, staring at her. He felt the air leave his chest, like a dune flattened by a desert wind.

The memory came back to him, slowly, painfully, as if ripping off a bandage. He had taken a boat to the Verani king's coastal home. It had been easy to stun the guards. When he finally found the king's bedroom, he had already killed six of them.

The bedroom had been unusually long, with a fire smoldering in the hearth. In the far end of the room, the Verani king slept alone, his large stomach rising and falling beneath the purple covers. Something had gone wrong, something Yassen hadn't noticed. Intel had told him the king would be alone that night, and he had been except for the hawk sitting by the open window.

It was tied down to its perch by a small chain. Its sable plumage absorbed the moonlight, and it looked at him with its golden eyes. Yassen had frozen when he saw the hawk. Its eyes bore into him, drowning him, and then it shrieked.

The sound woke the king, who, upon seeing Yassen, had reached for his pulse gun and shouted for his guards. But Yassen's eyes did not leave the hawk's. It beat its large wings, cawing, its gaze burning into him.

The king had fired a pulse and hit the hearth. The fire burst forth, grabbing Yassen's right arm. White-hot pain had pierced his skin and bones, and he howled. Guards rushed into the room. One tried to disarm him, but the flames beat the guard back. Yassen had stumbled to the window, the metallic stench of burning flesh searing his senses, and tumbled out.

He landed on the adjoining roof with ash in his hair and eyes. The flames had nearly made him blackout, but the heat drove a wild, animal-like fear. Yassen ran. He beat the flames as guards shouted to search the grounds. By some miracle, he had managed to find his way back to the shore. But the pain seared through him. It was as if the heat of the sun was trapped within his body, ensnaring him with fiery red whips. Without thinking, he had dived into the water.

The cold jolted him, and for a moment, Yassen forgot his pain. But then adrenaline had kicked in, and he rose to the surface, gasping, climbing into his hoverboat. He sped off, the coast guards staying behind. When Yassen had raised his eyes to the heavens, he saw why: thick, grey clouds lumbered over the horizon like a brooding god. The storm took him at once. Large waves had tossed his boat, drenching him until his fingers turned blue. But it could not drench the heat in his body, and the pain had redoubled until Yassen collapsed.

The Arohassin had found him floating far out at sea. For three weeks, he slipped in and out of consciousness, and the memory of his recovery had blurred around the edges. But the hawk. Yassen could not forget it. It was as if it had seen right through him, jolting him awake and forcing him to shed his garb of studied impassivity.

"I lost my nerve," he said and looked down at his arm. It had become a constant reminder of that night. "When I got burnt, it was as if something had smacked into me. It beat everything out until only I remained. No training, no walls, just me. And I couldn't face myself." He remembered Akaros's face the day he had woken up. He had looked at Yassen as if he were a mangled shobu that needed to be put out of its misery. "The Arohassin didn't think I had much more to offer. So I made a deal. They wanted me to reach out to Samson for the Ravence job, to help them take down the throne. In exchange, I'd free my hands of them."

"So you intended to not only betray Ravence, but also Samson," Elena said thickly.

"No," he said, but the word tasted sour. "I told myself that when the time came, I'd help Samson. I'd make sure he lived."

But Samson was dead. Yassen sank back into his seat, a bitter taste filling his mouth. Of all the people he had conned, of all the people he had hurt, Yassen only regretted two: Samson and Elena. Of all people, he sought forgiveness from them.

Elena slowly lowered her knees, her gaze dark, steady—the gaze he had grown to know like the back of his hand.

"Someone once told me that ghosts are memories that haunt us before we can let them go." She touched his knee, reaching for his clawed hand. "I think you have a lot of ghosts to address, but they'll forgive you."

Elena carefully uncurled his fingers so his palm lay flat. He glanced at her. There were specks of gold in her eyes. A trick of the light maybe, or a quality of a Ravani royal.

"You're free now," she said. "Yet you remain here with me. I'm sure that'll get you good graces somewhere in the heavens."

Free. What an awful word. Yassen had resented it because he had never known it, not truly, yet the soft light in the cabin and the song of the mountain larks told him otherwise.

Their chorus spread through the morning sky, filling the treetops with joy.

They sang three notes.

No danger—just expanse.

40
ELENA

Upon seeing the Holy Fire, one cannot help but kneel in reverence.
For here in Sayon, we have been blessed with the gift of the gods.
Fire is the mainstay of civilization. If it perishes, so shall we.

—FROM THE ANCIENT SCROLLS OF THE FIRST
PRIESTS OF THE FIRE ORDER

In the shade of the retherin pines, Elena rolled back her shoulders and widened her stance. Her visor itched against her forehead, but she did not take it off. After Yassen told her about the Arohassin, he had disappeared into the forest, claiming to close the tunnel—but Elena knew better. She noticed the soberness in his eyes, the tension in his mouth.

She raised her arms, extending her right hand in front, her left hand behind. The wound on her shoulder still smarted, but after Yassen had applied the skorrir balm, the pain had lessened.

With a deep breath, Elena spun toward the cabin. She had expected the abode of Yassen Knight to be full of traps and hidden doors, and in a way, it was. He had grieved for the death of his parents alone. He had transformed into a thief and criminal only because Ravence had failed him. Elena could see why he had resented her. While he stole and begged, she had enjoyed halls full of spiced meat and gardens full of birdsong. It reminded her of the Jantari boy foraging for his next meal, the people in the bazaar stiffening whenever a Palace guard rounded a corner.

The Arohassin and Jantar claimed that the Ravani family had failed its people. Maybe they had. She had been so concerned with proving herself fit to be queen that she had failed to notice the struggles beyond Palace Hill. Maybe that was why the Eternal Fire had laid waste to her land. Maybe that was why it had claimed her father—for the lies he had spun.

But it had spared her. Surely that meant something.

Yassen had revealed his grief. She could tell how it had shaken him, but also how, despite the suns of quiet anguish, it had freed him. There had been a lightness in his step when he had left, and she imagined him wandering across the carpeted forest floor, slowly becoming aware of his truth.

Like a spark slowly reviving.

Elena sank her weight into her heels and breathed out.

A flame unfurled in her outstretched palm like a bird hatching from its shell.

The Warrior.

She pivoted and kicked up her left leg, balancing on her right foot as she folded her arms behind her like the Desert Sparrow. The flame sighed and kissed her fingertips. She could feel its pulse, its desire to live as she flowed into the Lotus, the Spider, and then the Tree, the flame growing in her hand.

When she had burned down her room, the fire had burst from her fingertips like a sandstorm on a summer day. Sudden and destructive. Its power had surged through her body like an electric shock. She had used her anger to call it, to drill a hole in the world, and it had responded in kind.

But as Elena unwound from the Snake and once more extended her arms, she could feel the fire's energy coursing through her with a quiet, intense hum. Her senses sharpened. She could hear the skitter of a rodent in the underbrush, the flap of wings as a mountain lark took to the trees. She could feel every hair on her body prick against the mountain breeze and sense Yassen's heat at the bottom of the hill. As the fire looped around her arms, she spun. The flames arced across the sky before falling back into her hands. In their wake, a trail of sparks glistened like the stars.

Agneepath netrun. Fijjin a noor.
The path of fire is dangerous. Tread it with care.

Everyone had told her that. Ferma, Leo, her mother. They had all warned her of the madness of fire. But this, this concentrated energy, this buzz—it did not feel like delirium. It felt natural, as if she had finally found something equal to her.

The fire bowed, folding into itself as Elena drew it close to her chest. Slowly, she brought her palms together, and the flame died with a soft hiss, its heat spreading down her arms and across her shoulders like wings coming to rest.

A drone rippled down the mountainside as the miners resumed their drilling. Elena looked up to see a hoverpod take to the air. Even from this distance, she could spot the insignia of the winged ox. The sun struck the mountain, and, everywhere, the world glittered. Elena squinted despite her visor. The hoverpod likely contained soldiers and their precious ore. They would take it back to the factories, where they would turn it into crude weapons to be used against her people.

Every day she spent on this mountain, more Jantari soldiers invaded her kingdom. More Ravani were herded into camps. Elena knew she could not reveal herself, not yet, but she could not sit still while her people perished. She looked down at her hands. Her skin prickled as a flame emerged from her palm.

Jantari metal, when properly manufactured, was strong enough to withstand a low-level explosion, but its raw ore was vulnerable. Combustible. It was why each mine was equipped with tanks of water to cool down machinery. Elena watched as a plume of hot steam spouted into the sky. The flame hissed in her hand. She estimated that the nearest mine was ten miles to the east, if not more. If she could somehow set it afire, the combustible rig would blow clean off.

Elena curled her hand into a fist, smothering the flame. She went inside to the bedroom. The reflectors on the roof softened the afternoon sun so that it gently cast the space in a golden glow. Like most of the cabin, the bedroom was old, simple. A floating bed fit for two claimed the center of the room, and off to the right, two wooden shelves lined the wall. They were bare except for one holo, frozen in a crystal like a traditional photograph.

She had not noticed it last night. She had just fallen into bed, stared out the window to the dark sky and unfamiliar forest. Elena did not know when she had started to cry, only that once the tears began, they did not stop. It had hit her then, lying alone in a strange bed, just how much she had lost.

Elena approached the shelf and studied the photograph. There was a tall, burly man with straight, pale hair combed neatly to the side. Next to him stood a small woman with desert black hair and kind, green eyes. She had a soft smile, and that alone seemed to balance the man's cold, stern expression. Between them stood a small boy, perhaps six or seven suns. He had the same pale hair and eyes of the father, but his smile was that of his mother's: soft and easy, uninhibited by the demands of the world. The boy seemed to lean away from the man, as if to shirk his influence, but Elena recognized the similarities in their posture, the clarity in their eyes.

She lifted the crystal and brought it closer. Though the boy stood closer to the woman, he was more of the father than the mother.

"I'd forgotten about that picture."

Elena turned to see the boy in the crystal standing in the doorway. Except he was older now, stronger, and more haggard.

"Where were you?" she asked.

"That was taken the summer before my father died," Yassen said. "He brought us here for a hunting trip, but my mother couldn't stomach it, so she stayed in the cabin."

Elena replaced the crystal on the shelf and examined the small woman with the dark eyebrows.

"You have her smile."

He stood next to her and lifted the crystal. "I wish they were here now. A queen in their cabin!" He gave her a small smile. "They would've been beside themselves."

She glanced at him. "I think they would've been more excited to see you come home."

Yassen set the crystal back down. She noticed a slight tremor in his hand before he shoved it into his pocket. She touched his elbow.

"We need to take out the mines."

"Not again, Elena," he said. "You're out of your mind."

"I know," she replied.

She imagined the mountainside covered with fire, just like the day the Temple had burned, and a bitter vengeance filled her. Farin had taken what had been most precious to her. She would take the same from him. These mountains were the lifeblood of Jantar. The country's economy revolved around the trade and manufacturing of its ore. If she were to destroy it, even a part of it, the kingdom would begin to crumble.

She may not be able to hit all the rigs in the Sona Range, but it would be a start. Smoke would leach out the sun, and the Jantari would know darkness. They would know the same anguish she felt as she saw the fire take her father, her guards, her people. They would know what it felt like to lose a home.

But then Elena thought of the old man who had sold them their furs, the woman who had rented them their brenni. The explosions would surely rock the mountain or, worse, cause landslides. They would die by her hand, her fire. A coldness slithered through Elena as she clenched her jaw. She would be sending the entire town to its death. Those people had no role in the war, yet they would suffer.

Leo had told her to be ruthless. To become the villain if only to emerge as Ravence's hero. If war was the means and peace was the reward, the lives lost in between were necessary casualties. She was queen now, not a princess who relied on her father. The throne demanded sacrifice. It demanded cruelty.

This was her fate.

This was the only way back to her home.

"We have to buy more time," she said, forcing her voice to stay steady and sound strong even though her stomach twisted into a knot.

"This is madness," Yassen insisted. "Do you know how many soldiers will be here? If they even *think* you're alive, they'll hunt us down."

"But we have something they don't," she said and raised her hand. Sparks flashed between her fingers. "I can do this, Yassen."

He shook his head. "It's not that I don't think you can. I'm afraid you *will*."

"You're better than me." She gave a pained smile. "You spared that boy. You don't have to follow me."

Yassen looked down at her, and she could see in his eyes how he warred between fleeing and fighting. He'd sworn himself to her, taken the Desert Oath, but she could release him from it. Ravence had failed him, and she owed him his freedom. He *deserved* his freedom.

Yassen stepped closer and took her hand like he had last night.

"I go where you go," he whispered.

He drew her into his arms, and she pressed her face into the nook of his neck, breathing in his smell of ash and fresh mountain air. Felt the thrum of his heart beneath her cheek. They held each other for a long time, drinking in each other's warmth. And somewhere in that black ether of grief, Elena felt a heaviness lifting. A sliver of solace. Of all people, he understood her grief. How could she ever let him go?

When they parted, Yassen gave her a small smile.

"Shall we—" he began.

She leaned up and kissed him.

His lips were warm, sweet. He tasted of spice and honey, of the desert and the mountain. He tasted of home.

When she drew back, he looked at her, hesitant.

"I—"

She shushed him with another kiss.

"Elena—"

"Be quiet, you idiot," she whispered. She cupped his face and kissed him again. Slowly, he rested his hands on her waist and when she drew him to the bed, his touch was soft and gentle, as if nothing in the world mattered, not Ravence or Jantar, but her, but them.

Elena curled into Yassen, her arm draped across his chest. She could feel his breath dance against her hair. His chest rose and fell in slow, steady beats, and she heard the song of his heart in her ear. She could just stay, wrapped in this bliss. Forget about the world outside, the games of brutal kings and wayward queens. What did it matter anyway? But as she saw the light gradually seep out of the room, Elena knew she would have to go. People like her did not deserve bliss like this.

She tried to disentangle herself without waking Yassen, but he stirred against her.

"What are you doing?" he murmured.

"I have to go," she whispered.

"Why?"

She smiled wanly and touched his cheek, tracing the arch of his eyebrows. He smelled of sandstone and musk.

"Dream well," she said softly.

She rose and pulled on her clothes, knowing he was too tired to fight her. His eyes fluttered. On the shelf, the crystal glimmered in the growing darkness. Though she was not one for prayer, Elena whispered one.

"Watch him," she told the ghosts.

She took his gun by the bedside and tucked it into her waistband. As the cabin door shut with a soft click, a pang of regret cut through her chest. Elena stifled it down. The twin moons hung heavily in the sky, as if swollen with the weight of what was to come. Her brenni snorted nervously as Elena tightened its girth. She jumped on, and then with a solid kick, they set out into the forest.

Shadows stalked through the trees like the shards of a nightmare, cruel and unshapely. Despite herself, Elena shivered. The twin moons were full, but the thick canopy blocked out any hope of light. A chill crept through the forest, dampening the foliage. Elena cursed as she passed the amethyst pine for the third time.

From her calculations, the rig was ten miles to the east. She should have arrived along its outskirts an hour ago, but she had foolishly forgotten to take Yassen's holopod. Without it, she was lost.

Something stirred in the tree above her. Elena twisted in her saddle, yanking out the gun. A shadow darted through the branches, and she recognized the blue wings of a mountain lark. It sang three notes. Elena relaxed, but did not holster the weapon.

Pine needles and leaves crunched under the brenni's hooves. All her life, Elena had trained to survive in the desert, to withstand its harsh demands—from the grueling sandstorms to her own dry, brittle thirst. She had learned how to move without detection, how to find shelter from the sun, but there were no dunes here.

Elena nudged her steed to follow the roots of the trees just like Yassen had. She needed to find higher ground. Her brenni panted, and

Elena tried to lean forward in the saddle to ease its strain when she saw a glimmer of light. She halted just as her mount snorted.

Elena clicked back the safety and aimed the pistol in the light's direction. She squinted but could not make out the source. She held her breath, her finger on the trigger as her brenni shuffled its feet anxiously.

"Easy," she whispered.

The light flickered. Elena realized then it was not merely a light but a reflected moonbeam. Given the angle, moonlight was bouncing off a smooth surface, which could only mean one thing. She was getting closer to the mine.

Elena squeezed her calves, and her mount marched forward. She went in the direction of the light, hoping that once she reached it, she could see where the rig stood. They trotted past glades of neverwood and ganshi until they reached a clearing. Up ahead, the ground rose to form a steep hill. Elena jumped down and tied her brenni to a tree before creeping up the grade.

She climbed slowly, steadily, but as she neared the top, she lost her footing. Elena yelped, loose dirt and stone tumbling down the hill. A mountain lark cried out. She pressed into the grade, holding her breath, but the forest remained still. With a soft groan, she hauled herself up to the summit.

The rig sat in a clearing to the east like a giant parasite. It loomed over the treetops, glinting. Two glass-armored chutes dissected through its middle and descended into the depths of the mountain. Elena spotted four guard posts at each leg of the rig. A hoverpod floated on the landing beside the mine, likely full of sleeping soldiers. She was not surprised. The Jantari were deep in their territory. They had no fear of a lost queen and her insatiable fire.

Elena leaned forward and studied the mountain face. The trees reached the feet of the rig, but the pines had been cut down where the chutes dug into the mountain. If the guards were awake, they would have no trouble spotting her. Elena bit her lip. Heat buzzed through her hands—and then the idea came to her.

She trekked back to her brenni and untied it. They set off once more, but instead of going straight to the edge of the forest, Elena steered her steed south. She dismounted and tied her mount securely. She skirted along the edge of the forest to the southern part of the rig. Neverwood branches clawed at her hair and clothes, but Elena paid them no mind. She stopped before a thick huddle of molorians with slightly damp and wilted leaves.

Perfect.

The mine towered above her, blocking the twin moons. Two guard posts stood several yards away on her left and right, the other two standing in the distance. A guard patrolled the post on her right, his pulse gun glinting gently in the moonlight. She slunk further into the neverwoods. This close, Elena could see the giant water tanks and the gleam of the glass chutes. No carts descended into the mountain, but she spotted them hovering at the top, ready to send poor Sesharians into the depths of Sayon.

Elena took a step back and began her dance.

Heat jolted up her arms. The intensity frightened her, and Elena thought of the sleepy town hunkered within the mountain foothills. How would they die? By landslide, or by inferno? Which was worse if they were both by her hand?

She tried to breathe, to calm her mind, but doubt wormed its way in her chest. If she did this, she was no better than the Jantari. *Seven hells*, she was no better than even the Arohassin. They killed innocent people for their own gain. She was supposed to be the Golden Queen of peace. But here she was, sparks flitting in her hands, fire on her tongue like the goddesses of lore, like her namesake, the Burning Queen.

Be ruthless. Become whatever Ravence needs you to be.

Elena closed her eyes. She saw her father and the horror on his face as he fell into the flames. The twisted, mutilated bodies of the Palace guards on the Temple steps. Blood blossoming on Ferma's chest. She saw it, and she let her fire bloom.

The movements came to her as easily as sand spilling down a canyon. Sparks fizzled in her hands, and then a flame burst forth. She willed it to grow stronger, unwavering like the fire of the desert, like the fire of a Ravani.

The flame swooned, listening. It flared and hissed at the air. With a sharp jab, she hurled it onto the molorians.

The blaze sang and licked the base of the trees. The damp roots emitted steam, but they did not catch. Elena raised her hands, her brow furrowed in concentration as sweat beaded down her forehead. She could not doubt herself, not now; doubt would kill the flame. She could do this.

She had to.

Straining, Elena focused on the blaze growing taller. She stretched her hands, and the flame yawned. *Again.*

She thought of Ravence, of Ferma, of the energy that had buzzed through her body when she had first wielded an inferno.

The flame lengthened.

She thought of Yassen and the way he had held her, the warmth of his embrace. The touch of his breath as he had whispered into her ear that he would follow her, no matter what.

The flame howled.

Elena stepped back and closed her eyes. She felt the hum of power, the song of fire, coursing through her body. She imagined it strengthening, solidifying as a spear flashed in her hand. Her eyes flickered. The flame danced, waiting.

With a cry, Elena threw the spear of fire.

It struck the canopy, the wet leaves immediately catching. The blaze at the base doubled and then tripled before leaping up the grove. Wood snapped, and Elena grinned.

Sweat drenched her face as she pulled the blaze higher, willing it to grow brighter, and soon the treetops were filled with flames. Smoke buffeted out, dispersed by a sudden wind. Elena spun, and her inferno roared at the heavens.

Smoke alarms blared, waking the miners and soldiers. They were too late. Elena's grin widened, her arms shaking as she pushed the fire toward the rig. The flames tumbled and spat, growing louder, stronger. They reached the base of the mine, and then Elena let go.

The inferno raged on.

In the distance, men and women stumbled out of the guard posts toward the glass chutes. She saw their panic, but she could not stay to enjoy it. Elena whirled around and sprinted back south where she had left her steed. Her brenni neighed, its eyes widening in fright at the smoke writhing through the trees.

"It's okay. We're going," she gasped.

She jumped into the saddle and kicked hard. Her brenni shot into a gallop, and Elena squeezed her thighs to hold on. The inferno grew behind them with an insatiable haste. The high-pitched wail of the alarms and the roar of the fire filled the air, but Elena pushed her mount into the thicket of the forest, into the cool shadows that awaited. The alarms and smoke grew fainter as they hurtled deeper into the pines.

Suddenly, a roar ripped through the heavens as the mine exploded with a blinding flash. The mountain groaned. Her brenni shrieked, and they tumbled to the ground. Elena fell out of her saddle and rolled, coming to a stop beneath a molorian. She gasped, trembling. Her brenni nickered.

"It's alright," she called out. It stayed, listening to her voice. Slowly, Elena lurched back to her feet. Her ears rang. Blood trickled down from a cut on her forehead. Thorns pierced her arms, her face. But the ground did not rumble again. There was no landslide.

Death by fire then.

She fought down the sudden rush of guilt. This had to be done. Farin must feel the same loss that he had brought upon her. If the townspeople were lucky, the authorities would evacuate them before she destroyed the other mines. If not, well, then the Jantari would know the pain of burning.

Elena looked down at her hands. Her fingertips glowed like embers. *She* had single-handedly blown out a mine. Repulsion bit into her, but Elena also felt the steady, intoxicating beat of pride.

This was real power. She, Elena Aadya Ravence, could wield fire. Whatever doubt, whatever inhibitions she once had fled from her mind. She could lead her kingdom to victory. She would make Farin burn for his sins.

Forget the Phoenix and the Prophet. *She* was blessed by fire, and that was something no one could take away.

41
YASSEN

To be forgiven, one must be burned.

—A RAVANI PROVERB

Yassen awoke at dawn to the smell of smoke. It permeated the cabin, lining the floorboards, and when he saw the bed empty beside him, fear leapt up his throat. Had there been another attack? Had the Arohassin already taken Elena? He threw on his clothes, dashed out of bed, and stumbled down the stairs.

Elena's brenni was gone. With a groan, Yassen lifted the saddle and threw it on his steed. It neighed, nostrils flaring. Yassen fumbled with the clasps of the girth with his one hand. His fingers felt swollen, obtuse. He cursed. He tried to use his shoulder and lean against his brenni while he yanked up the girth, but the animal threw back its head.

"Easy, easy," he said, but it backed away from him.

Just then, he heard hoofbeats.

Yassen turned as Elena cantered up the hill. Soot coated her face, but she was smiling with triumph. The pressure in his chest burst. As soon as she jumped down, he grabbed her and pulled her close.

"It's alright. I'm fine," she gasped.

She was alive. She was here. The Arohassin still hadn't found them.

"You idiot," he whispered into her ear. "You stupid, beautiful idiot."

Elena blinked. "What do you mean?"

"They're going to search the mountain now," he said. "We have to leave."

"No, I have to take down the other rigs. Besides, they don't know it's me. It could just be a summer forest fire."

"Did they see you?"

"Only smoke," she said.

But Yassen knew it would not be long. He was no fool. The Jantari might be dull enough to think it was a forest fire, but the Arohassin were smarter. How does a damp forest at the end of summer catch on fire? Especially this high in the mountains? If the Arohassin were here, they'd track down what started the fire. And then they would come for them.

When he finally let her go, Elena laughed, touching his cheek.

"I got soot all over you," she smiled.

"Elena..." He shook his head. How could he tell her that *she* was the fool? That she had endangered them for a stupid stunt. In one stroke, she had broken the little peace they had found, and for what? A small bout of revenge? "What happened to the mine?"

"It exploded. The townspeople..." She shook her head, guilt flickering quickly across her face. "Yassen, this is our chance. We have to burn down the other two rigs. We can coordinate an attack tonight, and then we'll escape."

"We don't have time *now*," he said. "The Arohassin are coming. They'll know this wasn't some wildfire."

"Then let's burn it all down before they find us," she said. Early morning light stole through the canopy, highlighting the dirt and ash in her hair. "Yassen, we *must* do this. You saw the army. You saw what they're doing at the hovertrain stations. We'll buy Ravence more time."

"But the tunnels," he said, his voice dry. "If we blow up the other mines, they might collapse. How will we get to the Black Scales?"

"The mining tunnels might, but not the ones we need to take," she said. Her eyes glimmered as she stepped closer. "You know we'll find a way."

Yassen chewed his lip. He did not trust himself to say anything, not right now. She was wrong. He knew it in the core of his being. Nothing guaranteed the red tunnels would not collapse. A part of him, the assassin skilled in the art of deception, screamed for him to turn and run. To leave *now*.

But hadn't he been running all his life? From Ravence, Veran, Jantar, the Arohassin... His was the life between edges, between countries, between identities. And he was tired. Tired of hiding, from others and from himself.

"I—" he began. He looked to the sky, to the smoke that was already eating the horizon.

She touched his blackened hand, and he met her gaze. Her eyes looked even darker with ash coating her lashes.

"Stay with me," she said.

Yassen looked down at her hand on his. Not long ago, she had vowed to kill and make a statement out of him. When he had revealed what he had done, she had hurt him, but she had spared him, too. Yassen knew he was never destined for a quiet life. He had cursed himself ever since he had shot that prisoner, ever since he had let Samson escape and had not followed. Time and time again, fate had given him crossroads; time and time again, he had allowed it to push him down a path of its choosing.

But as Yassen looked at Elena and saw the burning conviction in her eyes, he understood he had a choice. Unlike him, Elena did not like to hide.

But just like her, he had a home worth fighting for.

Elena kissed her three fingers and placed them on his forehead.

"Fight with me," she said.

He closed his eyes and leaned into her hand.

"So we the blessed few," he said. The words fell like stones that sealed his decision.

"So we the blessed few," she whispered back.

They pored over the map, memorizing the network of tunnels that snaked beneath the mountain. The two mines lay fifteen miles north, high up on the ridge line, separated by only two miles of forest in between.

"Why would they be so close?" Elena asked as she peered at the holo. She had washed the soot from her face with an old bar of jasmine soap but had missed a spot beneath her ear. Yassen reached to wipe it off, and she turned, surprised.

"You missed a spot," he said.

She smiled and leaned into his hand.

The horizon thickened with smoke, blocking out the fading sunset. Their brennis nickered anxiously as shadows crept down the cabin walls. It was the fragile calm before the storm, but Yassen wanted to stretch it like the twin moons had stretched the long night for Alabore. To remember the way she looked at him now, her eyes dark and liquid, and lock it forever in his heart.

"What is it, Knight?" she whispered, holding him in her gaze. "Are you getting cold feet?"

No, he wanted to say. *I just want this.*

Yassen withdrew his hand, turning back to the holo. "Maybe they found a large deposit of ore up there, and that's why they need two mines." He pointed at the silver dots indicating the location of the rigs, and the red tunnel that sliced between them. "This is what we'll need to take. The entrance is hidden at an old campsite, beneath the fire pit. Once we blow up the first mine, the fire should spread to the second. We can escape before then."

Elena traced the tunnel, the shadows curving around her face, her lips. "And it won't collapse."

"It won't collapse," he repeated, hoping that by saying so would make it true.

They rode at night. The trees and the smoke began to thin as they pushed further north. Thin moonlight filtered through the forest, coating the pines in an eerie hush. Yassen slowed his brenni to a stop at a dry ravine filled with dead leaves. The old magazine bullets dug into his waist. He had found them in the hallway closet, underneath his father's hunting clothes.

"We're close," Yassen said as Elena drew up beside him. He could see the ridge line peeking between the trees. It skirted around the mines and would lead them to their western border. From there, they would steal through the forest and set them ablaze.

"If the soldiers start shooting, we run," he said, turning to her. Her face was hidden behind her scarf, but her eyes met his. "Understood?"

She merely dipped her head and marched her brenni forward. She led the way as the lower ridge crept northwest, taking them past thick groves and thin streams. Yassen held his gun against his thigh, his finger curling around the trigger. So far, they had encountered no soldiers nor assassins lying in wait. The forest was quiet save for the occasional scuttle of a rodent or the whispering of the wind.

His brenni grunted as it hopped over a fallen tree. Yassen stood up in his saddle and peered down through the heavy foliage. The cliff now rose above the trees, but he still couldn't spot the telltale glimmer of metal. Suddenly, Elena whistled. He turned to see her standing further up the ridge line, pointing down.

There, partly hidden by the trees, lay a stone path. It snaked down the bluff, weaving between the pines for the forest beyond. He opened his mouth to tell Elena to hold back, but she was already urging her brenni down the ridge.

"Wait!" he called out.

Cursing, Yassen chased Elena into the forest. She rode faster, cutting through the trees as the path curved further west. His brenni threw back its head.

And then it hit Yassen.

The acrid stench of burning metal and flesh.

The second rig rose out of the pines, glinting from the light of the flames beneath it. As Yassen neared, he saw the fire flickering under the eastern leg of the mine. The shadows of men danced around it as they tried, vainly, to dig a trench between them and the oncoming blaze.

But it was too late.

The fire from the east had already spread.

Yassen reined his brenni to a stop at the forest edge. Across the clearing, he traced the burnt path as the flames spread from the east. Soldiers streamed out of hoverpods docked on the northern platform. Some stood on the upper stairs of the rig, redirecting the water tanks toward the blaze.

Elena had tied her steed beneath a molorian and was already dropping into the first form of the fire dance. She looked up at him with a tight smile.

"I can feel it," she said.

He tightened his grip around his gun. His brenni nickered nervously.

"The other mine," he said and trailed off. The third mine lay in the path of the blaze. Had it already burned down? Had the tunnel in between already collapsed? He had heard no explosion or sirens. "Elena, we have to leave."

"No."

She raised her arms, sparks raining down from her fingertips. She twirled, and the sparks flared into a flame that leapt onto the canopy. The branches wilted and blackened like his arm, the leaves curling into ash. Elena coiled her wrists. The fire snaked up the spine of a retherin. The pine groaned, resisting, but then its trunk snapped with a loud crack that resounded through the forest. Everything fell to the inferno. Even the stones darkened as flames devoured the underbrush, the leaves, the trees.

Yassen shrank back, heat buffeting his face. When Elena turned around, he saw a bewitched look in her eyes as the flames spat behind her.

"Now we can go," she said. Her brenni reared as she grabbed the reins, but she easily swung onto the saddle and rocked it back to the ground.

"Elena—" he started.

"Ride, Yassen," she said and spurred her brenni. She looked over her shoulder and gave a mirthless smile. "Ride before they catch you."

Yassen nudged his brenni, but it needed no encouragement. It shot forward into a gallop. He could barely make out Elena in the thickening smoke. He wanted to call out to her, to stop her, but he only coughed. His eyes stung. Worry nagged at him in the darkness—a slither that ran through the pit of his stomach. *If the fire came from the east, what happened to the third mine?*

Yassen did not see the neverwood; its branches raked him across the cheek, and he ducked. He felt something warm drip down his jaw as his brenni brayed and vaulted to the right. He nearly fell out of his saddle, his left hand scratching at the reins.

Elena twisted in her seat, slowing her brenni. With a grunt, Yassen hauled himself back into the saddle, blood dripping down his jaw.

"Are you alright?" she called out.

Suddenly, the drone of a hoverpod filled the mountain. It appeared above them, a dark, smooth shape against the rolling grey sky. A large searchlight swept across the treetops. Yassen turned to Elena, reaching for her when light flooded the grove. His brenni brayed, blinded.

But then the mountain shrieked as the rig exploded.

A force wave rippled through the forest. Yassen hit the ground hard, the air rushing straight out of him. He gasped. His mind spun: the mine, the explosion, *get up, run, run!* But his body was slow to respond. Ash rained down and blotted out the pale moons, covering the sky. It reminded Yassen of the Temple, of Samson, of Elena. He scrambled to his knees. Black dots danced before his eyes as he felt around for his gun. His fingers grazed metal, and Yassen grabbed it. Blinking, he brought it in front of his face and realized it was not his gun, but a stray scrap of the rig.

"El-Elena!" He vaulted to his feet. The heavens swam, and Yassen reached out to steady himself. Instead of bark, he found flesh. Elena pulled him, her hair covered in bramble, her eyes wide, her mouth moving, telling him something. He shook his head. Sound came roaring back.

"The brenni!" she shouted.

He looked around but did not see their steeds. He felt his empty hip. *Where is my gun?*

Elena grabbed him, and they ran into the trees. Many of the pines had snapped in half from the blast, and the ones that were still standing leaned precariously. Yassen saw no sign of the hoverpod, only ash and shadow.

"This way," he croaked. He tugged her to the left, and they tore through the bramble. Elena kicked something, and Yassen saw a flash of silver.

The gun! He shot forward as it fell in a patch of splintered neverwood. Yassen winced as he pulled out the pistol, thorns digging into his skin. Elena slid to a stop beside him, doubling over.

"The rig, it's east of here, right?" she panted. When he did not respond, she shook him.

"Yassen! Yassen!" she yelled, but he had finally answered his question.

The blackened path. The unkempt fire.

Dread spread down his throat and chest.

"The Arohassin."

It was the only explanation. The Jantari soldiers must have created a fake fire to lure Elena and him to the mines. They had deliberately burned the forest between the two rigs—that was why there had been no sirens. They had feinted a distraction because it was a trap, and only Akaros could have designed a trick like this—a trick that came with sacrifice and reward. Farin hadn't betrayed the Arohassin after all. They still worked together.

The trap had cost Farin a mine and a few soldiers, but now Yassen and Elena were forced out into the open. The Arohassin knew about Elena's ability to wield fire. He had told them. And now they knew for certain this was no regular wildfire.

The queen had finally shown her face.

"The second mine was bait," he said. "They started the fire there only to smoke us out. They know we're here."

A familiar drone cut through the roar of the fire, and Yassen looked up to see two hoverpods flying up the mountain. *The reinforcements.* The Arohassin and the Jantari already had their soldiers trekking through the mountain. They had nowhere to run.

"Then we have to take out the third mine," she said.

He spun, his words hot and fierce. "Elena, *stop.*" He gripped her shoulder with his one hand. "There's no time. We need to get to the tunnel."

"But—"

"Do you want to die on this mountain?" He was shouting now, his voice dry and cracked. "Do you want to leave Ravence without a ruler? Without hope?"

He could see the wheels turning in her mind, could see her weigh the options: fight or flight, survival or triumph, a battle or the war. The tunnel was their only chance at survival, and when Elena's mouth hardened into a grudging scowl, he knew she saw it too.

"Let me at least make these bastards burn for it."

Elena whirled before he could stop her. She widened her stance and raised her hands. A hiss slithered up the trees. He saw a wink of red in her palm, and then it grew into a flame. With a jab, Elena threw the flame onto the molorian that sheltered them. It lit up like a torch. Elena turned, and the fire moved with her, leaping down the mountain.

He could not deny her power. He could feel it ripple off her like heat waves over a dune. Perhaps the Arohassin were wrong after all.

Perhaps there truly was a Phoenix and Elena was Her Prophet. But then all the stories and myths he had been told were lies. The Arohassin spoke of vengeful Prophets who cleaned the land of its sinners. Fire was cruel and so were its masters, they had preached. But Elena was not the hell and brimstone he had been taught to fear. She could be harsh, but she was a queen. She had a responsibility toward her people, and he believed she would never use her power to send them to a fiery doom.

"We have to go," he called.

For a moment, she stared at the burning branches and the smoke, her shoulders outlined by the light of the inferno. She stood tall, erect, and so alone. *The Burning Queen*, the servants had called her. But then she turned to him. This time, the bewitched look was gone from her eyes. There lay only somberness.

She touched his hand. Her skin was hot, as if it too were burning.

"The fire will find its way," she said.

He was not sure what she meant, but he felt himself answering, "Fire always finds a way."

Slowly, she nodded. "Then let's go."

They headed east. At some points they ran, at others, they crawled. They stumbled along the edge of a dry ravine as the fire followed, surrounding them like a shield. Hoverpods flew over the mountain, their searchlights vainly sweeping over the broken trees. Yassen coughed as they came to a bend in the ravine. The heat dried his eyes and lips. His cough intensified, and he doubled over, spitting out blood, when a pulse sliced into a branch where his head had just been. Yassen hit the ground, crawling behind the tree.

Pulse fire shredded the air. The fire roared in return. Ahead, he saw Elena raise her hands, the flames curling, but then a pulse cut through the pines, and she yelped, tumbling into the ravine.

"Elena!"

The fire moaned and swept past Yassen to surround her. Pain shot up his right arm. It felt as if his bones were ripping apart. He stifled a cry as he inched forward on his stomach and rolled into the ravine.

The flames circled them. Yassen dragged himself forward to where Elena kneeled, clutching her arm.

"Are you alright?" he panted.

She looked at him with glazed eyes. Blood streamed down her forearm. Her wrist hung at an unnatural angle, and the sight made Yassen's stomach roil.

"It's alright," he said to assure them both.

She had been hit right beneath the elbow and had broken her wrist during the fall. Yassen quickly took the scarf around her neck and tightened it around the wound. He then ripped off a part of his cloak to make a sling for her wrist.

"Mother's Gold," she rasped as he pulled tighter. "I'm going to kill them all."

Pulses zipped overhead. From their direction, Yassen estimated that the shooters lay south of them but were rapidly approaching. The tunnel entrance lay just to the east, past the flames and fallen trees.

Plans, escape points, battle tactics, and backhand maneuvers darted around in his mind. The soldiers would surround them soon. In the ravine, they were easy prey for slaughter. The fire would buy them time, but they only had one gun. Yassen stared at the flames as the pulse fire screeched overhead, as the forest crackled and burned, as Elena hugged her bleeding hand, and the decision came to him with a quiet, unwavering gravity.

Fire always found a way.

Yassen thrust his holopod into Elena's hand, his words clipped and rushed. "Follow the ravine. Stick to the trees for cover and you'll find the campsite. Take the tunnel and head south until you find the dragon. They'll know you've arrived even before you do."

He watched the realization dawn on her as her eyes widened.

"No," she said.

"Remember before we went up the mountain? I said you had to listen. If I told you to run, you run. If I told you to leave me, you leave me," he said and tied the knot of the sling. "Now for once in your life, listen to me."

"We're supposed to get out of here together!"

"Plans change," he said as he fumbled with the bullets strapped along his waist. "I'm expendable, and you're not."

"Not to me," she whispered. The fire hissed around them.

"I burned my name in the sand. Remember?" he said and cracked a tight smile. He checked the chamber of his gun and slid back the safety, but when he met her gaze, his smile faltered. He did not want to let her go. Of all things, he wished he could turn back time to that moment in the cabin, the moment when he had held her in his arms, and she had pressed her face into his neck. They had time then. They had had all the time in the world. "Ravence needs you. Your people need you. Now go."

Slowly, Elena rose to her feet. The flames drew back. He tried to smile again, but his chest was too heavy.

"I'll find you," he said, and he wondered if she noticed the tremor in his voice.

Her mouth tightened, her eyes glimmering. Finally, controlling herself, she spoke.

"You'd better."

Elena took a step back as the fire crackled. Still, her eyes did not leave his. A pulse smacked into the edge of the ravine, dislodging soil and rock. Still, his eyes did not leave hers.

Another pulse hit the tree above, and the molorian groaned as it snapped in two, crashing between them.

And then Elena turned and ran. Farther and farther away, around the bend.

As he watched her go, Yassen felt a quiet settle in his chest, a calmness that came with finality.

He turned and climbed the ravine bed. He crouched just along its edge and trained his gun. Through the flickering flames, Yassen could make out movement. They had spread out around him, just like he had predicted. Yassen breathed in smoke. Let it curl in his chest. And when he breathed out, he pulled the trigger.

It hit true.

A shadow fell. Yassen turned and found another. He fired twice to bring it down. The flames crawled up the fallen molorian and licked at his feet. He breathed in more smoke. Shot down another shadow and its partner.

A pulse zipped past his ear, cutting through a pine on his left. A soldier ran between the trees and Yassen fired, but he missed. The man ducked behind a fallen pine. Yassen waited, the flames crawling up to his ankles, and when the soldier reappeared, he fired twice. This time, the man fell.

Yassen crawled forward on his stomach as more soldiers fired, lighting up the forest with the blaze of their pulses. He huddled behind a smoldering neverwood bush, coughing. Heat and exhaustion tightened his throat, but they did not unseat his sense of clarity.

Peering through the smoke, Yassen spotted movement in the thicket of the trees to his left. He fired, and his assailants responded. Pulses slashed through the trees, cutting deep wedges in the bark. They all came from Yassen's left, and he fired twice in that direction. A man cried out. Yassen pulled the trigger again, but the chamber only clicked, empty.

Cursing, Yassen unlatched the empty magazine. It clattered to the ground. He tried to grasp a new magazine with his right hand, but his fingers turned inward like a frozen claw. *Damn this arm!* He gripped the pistol between his knees and pulled out a new magazine with his good hand. A pulse slammed into the pine. A branch fell just to Yassen's right. He gritted his teeth. *Focus.* He finally managed to line up the magazine, and it slid into his pistol with a satisfying click.

He turned, searching the smoke, when a bullet rang out. It ripped through the forest. Tore through branches. Sliced through his dead arm and out of his side.

Yassen tumbled into the ravine. There was a warm, liquid sensation in his chest. He rolled onto his back, struggling for breath as he looked up and saw the burning heavens and the sky full of smoke. The stars glinted like uncut gems. The fire surrounded the ravine, but this time, its heat did not suffocate him. It kissed him.

And in that swath of darkness that came after, Yassen Knight saw a light.

He did not fear it.

Finally in his cursed life, he would find untroubled sleep.

42
ELENA

Though I have the memory of you, I see you from before, in a land where roads are rivers and the sun is aglow, and we will wade to that wilderness that claimed us forever ago.

—FROM A SAYONAI FOLKLORE BALLAD

Elena tore through the forest of fire and smoke. She did not know where she was going, but she followed the ravine as Yassen had told her. Pulse fire carved through trees as mountain larks screeched singular notes. A pine groaned and snapped in two, sparks raining down. Elena yelped, falling. She rolled in the dirt, the world spinning, the flames hissing at her feet. The inferno came to her as if urging her to get up and move. With a grunt, she pushed herself up onto her knees.

More pulse fire sliced through the forest. It was like the Temple all over again, except this time, she didn't have Yassen.

She was alone.

Elena stared up at the burning sky, blood wetting the bandage Yassen had made. Her elbow throbbed, and the pain set her teeth on edge. She tried to rise only to fall again; it was as if her body had given up. All she wanted to do was sleep and wake up back in Ravence. For Ferma to tell her it was all a bad dream.

But the flames crackled around her, nipping at her feet. If she died here, no one would weep for her. She would be known as the shortest reigning monarch of Ravence, a scribble in history and nothing more. Would they sing of how she died? Would they say that she had put up a good fight, and that when all was said and done, she had died to buy Ravence a little more time?

Ferma had told her once that when you die, your life plays back to you to show your pleasures and your pain. But all Elena could see was the sky.

It had burnished into shades of orange like a glowing ember. Like the desert sky after a storm had passed, but was not completely gone. She could still see grains of sand in the air, still taste salt on her lips. Her desert, her home, connected by a sky just like this.

She had to reach it.

Slowly, Elena clambered to her feet. Placed one foot in front of the other because fighting was all she knew. Because to fight was all she could do.

Her chest clamored for air, but she put another foot forward. *Don't look back.*

With every step, her heart cracked. With every step, she abandoned Yassen. *Don't look back.*

If this was strength, if this was weakness, she did not know. She could only fight against the pressure in her lungs and the tears clouding her eyes. She could only put one foot after the other, again and again, until she was jogging, running because to fight, to move, to survive was all she could do. *Don't look back.*

She thought she heard a man scream, but then a pulse ripped a branch clean off, and it toppled down in a furl of sparks. *Yassen.* Elena swallowed the grit in her throat, but she did not stop. All she could see was the path ahead and the smoke behind.

The ravine curved off to the east and Elena climbed the bank. She hauled herself over the edge. The flames crawled up the trees, shaking the dead leaves with a sadistic hunger. Above the canopy, she saw the third mine. It jutted out, cold and silent, and for a moment, all Elena wanted to do was to hurl fire onto its metal face. She didn't just want to see the mine implode; she wanted it to melt before her, to ripple down the mountainside, dragging away Jantar's sweet, sweet ore.

The flames swooned, sensing her desire. Elena reached out and they curled around her hand, ready to leap, but instead of sending the inferno down the mountainside, Elena made a fist. The flames flattened, hissing in displeasure. She did not care. She opened her palm, and the flames peeled back as she walked forward. Over the flickering tips of the fire, Elena spotted the flat ground of the campsite.

She ran for it. The flames rushed in, covering her flight as she skidded into the clearing. In the middle of the campsite, the ground hollowed into a stone pit. Rocks marked its edge. Elena fell to her knees, searching for a lever, a hinge, and she recalled how Yassen had followed the roots of a tree; how he had pressed his pale hand into the knots; how the mountain had listened and opened for him.

The memory threatened to break her.

Her throat tightened, but Elena forced herself to concentrate on the task at hand. She felt the stones for irregular marks. Her fingers brushed over their rough surfaces until she found it—a dip in the stone, a notch that perfectly fit her thumb.

She pressed it.

The pit rumbled as the false stone beneath it slid back, revealing a deep, gaping darkness.

Elena hesitated. The forest groaned as the fire ate up the pines, the molorians, the neverwoods, everything. She thought of the cabin and crystal and the family frozen within. She thought of the boy who now lay somewhere on this mountainside, dead or alive, to buy her time. And she thought of Ravence. The shifting dunes. The cluttered, winding bazaars full of trinkets and spice. The expectant faces of the crowd when she had stepped onto the platform and hushed them with her raised hand. Ravence lay at the other side of this. Ravence was waiting for her.

Elena jumped into the pit.

She plunged deep into the mountain, wind rushing past her ear, stone scraping her elbows, before she hit the ground. The impact shocked her. Elena moaned, rolling onto her back. Above, she saw fire dancing over the opening of the tunnel, and then the stone slid back into place with a resounding boom—locking her within.

Slowly, she sat up.

The darkness was so vivid, so textured that Elena almost thought it was alive. As her eyes adjusted, she could make out jagged stones and a path snaking from the ledge she stood on. She did not know if it led south, but it was the only path she had.

She took it.

It was as if she had stepped into a different world. The shadows weren't shadows. They were pools of black liquid that rippled as she walked. A spider as large as her hand scuttled over a rock. It stopped and watched her with a hundred inky eyes as she scooted past it. Large, sharp obsidian jutted out from the bowels of the mountain like frozen innards. Perhaps it was the darkness playing tricks on her, but the rocks seemed to glow. Elena peered at them and realized with a start that actually, they were glowing.

Everything was.

As the tunnel veered deeper into the mountain, a blue, subliminal light emanated from the obsidian. Some stones shone brightly, others so faintly that they seemed to disappear. It was the ore; it existed in every part of the mountain, from the tiniest pebble to the largest boulder. Manufactured Jantari metal could blind a man if he weren't careful; the ore alone merely trapped tiny flecks of light. For this, Elena was grateful.

With her other hand, she felt for the holopod. Its side bent inward, but when Elena pressed her finger against the sensor, it flickered open. Yassen must have programmed her biometrics before he had given it to her, and his foresight made her shudder. Perhaps he had known that one day, she would have to go on without him. Perhaps he had already seen his death written in the palm of her hand.

With shaking fingers, Elena traced the red tunnel. It bore south to a black dot, the juncture where the tunnels connected in the middle of the Sona Range. There lay the Black Scales, or so she hoped. There was always the possibility that they had abandoned their posts or had been killed.

Suddenly, the mountain quaked, dust and dirt raining down into her eyes. *The mine.* It must have exploded. Elena grasped the wall, fear bounding through her body as the tunnel quivered. A deep groan echoed through the chamber. The shaking intensified, and the mountain seemed to moan, guttural and deep, as if it had lost some part of itself. And then Elena realized why. *Landslides.* The third explosion had finally triggered what she had feared.

The mountain shuddered again. Stone fell from the ceiling, but the tunnel held. After several minutes, the shaking finally stopped. Elena cautiously pushed herself to her feet.

Impossible.

Except for loose dirt and crumbled rocks, the tunnel lay intact. She pressed her hand against the stone, and the wall quivered. She gasped, shrinking back. The blue light from the ore pulsed, but when Elena touched the wall again, it lay still.

She was going mad.

Elena slid the holopod into her pocket, her muscles tensing. Nothing crept through the darkness. The tunnel lay as quiet as it had before the rumbling. Still, she was hesitant to wield her fire. The ore around her was highly combustible—one spark, and she'd bring the whole mountain down.

With one last look, Elena turned and continued on the path. It snaked deeper and deeper into the bowels of Sayon, and she walked until she collapsed in exhaustion.

She slept fitfully, dreaming of people choking beneath the earth. The old merchant. The brenni handler. Yassen. Their eyes were red and leering.

Burning Queen, they sneered. *Burning Queen.*

She woke to the sound of her own screaming. Her voice echoed through the mountain, but no one answered. No one was listening.

Elena stumbled in a delirious state, her eyes swollen, her chest tight. The blood on her elbow crusted over. Her broken wrist grew stiff. Hunger gnawed her stomach until it became familiar. She walked until she fainted, slept until she woke from nightmares. She had no sense of time but felt like she had been walking for days, weeks. She felt a strange presence throughout the mountain, as if someone were holding a deep breath.

But it could also be her madness.

Her throat was so dry it hurt, and her eyes were raw from tears. She did not know when she had started crying, only that it felt as if she had never stopped. She saw their faces: Ferma. Leo. Samson. Yassen. They peered through the obsidian rocks, but when she tried to call to them, they disappeared.

All her life, she had learned to swallow her tears and hide her grief. She had never openly grieved for her mother; the throne did not allow it. She had not grieved for her father; the desert made no room for it. When Yassen had found her curled in the bed, she had thought then that had been grief.

But this, this was something more. This created a creeping wail that threatened to spill out of her throat. A wail that hummed in the deep marrow of her bones. A wail that defied even the strongest of desert winds, the deepest of tunnels.

When she awoke, she let it out.

It reverberated through the bellows of the mountain and beyond. So keen was her cry, so sharp her anguish that the mountain trembled. It seemed to sense her loss. But the tunnel still stretched on, the same as before. No matter what she endured, no matter how many lives she sacrificed, Elena could not change the path ahead of her.

But she dared not stop. For she knew that if she did, she would not be able to start again.

Elena slept and walked, sometimes at once. Faintly, she registered the tunnel was beginning to rise. The path snaked past stalagmites shaped like dripping fingers, curling upward. Elena raised her hand to push back a lock of hair and saw a jagged line of dried blood from her index finger to her elbow. She touched the wound, and fresh dots of blood oozed out. One grew heavy; she watched as it fell from her broken wrist to the floor.

Somewhere deep in the mountain, there came a growl. Elena froze. Was she still dreaming? The sound seemed to have come from far below, from beneath the ground itself. The darkness before her rustled like a fabric being pulled tight. Again, Elena had the odd feeling that something was holding its breath, but now, as the growl came again, louder this time, she realized it wasn't waiting anymore.

It was coming toward her.

Elena began to run. The tunnel narrowed as it rose higher and higher. The walls closed in on her, and she was forced to crawl on her knees. Her heart pounded in her ears, but to Elena, it seemed to echo through the mountain itself. A sharp chill cut through the air. It knifed down her throat as she clawed her way through the tunnel. Suddenly, she felt something touch her ankle, and she almost shrieked. She began to scramble faster, her shoulders rubbing against the walls. Finally, the tunnel widened. Elena launched back to her feet and dashed forward, following the curving path.

It led her to a tall chamber full of light. Ore trapped within the rocks glinted, as if vibrating to the thrum of her heart. As if it were listening. Stalactites stretched down from the ceiling. A staircase chiseled out of the wall rose to a gate twice as tall as a man.

She sprinted up the stairs as she heard something scraping in the tunnel behind her. It growled, and the mountain shuddered in response. Elena took the steps three at a time. Runes were carved along the staircase, and she recognized the symbols of the inward storm and the fire.

Finally, she reached the landing as the mountain moaned. It was a frightening sound, cold and jarring like a metal nail dragging across a tin roof. She turned to the doors. She could tell at once it was an old gate, one that had been fashioned out of pure silver rather than Jantari steel. Several gears and bolts lay across the doors in an intricate pattern. She saw no doorknob, no handle. There was no inscription above the gate, no runes to give her clues.

The growl came again, louder now. Stalactites snapped and shattered on the floor. Elena turned back to the doors, grasping the gears. There had to be a key, there was always a key on this damned mountain, but as the shadows pressed around her, Elena realized there was no special stone, no pear-shaped tree root. The gate towered above her, silent and still.

Elena stared at the doors and their bolts. She dragged her hand down the gears, feeling the sharp grooves. *Odd.* The gate seemed as old as the mountain, yet the gears had not dulled with time. Elena studied how they snaked and twisted, slowly creating a figure, and then she saw it—the dragon.

"Head north until you find the dragon," Yassen had said. "They'll know you've arrived even before you do."

Samson.

Elena banged on the doors as the ground shifted beneath her feet. The shadows around the room shrank back from what came from beneath the mountain. She could feel its presence, or rather the absence of air behind her, but Elena dared not look back.

"Hello?" she yelled. "My name is Elena Ravence! I'm here!"

The gate stood still. The air around her grew bleaker, thinner. Elena looked at the silver doors that loomed in the swath of darkness, at the coiled dragon hidden in its gears, and tried again.

"My name is Elena Ravence, daughter of Leo Ravence and Aahnah Madhani, Queen of the Desert Kingdom."

The door did not move.

The world grew colder. Her eyelids felt heavy, her body weak. The mountain moaned as the darkness slithered behind her.

But Elena kept her eyes on the immovable gate and wet her lips.

"My name is Elena," she whispered.

The gears turned and the bolts receded back. Slowly, the doors swung open. A gush of fresh air and light hit her, and she stumbled forward.

At first, she was blinded by the sun and how it bounced off a silver body spilling between the mountains. Little by little, the world took shape around her. She saw that she was standing on a bluff and that the silver body was actually a large blue lake, bluer than the sea or the sky. A stone compound sat on its bank, flanked by hoverpods.

The Black Scales.

Suddenly, the gate slammed shut behind her, trapping whatever lay within. The mountain groaned. Elena shuddered to think what would have happened had the doors not opened.

She stepped toward the edge of the bluff, surveying the snow-capped peaks. She had no idea what day it was, whether the Black Scales were in this compound, whether the Ravani kingdom still existed—but she was alive.

Elena sank to her knees. Raised her face to the sun. She drank in its warmth and savored its light. A wild, desperate laugh shook her, and she realized she was crying all over again, but she did not care. The sky was a deep blue, an endless expanse. A part of her wondered if Yassen saw it, too.

"Hold," a voice came from behind her.

Slowly, she wiped her tears and turned. There, on the ridge above the door, stood a soldier, and then another, and another. They were dressed in combat black and had their pulse guns trained at her head.

"What did you say your name was again?" one asked, and she saw the blue insignia of a dragon on his chest.

She almost cried in relief.

"Elena Ravence." She stood and looked at them with clear eyes. "Queen of the Ravani Kingdom."

"Good," the soldier said. "He's been waiting for you."

EPILOGUE: CORONATION DAY

It was a pleasure not to burn.

Samson sighed as the inferno raged around him. Underneath the Phoenix statue, he watched the sky redden. The Eternal Fire ripped down the Temple, filling the mountainside with agony and smoke.

Flames wrapped around his arms, healing the burn on his hand.

"I know," he said as they crooned, "I shouldn't have let him burn me."

He closed his eyes. Felt the quiet, steady hum of energy coursing through his veins. The rush of power. It was cool, calculating. It knew when and how to burn.

When Samson opened his eyes, blue embers danced in his palm. He let them fall from between his fingers.

He climbed onto the back of the Phoenix's statue. A woman called his name, but when he turned, the inferno washed over him. The heat buffeted his face, warm and sweet like a lover, the crackle of the fire like a song. It whispered to him about how many men it had caught, how many trees it had burned. It even told him about the assassins crawling up the mountainside.

He had expected the Arohassin to keep their word about attacking Ravence today; what he hadn't expected was Yassen's role in it. *Poor Cass.* Even when freedom dangled before him, Yassen still chose to live within a cage. Samson had tried to show him the desert that lay beyond, but some men were just bound to their miserable fate. Still, if Yassen managed to live, he'd finally give his friend the peace he had earned.

The flames hissed, and Samson turned to listen. Suddenly, he felt an inferno flare down the mountainside, a blaze of heat that ripped through his body, and he knew at once it was Elena.

Despite himself, Samson smiled. He had sensed the Fire within her. When she had touched his hand, her energy was like a low buzz, humming every time she came near. She was Fireblood, the same as him. When he closed his eyes and felt for her Fire, he saw a deep, red soil and white sandstone. There was something ancient to her spark, something raw and untamed. It tasted of salt and hearth. In his mind, he reached out to touch it, but then the flare flickered and began to grow faint.

Samson dipped his hand and lifted a flame. He whispered to it. The flame purred and then leapt back into the inferno. The fire swooned as his message spread down the mountainside.

Bring her to me, it hissed.

Samson turned back to the desert. The dunes were still. The heavens burned a deep incarnadine as smoke coiled through the air like a snake ready to strike. Somewhere across the desert, across forest and stone, deep within the mountains, the old power rumbled. Samson felt it call to him. The flames around him quivered, sensing his desire.

Samson swung down and looped his arm around the Phoenix's neck. The inferno danced in its mirrored eyes.

"Am I all you ever asked for?" he asked, and then, with a snarl, he shattered the red eyes of the bird. The glass popped as it fell into the fire.

He hopped down and began to climb the stone steps. The flames bowed and touched their heads to the floor. When he found the High Priestess burnt and curled beneath the debris-laden boughs of a banyan tree, he nudged her with his foot. She stirred, moaning. Half of her face was burnt down to the bone.

Samson slowly cupped her bloodied cheek. She opened one bleary eye. Blue embers sparked in his hand, undoing the damage of the burns, knitting back the skin and soothing her scalded flesh.

As he stood, Saayna opened her eyes. Her hands flew to her face. The new skin stretched tightly over her cheek, marked by the sign of his Fire.

The black serpent.

It slithered down her cheek and throat. Her mouth curled into shock. Saayna looked up at him and, at once, threw herself down at his feet, her body quivering like the flames.

"Prophet," she cried.

Prophet. What a strange word.

The people wanted their Prophet, and so he had come. He, the Landless King. The orphan who they had spurned. The Sesharian they had tried to enslave. Yet, when he stepped out of the Fire reborn, they flocked to him as waves bowing to the shore.

Samson walked past the High Priestess without bidding her to rise. He came before the fallen Temple. The walls caved, the dome crumpled inward, but the gate still stood. Only thin hairline cracks slithered down the pink marble.

Samson slashed his arm down, and the inferno tore the gate apart. It collapsed with a boom.

Saayna gasped as she crawled up behind him.

"Why?" she croaked.

Samson turned to her. As he spoke, the flames cackled, their song lending to his voice.

"Because we will no longer pray to false gods."

GLOSSARY

Agneepath: The path of fire.

Agnee Range: Mountains that create the western border of Ravence. The Agnee Range is lush and covered with diverse plant species and trees. It stands in sharp contrast with the Ravani Desert.

Ahi Sea: A large body of water that splits Sayon in half.

Alabore's Passage: A long lane that runs east to west in Rani.

Alabore Street: A long lane that runs north to south in Rani.

Alabore's Tear: A long, dark valley north of Palace Hill. Legends say that it was created by Alabore Ravence himself when he met the Phoenix.

Almanys: High-tech robot dummies used to train soldiers.

Arohassin: An underground network of criminals and terrorists who are known to assassinate leaders and take down governments. The leader of the Arohassin goes by the name of Taran, but no one truly knows his name.

Ashanta ceremony: A fire blessing ceremony used to bestow the ruler(s) of Ravence with the power of the Phoenix.

Astra: The closest advisor and right-hand man of the ruler of Ravence.

Ayona: A large island nation in the northern Ahi Sea. The Ayoni do not welcome outsiders.

Azuri: A delicate tree whose white branches are often used to build pyres.

Banyan: A tree that can grow to be several feet wide, while its roots can be several miles long. It was introduced to the desert after intense years of environmental development under the rule of Queen Tamana.

Beuron: A southern city of Cyleon.

Birdsong: A small festival celebrated a week before the official opening day of the Fire Festival. It is meant for Ravanis to open their hearts and fill their spirits with song.

Black Scale: A soldier of Samson Kytuu's army. Known for their strength and skill, Black Scales have never lost a war.

Brenni: Furry, llama-like animals. They are often used to transport heavy loads in the Sona Range.

Casear Lunar: The Moon Palace, otherwise known as the abode of Samson Kytuu.

Chhatri: An elevated, dome-shaped pavilion often found within the architectural style of Ravence.

The Claws: Curved metal fixtures that are stationed around the track of a hovertrain station. When a hovertrain docks, the Claws latch on to the sides of the train and recharge its engines.

Coin Square: A popular square in the Thar district of Rani.

Collar platform: An immigration and customs platform within the port of Rysanti used to admit Sesharians. Sesharians are then driven from the platform to the Sona Range.

Cruiser: A floating vehicle used to transverse the desert.

Cyleon: A kingdom that lies north of Ravence. Cyleon has been an ally of Ravence for nearly two hundred suns.

Desert Spider: The band of female warriors chosen by Alabore Ravence to protect the Ravani Kingdom. It is also the name of a secret base located north of Rani.

Desertstone: A fine, purple crystal found within Ravence.

Dhol: A large drum used in Ravani music.

Diya: An oil lantern fixed at the end of every petal in the Temple of Fire.

Dupatta: A long scarf.

Enuu: An entity considered to be the evil eye by the Jantari.

Eternal Fire: A large inferno that burns within the Temple of Fire. It is said to have been created by the Sixth Prophet to remind men of the wrath of the Phoenix. It needs no fuel but demands sacrifice from all those who wish to claim its power.

Featherstone: A large gem that contains the only Phoenix feather given to men. It rests in the center of the Ravani crown.

Floating bladers: Metal and/or wooden boards that hover slightly above the ground. They are powered by batteries and can go up to thirty miles per hour with a full charge.

Fire chain: A gold-like metal mined within the canyons of Magar.

Fire Festival: A week-long festival that celebrates the founding of Ravence by Alabore and his followers.

Fire Order: A religious order of priests who serve the Phoenix and protect Her Temple.

Fire Palace: The royal governmental home of the ruler of Ravence.

Five Desert Wars: Five bitter years of war between Ravence and Jantar during the reign of King Fai of Ravence and Queen Runtha of Jantar. Both kingdoms lost thousands of men, but Ravence emerged victorious in the end.

Fyerian: A bush that grows within the Agnee Range and produces vivid red flowers.

Fyrra: A large white wolf known to live in the Sona Range.

Gamemaster: A trained official who can code gamesuits and create obstacles within the training field.

Gamesuit: Thin yet sturdy armor that is specifically programmed to fit its wearer. Gamesuits can reknit broken bones during training sessions. They can only be used within the constraints of a training field, due to the magnetic fixtures that help power the suit.

Ganshi: A long-leaf plant that grows along mountain creeks in the Sona Range.

Garian: A red flower that grows with the Ravani Desert.

Gemini: Crystals found within Seshar.

Gold cap: An ardent supporter of King Leo. Gold caps fiercely believe that King Leo is blessed by the Phoenix and has the divine right to rule Her desert kingdom. They are often vocal (and sometimes violent) in showing their support.

Gulmohar: A tree with fiery red leaves found within Ravence.

Haloscent: Tube lighting, often found in hovertrains, buildings, and residences.

Herra: An ancient language that used to be spoken in Ravence. It is the language that the first priests of the Fire Order used when creating scrollwork within the Temple.

Hiran: Deer found within Ravence.

Holoframe: A rigid, glass structure that holds a holo photograph.

Holopod: A small circular, handheld device that is activated by scanning one's fingerprint. One can store personal data, money, images, videos and more in this device.

Homeland platform: The main dock within the port of Rysanti. It is full of shops, restaurants, and entertainment. It is often a newcomer's first glimpse of Jantar.

Holosign: A floating, holographic poster and/or advertisement.

Hoverboat: A boat that slightly hovers over the sea.

Hovercam: A camera that can float in the air and is controlled via remote.

Hoverpod: A powered flying vehicle shaped like a large black oval. These vehicles vary in size, depending on its escort type: civilian, governmental, and/or military.

Hovertrain: A train that flies through the air. They can travel a great distance if properly charged (see **Claws**).

Hyuku River: A long river that cuts through the western regions of Nbru.

Iktara: A southeastern city of Ravence known for its fine artisans and scholars.

Immortal: Ancient beings of Sayon who never die. So far, only two have been discovered: the Phoenix and the Dragon.

Jade berry: A type of bush found within Ravence that produces bright green berries that taste slightly sweet. If a person eats too many of its berries, they will go into paralytic shock.

Jantar: A kingdom that lies east of Ravence. Jantar is known for its metal and brass cities. Jantar was founded before Ravence and believes the desert should be a part of its kingdom. Throughout the centuries, Jantar has waged countless wars against Ravence, but it has never won.

Jantari: The people of Jantar. They are known for their pale skin and white, colorless eyes.

Junhni 2000: A robot dummy that was used in training fields, but was later replaced by Almanys.

Jutti: Shoes with thin soles often worn in Ravence.

Karven: A kingdom that borders Cyleon and Jantar. It has been a steadfast ally of Jantar.

Karvanese: The people of Karven.

Kavach: A gamesuit designed by the Arohassin.

Knuckled bus: A metal, pulse-proof, armored bus used to transport Sesharians from Rysanti to the Sona Range.

Kurta: A long, loose collarless shirt commonly worn in Ravence.

Kymathra: An ancient fighting style of the Ravani.

Lehenga: A large, embellished skirt commonly worn in Ravence.

Lilliberries: Berries that grow off the deep roots of a skorrir bush.

Loyarian sparks: Floating specks of light that appear in shadowed areas during the summer in Ravence.

Lynthia: Long, blade-like grass that grows within the southern regions of Ravence.

Lynthium: A psychoactive drug used primarily for medical and recreational purposes. It is harvested from the Lnythia plant found within the southern regions of Ravence.

Magar: A southwestern city of Ravence known for its red canyons and bountiful gems.

Mandur: A kingdom across the Ahi Sea that borders Nbru and Pagua. It is well known for its outstanding navy. It has been in constant conflict with Pagua.

Marin Light: A champagne created within the foothills of Cyleon.

Mero/a/i: A term of endearment spoken in Jantar. Its masculine form means boy; its feminine form means girl; and its third form means a genderless person.

Metalman: A colloquial name given to the Jantari.

Mohanti: A horned, winged ox, the national symbol of Jantar.

Moksh: A kingdom across the Ahi Sea that borders the volcanic region of Pagua.

Molorian: A tree with purple leaves and dark bark found in the Sona Range.

Monora: A northwestern city of Jantar.

Monte Gumi: A mountain within the northern parts of Veran.

Moonspun ganshi: A mild psychoactive drug often smoked with a pipe. It is harvested from the Ganshi plant, found within the Sona Range.

Moonspun flowers: Lavender buds that bloom when touched.

Mutherwood: A pine that grows within the mountains of Seshar.

Nbru: A kingdom across the Ahi Sea that borders Mandur and Pagua. It is often the peacemaker between Mandur and Pagua, and never participates in wars.

Nero-granite: Black stone with veins of red. It is found within the southern parts of Ravence.

Neverwood: A thorny plant that grows beneath the underbrush in the Sona Range.

Nightdew chocolate: A sweet made exclusively in Rani.

Pagua: A kingdom across the Ahi Sea that borders Nbru, Mandur, and Moksh. It is well known for its stealthy air force. It has been in constant conflict with Mandur.

Palace Hill: The large rise north of Rani where the Fire Palace sits upon.

Palehearts: White flowers shaped like tiny hearts that grow within the Sona Range.

The Phoenix: The fiery god known for Her vengeful fire and penchant for justice. The Phoenix is said to choose a Prophet when the world is full of strife. She is worshipped by the Ravani.

Prophet: A man or woman chosen to enact justice as ordered by the Phoenix. The Prophet can wield fire and cannot burn.

Pulse gun: A weapon that shoots out "pulses," or bursts of lasers. Depending on the size and weight of the gun, some pulse guns can cleanly cut off limbs.

Radhia's Bazaar: A large, teeming network of shops, restaurants, and alleyways located south of Rani's city center.

Rakins: Thorny bushes that grow around the Temple of Fire.

Rani: The capital of Ravence.

Rasbakan: A port city that lies on the eastern border of Ravence.

Ravani Desert: A large swath of dunes and canyons. The southern desert is lusher and better suited for crops; the northern desert is harsher. Desert storms are known to appear and disappear suddenly within the northern regions.

Ravence: A desert kingdom founded by Alabore Ravence three hundred suns ago. The kingdom is considered to be part of the holy land created by the Sixth Prophet. Alabore Ravence named the kingdom after himself, bestowing his bloodline the burden of maintaining his dream of peace.

Receiving platform: An immigration and customs dock within the port of Rysanti used to check non-Sesharians visitors.

Red Rebellion: An uprising within Ravence led by rebels who wished for a democratic government. It was crushed by Queen Akira.

Registaan: A six-month-long desert test in which the Ravani heir is given no food, water, shelter, or protection. It is a rite of passage in which the heir must learn the sands of her home and why it runs through her veins.

Retherin: A pine with a velvet blue trunk and tawny orange leaves located within the Sona Range.

Rhini: A cattle-like animal used to drive carts within Ravence.

Royal Library: A tall chamber built underneath the Fire Palace that houses ancient scrolls and texts.

Rysanti: The Brass City of Jantar; it is a port city and popular immigration access point. All of its buildings are made out of brass, glass, and shining steel.

Sand raider: A Ravani soldier who is skilled in operating a cruiser and fighting underneath the surface of the Ravani desert. Sand raiders were formally a unit within the army; however, Queen Jumi created a separate branch for the sand raiders after expanding the kingdom's underground tunnels.

Sandscraper: Tall buildings made of sandstone and steel within the Ravani Kingdom.

Sandtrapper: A large, scaly tree found within the Ravani Desert.

Sari: A garment of unstitched fabric that is wrapped around the waist and draped over the shoulder, exposing the midriff; it is commonly worn in Ravence.

Sayon: The name of the world.

The Seat: The center dome within the Temple of Fire.

Seshar: A nation of three islands that lie within the middle of the Ahi Sea. Jantar invaded the country, turning the three islands against each other. Jantar emerged victorious and has maintained a thirty-sun colonial rule over Seshar, forcing its citizens to work within the mines of the Sona Range.

Sesharian: The people of Seshar. They are known for their raven-black hair and insurmountable strength.

Shagun: Presents given by the bride's father to the groom and his family.

Sherwani: A long coat-like garment often worn by royals in Ravence.

Shobu: A small dog with two tails and the mane of a lion, often found within Ravence.

Silver feathers: A colloquial name for the capital police of Rani.

Sixth Prophet: A priestess of the Fire Order believed to exist five hundred suns ago. She burned down the forest beyond the Agnee Range, creating what is now known as the Ravani Desert. The Sixth Prophet killed many kings, queens, generals and Yumi as punishment for constantly waging war. After many suns of burning, the Sixth Prophet disappeared.

Skorrir: A thorny bush found within the Ravani Desert. Its buds recede when a predator walks by.

Slab grenades: Explosive devices that shoot out spikes; they are detonated by pulling out a pin.

Slingsword: A weapon with a long, sharp blade and a trigger in the hilt. When pulled, the trigger releases the blade. The blade is connected to the trigger via a steel rope. A user can recall the blade back to the hilt by pulling the trigger again.

Sona Range: A mountain range located within the southeast regions of Jantar. The mountains have a rich deposit of metal ore. Before the Invasion of Seshar, Jantari miners worked the rigs. Now, Sesharians work the mines while Jantari soldiers keep watch.

Soothsayer: A type of tea grown within the sands of Rani.

Spear: The head guard of a Ravani royal.

Sudani: Ancient warriors that created a weapon that later morphed into the slingsword. They are also attributed to developing **Kymathra** and **Unsung.**

Sun's breath: Dawn.

Tabla: Twin drums often used in Ravani music.

Temple of Fire: The place of worship of the Phoenix. Shaped like a large white lotus with a dome in the center, the Temple was built by the first priests of the Fire Order.

Teranghar: A southern city of Ravence known for its rolling hills and training bases for Ravani and Sesharian soldiers.

Thar: A southern district of Rani.

Tsuana: A kingdom that borders Veran. Like Nbru, the country has sworn off war. Peace treaties between other countries are often signed with Tsuana.

Unsung: An ancient fighting style of the Ravani.

Veran: A kingdom that lies east of Jantar.

Vermi: A type of tea grown within the Agnee Range.

Vesathri: An ancient, mythical creature with the body of a scorpion and the head of a stag.

Vesseri: The common day language spoken in Ravence.

Visor: Made of plastic and/or fiber sheath, visors are used to shield the eyes from blinding Jantari metal.

White Lotus: A large, lotus-shaped sculpture that sits directly in a garden in the heart of Rani. A gas-powered flame burns in the center of the sculpture.

Windsnatch: A game in which two opposing teams ride floating bladers above a smoldering field. The goal is to get the ball into the opposing team's net.

Yeseri: A desert lion.

Yoddha Base: A Ravani military embankment that sits along the Ravani southern border.

Yron: A type of cigarette only found on the black market. Its nicotine is harvested from the Beldur plant, which can be found within the volcanic regions of Pagua.

Yuani: A sand-colored desert bird.

Yumi: A race of skilled fighters. The Yumi women are known for their long, silky hair that can suddenly harden into sharp shards; their hair can cut through diamonds. The Yumi men are known for their healing abilities. Once plentiful, the Yumi were nearly wiped out by the fires of the Sixth Prophet. Now, many serve as soldiers, guards, or mercenaries.

Zeemir: A long weapon with a sharp blade and butt of a gun. They are often used by the Jantari army.

Acknowledgments

I've always skipped the acknowledgments of a book, but only when I began to write one myself did I realize the importance of the people behind the story. So dear reader, stay a while. See the magic these people have spun.

First and foremost, I want to thank my editors Kristin Gustafson and Clayton Bohle. Thank you, Kristin, for your sharp, poetic eye and patience as I maneuvered this manuscript from barely readable to the story it is now. Your excitement for the story and its characters picked me up in my moments of doubt. It fueled me to create something better. I will miss our random musings about craft, horses, and Yassen's sad boy hours. To Clayton, thank you for shepherding this manuscript from the very beginning. Thank you for believing in this story. Thank you for believing in me. Without your guidance, your passion, and our hours-long conversations, this story wouldn't be as wicked and as powerful. Though I'm sorry I killed off your favorite character, there will be more! Fire always finds a way.

To the team at New Degree Press, thank you for believing in my book. I would like to especially thank: Kyra Dawkins, Emily Vander-Bent, Haley Newlin, Susan Levey, Leila Summers, Stephen Howard, Gjorgji Pejkovski, Nikola Tikoski, Eric Koester, and Brian Bies. A *huge* thank you to my cover designer Mario Jeric for making a jaw-dropping cover. You went above and beyond. I still can't stop staring at it as I write the next book.

Writing can be a lonely journey. I have been blessed to have friends and family to mitigate that loneliness. To David Snyder, thank you for your love, your patience, and your belief in me. I'm grateful for you, desert boy. To my friends who saw the early versions of the book, Sarah Schisla, Anthony Flores, Adesuwa Agbonile, Diego Dew, Hridu Jain, Danna Gallegos, and Julia Wierzbinska, thank you for hyping me up.

Your genuine love and excitement for this story humbled me, and it reminded me of why I started in the first place.

To my cousins Nikki and Neha, thank you for fangirling over the characters with me. To my brother, Romi (or as the girls on the block say, "Romeo"), thank you for pushing me to explore new narratives. You inspire me, though I won't tell you this in person. To my parents, thank you for never forcing me to pursue an engineering or medical degree like most Indian parents. You both recognized my love for storytelling, and instead of crushing it, you nurtured it. Papa, your tenacity inspires me. Mama, your gentleness protects me. Thank you for driving me to the library when I was younger. Thank you for *constantly* re-reading the Ramayana to me even when I complained. You helped me build the foundation of my stories. Maybe that's why I'm so obsessed with myths.

To my sisters from another mister, Ravjot, Natasha, Lauren, Megna, Gurkatvir, thank you for your constant love, your steadfast support, and your badassery. I thank the universe for bringing us together. Your creativity, your activism, and your kindness inspires me. I am blessed to know you all.

To the online book community, thank you for championing *The Boy with Fire* before pre-orders or early chapters were even available. Thank you CW and friends at The Quiet Pond for helping me unveil *The Boy with Fire* to the world for the first time. A huge, huge hug to Lexi @ redemptionarcs, Frid @ seraphicmavenn, Steoh @ steohsama, Jon @ youthfullyfelt, Hera @ acupofstarspls, Anastasia @ ahnnyjekyll, Angelika @ colouranomaly, Lolly @ f_ingspacequeen, @ yellowbirdie721, Bree @ BookwormDazzle, Nick @ sidsellie, Isabell @ ladykelsier, Celina @ immersedinpages, Luiza @ huccistyle, Sam @ ghafaxcx, and Krupali @ Chimings_.

To Ngoc, thank you for bringing my characters to life with your amazing art. To Angela from Dattura Studio, thank you for creating the beautiful merch for *The Boy with Fire*. You both made Yassen, Elena, and Leo far cooler than I imagined.

I want to thank the early supporters of the book, those of you who contributed to my Indiegogo campaign and bought the book before there was a cover, a summary, or a finalized manuscript. They are:

Vandana Srivastava
Katherine Snyder
Victoria Yuan
Emma Master
Emma Rashes
Stephen Garten
Lina Cordero
Laurie Snyder
Hannah Scott
Tom Joad
Erica Scott
Dylan C. Juarez
Onyi Moss
Samuel Good
Eli Peters
Christina Li
Alan Tomusiak
Chuqing Yang
Eli Navarro
Nylah DePass
Elvira Prieto
Samson Yemenu
Ana Cabrera
John Rees
Sonal Chokshi
Catie Brown
Stone Kalisa
Tom Kealey
Josh Cobler
Hannah Knowles
Margit Wennmachers
Kaavya Muralidhar
Julian Pena
Maya Mahony
Karunya Bhramasandra
Vaishali Swami
Andrew Radford
Madison Tivvis

Geraldine Moriba
Frank Masel
Jackson Roach
Andrew Milich
Ranjit Kumar
Jerrell Taylor
Jeff Tribble
Eric Koester
Brandon Jaimes
Rebecca Moretti
Danish Shabbir
Rachel Thomson
Sarah Dobbins
Amy Hoemeke
Virender Verma
Vivian Beebe Sana
Nicolas Martell
Isaac Vaught
Drake Hougo
Vikas Grover
Jack Kramer
Tiffany Naiman
Michael Spencer
Sanja Savic
Kunal Bisla
Sonja Hansen
Ekalan Hou
Meera Srinivasan
Erika DePalatis
Natti Robinson
Emily Wilson
Ethan Chua
Javier Aguayo
Nancy Xu
Katiana Uyemura
Kevin Chang
Haley Moreau
Donna Knutson

Christopher LeBoa
Joey Hurlocker
Anthony Flores
Caroline Flores
Matthew Bedick
Patricia Arcellana
Anna Self
Lindsay Bjerken
Marshall Snyder
Surbhi Sachdeva
Michael Solorio
Anastasiosa Angelopoulos
Gabe Rosen
Evan Tuchinsky
Rushali Patel
Ritesh Verma
Alexa Amita Ramachandran
Adesuwa Agbonile
Patty Snyder
Sharon Huang
Megan Catherine Calfas
Sam Duke
Josh Smith
Al Sexton
Caitlin Hepp
Maggie Isaacs
Aashish Maru
Sonja Stevenson
Emily Schmidt
Nikhil Prabala
Avery Segal
Christian Martin
Braedon Martinez
Karen Oropeza
Marcella Renteria
Royce Wang
Keaton Ollech
Paul Serrato

Krishna Verma
Dheerja Kaur
Will Shan
Gilda Geist
Isabella Tilley
Jimmy Le
Nestor Walters
Luis Govea
Melina Walling
Joel Brusewitz
Neha Bhagirath
Deeksha Walia
Sarah Schisla
Mai Wang
Adi Patel
Amy Chiu
Amelia Salyers
Aditya Arya
James Pillot
Sunita Verma
Lauren Hess
Ravjot Singh
Danna Gallegos
Gurkatvir Uppal
Gaby Li
Tanay Kothari
Josh Payne
Hridu Jain
Veer Shah
Javier Andres Garcia
Kelsie Wysong
Christy Hartman
Jaime Gomez
David Snyder
Doug Albright
Carlos Ciudad-Real
Aditya Raj Jain
Eric Singh

Nikki Kumar   Gregory Hill
Kevin Skinner   Sandhini Agarwal

I kept writing all these suns because a part of me always believed someone out there in the world would read my story. In moments of self-doubt, I always thought of you, dear reader. So last but not least, I want to thank *you*, whoever is holding this book right now. Thank you for giving this story a chance.

CPSIA information can be obtained
at www.ICGtesting.com
Printed in the USA
LVHW052047200921
698279LV00012B/2158